"To simplify the concept of relativity, I always use the following example: if you sit with a girl on a garden bench and the moon is shining, then for you the hour will be a minute. However, if you sit on a hot stove, the minute will be an hour."

ALBERT EINSTEIN, 1948

RELATIVITY

THE GODDAMNED LONELY UNIVERSE SAGA
BOOK ONE

A JANOSCORP PUBLICATIONS RELEASE

BY HENRY ABNER

THE JANOS CORPORATION
FROM THE PAST & TO THE FUTURE

http://www.janoscorp.com

ISBN (PAPERBACK) 978-0692665916

Cover by Dylan Werner, courtesy of Antipodes Press
antipodespress.com

Printed in the United States of America

For L,

Who didn't believe Einstein but always believed in me.

In 1535 a small fleet of Janos Corporation vessels harnessed the latest in sailing technology to safely and swiftly deliver the first viceroy of New Spain across the Atlantic Ocean, ushering in a triumphant new age of exploration and discovery.

That spirit is carried on today, as our luxury TimeResorts embrace the power of relativity to deliver guests in comfort to their next frontier: the future.

As an enduring symbol of sophistication, style, and legendary service, The Janos Corporation creates unparalleled experiences with an ever-growing stable of world-class amenities and destinations, including our newest addition:

The TimeResort at Seren Luna.

Whether you're traveling to tomorrow or beyond, the choice is clear.

THE JANOSCORPORATION

"From the Past / To the Future"
Copyright MMDCXVI JANOSCORP LLC

ONE

Little old lady called it in, or so they tell me.

"A magcab left in a back alley all night? You'll have to do better than that."

I yawn and get vertical, click the line dead. Parked cabs aren't my racket. Either this one's got a trunk full of raw meat or I've been knocked down a peg or two. Lucky me, the smart money's on the former. That crowd down at Central knows I'd make a lousy meter maid. Don't have the legs for it.

I dig around the sink for the razor module but think twice instead. The mirror says I've only got a day or two of stubble, and besides, the sun's not even fully up, why the hell should I be? If I strain, I can remember a time when this job used to mean something, but only just barely.

I grab the last cup of cheap McDunkRoast and hop the first tram uptown. Sergeant Ruffner is already on the scene, laying tape in the cold drizzle. It's a lazy rain. The kind that will ruin your day but not your shoes. Ruffner's not exactly my type, but then again, who is? I work alone, and for good reason. Central's not too keen to hand out partners to guys with a habit of misplacing them. Good cops don't grow on trees, at least not since I've been carrying a badge they don't.

"Nice to see a friendly face around here, Ames," Ruffner says. "Hell, it's nice to see a face at all. Even yours. I wasn't sure if you or your partner would show first."

I take a sip and shrug. Ignore his laughter. Ruffner knows me well enough to know I won't bite back this early in the morning. He's safe for now, at least until I get a little caffeine in me. Thankfully, the coffee is still lukewarm. I'd need a third mortgage to score a refill this far uptown.

"You're lucky anybody showed at this hour," I say, holding the joe close. A wide brim pulled low on my brow keeps the rain out and the acid-burn flavor in. "What do we got here?"

I gesture to the taxi with my mug. It sits lonely on the slick pavement, under the watchful gaze of a JanosCorp holoboard advertisement. The bearded corporate logo on the glowing sign stares left and right with his twin faces—*from the past and to the future*—but refuses to acknowledge the crippled cab directly below him. The electronic eyes dotting the frame are a different story. They're fixed on me. Racking focus. Counting every face as a potential customer, even one as broke as mine. Ruffner stops with the tape and eyeballs me too, hands glued to his hips.

"You tell *me* what we got here," he says into the rain. "Ain't any of my business what's in the back of that cab. They don't pay me enough for that. I just happened to have the lousy luck to get here first. Took one sniff and called for the heavy hitters in Homicide. That's you, ain't it, Ames?"

I grimace and shake my head.

"Swing for the fences, Detective."

Ruffner finishes tacking up the blinking yellow tape to a slick brick wall. We're sealed in now. Separated from the manic, screaming neon and expensive thrills of the uptown world outside our little alley, if only by a single strand of flashing plastic and an even thinner streak of duty. He grunts as he unpacks a fat, padded crate, then starts to work hanging the V-Cap scanners hidden inside.

Skinny silver legs drop out of each device as he raises them into position in a sloppy arc around my scene. "I've been busy keeping everything nice and pretty for you, Ames. Virginal, even."

He spits into a dark puddle and it gets darker.

"Thanks," I say. "You're a real sweetheart."

I set my mug down on the taxi's cold hood and step to the rear. The back door is already swung up and open, like a gaping mouth in some demented dentist's chair. I peel my lid and peek inside.

Splatsville. Population: four. Five if you count the synthetic driver. I don't. Four former humans: three Johns and one lonely Jane Doe. They left quite a mess for me. Not an intact cranium between the lot of them. Everything above their necklines is now a fine mist soaking into the cheap upholstery and their richo duds. I slip the retinal scanner back into my coat. Rules out a dental record lookup, too.

I pop on some latex and check the closest wrist. Slide back a nicely tailored silk sleeve. Nope. Mr. Doe's ArmPod is missing. Just an empty scar-tissued cavity with a couple of dangling power leads. No surprise there.

We're going to have a lot of fun identifying these four. Like I said, a real mess. No faces. No teeth. No electronic identification. It's too bad monograms went out of style last Tuesday, might help me cut down the options. It won't be impossible to pin names to these stiffs, just a pain in my already sore ass. I'm suddenly nostalgic for the days when folks carried paper ID's around in their pockets. That's the trouble with technology: when it stops working, you do too.

I unfasten the forearm panel on my coat and access my own multipurpose device. My government-issued ArmPod® brand MPD doesn't impress the kids down on the corner, but it gets the job done for a dinosaur like me. I thumb the red button on the recorder app and make with my initial findings.

"This is Detective Stockton Ames reporting. Badge number oh five six adam six three two. We've got a quadrup—"

My arm vibrates.

Incoming voicecom. Who could be calling at this hour? It's far too early to be anybody from the precinct. They won't get moving until I get back with a prelim and a head cold. Those lucky bastards are all sipping DunkRoast in their dundies, catching up on the morning's newstream. The trace display on my arm doesn't return a name. *Unknown* it says.

Unknown can leave a message.

"Quadruple homicide. WestEnd Uptown. Richter Street between 7th and 8th. Victims are unidentified: three males, one female. Bodies recovered in the passenger compartment of magcab dispatch number—" I take a step back, examine the markings on the rear quarterpanel. "—Adam Mary Boston Three One Four Charlie. MetroWest Magcab. Multipurpose devices were removed post-mortem. Cause of death for all four victims is severe head trauma, and I do mean severe. Source of trauma looks like small arms fire, uhh—"

Ducking into the cab again, I put a hand down on Jane Doe's thigh to steady myself. Her slashed silk stockings and unlatched garters say mine's not the first to be there tonight. "Apologies, ma'am."

I swab the rear windscreen with a clean handkerchief. Amongst the blood and gristle is a single fat band of fine white residue, stretching the width of the bench seat, from window to window. I give it a sniff and cringe. Blast powder. What else will take a head clean off?

"Source of the trauma appears to be a dustgun. One shot for the vics." I poke my head in once more and glance up front. "A second for the synthetic driver."

Must be hard times. Even the crooks are getting chintzy. In fact I'm surprised they spared a round for the synth at all. Half the dead robots we find have their heads pried off with nothing more than a screwdriver and a pocket torch. We don't pay the synthos much mind at the Homicide desk, dead or alive. You can't take a life that was never technically living—and that's official department policy, but it suits me just fine. Broken robots get left for the beat cops and garbage collectors, that is, if a crafty hobo doesn't get to them first.

Ruffner approaches, his V-Cap tripods all set up behind him. Their little scanning heads buzz left and right, capturing the scene in perfect detail. They turn in sync, like spectators at a StockRocket race. Between the six of them, they won't miss a print: finger, foot, or otherwise. Part of me wonders why I haven't been completely hotswapped for a machine already.

"Stick up?" he says, grimacing at the carnage.

I nod, fish out a variety pack of flavored toothpicks, and for the thousandth time in as many days, wish they were a deck of butts. Between the city smoking ordinance and the precinct's employee health screens, this lack of 'bacco will be the death of me. I shake one stick loose and bite down, but spit it back out onto the wet pavement.

Curryspice. Gag me. I make for the coffee instead.

"Wouldn't bet against it," I say between sips. "Clothes like these? This part of town? I've got a week's pay what says those MPDs were top of the line. They'll be wiped clean and in new wrists by suppertime. A good old-fashioned robbery with a dash of homicide to cover the tracks."

"The Uptown Special," he says.

I nod and take another pull of java. I have a hunch it's not the only thing that's gone cold. "Any word from MetroWest? I'd love to get my hands on the cab's dome recorder feed." I take a swallow and point to the two-faced man watching over the alley. "Or how about those holoboard cameras? Anything from JanosCorp?"

He laughs.

"Yeah and I'm sure you'd like a raise too, Detective."

Our work here is done.

I catch the express and book it back downtown. Ruffner has the V-Cap data in the network before I can even slink into my desk. I spend the rest of my morning scouring a virtual mock-up of the alley and drinking bad coffee. There's not much else to go on. MetroWest lost contact with the cab in question just after midnight. Driving up Ninth one minute, a quick stop, the feed goes dark the next. Of course, no physical witnesses step forward, either. They're beginning to become a bit of an endangered species around these parts. Violent crime is more popular than soda pop, and yet no one ever sees a thing.

The mock-up is just as worthless. It turns up a couple sets of generic hoofprints that could belong to anybody with a pair of cheap sneakers. No hits on the dustgun chem signature either. By law, the ammo has to be registered with SHOTnet, an interglobal law-enforcement database. But according to my trace, the cartridges in question are still sitting on the shelf at a Novo São Paulo warehouse, half-a-galaxy away. In other words: none of it's any help at all. About what I've come to expect from an average case these days.

Around lunchtime the eggheads in the basement deliver some names for Misters and Mizz Doe. Not a bad turn-around for a genecrack. I ought to send down some pie. Since we don't have any faces to match, those pale-skinned geeks saved me an afternoon of cross-referencing the missing citizen query by hand. Not exactly buckets of fun in anybody's book.

I glance over the nerds' handiwork. All four stiffs are local. The fellas are well-off richos with cushy uptown finance gigs. They fit the profile to a tee, and then some. Young, wealthy, and careless. Perfect posterboys for the crime prevention PSAs.

The female has a handful of priors. Well *had* anyway. A working girl with the goods to cater to the smart set, but not the smarts to stay out of trouble. Did she get these boys into hot water? Was that last turn down the dark alley her idea? It's as good a guess as any. Even if she wasn't the street-walking type, she was still a woman.

In the end it doesn't matter. We've got files full of victims that read just like these four. Only the names and faces—or lack thereof—change. Hit-and-run snatch jobs are about as common as a McTasty's franchise these days. There's one on every corner.

I've got nothing to go on but I spend six-and-a-half hours parked in paperwork anyway. Funny name, paperwork. There hasn't been any parchment in the equation for ages, but old habits and catchy names die hard. The lack of physical documents doesn't make my job any easier. Doesn't make it worthwhile, either. Digital or analog, no amount of paper pushing ever collared a perp in a case with no leads. Today, like every other day, is no exception. This case goes right into the big bucket marked "unsolved." It sits beside two dozen just like it from the past month alone.

At closing time I pop on my slicker and catch the usual tram back home. The walk to the station is wet and the express is late. When it finally shows, I squeeze into a child-sized spot in the corner, my back pressed against some colorful graffito burnt into the plastic paneling. I run a thumb over the letters. *Syntho shit is better than no shit at all*, it reads.

I smile. Everybody's a poet these days. The tram squeaks and squeals through the dying daylight, her passengers packed on top of each other like sad little sardines. I keep a firm grasp on the loop above me and hold on for dear life. Somewhere, there's a beautiful sunset in purples and pinks and oranges. But at my stop, the sky is just a slightly lighter shade of gray.

I lean over a puddle and scan my ArmPod at the front door, in the off chance the deadbolt is working today. 87665 Avenue F South. Three blocks from nowhere. To my surprise, the slidelock accepts my AccessKard, beeps with recognition, and slips out of sight. I breeze through the lobby, ignoring the sad collection of crooked-hanging holos—the ones that came preloaded in the frames, no doubt. Portraits of people nobody knows, landscapes from vacations that never happened. Still dripping, I step into the waiting turbolift.

My building's rickety old elevator lumbers upward, stinking of sweat and sticking ever-so-slightly as we pass floors six and thirteen. Twelve years I've hung my hat at unit 2612B, and for twelve years it's hiccupped at floors six and thirteen.

I'm not holding out for the LiftDoc anytime soon.

I take a deep breath and try to enjoy the quiet thrum of the ride up. It's the first time I've been alone since I stepped out the door this morning. It feels nice. The city's not the kind of place for folks that don't like being around other folks. I oughta know. Your only privacy is in your anonymity. In the fact that you are one of a hundred million other sheep, and you don't matter one bit to the rest of them.

The lift shivers to a stop at twenty-six and I exhale.

My one-room castle is at the far end of a particularly treacherous stretch of corridor. You'd think I'd be happy—what with only the one set of noisy neighbors right next door to cry about—but you'd think wrong.

Crossing my fingers and then myself, I step out into an empty hallway, thank the Lord. I'm a few feet from sliding into home and a nice tall glass of Jensens Family Brand corn mash over ice. In my mind I'm already kicked back on my worn-out corner of the lounger, catching some pregame analysis for the Knights' big matchup this weekend. I round the bend, entering the homestretch.

Ambushed!

Mrs. Johnston stalks the hallway in her housecoat and curlers. Might as well be a uniform for as much as I've seen her in anything else. Just like all the other slum dwellers that can't afford neighbors nicer than these, old Edna Johnston is nothing if not a creature of habit. Hands on her hips, she taps a slippered foot on a mismatched linoleum tile. She's on the prowl, and I've fallen right into her trap.

"Mr. Ames!" she says.

I try not to sigh out loud, but I don't try hard enough.

"Mrs. Johnston."

I tip my hat a touch too low. A few drops of rain slide off the brim. She watches them tumble down to the floor with bulging, bespectacled eyes before regaining her train of thought.

"Mr. Ames, I hate to bother you."

Sure she does. "But someone has been leaving their garbage out in the hallway again, which, as I'm sure you're aware is a direct violation of the tenant association bylaws—"

She could go on like this for days, but I learned years ago not to let her. "Wasn't me," I say. "My compressor and chute work just fine. Promise. AstroScout's honor."

It's a feeble attempt, considering my adversary, but I move to escape anyway. I can just barely see my door from here. It looks like sweet, rusty freedom. The old bat won't have it though. She snags my arm as I brush past the black plastic bags stacked high against the sagging wall and peeling paint. I'm juicy prey, and she's got her fangs in my hindquarters alright.

"I'm not accusing you, Mr. Ames," she says.

Could have fooled me.

"Well then what do you want?"

She glances away.

"Well... aren't you... a police officer?"

Yep. Sure am. And I've got nothing better to do with my time off than solve The Great Trash Caper. The future of our fair city hangs in the balance. I poke at the villainous sacks with soaked loafers. Guess I was wrong about the rain.

"Did you try looking in the garbage, Mrs. Johnston?"

"Well of course not," she says. "Could be all manner of illicit substances in there and I just don't think—"

I pop open my pocketplasma and make a hasty incision along the top of the nearest bag. The plastic sizzles at the touch of the torch. I wait a moment for it to cool, then reach in and snatch a padded envelope. She winces at the stick of a dirty needle that my fingers never find, but her eyes stay glued to that envelope. She adjusts her glasses. She's hungry for justice.

I read the warrant.

"Looks like your culprit is one... Mr. David H. Johnston." I purse my lips. "Say, isn't that your husband's name, Mrs. Johnston?"

Her cheeks go red. She reaches down and grabs a bag in each hand before turning back to her door. The shrill chattering of a trashy talkstream squeaks through the open slidelock. It's quickly drowned out by some shrill chattering of her own.

"Wait now, ma'am! Are you sure you don't want me to bring him in for questioning?"

RELATIVITY

The door slams shut and I'm free to go.

I don't need a perfect job. A beautiful life. Just something better than this.

TWO

Home-sweet-hole-in-the-wall.

The door shimmies open with a dull rumble and a whiny squeak. It needs a good lubing. Has for months now, but shame on me if I schedule one more service appointment with that lousy syntho super of ours. A robot that rusty is a menace with a wrench, and I'll keep my distance, long as I can help it.

I file past the cooking closet, toss my coat and hat on a lonely, crooked hook, and hit a switch on the cracked interface panel. With some hesitation, the somnopod and wardrobe unit fold down into the floor. A familiar clunk grinds behind the wall.

I give it a good pounding with my fist. While I wait, I straighten the only holo hanging in my place: a cheap mugshot of our Lord and Savior that came free with the purchase of one personal salvation down at the Local 3640. The grinding eventually quits as the servos slip behind the wall and kick back into gear with a soft buzz. The picture of the Big Guy goes sideways once more, and a lounger and holoprojector crawl out onto the stained, beige linoleum.

Just like that my bedroom becomes a living room. The realtors call it a "multiuse space." I call it all I can afford on a municipal salary.

I sigh and step into the tiny room. My favorite Knight's sweatshirt is caught up in the lounger. Well most of it is, anyway. One of the arms lies ripped off and dangling from the transfer port in the wall. A floppy tube of jagged, black fabric, mocking me. Not a good omen for the big game on Sunday. I leave it hanging. Flip on the holo to the sportstream and pour myself a tall one from a bottle buried in the cushions. "*Ahhhh.*" Finally. I fall into the lounger as the whiskey kisses my lips.

Bzzzzzz.

Someone's at the damned door.

I sigh and stand up to answer it.

"Look Mrs. Johnston," I say, thumbing the panel and staring into my drink. "I really don't care who put—"

I don't see slippers.

"You're not Mrs. Johnston."

It's a young guy. Light skin. Dark, buzzed hair. Padded, strappy jumpsuit and thick-soled boots. Like a RocketSled driver, but missing the corporate insignia covering every inch of him like colorful camouflage. A clean-shaved fella, he's possibly military, certainly militant, and definitely not a resident of *this* building.

I reach for my hip but stop short.

"Stockton Ames?" he says.

"Yeah, that's right. Who wants to know?"

His hand disappears into an unzipped breast pocket. This time I do palm the magnum. He raises an eyebrow. Pulls out an unmarked silver envelope.

"Personal letter," he says. "From JanosCorp and USG."

I drop my gun back into the holster and Buzzcut hands me the shiny plastic envelope. "Personal letter?" I turn it over in my hands. "Nobody sends these things anymore. At least not to a working stiff like me. Not even for my birthday."

"Yeah," he says. "I know. You ought to answer your voicecoms, bru. Would have saved me a trip."

I shrug and step away.

The slidelock slips shut automatically between us, and I rip into the envelope from a perforated tab. Sure as Pheggs® is eggs, it's a handwritten note, smeared ink and all.

Ha! How do you like that? The note instructs me to check my inbox and dial a JanosCorp rep.

I do like it says.

The message is from a sweepstakes. I can't believe it got through the iFilter. The courier, the handwritten letter. These scams are getting more and more ridiculous every week. But of all the suckers in all the world, they sure picked the right one. I'd suffer a thousand spammy scams for just one chance at the big time. For a chance to leave all this behind. I listen to the VM.

Pack your bags, Stockton Ames. Congratulations! You've won an all-expenses paid trip to The TimeResort at Seren Luna, courtesy of The Janos Corporation and United SpaceGate Conglomerate. Voicecom a booking agent right away to claim your prize. And remember, Seren Luna isn't just a destination, it's the voyage of a lifetime!

I chuckle. Not a chance in hell it's legit. I've never won a thing in my life. Not even the goddamn lottery to *buy* Knights tickets. I vaguely remember accepting some gaudy contest outlink in some gaudy infocom a couple months back. It sounds like something I'd do. With a few drinks in me, anyway.

So against my better judgement, I make the call. An actual human being answers. Those synthetic voicecom simulators sound decent enough these days, but they still have a hard time understanding real human input. Make you repeat words left and right like you're some kind of limey New Union immigrant. Not this booking agent though. She's got a raspy, familiar voice, as if we're old friends. Knows my name and everything. I expect to be scammed for money or recos, maybe sold something I can't afford. But no. She doesn't want a thing from me. I won.

At first the snoop in me refuses to believe it, wants to find something fishy, some sinister plot underneath it all. But the overworked cheapskate in me won't hear any of that gripe. Everything is paid for. One round-trip ticket for a week at the galaxy's most overpriced TimeResort. I just need to show up.

It's not quite as simple as all that, though. Traveling to a TimeResort isn't your everyday trip down the shore. You don't just pack a bag and remember your UV pills and your dentascrub module. You pack up your life, because when you get back, it won't be there.

TimeResorts are all built near the edge of the galaxy, or maybe it's the center. About as far from Earth as mankind gets, anyway. Even farther than the most remote offworld colonies. Something about being way the hell out there makes time work differently—relative rotational velocities and gravitational coefficients and theories of this and laws of that. My orientation infocom explains it all in microscopic detail, but that's not my language. I speak in results. And the result of visiting a TimeResort is that life on Earth gets fastplayed while you're gone. Go for a month, and when you get home, four years have passed by for everyone else. The further out the TimeResort, the more time gets skipped. And Seren Luna is the furthest yet. Spend a week there, you come back some twenty odd years into the future.

I shake my head and laugh. It's not for everybody. You have to decide if the price is worth the payoff, and we're not just talking dollars and cents here. Sure, it's the most expensive vacation money can buy. Hell, only the upper crust of the upper crust can afford admission anyway. But there's an additional tradeoff. An expense that won't show on any financial ledger or stock portfolio.

You need to cash in your life and everything in it to take the trip. One of the quirks of travelling to the future is that your present very quickly becomes the past. And there's no getting it back once you go. It's a one-way street. Modern technology can bring you to the future, but not the past. At the end of the day though, the rewards are rich. In return, you get even more fabulous wealth and a fastpass to all of the scientific and social advances that the future promised us. You get a chance to get away from today.

Most folks need to weigh the downside—especially for a resort as *progressively relative* as Seren Luna. That's what they call it: *progressively relative*. Never "fast" or "speedy", or goddamned crazy. The downside is that you have to wave goodbye to everything you know. Your friends and family and neighbors? They get old. Sometimes they die. The city you live in, your neighborhood, the corner bar? Remarkably different when you get back. The media you crawl, the politicos you vote for, the tech you use—all of it—your whole damned life becomes obsolete. Sometimes that's just too much to ask. Sometimes you bring your family along, and anything else small enough to fit in a suitcase. But it's always a hard decision. There's always a sacrifice.

That is, it's a hard decision if you've got anything worth holding onto. Most richos do. Not so much for a charity-case like me. On paper, I just may be the perfect candidate. But the decision is mine to make all the same, and I take my time to make it.

I chew on the choice over dinner. I need to taste the world I'm giving up. To weigh my current life against the possibilities of a better tomorrow. If I'd bothered to ask myself twenty years ago where I'd be today, this sure ain't the answer I'd have given. 'Sad, poor, and lonely' wasn't even an option for the young and gullible Stockton Ames of twenty years ago, that optimistic asshole. I take the present in with deep breaths.

Today smells like the curried stench of the neighbors' cooking. It wafts through the paper thin walls along with their Hinky chatter. Their exotic, offworld stink overpowers my own meal. Leftovers. The fifth day of EasyNuked beef noodles. My life tastes like bad dessert: a lemon pie-flavored toothpick and the bite of cheap bourbon from a cracked glass.

In the other hand, I have the chance of a lifetime—several lifetimes even—to try something different and come back a very rich man indeed. It's the main draw of a joint like Seren Luna, at least for a working stiff like me and the billions of other dreamers that could never afford the ticket in the first place. Put your pennies away and come back loaded, thanks to compound interest and the oodles of time that relativity buys you. I've seen the newstream specials, the banking adverts. Even a bottom-feeder like me can clean up with the racket Seren Luna is offering.

For most of the regular clientele, though, the dough's a very distant second. They always had it and never needed it. These snobs are bullish on the tech growth. Got an incurable disease? Visit the TimeResort. Someone will have a treatment all sorted out by the time you get back. These are the kind of people that print their own money. But a vacation as a shortcut to immortality? It's an easy sell for anybody.

In the end, the decision makes itself. It just takes a half-a-handle of corn mash to help me swallow it. I toss my dinner tray in the compressor when it hits me; my mind is made up. I'm going to Seren Luna, the ritziest goddamned resort in the whole goddamned lonely universe. And I'm giving up my life to do it.

So long shitty job. Goodbye crappy, cramped apartment. See ya next time dirtbag friends, distant cold family, non-existent love life. I'm going away for a bit. When I get back, I'll be rich and you'll all be gone.

I book the trip and chase the last few drops of hooch out the plastic jug. Then I call it a night, still sprawled out on the lounger. The latenight sportstream pundit on the holo chitters me a lullaby. The somnopod—and a night of restful sleep—stay tucked away below my backside.

I wake with a stiff neck and hock my life at the local pawn dealer, all at once. Any clothes that won't fit in my bag, the Murphy lounger somnopod and holoprojector wardrobe unit. The cooking nook EasyNuke. This small pittance—the only sticks of furniture in my place and a few tattered rags—make up the majority of my life savings. But it's enough. I transfer the take to a PeoplesBank long-term interest fund, The Time Traveller's Package. Everything else goes in my old, rust-stained packbot. The antique P280 model I've had since I was just a boy. It's the only piece of my life I intend to bring back.

I don't even say goodbye, with a single exception. I catch the midday express over the river and slip down through miles of sprawling industrial park to the memorial gardens. Drooping smokestacks crawl over the gates and bare-limbed trees as I stroll to a familiar plot in subsection 42C. The grass needs a mow, but the landscaper could say the same thing about my chin. Smiling, I snap the stalks from some wilty irises and toss them on her stone. Just like a young Stockton Ames was once upon a time, these flowers were her favorite.

I stand tall and stare at the headstone, my coat flapping in the stiff breeze off the stinking river. The lease on her plot will run up before I get back, so I won't get another shot at this. There won't be a second goodbye, not that there was anything 'good' about the first one. I don't say much. Never do. She deserves better and always did. Her only child, I never was much of a son and I don't have the time to start being one now. "So long, Ma."

I skip the station on my way back to my empty apartment. No note for the boys in blue. They'll be looking for me down at the precinct come Monday. Well, they might check a few of the local watering holes first. I might even make the missing citizen query. That's rich. As far as the government knows I'm just another lost soul, swallowed up by the tough times and the big, ugly city.

I stand in my apartment, completely bare, and breathe in what's left of my life. Some peeling paint, a pile of dust and dead bugs. I even hocked the holo of The Big Guy. Is it worth it? A vacation will be aces, but am I going to enjoy what I find when I get back? Or was the problem something inside *me* all along? I peek under the sink, where the half-broken hinge lets the cabinet hang loose. The trash peeks out. I gather the big bag and smile to myself. Then I toss it outside the Johnstons' door on my way out.

I hail a cab to the terminal, and why not? I'm a big shot now, I'll save the tram for all those poor suckers I'm leaving behind. We pass no less than five holoboards hawking Seren Luna on the way there. They're not the kind of 'verts Madison Ave whips up for a guy like me. Classy, simple affairs. Big glowing signs with black and white waifs staring into each other's sparkling eyes. Understated. Elegant. They belong to that hoity family of ads that don't even have the courtesy to tell you what they're selling. What Seren Luna is. And they don't need to; if you don't know already, you can't afford to go.

As we cruise uptown through the familiar stop-and-go, break-neck traffic, I roll the window down and look out over my city. A toothless hobo gives me the finger and shakes a tiny gun at the cab as I let the wind blow through my hair. I can't help but smile. She's big and crowded and ugly and dirty, and the air in this neighborhood always stinks like boiling cabbages and burning tires—but she's mine. She's all I've ever known and I'm afraid, just the teensiest bit afraid, that I might miss her while I'm away. Deep down though, I know she'll still be here when I get back, and that she won't even notice I was gone at all.

I swipe my ArmPod to pay the fare and the drivebot synth mumbles an incoherent thanks. I give his hollow rubber head a healthy smack on my way out. I miss the human drivers from when I was a kid. Never had to worry about them having a malfunctioning vocal modulator or missing a critical routing patch. Human hardware is more resilient than modern times gives it credit for. Nobody trusts a real person to do anything a piece of software and a hunk of plastic can do for them anymore.

I step out onto the terminal plaza curb. Another JanosCorp ad scrolls across the awning overhead. The corporate logo materializes on the margins. The two-faced man, looking to the past and to the future. I wave to him, hello and goodbye, and step into the station.

Everything I still own is tucked away safe in the packbot at my side as it follows me through the crowded entrance. It's my first time at the SpaceGate terminal and I'm not quite sure where to go first. I stop inside to get my bearings. Suits and skirts blow by me with that universal snobbo sneer, noses high, on their way to the gates. These are supposed to be the beautiful people, but you'd never know it from the constant grimace smeared across their pretty faces.

I look around. The SpaceGates are mostly used for long distance stuff, and I've never even been off-planet before. Unless you count a couple of low-orbit dinner dates with the occasional badge bunny: sisters that needed an inside man for a spat with John Law. Hell, I'd never even sunned myself on the decks of a YangtzeSystems' star-liner, the poor man's TimeResort. What can I say? I like to keep firmly grounded. Finally, I spot the signage for the security checkpoint.

I hop in at the end of a long line and look forward to spending the next thirty-five minutes staring into the greasy neck of the shlump in front of me. For all the cash these people dropped on their tickets, USG did their damnedest to hire the least amount of the least educated, least pleasant baggage screeners they could get away with. I watch one uni-formed dropout spend the better part of three minutes staring aimlessly at a closed zipper. Either unwilling, or unsure how, to open it.

After ten minutes in queue, I'm suddenly skeptical about the need for security for this kind of travel. We shoot the void single file after all. But then I remember what those jihadi commie bastards did to Phoenix when they dropped a bomb through the gate back in '39. Popped a dimensional rift. Sucked the whole damned valley and every-one in it down some swirling vortex, and ain't nobody seen 'em since. They say it's much nicer to visit Arizona now, but still. These security shmos should be screened themselves for basic human intelligence if it's a whole city on the line.

I pass the time soaking in the orientation media that I skipped at home and digging at the dirt under my nails with a half-chewed cherry flavorstick. Lord knows the grime will show in the security scan. I've never used one before, but I'm vaguely familiar with the SpaceGate process. I know enough to know it isn't something I want to screw around with, Phoenix besides. A whole mess of holos lays it out for us in the line as we wait like sheep at the department of mutton vehicles.

First they deepscan you, every molecule, inside and out. Then they give you a sleeping pill. Then they pull you apart with something called a resonance de-harmonizer, until you're nothing but a cloud of floating particles. The particles in the orientation stream all have little smileycons on them. Adorable. Then they take your particles and the deepscan data and pass it through a great big whatsit that sits deep below the terminal. A wormhole field generator, they call it. A WFG. This big machine rips a tiny hole in the very fabric of space and shoots you right in, one atom at a time. You take a short ride at the speed of light, straight into the terrible emptiness of the fifth dimension. An interstellar shortcut through The Great Big Nowhere. Then your particles and data pop out from an identical WFG at your destination and they staple you back together with a resonance re-stabilizer. Simple as pie.

"Wonderful," I say aloud. "What's to keep my particles from getting all mixed up with some other sap's?"

This guy next to me, a real well-off asshole in an ugly, hundred-thousand-dollar coat, turns to me. "The particles aren't what's impor-tant, bud. Your particles? My particles? They're all the same. It's the datafeed that matters…. So they can put you back together again?"

Mr. Moneybags says it like a question—a question a child should already know the answer to. He even rolls his eyes at me, the smug bastard. I have half-a-mind to pop him one. "Thanks pal, I feel much better. So forget the particles, it's only the goddamned datafeed that's keeping me from coming out the other end like so much McTasty's Brand meatpattie."

I move on, the packbot wheezing after me.

A lifetime later, it's my turn. A youngish, barrel-shaped broad with an accent thicker than Jupiter Stew stands before me. She twirls plas-tic-looking, bottle-blond braids with two-inch fingernails that look like a Princess Rainbow Pony got sick all over them.

"Good afternoon, my lovelies," she says, blowing a fist-sized bubble of bright pink gum. "Welcome to the security checkpoint."

I approach with my sleeve pulled back, ready for my MPD to be scanned. She passes the scanner over my wrist and tosses her hair. "Hi there, sweetness," she says. She waves me forward with the candy-polished fingernails gleaming like signal beacons. Then she points towards an ominous machine: the Universal Hazard Detector. It's big and mean and the opening looks like it wants to swallow me up and spit me out in several pieces on the other side. I see the smartass fella in front of me disappear into the gaping maw.

"Don't be scared, honey," she says. "When you walk through con-fetti's gonna shoot out."

I eye her cautiously and step into the dark tunnel. A blast of air nearly lifts me out of my shoes and a buzzing static charge makes the hair on my arms benchpress my sleeves. A terrible siren starts to scream. I cover my ears and glare at the woman.

"That ain't confetti," I say.

She returns my stare with a hand on her hip and a shake of her stupid head. "No, baby. No it's not."

After a quick date with a security ape with cold hands, I'm through the gauntlet. I've managed to convince this team of highly-trained professionals that I do not pose a danger to myself or others—or that it's not their job to care one way or the other. It was the bolts in my bum knee that threw the alarm, honest it was. It takes the pinhead ten minutes to scan my legs up and down twelve ways from Tuesday. His beeping wand bitches enough to make him happy and he lets me walk, packbot in tow. I'm just glad he let me leave my pants on until he could get me someplace 'private.' There are children in the terminal, for crying out loud.

I step out from behind an uncomfortably sheer curtain and give my trousers a quick zip. A ServRep skirt in JanosCorp navy and orange waits for me at the ticketing lounge, just ahead. She's got shoulder length locks the color of my morning DunkRoast, no cream, and legs that go all the way up. A couple of jade jewels light up her face, my libido. Her top lip is a touch malnourished for my taste, but the bottom one is oh so right. Plump and sassy. In fact I'd love to give it a tiny taste, if she'd only be so kind. I won't hold my breath though. That upturned kisser parts in the middle of an otherwise uptight face as she calls out to me.

"Over here, Mr. Ames."

I'll be damned if it's not the same girl from the voicecom. How could I forget that raspy familiarity? That curt intonation? Like she wants me to know she's a ServRep, but not a servant.

I take a long drink of her as I waltz over. She's a pretty young thing. Delicate but fierce. Athletic frame. Soft features. Nice trim package too, like a well-appointed sportscar. Just the type to test drive, but not something you want to keep in the garage; I couldn't make the payments. She wouldn't be a half-bad catch either, if she'd let her hair down and stop calling me Mr. Ames.

I tell her as much, on both accounts.

She frowns and gives it a go.

"Stockton, then," it comes out awkward, like she's speaking English for the first time. "My name is Audrine DeMarco. On behalf of The Janos Corporation and United SpaceGate Conglomerate, congratulations. I'll be your guest services liaison. It's my duty to assist you in any way you desire for the duration of your stay. Here is your itinerary and gate pass."

Our MPDs kiss as she handshakes the data to me. I tell her thanks. She motions towards the gate but I stop her before she can get too far ahead of herself.

"Say doll, haven't we met before? I've got an itch like we're old pals." It's not just a line. This broad is familiar as failure. I know I've seen that face before. Heard that gravelly voice call my name. And not just in my dreams. This whole scene is playing out like a cheap rerun.

"We spoke over the voicecom…"

"No, that's not it," I say, shaking my head. "Spend any time downtown? Off the N-tram? Shakey's? The Wellton? …Twitchy Bill's?"

She frowns. "I'm positive you're mistaken," she says, but in her eyes—and in my heart—I know she doesn't mean it. She spins on her heel a little too quickly, and changes the subject as we march. "Are you sure we can't offer you a new packbot? Courtesy of The Janos Corporation of course. Yours seems to be… limping." She says it polite as she can, still twice as rude as she'd like, I'm sure.

I take a look. The old guy does seem to have a bit of a wobble to his float these days. One of the first Lev models, practically an antique with this crowd. "He'll be fine," I say. "Ain't missed a train yet."

She smiles, although clearly unhappy with my decision. If I know anything about women, it's that the lips may say one thing, but the eyes never lie. She bends over to examine the packbot more closely, fiddles with his casing. I do an examination of my own.

"I'll take him from here," she says. "How do I activate the PRP?"

"The whatnow?"

"The pheromone recognition protocol?" she says, trying too hard not to sound surprised by my ignorance.

"Not on this model, honey," I reply. I fish the homing chit out of my coat pocket and drop it into her slowly outstretching palm. She looks at it like we weren't all using them twenty years ago. Nuts, twenty years ago she was just a kid. Audrine DeMarco nods and smiles. She begins to walk away. Limpy teeters after her.

"We'll be waiting for you, Mr. Ames," she says over her shoulder, "at Seren Luna."

I rush after her. Quite a dramatic exit, standing ovation, but I'm not ready for goodbyes just yet. "Just a sec, doll."

She stops. Turns to wait as I walk over with my hat in my hand.

"This is my first trip by SpaceGate..."

She stares back at me with a beautifully empty expression.

"Would you like me to review the orientation media with you?"

I shake my head. "Listen. All I want to know is, are these things safe? These wormhole fields and resonance wreckers and whathaveyou? Seems to me like a lot of messing around with important things we don't fully understand."

She sighs but tries to hide it midway through. This is a lecture she's been over before, although maybe not with many full-grown adults. "Things *you* don't understand," she corrects me. "I can assure you, Mr. Ames, travel by wormhole is incredibly safe. Statistically much safer than riding your N-tram, so long as you don't try to tunnel one through the middle of a star or a black hole or something idiotic like that."

I frown at her.

She sighs again; this time there's no holding it back.

"And you will most certainly not be doing any such thing, Mr. Ames. We are all professionals here. The wormhole network has been laid out and active for years now, used safely by millions of passengers. Our USG technicians understand the risks and take every measure to ensure the most pleasant, danger-free experience for all of our guests. I've personally travelled by SpaceGate hundreds of times without incident. I assure you, you'll be just fine."

I feel moderately better.

"Thanks," I say, "but just for argument's sake, what would happen if your boys were to screw the pooch, send my particles flying right smack dab into the center of a big bad black hole? By accident, you know? Humor me."

She doesn't have to think about it.

"I wouldn't know," she says.

I cock my head and wait for the explanation.

"No one's ever come out the other side to tell us about it," she says.

My jaw hangs limp. Not the answer I was hoping to hear.

"That's how black holes work, Mr. Ames. Things go in. Nothing comes out."

I grimace. Maybe this isn't such a great idea.

She picks up on my hesitation.

"If it would make you feel any better," she says, "I can arrange for someone to hold your hand."

She smiles and walks away again.

THREE

I saunter over to the gate, a gaudy affair draped in chrome curves and black velvet swirls. A lanky lackey hands me a bright blue SomnoTab sleeping pill stamped with a smileycon imprint. He leads me to an overstuffed hoverchair floating eighteen inches off the polished concrete floor. Is this actual leather? Color me impressed. I sink deep into the cowskin and think twice about popping the pill. It sits heavy in my palm: one last chance to pull out. Risks and rewards swap wallops in my head.

Forget it. I've only got one life to live. I spit-swallow the pill and switch out like a light, thank God. No time to second guess myself now.

I awake an instant later, standing in a perfectly empty white room. Something buzzes below me. A steady stream of smiling particles pours out of the floor and swirl around me, each one laughing like a pea-sized jackal. Cackling in my face. I try to swat the clouds away but my arms go gimp, hang dead at my sides. I stand there, helpless as a babe, as the miniature monsters begin to zip into my screaming mouth. I choke on them, coughing fits, unable to breathe.

And then I'm awake. *Really* awake. I gasp and sit up straight, Audrine DeMarco's emerald eyes only inches away.

"Good evening, Mr. Ames."

She smiles and stands up straight, leaving a trace of some angelic scent, like jasmine and the sea. I shut my eyes again and take her in. Like a rooftop garden after a rain.

"I hope your travel was pleasant?"

"Dreamy," I say, pawing at my lids with two fists. I know the room is hardly sunny, but I squint in the dark all the same. "Why's it seem so damned bright in here?"

Audrine takes my hands from my eyes and helps me to my feet. Her skin is soft but her grip is firm. My head swims a tad less at her touch, but I still feel a little like the packbot as I try to take a step towards her.

"A side effect of the sleeping medication, I'm afraid." She doesn't sound sorry. I've got a hunch this is a broad who doesn't make many sincere apologies. "Your eyes will adjust quickly, and your balance should return shortly thereafter."

She tells the truth.

My surroundings slowly come into focus, and at a glance, nothing appears all that different from the terminal back on Earth. Ritzier, sure, but done up in the same kind of classic stylings. All metal and stone and smooth, strong lines. It's simple in the expensive kind of way. Like a luxury sedan, or a good hat.

"Just so long as you put my peepers back together right," I say with a yawn. "I got a lot to look at."

She gives me a cold, hard stare, like she can't quite figure out if I'm ribbing her or making a pass. Good. Best to leave a twist like this on her toes. Keep some of my cards off the table.

Audrine leads me across the arrival chamber to a large display set into a rough granite wall. A sequence of square panels with illuminated markings sits perched inside a stony alcove. It reads *+00000Y000D00H00S*. Above the digits hangs an etched silver sign that spells *Relativity*.

"Looks like your clock is broken," I say.

Audrine takes my wrist—the one with the MPD—and holds it up to the display. There's a soft *beepbeep* as the clock clicks to life. It starts to count up, slow-like.

"You had to register with the resort first," she says. "Now that we've created a timestamp in your MPD, this Relativity Clock will calculate the amount of time dilation you've experienced since arriving. It's a function of our velocity, relative to that of the Earth, with a variant for the increased gravitational forces pre—"

"Right, right." I say, stifling another yawn. "Counting the days since I've been gone."

"The *Earth* days since you've been gone," she corrects me.

I shrug. "Why can't you just give me the grand total straight from the start? You know how long I'll be up here. Should be some simple arithmetic for a smart girl like you, no?"

Audrine smiles at me, but she doesn't mean it.

"If you hadn't interrupted me, I'd planned to tell you exactly why it's *not* so simple."

I motion for her to continue.

"There are a variety of tiny variables which can change the total time dilation each guest may experience. Variables about which you've made it abundantly clear you are not interested in hearing. We can give you the ballpark figure, so to speak, but your precise number may change as your journey with us continues."

"Precise numbers for a gig like this? Who needs 'em? Nobody knows what we'll head back to anyways. The world's a crazy place. Finding out what it turns into feels like half the fun for a fella like me."

"Regardless," she says, "many of our *paying* guests enjoy knowing exactly how much time dilation they've accumulated."

I nod. "It's why they shell out the big bucks to ship off all the way out here."

"Exactly, Mr. Ames." Audrine blinks twice, then motions back to the clock. "Now that you have the initial registry, you can calculate your personal time dilation at any Relativity Clock console throughout the resort. It can be useful for coordinating with events back on Earth."

"Eh," I shrug. "That's not really my cup of DunkRoast. I don't even wear a watch." I flash her my bare wrist and tuck the one with the MPD behind my back. She doesn't so much as smile at the gag.

"Do you have any more questions, Mr. Ames?" she says, barely stopping her eyes mid-roll.

"Yeah," I say. "Just one. Do you think we'll need all those goose eggs over by the year?" I point to the row of five zeros parked at the far end of the clock. "Seems a bit excessive, relativity or no, but what the hell do I know about it?"

Audrine turns her back to the flipping digits and walks away.

"Most guests won't," she says. "*You* certainly will not." She shuts her eyes. "Some of us employees though, that's another story." She motions for me to follow her. My legs still work, more or less.

"You'll see that your friend is still with us," she says.

Old Wobbles waits patiently by the doorway—something he was not programmed to do when we stepped out of the cab back on Earth. He limps after us as we walk out of the room.

"And here I thought you couldn't teach an old suitcase new tricks," I say. "Does he roll over and play dead now too?"

She shrugs. "I'm a great teacher."

Her heels *click-clack* down the checked marble floor of a long, low lit corridor. This joint feels a touch dated, but really kind of timeless. Like a nice suit. Well-made, but not showy. The kind of place you'd expect the politicos and their corporate constituents to hang. It's cool but not cold. Polished to a chic, mirror sheen. Every line is a work of art. Every work of art a committee decision. It's got class, but no character. Exactly the kind of house I never had the chance to haunt back home.

We reach the end of the hallway and step out into a huge atrium. It's all swooping beams and sweeping crystal facades. Not a single square angle or straight line in the place. And through that great glass bubble I look out and see the face of God Almighty himself. Now I've never been much of a believer, but a view like that will fill a fella with faith fairly fast.

What appears to be all of blessed creation sits splayed out before me like His dazzling countenance. A pair of broiling red stars fill up half the heavens, burning bright enough for me to squint but not so strong for me to cry about it. Like two lovers, the stars slow dance together in a sensual embrace. The rest of the universe turns in sync behind them, a swirling spiral of milky tears, stretched out to infinity. Delicate ribbons of color spill out from the nearest stars—a nebula, wrapped around itself in soft tangles and swaths of brilliance. A billion silky hues blossom in this cosmic cradle. My eyes feast on a buffet of colors they never even knew existed.

Somewhere out there, you'll find everything that ever was or ever will be. I'm perched at the edge of existence, and the view reminds me that we're all dancing to the same song, no matter where we stand. I feel incredibly small, impossibly young and insignificant. A speck of dust on a dinosaur's diamond ring.

The view takes the breath right out of my mouth. I stop dead in my tracks and forget about the girl, the sweepstakes, the resort. The life I gave up for it all. It's so damned beautiful my eyes start to water.

Suddenly she's behind me, whispering in my ear, my good ear. "Sometimes I forget," she says. "What it's like to see for the first time. The whole galaxy, laid out like a pic-a-nic, just for you."

I don't see them, mostly on account of not looking, but I know her eyes have gone a touch glossy too. She's a little girl again, full of hope and wonder for the world and everything she knows it can be.

"A picta-what?" I say, regaining composure. These kids and their newfangled gadgets. "It's real nice, yeah. Hell of a view." I force myself to look away.

She continues staring out the viewport, her eyes a little wet after all. I've got a hunch that this crabby demeanor is a practiced act. A carefully crafted shell over something softer and sadder than she'll ever let on.

Audrine shakes it off, continues the lesson.

"Those two big neutron stars make up the Calvera II star system," she says. "A binary system, of course. They're our resident eye candy here at Seren Luna. Our orbit on the resort is tidally locked at the best viewing angle, so they're always on display."

We both stare in silence.

Until a sharp dressed stick of a fella approaches, interrupting our little moment in endangered leather loafers. This guy tucks an antique golden fountain pen into a small leather notebook as he walks towards us, then pockets the whole kit and kaboodle carefully. He looks official. He smells important. His suit is slick as ice and just a hair shy of swishy. It fits him like a silk spraytan. Here's a guy vain enough to have enough work done so that even a stooge like me can see it. I'll be damned if he was born with that Greek beak, or that chiseled chin. His smile screams of plastic and expensive dental work. He's my favorite kind of guy to avoid.

I get a sniff like his introduction is phoney too. Scripted. The déjà vu comes roaring back, makes my head swim, just like it did with the dame. I could swear I know him, too. Like his smug, condescending face is burned into my brain right beside Audrine's gorgeous greens and sultry squawk.

"Welcome to The TimeResort at Seren Luna, Mr. Ames." His accent marks him exotic, though not exactly foreign. His voice is smooth as a chocolate shake, sharp as a smack to the face. "Miss DeMarco, would you kindly show Mr. Ames to the Imperial statesuite? I'm sure he'd like to freshen up after his journey. Hurry now. Supper will be served shortly in the Garden Dome."

"Yes sir, Mr. Proletti," she ducks her head, avoids his eyes. "Right this way, Mr. Ames."

She gestures towards one of the half-dozen hallways that feed into the lobby. Lets me lead, but tails close. I can feel Slick's eyes stuck to the back of my skull until we round the first bend.

I hate him already. Not because he's rich, and not because he's good looking. Not even because he thinks he's a better man than me. Hell, *that* I'm used to. What gets me all wound up is that he's managed to give me orders without sounding like he was telling me what to do. I'll take a hood with a heater over a creep like him any day. With the hood, at least you know to keep an eye on his trigger finger. Highpockets here could knock me off from any which way and I'd never even see it coming.

Girl, cop, and suitcase, our little posse tramps its way through all manner of fancypants passages. There's no view from here, but the decor isn't half bad. Everything looks hard, solid. Expensive. Oversized, important artworks that I'll never understand hang in golden gilded frames. It's the kind of place that makes me nervous, like I might dry my hands on the curtains.

I walk point, taking directions from my suddenly sullen little temptress. That Proletti jerk really got to her too, it seems. Old Rusty pulls up the rear, nipping at our heels like a good little boy. Silver slidelocks stand ominously shut in gaping alcoves every hundred yards or so as we breeze by.

"I gather you don't like Slick back there anymore than I do?"

"Is it that obvious?" she says. She frowns, and slows her pace to chat.

"Just a hunch." I shrug. "He doesn't seem the type to make nice with." She smiles.

"What's his story, anyway? He carries more puff in his pocket than your average mater dee."

"He does, doesn't he?" She muffles a giggle. "Stephon Proletti was a brilliant up-and-coming theoretical physicist. He left a cushy, tenure-track research grant to come work with us here at The Janos Corporation."

I take a stab at it.

"On first impressions, I'd wager it was the paycheck?"

"Maybe," Audrine says. "There were lots of stories floating around when he first arrived at the corporate offices. Experiments gone wrong, losing the love of his life because he was too wrapped up in his work—those kinds of rumors. Nothing with any solid evidence to support it. Some of us—those that have been around a while—we even wondered if he'd just flat out lost his mind to come work at a place like this."

I nod. "And he's been here, riding your ass ever since?"

She frowns at my turn of phrase.

"No," she says. "Not the whole time. He started in corporate research and development, doing E&M work, mostly. That's exploration and mapping, for new resort projects and the like. Seren Luna was his brainchild, and he jumped on board as soon as it got the green light. Moved into Operations. He insisted on personally overseeing every detail since the construction crews finished. Rode over with the first fresh produce delivery and never left. Not one time back to Earth since the grand opening, or so the staff likes to say. That was seventy-five years ago, relative time—just over a month here. You could say he's something of a control freak."

"Maybe that's why I can't stand him," I say. But deep down, I know it's so much more than that. This is a man I was born and bred to hate. It's already in my bones and I just met the guy.

We pick up the pace and march through the wide, cold hallways in silence. After a series of twists and turns that would make a fish dizzy, we pull up and park in front of one of the doors.

"The slidelock for your suite has automatically registered your biorhythm and will grant you access." She gives me a little shove towards the door. Friendly I'm sure, but with enough mustard to do a dog right. Just like she promised, it opens right up. Slides away silently.

That's a little funny to me. No MPD AccessKards, no handscans, no goddamn keys? "Automagically, huh? And just how does my room know what my biorhythm looks like?"

She stares me straight in the eyes, doesn't bat a lash. "While you were in transit, we took certain… liberties. We forwarded your deep-scan datafeed to the resort cloud. Only to better serve you, of course."

I snort. "Any other 'liberties' I should know about while I was squiffed-out in your custody, lady?"

I give her a quick wink but she ignores me.

"If that's all, Mr. Ames, you should find every accommodation in your Imperial statesuite. Truly the finest room in the resort, I can assure you. If you need anything at all, please don't hesitate to voice-com me. My outlink has been uploaded to your MPD. Good evening, Mr. Ames."

She turns and walks away.

I call out after her. "How do I teach my room to let you in?"

She doesn't stop.

"At least have dinner with me!"

Was that a slight hitch in her step?

No. She keeps right on walking.

"And call me Stockton!"

I retire to my 'Imperial statesuite', the packbot in tow. She never returned his homing chit. Guess she did show him some new tricks after all.

A marble-lined turbolift carries me up some unfathomable distance. I'm not in the lift long, but these luxury models can really book it. I run my hands along the wall and wonder how many moons they hollowed out to get all the pretty, polished stone for a place like this. Rusty and I glide to a halt and the lift opens wide to reveal my room in all its 'Imperial' glory.

Apparently I'm sleeping in a giant goddamned terrarium. A real palace, this place, under the same type of framed, clear dome as the lobby. Abstract and asymmetrical and absolutely bananas. My suite rises high above the rest of the resort. And judging by the other structures dotting the landscape, it's shaped like a huge mushroom. The living quarters are a round, flat-bottomed cap sitting above the skinny lift-stalk I just rode up.

From the look of things, I'm King Shroom. Hundreds of subjects bow in reverence to his Imperial Suite-ness. They spread out across the smooth surface of this rock to the horizon. It's a relief to see a slab of stone down there under the fungal towers. Means there's a planet below me. I know some of these TimeResorts are fully fabricated, artificial satellites. Glorified rocket ships. No thanks. I prefer to take my vacations on solid ground, thank you very much.

Audrine didn't razz me about the room.

It's about as big as my entire floor back home. All twenty-four tiny housing units would fit quite comfortably in this castle. I think briefly about my neighbors gawking around in here and shudder. Well, it's as big as my floor *was* anyway. They've probably already knocked down the crumbling, old stack of crap. Mrs. Johnston won't know what to do with herself without her favorite detective to pester. I try to figure how much time has passed back on Earth. Is old Edna J. even still kicking? If one week equals almost eighteen years and I've been here for an hour… The calculations crumble to dust in my head. A lingering, dull headache is my reward for the effort.

I'd love to nap it off but I can't find the somnopod. Where the hell do you sleep in this palace? There's a mountain of pillows on what looks like a huge stretched-out lounge unit over in goddamned Sector C, just past the pool. A closer inspection reveals a handwritten note pinned to one of the pillows. I haven't seen so much handwriting in my whole life since I met this dame.

This is a 'bed.' You sleep on it. Enjoy.
            -Audrine

Bed, huh? I sit on the edge and Wheezy totters over to me. Not sure how much shut-eye I'll catch in a convertible like this. A guy like me gets pretty attached to dozing with the help of automated oxygen control, not to mention the half-dozen other features afforded by the last thirty-five years of somnopod technology. These richos go ape over outdated styles, but they might just find out how grumpy I get without my beauty sleep.

May as well put my things away instead. I crack Rusty's hatch and start with an industrial-sized box of multiflavor chewsticks. Then I work on pulling out my tropicos and my best suit—the one that's only been patched up a couple of times. I have a hard time finding a button-down without any DunkRoast stains.

I pop open the wardobe storage unit. Damned thing's just about as big as a house. And looky here, there's already something inside. The return servo slings it up to me from the cavernous depths of the stupid thing. A single hanger quivers to a sudden stop. It's a tux. It's the tux of tuxes. Creased and crimped a thousand times over, in the latest and greatest fall fashion. I run my hands over the jet black fabric, soft as spun butter. I've never even *seen* clothes so nice, not even on the awardstreams.

There's another little note pinned to the collar.

Courtesy of The Janos Corporation.
            -A

Another one of those liberties? I'm sure it fits like a dream—better than Slick's ensemble even—but I put on my old patched-up suit and the only unstained shirt instead. It fits like a sack but at least it's mine. And besides, I hate pleats. My tie found the DunkRoast that the shirt missed so I snatch the jeweled cravat from the Imperial tux. A frilly ridiculous thing, but what the heck. When in Rome, right? I want to look my best at dinner, if only for my own sake.

I take a swill of corn mash from the plastic jug in my packbot, then, against my better judgement, leave it on the little ledge next to the somnopo— next to the 'bed.' I head back over towards the turbo-lift. Takes me five minutes just to find the damned thing. This place is beginning to make me feel small *and* slow.

I point at Wheezy.

"Stay," I tell him.

He does. The door shuts. Yesterday he would have smashed up into the closed slidelock until I got back or his batteries died, which-ever came first. I run my fingers over the delicate embroidery of the cravat around my neck as the lift descends. I smirk to myself. "What a difference a day makes."

A short ride later, I emerge into the hallway and I come to the sudden, horrific conclusion that I have absolutely no clue where to find the mess hall. 'Garden Dome,' Slick said. I look around for some sort of directions. Turn up empty. These rooms don't even have numbers. I search for help down the hallway, but nobody's home.

I tap my teeth. The only thing to do is pick a direction and start hoofing. I've got about as good a chance as an augmentation-free sprinter in the Vertical Mile, but I'm not one to take my licks lying down. I set out down a long, empty passage. It's amazing just how quiet this joint can be. Could almost make a fella miss the hustle and bustle of the big, ugly city back home. The traffic and the honking and the babies crying and the couples fighting and the chittering neighbors with their lousy, off-world accents.

For the first time the reality of my situation sinks in. I may never hear any of those sounds again. When I get home, a hundred years from yesterday, it may very well be to some idyllic wonderland. Some peaceful haven of quiet contemplation and perfect social structure. A place where it's illegal to raise your voice. Like the anti-honk zones for the magcabs and hovertrucks, but spread across a whole planet, and with better enforcement.

I shut my eyes as I walk, try to remember what I've left behind. The good and the bad. I remember the sad, dirty crowd on the weekday N-tram, the busted yellow taxis and their busted rubber drivers. The uptown view from the SkyPark and the smell of the steaming, dirty-water-dogs they still sling up there. The unsure shuffle of fat packs of dipshit tourists, and the professional strut of the wisest of the working girls. Hell, I might even miss those noisy Hink neighbors and the dozen odd brats they packed into the rathole next door. I remember the lot of a middle-aged blue collar nobody, and fifty million more just like me, because—if for no other reason—*somebody* should remember it. When I return, I may be the last living remnant of a life in the shitter.

I wander aimlessly through a labyrinth of identical hallways until, eventually, I hear a soft hum from up ahead. It's good to hear anything at all. Means I haven't wandered myself right onto an episode of *The Forbidden Dimension*. I haven't seen a soul or heard a peep since I left my room twenty minutes ago, and it's starting to eat at my nerves. Like that feeling when you aren't sure if you locked your front door, but you're too far away to do anything about it. I round a big bend to find an old synthbot hunched over, scrubbing a spot on the floor. He's not human—and that *never* sits well with me—but I guess I can trust him enough for directions to the diner.

"Hey bub," I say.

A creaky bucket of bolts whirls around to face me. He's vaguely human-looking. Two arms. Two legs. A face. Got nothing on the late models though, especially those AutoDyne LexSynths. Rumor has it half the pro ballclubs have secretly-syntho players on their rosters. But the robot rising to his feet before me couldn't pass for the real thing if he choked to death on a ham sandwich. He's a classic model. An interesting choice for a joint like this, but I guess these richos do love their antiques. His skin is rubbery and dry under a long-tailed butler-tux as his twitchy, robot eyes look me over. He moves with a clunky efficiency that's far too precise to be natural. Something in my gut crawls up into my fists, nearly fighting-mad at the sight of his plastic face.

"Hello sir." His voice modulator is a little rough around the edges. A nice touch. Reminds me of the syntho sexbots working the poorer corners back home. "How may I be of s-s-s-service to you?"

"Looking for directions, chief," I say. "To the Garden Dome." I tap an invisible wristwatch. "It's dinner time, so let's be quick about it, huh buddy?"

"Why y-y-y-yes sir, of course." He whips around nervously. I've never met a jittery robot before. It's a little funny, a little sad. "Ummm, sir have you checked your multipurpose device? I believe resort p-p-p-policy is to provide each guest with a full c-complement of facility infographics modules."

I glance down at my MPD and shrug. Why not? She took care of everything else. Doesn't seem the type to leave a cookie on the counter. I'm not the type to lean on my ArmPod when the going gets grimy, but then again, I'm not the standard breed, especially for a ritzy joint like Seren-freaking Luna. I swipe around a bit. Sure enough, there's the routing protocol, right on my feed screen, right where she left it.

"Thanks, buddy." I give him a pat on the back. Normally I'm no bleeding-circuit activist—they're just machines, after all—but something about this creaky unit puts my normal qualms at ease. "What's your ID pal?"

"Of c-c-c-course, sir. I am an Automated Dynamics model G-G6, d-d-designated SAMM-E." He sneaks a peek at that same spot on the floor. Eager beaver. "Enjoy your d-d-d-dinner, sir."

"Well, thanks Sammy." I tip my non-existent hat to him and get going. Leave him to his mop job. The routing protocol gives me step-by-step directions through another maze of snaking spaghetti corridors. I'm up a creek without it. There's not a single infograph or datahub anywhere in this joint.

After a short hike where I'm sure I've lapped myself twice, I approach a grand arch of light shining above the end of a chrome hallway. Looks about right.

A wide ramp leads up to yet another clear-roofed atrium. This one's similar to the lobby—just another big glass bubble with one hell of a view—but it's absolutely crawling with flora inside. Not that plastic crap either. Real live plants. I snap a leaf and sniff. Not too shabby. I feel like a character from one of the old adventurestreams, strolling into the goddamned jungle. It's all I can do to keep from beating my fists across my chest, howling like a wildman, and riding a vine to the table.

A guy in a monkeysuit clears his throat.

I quickly stash the leaf in a pocket.

"Ahem," the guy says, raising his eyebrows at me. He takes a quick breath. "Right this way, Mr. Ames. Your guest is waiting."

FOUR

"My guest, huh?" Wonder who that could be?

Monkeysuit leads me through a swank jungle swarming with all kinds of richos and richograndes. Dames dripping in fake tits, real jewels, and dead animals. Fellas sporting championship rings, high-flying designer hairdoos, and academy awards. Everyone in this zoo's got more money than sense. It's amazing what it costs to look utterly ridiculous these days. The crumpled tux hanging in my closet would sit firmly on the conservative side of the scale in a place like this. Squinting through a sea of sequins and sparkling stones, I glance over a hundred faces I recognize from the newstreams and mediafeeds. This must be the most important dining room in the galaxy, and don't they all just know it.

I shake my head as my eyes dance around the tables. It's no wonder there's no talent left on Earth. Here's where it all disappeared to. All the best ballplayers, 'stream stars, and musicians from the last fifty years are cram-packed onto this rock, into this restaurant.

RELATIVITY

Here's a crowd of dinosaurs, still in their prime, living it up with like-minded company in this 'so-fast-it's-frozen-in-time' fishbowl of a resort. It's like Hollywood heaven, except each celeb-u-tarian is only biding his time, waiting to make a glorious return to save the rotten soul of a planet he's nearly forgotten. 'Pop culture purgatory' sounds more like it.

There's Margalene Del Monte dining with Sonny Marone. Staring wistfully into his eyes like they had never left the set of *The Cruelest Facade* some thirty-odd Earth years ago. Like the script was real and they hadn't gotten to the backstabbing bits yet. I stroll past Frankie Wonder tapping glasses with the entire rhythm section from the Matchstick Circus Orchestra. The MonkeyBoy tells me both Victor Harvey and Harvey Victor are in here somewhere, but not together. Their fighting careers are so old even an aficionado like myself can't tell you which man is which, or why I should care. "Who?" I say.

As we brush by one particularly boisterous group, a flabby arm shoots out and snares my wrist. The laughter from the table slows to a rolling boil. The arm is attached to a moon-faced broad, older than the rest of the crowd by two decades and weighed down with a galaxy of glittering gemstones. She's the only woman in sight with wrinkles that show, and I can't for the life of me think of who she might be. Someone's wife maybe. This dame motions at me with a wobbling glass of bubbly. Her champagne misses my shoe, but just barely.

"This man here," she says to her friends, throwing an arm around my waist. "This one I remember." She looks up at me. "What's your name, dearie? You were just darling in all those early interactive holos. I never forget a face."

I narrow my eyes and rack my brains. Try to come up with anybody at all she could possibly have me confused for. I turn up empty, but that's never stopped me before.

"That's right," I say. "The primitive pictures."

A skinny bim with a nose like a vulture is impressed. "Were you any good?" she says from across the table.

The waiter tugs at my sleeve, but I pat his arm away. "Was I any good? Trust me, Duchess. When you're born with a mug like mine, you have to be good."

Giggles from all around. But the wrinkly matriarch doesn't bite. Instead, she rubs at the cheap fabric of my coat between her chubby fingers. The look on her round mug says she thinks my story might be even thinner than the suit on my back.

"What was your stage name then, darling? Maybe we'll catch one of your holos after dinner."

I put out a paw for a shake but the glittering sow only frowns at me. "They used to call me 'Sedso' back East."

"No that can't be right," she says through squinting, beady eyes. She fingers a curl of her massive bouffant and nearly loses her champagne again. "Why would they call you that?"

I flash a fifty-cent smile and snatch the flute from her hand before she can pour the rest of it down my pantleg. I slug her bubbles and shove the glass back inside her fat paw. "Because I said so," I say. The table is silent. The cow scoffs and I boogie with a wink.

MonkeyBoy bows an apology to the table before he drags me off through the bustling garden to a small space tucked away, way in the back. This corner gushes with greenery and bright yellow flowers, nearly hidden from the rest of these done-up diners. In other words, real private. Don't know if this segregation is for my sake or for theirs, but I've got a good idea.

A sharp-dressed chap in a white dinner jacket stands over a lonely table with his back to me, conversing with someone hidden behind a flowering bush. Something about his stature tells me he's not the help. This fella hears footsteps and scurries past as I walk up. Puts a hard shoulder into me and disappears.

"What's the rush, bub?" I don't get a good look at his face, but he feels sort of familiar just the same. I approach an empty chair, rubbing my arm and frowning after him. Someone clears her throat at the table.

And there she is, just poured into some shiny, slinky number. Glowing green, it matches her eyes. Dark brown curls sit tied up tight in sassy rings that hang high around her face. She's painted-on, dark around the lids, light around the lips, like some golden era starlet from the 'streams. Like she belongs amongst all that old-time tinseltown royalty I shimmied by on the way in. Holy hell, she looks like a hundred million bucks. Forget it! She makes a hundred big ones look cheap.

Candlelight bounces onto her face as she glances up at me from under a springy brown ringlet. It's not just some simulamp, either. This puppy is genuine burning flame, smoke and all. It gives her eyes a shine that should make the stars out the window jealous. Any fella in the universe would be lucky to be sitting across from her. A sly smile crawls across my face as I slide into my seat. "Hiya, beautiful."

She frowns when she sees me.

"Good evening, Mr. Ames."

"Call me Stockton," I say.

Audrine continues without acknowledging the request.

"I hope your accommodations were satisfactory?"

I can ignore her just as easily. "Sorry I'm late, doll. Would you believe I had trouble finding the place?"

She sighs and speaks into her water glass.

"Actually, I would. You could have called."

She gestures towards her MPD.

"Not really my style," I say with a shrug. "Took everything I had to stop and ask the janitor for directions."

"How very proactive of you." It would appear it's up to me to carry this conversation. Not a bad burden for a fella that likes to run his mouth. I lean back in the chair. "Say, who's your pal with the poor manners? I wouldn't mind a word with him."

"Just a colleague." She refuses to look at me.

"He was in an awful rush, huh? What am I, interrupting?"

She says nothing.

We sit in silence for a moment. I break it before they bring the bread out, but only by a sliver. "I didn't think you'd come."

She turns to face me. Glares into me like a twenty gigawatt spot. There's nothing in the world like a pretty woman all done up and pissed off. The waiter drops a basket of butter and baguettes and scampers away lickety-quick.

"My function," she hides the anger in her voice and tries again. Her eyes are burning balls of fire. Almost as angry as the Calvera II system out the glass behind her. "My function is to ensure your complete satisfaction for the duration of your stay."

And boy ain't she happy about it!

"I see." There's genuine regret in my voice and it strikes a chord. She shakes her head and changes the subject.

"I'm sorry, didn't you see the tuxedo we left for you? I should have said something but I was sure you'd find—"

"I found it," I say. "I prefer this one."

She nods and throws me a look that says "I'm sure you do."

"Besides," I say. "I didn't leave it all behind."

I flash the frilly tie as I take a sip of fizzy water.

She's not impressed.

"Wonderful," she says. "You wore the least expensive, most insignificant part of a five-million-dollar suit."

I almost spit the water out. Five million bucks? For one suit? That's more than I took home in two years with the precinct. My mind wanders as she stares out the window. How long does it take for a year to go by back on Earth? A few hours? A few minutes? I was never great at math or econ or physics or whatever class could help you answer a question like that.

She concentrates on ignoring me until another MonkeyBoy strides over to take our wine order. His plumage is brilliant. A smart white coat with long, fuzzy tails dangles halfway to his knees. This jungle is just hopping with wildlife, but I'm not so sure this dame and I aren't the strangest specimens of all. Audrine offers me the list, a gorgeous leather bound jawn with gold leaf pages four inches thick. A gilded bible from some secret sect of mystical, pinky-raising boozebags. I leave it shut. "Can you recommend something that pairs well with the lady's lipstick?" I ask the waiter.

Audrine glares. "How about a smack in the mouth?"

I shrug and hand the heavy list back to her. "Why don't you just do the honors then?"

She puts the book down and orders from memory. Something from the bottom of the cellar that I can't pronounce. I don't understand why the guys vending vino didn't get the infocom that the whole world has been speaking American English for the past twenty-some years. Since the T-Wars turned the whole language barrier out on its ass once and for all. Hell even those snooty, New Union Brits cop from a Yank dictionary these days. I look out the window. I stand corrected. The whole *galaxy* has been speaking American English for the past twenty plus years. Well, twenty years back on Earth, anyway. I tear away from the window. This will take some getting used to.

"So, Mr. Ames," Audrine says, folding her hands neatly in front of her. "What was it that you did back on Earth?"

I smile and stare right into those big green beauties. She meets my stare with a lazy, uncaring expression, her eyes half shut. "I'll only tell you, if you promise to stop calling me Mr. Ames."

She breaks my gaze and studies her palms.

"I'm sorry," she says. "It's hard to ignore old habits. We don't have many guests in this line of work that want to get on a first name basis with the help."

I grab her hand. She stares at the floor.

"Look at me," I say. She does, but she doesn't like it. "Do I look like the rest of these schmucks around here? Do I?"

She shakes her head softly but her eyes burn.

"Well I want to be on a first name basis with you. And I'm the guest, so you have to do what I say. Got it?"

I give her a playful smirk and double-click my tongue.

She finally smiles. There's a cute little gap between her two front teeth that I missed before. She ought to smile more often. I didn't take her for the type of skirt to get so worked up over what anybody else thought of her, at least not so anyone would notice. Maybe I'm wrong about this broad, though. Maybe she just doesn't care what *I* think of her.

"So, Stockton," she says. It sounds good on her lips. "What was it that you did back on Earth?"

"I was a dick," I say. "For the city."

"Well, yes of course," she replies. She lifts her water to her lips. "But what did you do for a living?"

She takes a sip to muffle the giggles. Saw that one coming a mile away. It's not my first rodeo but I let her rope me anyway. I always was a sucker for dames that want to kick me in the kidneys. She swallows and serenity returns to her face. "Did you enjoy being a detective? I mean, it just seems so... unpleasant. All the crime, all the violence?"

"I enjoyed it about as much as the next guy." I shake the cubes in my glass. "That's to say, not much at all. But it wasn't the gore that had me crying into my cocktails every night."

She's interested, or trying very hard to appear as such.

"What then?" she says.

I shrug. "I guess you could say I always wanted to do something more. Something that matters. Something that made a lick of difference for folks that still had their lives to live."

"But taking criminals off the street, solving crimes, surely that's important work?"

"You'd think so, wouldn't you?" I set my glass down. "I thought so too, once upon a time, when I was young and hungry and more than just a little naive. A career on the streets will prove that's just not the case. Hammer reality into your head no matter how idealistic you leave the academy. I learned quicker than most; cleaning up after crooks is a fixed game."

"What do you mean by that?"

"I mean you're always a buck short and a day late. I never brought anybody back to life, and neither did any other pro snoop. As a cop, I left plenty more killers on the street than I could ever hope to catch, not in a hundred years of wearing a badge. It's a losing fight, doll. Always has been."

Her eyes go soft on me. "Didn't you ever get tired of it?"

"Wouldn't be here if I didn't," I say.

MonkeyBoy #2 returns with a dusty bottle, coat tails a-flailin'. There's a big to-do about presenting the label and pouring a sample. He describes the ruddy, red liquid with a string of words that have little to do with booze in my experience. Terms better suited for a barnyard than a bar top. Tastes fine to me, but what do I know about it? I motion for him to get on with it and get away.

He wants food orders. I search the table for a menu but come up empty-handed. Audrine stops me before I peek under the tablecloth. She fills me in. They run a full service hash house back there. Anything we want, they got it, made to order. The broad requests some kind of truffle oil salmon puff soufflé. The froufrou blue plate. I order a burger. Fancy place like this, they've got to use some high quality RealBeef. The genuine article. Something that spent some time in a field chewing cud and saying "moo." MonkeyBoy harumphs his way back to the kitchen.

"How about you?" I turn to Audrine. "You ever get sick of serving richos their Peen-O Shat-O and flying around the universe at half-a-million light years a second? Don't get me wrong, this place is plush for days, doll. But if all you ever see is luxury and beautiful people in nice clothes, doesn't it lose its luster after a while? Don't you ever miss the regular folks back on Earth?"

"I wouldn't be here with you if I didn't."

She says it with a sad smile and even sadder eyes.

The food comes in on steaming silver platters. Two teams of waiters reveal our meal with great flourishes and frequent floor-scraping bows. Of course my burger is piled nine feet high with all kinds of sautéed this and artisanal that. A fat stack of the finest cheeses from no less than six of Saturn's lunar colonies. A little old blind lady and her pet pig picked the mushrooms from some dirt farm without a name way out on New Utah. The chief MonkeyBoy takes great pride in explaining it all to me, much to the delight of his adoring waitstaff. I take great pride in slopping it all off the bun and asking him to fetch a bottle of GreenCap hotsauce, chopchop! He storms off and I go to town.

What a bite! It's been ages since I had any real meat. Everything affordable is grown in a VatLab these days. It's enough to turn a guy into a veggo.

I begin to ask Audrine how she likes her whatever-the-hell it is when the table starts to shake. It doesn't boogie too badly, but enough to rattle the dishes and spill the salt. The joint gets dead quiet. My eyes get wide. Then I get low and clutch the table. I lived through the T-Wars as a kid. I remember those commie quakebombs, and the obituaries the next day.

Suddenly bright burning streaks start to shoot past the window. We're smack-dab in the middle of a goddamned firefight! The other diners "*ooh*" and "*aah*" and get back to their regular conversations like they couldn't care less that we're under attack. My knuckles clench white on the table top. The rest of me crawls under it. Somebody needs to vee up the Orbital Defense Corps, if they aren't already on their way with an armada, and a division or two of dropship Marines.

"What the hell is that?" I shout.

Audrine peeks her head under and laughs out loud. "It's alright! It's alright!" she says, still snickering. "Get back up here! It's just a pulsar cyclosheet, a slight gravitational anomaly. Perfectly normal stellar radiation phenomena. Happens all the time at most of the deeper TimeResorts, Seren Luna included. Really, it's fine."

I climb back into my chair and adjust my tie. Try not to look too foolish, but I can only try so hard. The tracers are gone, but I can't stop staring out the window. Like the flashes are etched into my eyes, or my brain. "Goddamn!" I say. "You ought to warn a guy. Isn't there anything you can do to stop them? I mean, a fancy place like this ought to..." I trail off.

She regains her composure, for the moment anyway. At least she's not openly cackling in my face anymore. "I'm afraid there's not much we can do about our proximity to all of the enormous neutron stars in the galaxy, Stockton, let alone the two we orbit. We only catch a truly large show every few days or so. I'll spare you the details, which I'll go ahead and assume you skimmed over in the orientation package. But I assure you, they are perfectly harmless. Besides Stockton, most of the other guests find them... appealing."

"Appealing my ass." I keep any further complaints to myself and get back to the burger. We make the smallest of talk, finish our meal. When the last crumb clears the plate, Audrine excuses herself. Says goodbye for the night and bounces out of sight, and not a second later than she can get away. Probably back to that young hunk she was chatting up when I rolled in. I hate to see her leave, but I can't help but watch her go. They must have stitched that dress together right over her hide.

I tell Monkey Boy #2—or one of his disciples, anyway—to forget the fancy stuff and bring out a bottle of whiskey. He knows better than to ask for a brand preference by now. I strip off the tie and toss it in a bush. Then I sit quietly, slugging ryes. Staring out the window, I watch the universe float by.

The night gets hazy.

FIVE

The next morning I wake up early and alone. A steady kickdrum thump beats in my brains and my peepers feel like they might fall out of my head. It's too easy for a fella like me to tie one on when the whole tab is on the house. I've got unlimited credit at this snobbery, and easy terms: everything's included. The whiskey bottles will be telling scary stories about the night Stockton Ames came to town. I nearly tumble into my personal pool, then I flip on some flops, tie on some cotton trousers and a short-sleeved tropico, and hit the lift for the nearest bar. I need some hair of the dog, and I need it worse than the dog does.

My MPD knows the way and I stumble there in half-a-haze. The routing protocol leads me right to another one of those big glass bubbles. An empty, thatch-roofed tiki hut stands at the entrance, shining in the sunlight like the pearly gates. I plop myself at a stool and whistle for the 'tender with pinkies in my mouth. A syntho rumslinger pops through the door, sets down a glass, and greets me as warmly as his kind can.

"Howdy pal!" he says. "You're up early. What'll it be?"

I pry my eyes just wide enough to glance at a fancy holodisplay. A Bloody Ivan signature drink they call the *Beefy Rocket Buster*, that's the ticket, despite that awful name. I point it out to him and mumble something vaguely desirous.

"How do you want it, big guy?" he says.

I hold my hands over my eyes. "However it comes, but faster." I collapse on the counter and ask the robot to shake me awake when it's ready.

An eternity later he taps me twice and proudly presents the largest goddamned drink I've ever seen. It's a big bowl of booze and break-fast, all at once, and it's a damned beautiful sight to these bloodshot eyes. A full-blown T-bone steak sits speared through the top of the peppery tomato cocktail, seared to perfection and flanked by six smoked sausage links, a tiny burger in a bun, and no less than half a pig's worth of double-thick maple bacon. Next to this colossal cup he hauls a good-sized vegetable garden—fresh, pickled, you name it—and a whole army of hotsauces and horseradishes. I swirl the mammoth mug with spicy GreenCap goodness and take the straw to my lips.

"Not bad," I say, mostly to myself.

The synth nods.

"You planning on taking a dip today, sir?" He gestures over a shoulder with a rubbery thumb.

I plop a few monstrous olives in my mouth and lean to look past him. I smile between cheese-stuffed chews. Sure enough, there's a beautiful beach behind the bar. Must be half-a-mile if it's an inch, stretched out in a gentle curve worthy of a woman's stomach. Brilliant blue waves crash on a sandy shore as uniformed resort staff wipe down white loungers and tables. The view is so sweet I forget where I'm sitting for a moment. Rocky cliffs replace the great glass dome and the space scene outside. A brisk wind tussles my hair, smelling of salt and seaweed. Palm fronds sway and a gull cries and little black crabs scurry underfoot. I kick a crustacean away from my stool, but my toes slip right through the holographic illusion. A simulator, sure: a holo-beach. But a damned fine one.

The BotTender points to a schedule drawn up on a bamboo chalk-board beside the bar. "Saint Bart's today," he says.

I nod and soak a strip of bacon in my booze. The schedule out-lines a different holo-dressing for everyday of the week. Malaysian Monday. Tortuga Tuesday. Wednesdays in Waikiki. Wildcards on the weekend. It's a clever trick, and the projectors sell it well. Underneath the glitz and glamour of the illusion though, I know it's just concrete and chemicals, like any other inner-city public pool. Hell, even the sand is drawn on.

Still I snatch up my fishbowl with both hands and wander off towards the empty surf. The 'beach' gives with a softness to my step, but none of the grit and grime of the real thing.

"Sir," the robot calls after me. I slump to a stop, but just long enough to let him finish. "Let's not forget to wait thirty minutes before wading!"

I lumber onward.

"Don't get your circuits bent, pal. I ain't the swimming type."

I crash into a lounger and heave the drink to the gaudy thatch table beside me. The holobeach is nearly empty this time of the morning, and that's just fine by me. Just a steady trickle of richos swoop in by the time my ice gets dry. Stretched out in the chair, artificial sun on my face, I drift away to a deep and dreamless sleep.

I awake to some blond brat with a finger in my face. I swat at him like any other buzzing pest.

"What do you want kid? Scram!"

He glares down at me. "My mom says you're a loser!"

What a way to wake up.

"Yeah, and who's your mother? Or didn't your daddy tell you?" I snatch him by the wrist. Ready to teach him to respect his elders the way his folks never did. What's this though? Curious. "What's the matter kid? Your parents won't pony for an ArmPod? You're old enough aren't you?"

I let him go.

His forearm is smooth and bare as a baby's bottom. Where I come from, a kid's fifth birthday can't come soon enough: the big day when he finally gets his first MPD implanted. It's a subsidized surgery, even if you can't afford it. Everybody needs an ArmPod these days; it's a verifiable, disability-paying handicap to go without one. A medical emergency if it breaks down. Somehow, I think this kid's richo 'rents can afford it.

"Nobody wears an *ArmPod* anymore, duh!" he says. He taps at his melon. "It's all up here now, you rusted cork! Haven't you ever heard of the TotalNeural® Interface? Or are you too much of a loser? What's next? You want to borrow my cellular telephone?"

"Why don't you just scoot, Scamp?"

I wind up to smack him and he skedaddles.

I wouldn't have laid into the brat—not yet anyway—but his words have me vexed. Things have already started to change back home in a big way, and it's only been one day up here. These neuro-jobs are just what the world needs, all the corponational MPD manufacturers tinkering around in our heads, while all the stock-owning, board-sitting politicos look the other way.

I whistle for a dark-skinned cabana boy to bring me a whiskey and a bottle of UV pills. "Sure thing sir," he says, flashing brilliant white teeth. "But you won't need those pills. Our SynthRays are fully CHR."

I don't have the slightest idea what those initials stand for, but I get the gist. He trots and my eyes follow him, until they pass a pair of buxom beach bunnies, frolicing in the foamy surf. If I squint, I can just barely spot the scraps of fabric somebody sold them as bikinis. Maybe the future won't be so bad after all. I kick back and smile, let the whiskey and the sunshine do their job.

Days fly by and it's much of the same. Too much food, too many tall drinks. Simulated sunshine and holo-sand. The beach changes every day but my routine does not. In fact, the only thing missing is Audrine. I don't have the gumption to ring her—I'm not that fella—but I'd love to see her just the same.

Evenings I do supper for one in the throwback dining room. *Atomic Johnny's,* they call it. It's a real hit with the kiddies too, much to my aching chagrin: a kitschy, retro kitchen, at least for this crowd. For me though, it feels like home. Big, overstuffed vinyl booths and no frills fare. It's all I need and more than I'm accustomed to.

One night over eggs, I catch a youngish fella sporting a fresh Knight's jersey with a name I can't hardly pronounce stitched on the back. Must be a kicker. He saunters past me but I snag his wrist before he gets too far.

"Say pal," I say. "How are the Knights doing? I've been up here a while. They winning any?"

He smiles bright. "Great, bru! Great! They've been winning lots and lots. You oughta catch it then, friend. Swords up!"

His voice has more than a hint of that Hinky offworld timbre, which strikes me as strange. But what the hell? Lots of room for lots of folks on the old bandwagon anymore. I pound my heart twice and give him the swords up salute. He nods, then goes about his business, all smiles.

News only comes through in little spurts like that: from the new arrivals. We don't have much access to the world back home up in resortland. Our MPDs can only sync with the JanosCorp network; there's no downlink back to reality. Something about time dilation data-swell. Too much juice to fit through their skinny pipes, that's what I hear. All the resort-side infocoms and netcrawls just offer fluff about official activities and menus and services. I don't fit nicely into any of the JanosCorp targeted-advertising demographics, so I catch all the 'verts: for the kiddos' low grav jungle gyms *and* the geria-rotic couples' therapy spas.

They do offer nightly newstream updates in several of the cinemas to keep folks up to speed with everything that's happened back home in the decade since yesterday. I decide to take that fella up on his offer and attend a sesh the next day. A sports-themed catch-up.

I grab some refreshments and an empty seat near the rear. The lights go down and the holo spins up. The Knights win the WarnerBowl, the old Grand Dame herself. Twice even. Then they get sold and shipped off to the damned Hinks way off in Novo São Paulo, where they proceed to win three more championships in the Deep Colony Leagues. I dropkick my popcorn and walk out. It's my first and last update infosession.

Storming away from the theater, I find the nearest chapel instead. After news like that, a fella could use some salvation. Some time communing with the Big Guy, Junior, and Their Invisible Friend, if only to complain. The resort's multi-use WorshipCenter is half as big and twice as nice as the Local 3640 Meeting Hall back home—not that I've spent much time there recently. I kept up with my dues, but the Holy Roman Brotherhood of Municipal Service Workers isn't exactly my kind of support group. The coffee's bad and the confessional gives me claustrophobia.

I grab a seat on a long, empty glass pew. There's a handful of lonely souls in here. Each one with the dejected, eye-avoiding squirrelishness of a resort staff member. Not much room for religion in a richo's world. Us working stiffs though, we suffer our due-tithes and cling to the church-unions because we know they're the only thing keeping the greedy corporationals and their pet politicos off our backs. Somebody's going to reach in my pocket, and I'd rather it be the man upstairs that's answering prayers. At least on paper He is.

I intend to find out.

I swipe through the built-in MultiHymn catalog. Past the grocery-bagging Buddhist Sutras, the Hindu housekeeper Mantras, and the unemployed artist AntiTheos Affirmations. Eventually I flip to a section with the scriptures I grew up on—Ma was a school nurse—and click a random passage. Muni Catholic Bible, Second Peter, chapter three, verse eight:

But do not forget this one thing, brothers and sisters: With the Lord a single shift is like a thousand years, and a thousand years are like a single shift.

"Amen," I mutter to myself.

"Perhaps you should keep reading, child," a sickly-sweet voice says. "The Apostle gives tenable advice for how to live under the Lord's scrutiny. For making preparations for the end of days."

I look up. A priest in long green Scab robes stands before me. Fresh out of Protestant prayer school from his baby face and bad haircut. I click the MultiHymn interface closed and stand up. Don't know what I thought I'd find in here anyway.

"Sorry Padre," I say, shuffling out of the pew. "I was just on my way out."

He claps my shoulder and sees me down the aisle.

"Just remember, my son, the eyes of the Lord are on those that fear him. On those that wait for his hope and mercy."

Yeah, but what about the rest of us sinners?

I nod once and walk out the door.

∞

The rest of my week on Seren Luna zips by so quick it leaves me spinning dizzy. Leaves me with indigestion, too. After dinner at the diner on my second to last night, I've got the better part of a half hour to think it over as I reign from a porcelain throne. I sigh. One more day. Two more nights. Then it's back to Earth and whatever may be left for me there. Not my Knights—although I've tried not to think about them. Hell, the league was getting lousy anyway, or so I try to tell myself. Maybe I'll catch up with a few friends that I hardly cared for twenty of their years ago. See a world that I won't even recognize and didn't bother to see before I left it behind. Apparently JanosCorp offers a re-climatization session before departure, but I'm happy to let it all smack me in the face when I get there. Like the end of a bad date.

I glance around the palatial potty and begin to wonder if I may even start to miss this place some. Everything in here is dipped in chrome, carved from stone, or folded up in fancy shapes. The bath-robe sits twisted into a long-necked swan, staring at me from atop a pile of heart-shaped hand towels. Even the bog roll is cut up and creased into perfect little pairs of clam shells, stacked tall in single-serving silky puffs. They don't even expect anyone to tear their own TP in a joint like Seren Luna. I've come a long way from the half-ply life I left behind, and I'm not so sure if I'm up for the return in just a few short days.

I splash some cold water on my cheeks, then let the sink wash my hands. I dry them on a crumpled heart and toss it to the floor. The bathroom tells me goodbye with a sweet robotic voice and a flutter of pastel flashes and flushes as I step back into my room. It's another forty paces through a jungle of sprawling loungers and hid-eously twisted light fixtures. Modern art, my ass. I plop onto the bed and mindlessly scrub through the resort's mediacrawl offerings on my ArmPod. It's not an easy choice. They've got a great library, complete with all the classics.

But here's a story worth watching again. An early Skip McKendrick western. *Desperado Sundown*. One of the quick-shooting sheriff's best performances in my book. And this was a guy that never featured in a bad flick. As a kid, I would daydream that Skip McKendrick was the father I never knew. And even if he had run out on us, I still loved his work. Made me feel good to see him up on the big screen, saving the day—so what if it was for somebody else? He wasn't a bad guy, just busy. I toss the feed to the room's holo.

The projector spins to life.

There's Skip, noose around his neck, strung up and ready to swing. What a start! Warm nostalgia washes over me like a slug of rye. Just as they shoot the horse out from under Mr. McKendrick, there's a knock on the side of the wardrobe unit beside me. These damn silent turbolifts and slidelocks are enough to give anybody the bulge on a fella. Without thinking, I grab my piece from under the softest pillow my neck's ever known and draw down on the intruder.

I throw the safety and get ready to burn.

But it's just the broad. She's back to wearing the JanosCorp suitskirt. Navy wool. Orange trim and matching silk scarf. Little silver buttons with the two-faced man stamped on. Her skirt's just short enough to grab my attention but too long to hold it. A plastic bottle hangs limp from her left hand. Her right paw is planted squarely on her hip.

"Are you going to put that thing down, Stockton?"

"Jesus!" I say, flipping the safety catch, sticking the muzzle to the mattress. "Don't sneak up on me like that!"

"I guess your room recognizes my biorhythms after all," she says with a wink.

"Guess so, toots. You here for a swim?"

I gesture at the pool tucked around the corner.

"No," she says. "I don't have a suit."

I shrug. "All the better." I smile but she doesn't.

Her inky locks are slung low over one eye. Brushing them aside, she tosses the bottle to me. I drop the sidearm to catch it—the same plastic jug of Jensen's corn mash I brought from home but polished off days ago. None of the bars on the resort keep it in stock. They don't serve from shelves that low at a joint like this; I've asked around.

"What's this for?"

She frowns. "Most men would say 'thank you' when a lady brings them a bottle of their favorite brand."

"Thanks, doll," I say, inspecting the chintzy, oversaturated label closely. "Now what's it for?"

She walks over and sits beside me on the bed.

"I thought you might want it for tomorrow night. There's a big cyclosheet on the docket. Huge even. The rest of the guests are extremely excited. They're even throwing a little fête in the Garden Dome. I know you're leaving the next morning, but I thought the liquor might... help you cope. You can sleep it off back on Earth."

I pick at a loose corner of the garish label with my thumbnail and stare through the golden liquid behind it. "What do you think it will be like, Beautiful?"

"Earth?" she says.

I tilt my head and set the bottle down beside me. "I've never been to New Jerusalem, New Utah, or Novo Anywhere, so yeah, Earth's a good place to start."

She huffs.

"You've been in this same boat plenty of times, I'd have to imagine. Aren't you ever worried that maybe you missed something great while you were up here? That there's nothing left for you down there?"

She touches my shoulder softly, staring through the ceiling, at the dancing stars behind it. She opens her mouth, ready to spill her guts to the stranger sitting beside her.

But before anything authentic can leak out, she snaps it shut and gives me a guarded answer instead. "Don't worry, Stockton. I'm sure you'll be just as unhappy with the way things are going on Earth as you were before you left." She smiles and socks me in the shoulder playfully. "And if you're not? At least you can drink yourself to death with that rotgut stuff you're so fond of."

I throw an arm around her waist and twist her back onto the bed beside me. She gasps and pretends to be surprised. Silently dares me to kiss her. "Don't be silly," I tell her with a smirk. "That's what the gun is for." I make the motion of a man ready to end it all, then collapse to the mattress next to her.

She stands up and frowns. Picks up my pistol and runs her fingers along the barrel. It's not standard precinct issue but not a museum piece either. A nice weapon. Crafted like the ones from the classic Western mediastreams, but chambered in 6mm gaussian MagnumRails. Not unlike what old Sherriff Skip is whipping out up on the holo, burying banditos in a hail of bullets and a blaze of glory. You might call my magnum 'pretty', if you didn't know any better.

Now, I'm not normally one for gunwork, but it comes with the territory from time to time. A life in law enforcement has taught me that it's better to be a living cowboy than a dead saint. You can ask the last partner they ever gave me, Jay Mendoza, for the details. Or you could, if he were still around to talk. No, I've bagged my share of scum over the years, but I never once enjoyed doing it. Audrine's eyes are lost in the chrome hardware.

"Thanks for the hooch," I say, pulling the shiny red top with my teeth. "And for the heads up about tomorrow night. How's about we pour some stiffies right now and you can help me *cope*?"

I raise my eyebrows and pat the bed beside me.

She rises to her feet and slowly turns the magnum on me. There's evil in her eyes. "Didn't your mother teach you not to hit on a woman holding a gun?"

I stand up tall and snatch it away from her. Maybe I'm a bit rough, but I'm not experienced disarming dames that don't actually mean to bump me off. She shakes a tender wrist and backs away. The look on her face sells it hard: half shock, three-quarters anger.

"It's not a goddamned toy!" I say, popping out the chargemodule and tossing it aside.

"It's also against JanosCorp policy for guests to bring weapons into our facilities," she says, crossing her arms.

"So is that how it's gonna be? You gonna send some security ape up here to take it away?" I don't blink.

"If I didn't want you to have it," she begins to walk away, "it would already be gone. Goodnight, Mr. Ames."

I get back to Sheriff Skip, the bottle in my lap.

∞

I make the most of my last day at Seren Luna. I'm booked for a visit to the SpaceGate terminal the following morning, so I make double sure to get my jollies in. Holobeach. A few trips to the tiki bar. Kicked back in a lounger, I take in my once pasty thighs. Think I'm starting to get a little color on these milky whites. Who would have thought? Stockton Ames: tall, dark, and handsome-ish.

I've definitely got a little buzz going by the time the soirée begins in the Garden Dome. I could care less about the richos' party, but in my half-drunken state I figure I might run into the girl, sweep her off her feet. Rock her world and convince her to come back to Earth with me in the morning. I even sport that stupid, crinkly tux.

I swing through the jungle bubble but she's not there. Just a crowded, loud herd of yesterday and tomorrow's favorite public personalities. I leave the time-travelling wildlife alone, head back to my room, and gulp down what's left of the jug she left me. I'm not even conscious for the big event. Maybe I half planned it that way.

Morning comes sudden and ugly. The alarm in my ArmPod is less than understanding. Apparently it's never had a hangover. It whines and cries and buzzes with a single screaming message:

Time to go home.

I pack up Rusty and say my goodbyes. So long, enormous room. Personal swimming pool. Wish I'd taken the time to take a dip. See you later, hundreds of other mushroom subjects. Ta-ta, entire universe out my window, it's been swell. I leave a note for Audrine, scrawled across the brown butcher paper from a half-eaten hero. Ask her to look me up if she ever wants a shooting lesson. Hell, I might be long dead before she makes it back to town, but what have I got to lose? She sent me a handwritten message once upon a time, least I can do is return the favor. I just hope she can read my sloppy, unpracticed henscratch.

I head for the SpaceGate terminal but get logjammed behind a slow-moving herd of richos on the way. Four kiddies bitch and moan about having to blow so soon. I recognize their old man as he tells them to shut their damned yappers. A bigwig politico with the handshake to prove it. His tired-eyed wife calmly explains to the screaming brats that their father has important business back on Earth. They care about his reasons about as much as I do—that's to say, not one byte.

I shuffle through them, tipping my hat and grumbling false apologies. The packbot weaves through nimbly, even with a float that's wobblier than a drunk on crutches. If I've accomplished nothing else on this joyride, at least my suitcase has cashed in on some serious firmware upgrades. If I could just fix that gimpy levitator and buff out some rust, he'd be brand-spanking-new.

On my way across the gleaming marble floor of the main atrium lobby, I spot that Proletti prick behind the counter, jotting in his notebook, or at least pretending to. Old SlickSuit himself. He's looking for me. Got a target painted right on my keister. I can see it in his eyes, no matter how suave he is or how hard he tries to hide it. Reading faces isn't something they teach you at the academy, at least not in any way that's worth a lick. You have to learn it on the streets or you don't learn it at all.

"Mr. Ames!" he says, approaching me a little too quickly to be casual. "Good Morning, Mr. Ames. How are you today?"

"What's this about, Proletti?" I've got no patience for guys like him and I hope he knows it. I don't stop to chat. He falls in with me and doesn't miss a step in his Italian apeskin loafers.

"Wonderful news, Mr. Ames," he says, maintaining my brisk pace and waving that gaudy gold pen like a baton. "You've been selected by

The Janos Corporation to extend your stay with us. Fully complimentary, of course."

He holds out his hands, palms up, and smiles a little.

"Not interested," I say.

I must be crazy to bail on a joint like this—especially on the free—but something about his offer rubs me the wrong way. Like I'm not doing myself any favors by agreeing with the likes of him. Not for any reason. Like I need to jump ship while I still have half-a-chance.

"I'm sorry to hear that, Mr. Ames. Were our accommodations not to your liking?"

We're rapidly approaching the terminal, and I don't mean to tell him "no" the whole way home. I stop and spin to face him. "The place is fine, and you damn well know it," I say. "Here's the story, Chief. If you're full of hooey and I catch wind, I just might poke you in the teeth."

I reach up and straighten his collar for him with a wink. The SpaceGate techs throw hands over their mouths in the near distance. "And even if you're being straight with me, I can't think of a single, lonely reason why I should explain myself to the likes of you. I'm walking, and that's all you need to know."

I turn to go. The gold-suited wrench-monkeys tap at terminals beside a great big machine that looks like the world's fanciest shower stall. Everything's all set to scan in all the cheeseburgers and booze I've poured down my gullet, all that color I've picked up over the last week. I wonder if they could just reuse the old data, send me back as the exact same person I was when I arrived. Wipe my head of the tiny taste of luxury, the smell of Audrine's perfume. Proletti's footsteps follow me down the hallway, but I do my best to pretend he's not there.

One of the technicians waves me forward in a half-assed sort of way. His eyes dart back to Proletti, then back to me, then back to his boss once more.

"Are you, ummmm, ready to head back to Earth, Mr. Ames?" The tech asks it like he's not ready himself. He's still staring at Slick, over my shoulder. I may just have to wring Proletti's pencil neck afterall.

"That's right, pal. Send me home."

The tech swallows hard.

"That's really too bad, sir." It's Slick, speaking into my ear. My good ear. He tacks on a phony frown so thick I can hear his cheeks creak behind me.

"Miss DeMarco will be very disappointed. She was looking forward to enjoying her upcoming time off with you. She has seven days' vacation, beginning immediately. We were prepared to offer you a week's extension to match, at her request of course."

My jaw hangs, and then resets. My eyes narrow as the technician gets very interested in fingering buttons on the screen behind him.

Slick's hit me where it counts: below the belt.

"Be true to you."

JENSEN'S™
FAMILY BRAND
KENTUCKY-STYLE
ORIGINAL RECIPE
CORNMASH WHISKEY

A Division of Amalgamated Beverages, Inc.

SIX

I think of spending a week with Audrine at the holobeach.

"Is that so?" I say to Proletti through slanted lids.

He's got me hooked hard and he knows it.

"Of course," he says. A smug grin creeps onto his face. "Corporate policy requires I be forthright with all of our guests. Although, you should save your gratitude for Miss DeMarco. She is the one that put you in for the extension." He nods, knowing exactly what I've got saved for *him*. "She's waiting for you right now at the AlpineSimulator complex."

I shake my head. Pull my hat and scratch.

The bastard's done it again. Jugged me good, and boy aren't I miserable about it.

"Alright," I say. "I'll stay."

And why not? What am I in such a rush to get back to? A crowded, dirty planet worse than the one I left? Some perfect society that doesn't need me? Either way, Earth is not the same world I left a week ago—or twenty-three and a half years ago, depending on your perspective.

You don't need to be a brilliant theoretical physicist to see that I might not like what I find. Hell, you don't even need to be smart.

Proletti nods but says nothing. He turns on his heel, barks some official orders at a couple of dawdling bellhops, and smacks one upside the back of his cap as they scurry by. And yet I'm the one that's sore.

I send Rusty along to the suite and tap on my ArmPod to double check the location of this AlpineSim facility. I scroll around for a good minute before I find it, too: all the way on the other side of the resort. A good haul from here, measured in miles. They offer a hovershuttle service that will take me across the planet's "primitive, bare surface", but I decide to hoof it. I could use the exercise. All those RealBeef burgers aren't doing my physique any favors.

The AlpineSim complex is a monstrous feat of engineering "tucked away" at the western edge of the resort. From the glass tunnel leading up, it's a metal mountain rising high above the many-mushroomed resort skyline. Once inside, I find a lobby made up to look like an enormous, golden-era ski lodge. Rough-hewn wooden walls. Roaring holographic fire. ChocoHot in steaming mugs. The whole shebang. Even the staff is decked out in vintage, twentieth century ski-bum duds, and it's no wonder why—it's damned cold in here.

Two red-jacketed twenty-somethings saunter over when I enter. They give me the lowdown. Audrine is already "shredding pow" and waiting for me up in "the Lost Kingdom of Gnar." Then they deck me out in the full outfit. Goggles. Parka. Snowpants with built-in boots. It's "all the latest in high-end protective performance steez", whatever that might mean. All I know is that it looks expensive. A brand called SpektraTek. They point out the logos stenciled over every square inch of the stuff as I climb into it, one leg at a time. I draw the line at the fuzzy watchcap with light-up danglies; I brought my own lid.

I ask them if I need any kind of training. If a city boy like me is bound to get banged up out there, even on a virtual mountain.

"Nah," says the one with shaggy blond curls. "This SpektraTek gear is the brand newby-est, brooster! It's impossible to hurt yourself up there, even if you triple crank some gnarls, yard sale spillage. You're bullion, bru, straight bullion!"

They usher me onto a cushy silver hoverlift that's more davenport than sporting-good, tap some instructions onto an interface panel, and away I go. The chair whisks me out of the lodge and up a spruce-lined holotrail, with actual falling snow that kisses my face and a pumped-in pine-fresh scent that smacks me right in the beeze. First the beach and now the slopes; these richos really bite on their immersive experiences. What's next? Holographic hide-and-seek? You'd think maybe they'd just pony up for a trip to someplace real.

The 'slopes' are a series of shiny geodesic domes lodged in the side of a steep, snowy embankment. They're planted up the edge of the mountain as high as I can see. I spot a half-dozen other lifts carrying bundled richos to their own silver pods in the sky. The lift ferries me up towards a single flashing light. Ten years ago, the dizzying drop below would have sent shivers down my spine, maybe even soaked my shoes. Thankfully, I've long since outgrown my fear of heights. But just to be sure, I hug the railing tight and don't look down.

A hidden slidelock in my destination pod winks open as the lift docks. I hop off the floating sofa into a very dark room and the empty lift whisks away into the snowy aether, leaving me teetering. I can hear her breathing in here. Smell her sweet, musky perfume. Teasing me, soft and seductive. I've got a head chock-full of this dame, but it's so damned dark I can't see a thing.

Turquoise flashes in the floor guide me to my place in the center of the dome. More lights tell me where to put my feet: about shoulder width apart. When I step into the glowing ring on the floor, something soft drops from the ceiling and nestles up against the back of my neck. There's a quiet hum and a prickly chill down my spine and suddenly I'm standing on top of a purple peak in the goddamned Swiss Alps.

The wind bites at my bare cheeks in brisk, billowy gusts like a junkyard dog with a chain that's just too short to reach me. I rub at my arms and smile. A faint, menthol aroma of evergreens saturates the air and nips at my nose with none of the ham-handedness of that pumped-in garbage from the holotrail just a few minutes ago. This scent is rich, complex—with a hint of woodsmoke and several dashes of sweet sweat. A big yellow sun smiles down on me from a cloudless sky. The snowy blanket looks pillowy and inviting, like heaping scoops of mashed potatoes. It's all real enough that I reach for some UV pills in an imaginary pocket.

Looking around, I spot a lone figure in white, sporting laguna blue skis and tearing down the mountain like an over-achieving avalanche. Those blue planks slash through virginal mounds of freshly fallen white powder and leave a skinny trail snaking behind them. The skier skids to a sliding stop right on top of me and sprays a shower of slush into my face. Audrine pulls ruby red goggles up to rest on her forehead. Her brow is creased like a pair of accordion slacks and she bites her lip so hard it turns from pink to something paler than the snow.

"Follow me," she says and shoves off down the slope.

"Great to see you too!" I call out after her.

I manage to push off with the stick things in my hands and by God I'm skiing, although not terribly well. I fall all over myself in these damned clumsy things. There's no give for my ankles and my trick knee pays the tab. I can feel my bones rubbing around down there like a secondhand pepper grinder. Audrine is quite literally leaving me in her fine, white dust. Just when I think I'm gonna tumble into that yard sale Shaggy was talking about, a happy little chime sounds in my skull. *DING-DONG.* The skiing is immediately effortless. My ankles go free, the pressure on my knee splits. Even my sinuses clear up. I guess the autopilot finally kicked in on this stupid simulator, and not a tick too soon.

I shred like a pro. Perfectly balanced and rocketing downhill like I've been launched out of a torpedo tube. I play catch up and fall within spitting distance of the broad's beautiful backside. Her outfit hugs the curves even better than she does. We dash into a copse of firs and Audrine cuts a hard roger. I breeze behind her, thanks to the autopilot. We leave the established trail and bushwhack into the backwoods. The trees get thick. Fallen logs and stones start to poke their ugly little heads above the blanket of virgin powder. Even with my new skills, I catch a few stray branches here and there. I can't see but five yards ahead of me in this tangle. I dodge a low hanging limb that I have the better part of a quarter-second to outmaneuver. We're still barreling downhill at breakneck speed when I begin to worry our luck might start to run thinner than the mountain air.

"Hey!" I yell after her. "Do you think we ought to slo—"

Before I can finish we pop out of the trees. I stare out at about thirty feet of runway and then nothing but open sky. Before I can even think to put the brakes on, I catapult over the abyss, tumbling end over end after her. I can just make out the neon blur of her skis and about a half-mile below that, a very rocky looking outcrop. I scream.

∞

And then I'm back in the dark dome. I see Audrine's face, bathed softly from the floor lights. She clutches the neural interface cradle and yanks it away from my neck. It's got the look of a tiny plastic catcher's mask, and it buzzes with a green electric fury. I slowly realize I'm still screaming.

"Shut up," she says. She slaps me. So much for not being able to injure yourself in these things.

"Goddamn," I say, rubbing my cheek.

"We've only got about ninety seconds in here before the simulator resets and they start recording us again."

Her eyes are fixed slits, unblinking in the pale glow.

"Listen to me," she says. "Something bad is going down. Something must have happened last night, after the Garden Party. A security breach, a terror threat... something bad like that."

"Something bad, huh? What's got you shaking, kid?"

"This morning I caught a work detail unloading two cases of tactical psychometers. They didn't see me, and if they had, I don't know that I'd be here speaking with you. That's about the heaviest weaponry JanosCorp is willing to keep indoors at a place like this. There was nothing in the morning statcheck infocom about any kind of disturbance or threat or breach. There've been no security alerts before or since. Whatever it is, they're trying to keep it quiet—even from the staff—and *that's* what frightens me."

"Well those are tough breaks," I say. "What do I do about it?"

She grabs me by the shoulders and shakes.

"You said you were a detective back on Earth, Ames! Do detective work! Keep your eyes open. Shake someone down. Look for clues. Find out what the hell is going on!"

"Just like that, huh? Listen kid, this is a big place. You've gotta give me somewhere to start. Something specific to dig up. A mark to tail. A tail to chase. Something."

"Okay," she says. "How about Proletti? Keep a close eye on him, if you can. He usually has this green leather notebook on him—"

I know just the one she means.

"—with a gold pen, right?"

"That's it," she says. "He's keeping track of *something* in there. Something so secret he's afraid to type it up, or let that damned book out of his sight for a single second. Get your hands on that notebook, and we might just find out what the hell is going on around here."

"I don't know doll," I say. with a frown "I'm on vacation. And besides, I don't come cheap."

She rears back with an open palm, ready to smack me again.

I reach for her wrist before she can pop me a second time.

"Alright, alright. I'm on the case, for crying out loud. I'll nab his damned diary if that's what you want. Jesus Christ, woman. What do you think he's scribbling in there anyway?"

"I think he's looking for something. And I don't think we want him to find it."

"Sure, doll. Whatever you say. Do you always bully your way into everything you want?"

"No," she says, feigning offense. "As a matter of fact I have plenty of other tricks in my bag." She bats her lashes and leans close, then goes back to being angry, all in the blink of an eye. "Now the simulator is going to reboot, and when it does, they'll be monitoring us again. I'll approach you when it's safe to talk. Until then…"

She makes a hushing gesture, with her forefinger pushed up against those pouty lips of hers. She presses it up to mine next and for the briefest of moments I can taste her lip gloss, tangy and sweet, like a key lime lollipop.

The lights flash and I hear that faint hum kick on again. Apparently the system is reset. Audrine notices too. She leans forward, pulls me close and kisses me. Her tongue is tart and wet and then it's gone. She shoves me away, reaches back, and full on open-hands me across the mouth. My hat takes a tumble. She stands with her hands glued to her hips.

"Mr. Ames that was quite over the line!"

Her eyes motion towards an observation deck built into the ceiling. It's all an act for the cameras, even if I'd like to think otherwise. "I most certainly did not give you permission to kiss me! That kind of behavior is not acceptable between guests and staff at Seren Luna!"

"Sorry, toots," I say, rubbing that same cheek and bending to retrieve my lid. "I don't know what came over me."

Audrine storms over to the slidelock and exits to a swaying sofa lift. Flurries of snow drift in the door behind her. She turns back to face me before she boards. The brightness outside frames her body like a stained-glass saint. Like a sun-bleached angel.

"If you can learn to control yourself," she says through bared teeth, "perhaps I will see you at dinner. Our usual table."

She scoots, leaving me—and a cloud of confusion—in her icy wake.

I take a few more tries down the slopes to cool off. It's not half-bad kicks, especially when you stick to the trails. I can't exactly figure how much is the autopilot and how much is me, but it sure feels like I'm improving. I'll be a regular Virtual Olympian in no time flat. After a handful of long runs I decide to hang up my skis and call it a day. I tell an imaginary hot tub "so long" and pull the cord.

The lift ferries me back to the lodge where I shed the parka and pants. Shaggy tells me to keep the gear, in case I want to do any "future shredding." Nice kid, this one. He thumbs a button under the collar, and the jacket, pants, and built-in boots fold themselves up into a tiny packet that fits into the palm of my hand. "SpektraTek, bru!" Shaggy says. "Ain't it golden?"

I nod, bouncing the tiny package in my palm.

"Just make sure you take it off before you hit that button, bruski! We had to carve an old lady out of her suit just this morning."

The look on his face tells me just how much he enjoyed that little endeavor.

I stash the packet in a pocket and walk out.

All that fake skiing did a number on these old bones. I rub my bum knee, not so sure it's up for the hike back to the 'shroom suite. As I debate hoofing it, a lumbering hovershuttle pulls up to the window right beside me. Right on time, too. I step up into the welcome wagon and a gaggle of richos climb aboard behind me, a pack of vicious kiddies in tow. We pull off the dock before the snarling brats can change my mind about hitching a ride.

As the shuttle moseys along, I can't help but think about Audrine's request. What is she, nuts? Does she really think there's some kind of conspiracy going down at the fanciest resort in the goddamned galaxy? She must believe it, to throw a spat like that. She was genuinely scared. It's familiar territory for an old hawkshaw like me. I've worked enough late night beats to recognize honest-to-God fear in a woman's eyes.

I stretch out on a row of plush leather seats and growl at any youngsters that wander close enough to bite. I try to forget the look on her face—and the taste on her lips—when one of the gabby brats grabs my ear.

"Look at that, daddy," the little mop-headed raggamuffin says. "There's footprints out there on the ground."

Richo daddy doesn't give two beans.

"Yeah, yeah," Dad says, tinkering with his MPD.

I take that look for him. The planet's surface must be covered in some kind of silt or spacedust. The hovershuttle leaves a wide trail of rippled rug, stretching out behind us and in front of us like the leavings from an enormous space snail, traipsing between the mushroom stalks. I look closer.

Sure enough, there they are. A trail of evenly arranged little footprints crosses under the shuttle's slug track and disappears out into the open planet. They're faint. You'd never catch 'em unless you knew what to look for and right where to look.

Where did they lead to? And who left them for this eagle-eyed brat to find? He's an observant kid. I notice he doesn't have the MPD graft in his arm. Another one of those TotalNeural Interface jobs. Maybe he's sporting some serious optical enhancements in that souped-up noggin? Or maybe he's just a real smart cookie.

"Thanks kid," I say, pulling my hat over my eyes and kicking my legs up. "You just found my first clue."

SEVEN

I hop off the shuttle at the end of the line and waltz back to my room for a spell. As soon as I set foot in the suite, I feel a tiny tickle in the back of my noodle. That gumshoe gumption that something's sour, and it sure as sugar ain't the corn mash in my whiskey jar.

At first glance nothing is out of order, not in the slightest. I find exactly the same mess I walked out on this morning. Towels piled waist high on the plush, nanofiber carpets. Empty glasses for days. Dirty dishes with half-chewed hoagies left by the bed.

And then it hits me—that's exactly what's eating me.

The maidbot hasn't been by. Now I don't mind wallowing in a bit of my own, but that's certainly not how JanosCorp does business. The cleaning routine normally sweeps up around me on an hourly basis. The room *always* tidies itself up while I'm out.

Not once have I returned to a pigsty like this. Why should I start now?

I've got plenty of questions and not enough answers. Maybe I wasn't gone long enough for them to clean? But how could they know how long I'd be out? As far as I knew this morning, I wasn't coming back at all. But something tells me *they* knew, alright. That Proletti creep knew exactly where I'd be, and when I'd be there, too. My eyes narrow and my fists ball up, all on their own, when I start to think about that bastard pulling my strings.

It's fishy, to say the least, and unless I'm all wet here, he's been playing coy and the rest of the JanosCorp crew right along with him. They've been snooping around my digs, and trying too hard to keep me clueless. Or have they? The simple answer says the syntho maids just haven't gotten around to my room yet. The smart money says I'm just jumping at shadows. I blow out a deep breath and turn in place, searching the joint for anything to confirm or deny my suspicion.

This broad has me all wooly-headed. So where exactly does she fit in? Whichever side of the field Audrine's playing, it's her fault I'm involved. Security breaches? Terror threats? I'm supposed to be on vacation for crying out loud. How many times do I need to remind her? All I want to do is to relax, but she wants me running spy missions on the laundry service. I'd be happy just to nosh some greasy grub and maybe chase a tail or two. Is that so much to ask? I always did have a hard time telling the pretty ones "no."

What the hell would JanosCorp want in my room, anyway? I snap a cinnamon chewstick between my teeth and poke around some more of my mess. I slam a drawer shut and it comes to me in a flash.

The piece, that's what they'd want.

Where the hell is that damned packbot? He should have greeted me at the door, like usual. Well, 'like usual' since Audrine swapped his circuits out for a damned labrador. And now they've taken him and the magnum inside his rust-crusted hide. Wonderful. Just when things start to get hairy, I lose my heat.

Frustrated, I grab some of the tropicos lying crumpled around the floor and kick open the wardrobe. I plan to put them away—or at least throw the wrinkled heap inside and let the unit press and hang them for me. I knock the activator with an elbow and the unit whirls into motion. That ridiculous crinkled tux swings up into view, mocking me. I heave some of the shirts in behind it. All the way into the back. Out of sight.

And I'll be damned if the wrinkly bastards don't come crawling right back to me. What is this, some kind of new service? Automatic fashion police, built right into the damned furniture? Then I spot him. Buried under the button-downs I just tried to toss in.

"Good boy." I pat his casing.

He's been hiding from those snooping JanosCorp goons. I have to hand it to her, Audrine *is* a good teacher.

I squat low to block any view they may have from the observation decks I know are hidden throughout the room above me. Let's hope they don't have one in this wardrobe itself. I eye that tux suspiciously, but if they've gotten cute with the cameras it's too late now. I give Rusty's secret latch a sharp tug to release the stash tray. It slides out with a little more coaxing and a healthy smack or two. Snatching up the gun, I drop it into the tux jacket's breast pocket. If they've already checked there once they won't be likely to look again in the near future. I'm willing to wager they'd love to get their hands on the suitcase though. Give him a thorough pat down with a deepscan machine. And a plasmacutter, if it came down to it.

Ol' Rusty gets a swift kick back to the dark depths of the wardrobe and I step away. Let the unit slip shut behind me. The maidbot can let him out later. This whole shady operation only took a few seconds; here's to hoping they didn't catch a whiff. I've got an itch that bringing along the gun was a slick move after all.

I keep my head low, spend the rest of the day holed up at the holo-beach. They've got it dressed like the Dutch Antilles today. A rainbow of virtual reefs and smiling holofish canvas the turquoise water. A cheesy, parrot-poking YachtPop wank swoons about Gilmore's NativeSon® rum on stage, as fake broads tip back fake daiquiris on the decks of fake boats in the fake distance. No juice for me today, though. I'm trying to stay real. I need to keep a clear head and keep a look out for anything out of the ordinary, just like the lady said. Someone's keeping tabs on me, and I'd like to find out exactly who. But after an hour or two of baking like a beached whale, I change my mind. Just a few sips to cool off couldn't hurt. Plus, I wouldn't want to start acting suspicious now, would I?

I try the bar. "Double whiskey. Neat." I'm the only sap not dumping that Gilmore's glop down my gullet. I have to tell the BotTender twice where he can pour it, which is precisely twice more than I'd like.

I keep a close eye on the richos lounging poolside as I sip the sauce. There's a good flock of them flopping around today. Other than the crowd, nothing seems too switched up. Honestly, I hadn't paid much attention to the pretty bastards before today. I see a bunch of entitled adults generally enjoying themselves. And generally ignoring their spoiled children who run around like drunken little banshees. I'd wager most of these families aren't used to communicating without 'the help' to act as translator. Syntho nannies were a regular sight back home, herding well-dressed kiddies to uptown appointments and ungodly expensive prep-schools. But I don't spy any android babysitters up here. Maybe on account of the cost of admission. Or maybe the man who makes the rules doesn't care for the rubberguts syntho scum any more than I do.

I grab a fresh whiskey and the BotTender insists on stabbing a little pink umbrella into it. I thank him all the same, just as a rampaging scamp slams right into my kneecap. This little creep looks up at me with big scared eyes and drops a rubber football at my feet. His team-mates keep a healthy distance from the scene they're sure is coming.

Your typical richo parent is great at burying his head in the sand, that is, until it comes time for punishment. There aren't any robo-pairs resortside to act as judge, jury, and executioner; and the richos them-selves don't have any actual child-rearing experience on their resumés. These are all upper management types with no time in the trenches. Now I'm no expert on the subject, but I've caught more than my share of public whoopings since pulling into port at Seren Luna. This poor kid is positive his spanking is coming next, and I have a throbbing inclination to give it to him. I frown at him with one eye angrier than the other and rub at my sore knee. But hold on now, I've seen *this* brat before. I hand him the pink parasol from my whiskey, kick the ball into the waves, and give him a wink. "Now scram, Sport."

I take a walk and scan around for the knee-bumper's old man. Sure enough, I find him, sulking into a punchbowl the size of a waste-bin. Looking much too unhappy to be relaxing by the galaxy's finest holobeach. It's my politico friend. The one that was in such a rush to get off-resort and back to business on Earth, right around the same time I had half-a-mind to do the same. Now I'm a pushover, but why the hell is *he* still here? Did the thought of those brats bitching the whole way home change his mind? No, not a chance. If I've learned anything about these people, it's that they aren't really worried about their children. They're masters at tuning out the brood, like so many bad mediastreams or spammy infocoms.

No, this guy doesn't give a slice of pie what his kids want. *He* wants to be back on Earth. And this is a man that's accustomed to getting what he wants. He sponsored that whole PolarSouth shipyard merger, for crying out loud. He's important enough that even a lout like me knows his tricks. So why isn't he home?

Maybe Audrine is right. Maybe there *is* something going on here. First JanosCorp invites me, their most unwanted guest, to an extended stay—on their dime, no less. Now big shots that want to skidaddle are sticking around too? Something stinks, and it sure as schnapps ain't the holofish.

When I approach her in the Garden Dome for evening chow, I give her my outlook. "Listen doll," I say. "You're on to something. There's something slimy crawling around this resort. I'd like you and I to have a go at just what it might be, what do you say?"

We're back in our usual corner, tucked away for safe keeping. She gives me an evil eye and rips at the volume knob for our musical accompaniment. The golden era grimehaus track—her selection— spins harder, and the first of many bass-drops makes her fizzy-water quiver and bounce out of the glass. She wants to drown me out and she's doing a decent job.

"Well hello to you too, Stockton," she says as I slide into the seat across from her. "I'm sorry if you don't like the perfume I'm wearing." She practically shouts over the music. "Maybe we should *discuss it later?*"

Those emerald eyes burn craters into my hide.

I smile a silent apology, glance around for eavesdroppers, and eventually she lets me cut the beats back to a reasonable level. Audrine orders a bottle of something old, red, and expensive. Pours me a tall one and insists I drink it, too. And then something inside her switches on—or *off* maybe is more like it. She becomes a different dame altogether. She giggles at me. Reaches across the table, grabs both my hands and tells me what a wonderful time she's having. Even offers to patch up the split seams on my old, stained suit with an old-fashioned needle and thread. What's gotten into her? I'm not game for guessing what makes a dish like this tick, but I'm not ready to tell her to breeze off either. Maybe I can catch the low-down straight from this pretty little pony's mouth while I've got her in giggles. I set the wine aside and get to grilling.

"Where you from, doll?"

She smiles, but plays dumb. Twists a curl around her finger.

"I'm afraid I was never very good at keeping an address."

I lean in closer. I don't shake that easily.

"How about your folks, then? Where do they hang their hats?"

She swallows exactly once. Moisture wells along her long lashes and she stares out the window to keep me from seeing. "I'm afraid they're not around, Stockton."

She dabs at her eyes with a napkin then turns to face me. She'll never admit it, but the thought of Mr. and Mrs. DeMarco has her balled up like a wet napkin. Maybe I've touched on something solid here. I press harder. "Sorry to hear that," I say. "They been gone long?"

She smiles again, although her eyes still glisten.

"Long enough. Friends and family are the first luxury you lose in this line of work." She looks back out the window and sips at her wine, softer this time.

"This line of work? You mean being a time-travelling travel agent? Babysitting the rich and famous?"

"Sure," she says. "Why not?"

I nod and suck my teeth. "If your loved ones are the first to go, what's the last thing you lose?"

She blinks at the stars outside and lets the vino be, but only for a moment. "I'll be sure to let you know when I find out." Her voice is cold and distant, and I have a feeling it's not about to get much warmer. I still have prying to do. Answers to dig out. She hums a little tune to herself, under her breath.

"So when they were with us, where did Ma and Pa DeMarco park the car? I don't mean to be rude, doll, but I'll do it anyway. Call it professional curiosity."

She peels herself from the window and glares at me with diamond-hard eyes. "A little villa in the south of Philly."

She smirks and shrugs and recrosses her legs.

I nod and tap at my teeth.

"Way I hear it that's a colorful neighborhood, kid. How about your people before them? What kind of ship did they sail over on?"

"I don't know," she says. "I never met them." She meets my gaze and leans in over the table. "What's with the questions, Inspector?"

"Oh nothing personal," I say. "It just seems you won the genetic lottery is all. I want to know where to take my next vacation. Where they grow 'em good as you. If I had to guess, I'd wager someplace sunny and warm. How *is* Pennsylvania this time of year?"

She rolls her eyes and crosses her arms.

"Nothing personal my foot. If I didn't know any better I'd think you were trying to get to know me."

She turns her head towards the jungle, not looking at anything in particular, just trying her damnedest not to look at me. The tendons in her neck tense as they disappear down the plunging bodice of her dark dress.

"Why shouldn't I?" I say, swirling my wine in the glass. The red liquid races up to the rim and back down again, but I'm careful to keep it off the tablecloth. "If you and me's gonna be pals, I'd rather get it out of the way."

She snorts.

"Pals, huh? Alright, *buddy*. You can ask me one more before we change the subject. A lady likes her secrets sometimes."

"Just one more?"

She nods, mid-sip.

"Promise?"

She nods again. A single drop of wine perches on her ruby red lower lip before she licks it away. The dead parent angle isn't bearing fruit, so I move to another orchard altogether. "Okay, here goes. Pay attention now, it's a zinger. You've got business in the bathroom. A shower and a shit. My question is: which comes first?"

The practiced act comes back in a flash. She's coy.

"Mr. Ames! You're much too much!"

She folds her arms and leans back in the chair.

"Hey you only gave me one shot here! It had to be a whopper or it wouldn't work at all. Now fess up. We've got dinner yet."

"I don't think I can answer a question like that. I don't even know you." She frowns and squints, staring into the glass dome overhead. "What could it possibly even tell you about me anyway?"

"Lots, doll."

She nods sarcastically and taps her foot under the table. "Try me."

It's an old detective's trick, the answer isn't important. The real story is in the way she goes about the telling. But she doesn't need to know all that. "There's no right or wrong answer, doll. It's a dilemma. A philosophical conundrum. Pros and cons, either way. You can learn a lot about somebody from their values."

"Real highbrow dilemma there, Socrates. What's the benefit of showering first?"

"Well it smells a lot better, for one."

"Mmhhmm. And what does it tell you if I don't give you any answer at all?"

"Plenty." I take a sip. "It tells me promises don't mean much to you. So what is it?"

"What is what?"

"Your answer. Which comes first? The shower or the shit? Come on now, we don't have all night."

She looks me right in the eye.

"My answer is that it's none of your business what goes on in my bathroom." She uncrosses her arms, then leans over the table towards me. Her glittering necklace flirts with the wine. "But in general, my take is a shower's always more fun with a friend."

"That so?" I say.

Her eyes narrow.

"No. But, that's what you wanted to hear, wasn't it?"

She says nothing else but doesn't break eye contact until a MonkeyBoy approaches to take our order. The tension is palpable. Wrist-thick and humming showtunes. Without taking my eyes from her, I hold up a finger for the waiter to wait. He stands patiently by the end of the table and tries too hard to look like he's not listening. Finally she cracks. She smiles and shakes her head, then takes another swallow from her nearly empty glass.

"Seriously?" She lets out a roaring laugh. "How did you think that would go?"

Now it's my turn to shrug.

"Honestly I half-expected to be wearing your wine."

She tips her glass towards me. "You nearly got it right."

The waiter's getting antsy but I flash him a look that says he'll wait longer and he'll like it. "Isn't there anything you need to know about me?" I say.

"Who's to say I don't know everything interesting there is to know about you already?" She flashes a wicked grin and gives MonkeySuit the business. Taps at her nearly empty wine glass and nods. Then she orders dinner. My gut says she's got more to share than she already hasn't. I'm ready to keep slugging it out with Little Miss Mysterious here, but I'll wait until we're alone.

I decide to branch out for a change, order a steak. When they deliver it, I'm surprised to find it a little tough. Slightly artificial. Better than I'm accustomed to back home, but nothing like those RealBeef burgers I've been pounding all week. I make a mental note but keep it to myself for now.

I try to turn the conversation back to personal matters but she ducks my every prying poke with another slug of red and a hearty laugh. She keeps MonkeyBoy and his pals hopping back and forth in a frantic daisy chain of bottle service. Stacks 'em up faster than they can haul away the empties. She drinks with purpose and fervor, nearly puts me to shame. Nearly.

The conversation turns mundane—as discussions about simulated weather at holographic beaches often do—but I'm happy to keep her yapping. Let her get nice and comfy before I try and slice anything else out of her. Eventually I set my knife and fork aside with a clink. Audrine eyes me from over the top of her glass. "Listen honey," I say. "Let's skip the gristle and cut right down to the bone."

She raises an eyebrow, and appears, if only for a moment, to sober up. "What do you want to know?" she says quietly.

"I'd like to know about you, Miss DeMarco. But you don't seem too keen to share."

"Sorry, Charlie," she says. "Maybe you're just not my type."

"Maybe I'm not," I say. "So who is? What do you look for in a fella?"

The wobbliness of the wine leaves her completely, replaced by something confident and angry and sarcastic. "Oh I don't want anything any other woman doesn't, Stockton. For starters, a man that's as interested by what's between my ears as what's between my legs."

"You know, I always said you had nice eyes."

She smiles and nods. "Well how about a man that wants to know more about me than what I look for in a man?"

I lean back in my chair and spread my hands. "You're not giving me much of a chance here, doll."

"No," she says. "I'm not." The smarm bolts from her voice. The sharpness flees her eyes. She's back to playing the happy drunk again. Back to pretending to enjoy her time with a guy like me. She smiles again. "Now why don't you finish telling me about which one of our holobeaches is your favorite? Maui, was it?"

Soon enough we've cleared the spread and it's time to jet. Audrine polishes off her umpteenth glass and makes a big scene of stumbling out through the dining room, clinging to my arm as if I were the only stable chunk of rock in the universe. Is she actually zazzled, or is this all part of her sham? She sure tossed her share back tonight, but she's a tricky twist to pin down. She's crafty, and I won't forget it. From where I stand—half-carrying her slender, giggling frame through the flowery chow hall—this little show is at least half-bogus. Either way, I'm not going to lie; I enjoy the act. Baloney or no, she's quite the arm candy.

We traipse past the diners to the host stand, and she steps up on her tippy toes and gives me a big wet smooch on the cheek. The richo royalty couldn't care less if we were their neglected children, but her monkey-suited coworkers do doubletakes for days. She fiddles with her MPD and motions for me to lean closer so she can whisper in my ear.

"Meet me here," she says.

Her sweet lips brush my lobe and linger. I'm jelly.

She drunkenly rubs her MPD up against mine, transfers the digitized details. I glance down to see where she's leading me, but there's no description, just directions. A nightcap at her place perhaps? Poking around the map screen gets me nowhere in a hurry. Is *nothing* labeled around here?

I look up and she's gone, clickety-clacking down the hallway. From the sound of it she's not exactly walking a straight line. I snatch a couple of flowers from the blossoms vining their way around the Garden Dome entrance and catch a frown from one of the waiters. He gets a wink and I'm gone.

I stop by the Tiki Bar at the holobeach for a few slugs. Just to take the edge off and wash the sour taste of the good stuff out of my mouth. Smooth, island rhythms play in time with the crashing waves as I slide up to a stool between two lonely richos drowning in their three thousand dollar beers. The BotTender notices the flowers, asks if I've got "a hot date tonight." Whoever writes the personality code for these things needs to get paid more.

"I dunno," I tell him. I take the shot. "Ask me tomorrow."

He pours me one more and I'm off.

Audrine's routing protocol sends me scampering down more of the same identical-looking hallways to an identical-looking slidelock. The corridor is stark naked except for me. This could be her room, or it could be the airlock for all I know. Only one way to find out. I step in, and to my surprise, the turbolift pulls south. So they keep the help in the basement do they?

I straighten my hat and step out of the lift.

I emerge into a very dark hallway with a pale red light pouring from a tight turn up ahead. It's a sketchy scene from any number of seedy back alleys. A scene I'm well familiar with, in the professional sense. I half-expect a mangy cat to claw at me from a dented compost dumpster, or some chicken-headed needle-jock to take a pot shot with a homemade heater. Suddenly wish I had packed the magnum. Where is this broad dragging me? The trash compactor? I round the corner, bathed in a bloody glow.

The scene paints itself beyond the bend: I am not in the staff quarters. Or the trash compactor. A very attractive blonde stands behind a glass podium next to a gleaming slidelock. She's a tall thing, with long, straight hair that looks like it was cut with a laserbeam. As a matter of fact, her whole body looks rather carved from something hard. She wears a very form-fitting, very revealing little sheer number, a big smile, and not much else. That lacy negligée has got to be against corporate policy. But oh no, there it is. A tiny little two-faced JanosCorp logo right on the... err, blouse.

I almost look away.

She's all kinds of nice, but definitely not the woman I came to see.

"Hello, Mr. Ames," she says. Her voice is smooth as melted caramel, dripping down her chin and into my ears. "We've been expecting you."

I stroll over to investigate.

"That a fact?" I say.

She hands me a package wrapped in stiff, brown paper and points to a series of doors I hadn't seen before. "Why yes sir, Mr. Ames." She winks. "You can get ready over there."

Well, well, well. What's the story here? I walk towards the line of doors and one of them opens at my approach. Another pale red light kicks on when I enter. The room is small but comfortable. There's a sleek vinyl lounger and a big mirror and that's about it. I take a seat and rip the paper off the package.

Inside is a silk robe. Navy, with a finely embroidered, double-headed JanosCorp logo in silver and orange. Where the hell am I? I sit and stare at the robe for a few minutes. The smart money says I'm supposed to put it on. But why? Suddenly there's a knock at the slidelock.

I nearly hop right out of my skin. Now in my line of work, the bad guys hardly *ever* knock. But I'm so far out of my comfort zone I don't know my bare ass from a bran muffin.

"Do you require any *assistance*, Mr. Ames?" It's the ServRep from outside. Or whatever her job description might be. "I'd be more than happy to lend you a hand."

I have to think about the answer to a doozy like that.

"No, no, that's alright," I say. "But thanks for the offer just the same, toots. Be out in a flash."

I am.

I open the door and glance out of the changing room, feeling more than a little ridiculous. But the robe does feel oh so silky smooth against my skin. The blonde eyes me from her post by the podium. This look is a bit swishy for a mug like me, but I'd sport a striped skirt and like it for a chance with a looker like this one. I sweep up my duds and exit the dressing room posthaste.

"Miss DeMarco is waiting for you in The Grotto," sexy ServRep says as I approach the glass podium. "We'll have your things sent back to your room."

"Thanks," I say, handing off an armful of clothes to the beautiful broad before me. She flashes a smile before peeking into the pile. Her eyebrows arch.

"Mr. Ames?"

"Yeah, doll?"

"Protocol requires that we take *all* of your clothing before you enter."

She's not shy about staring towards the region in question. I quickly slide off my skivvies from under the robe and place them on top of the others.

"All yours," I say and step over to the door next to her.

"It's my pleasure," she says with a wink.

The door slips open. I'm enveloped in a cloudy mist.

"Welcome to ClubZero, Mr. Ames."

EIGHT

Darkness crawls over me as I step through the door. Pale red light peeks through the fog hanging heavy in the air like rush hour exhaust. It's warm in here. I'd almost call it steamy. Slow, sexy music with a deep, haunting bassline slinks through the mist and punches me in the gut. They must have woofers inside the woofers, and big ones at that. I keep walking until a cool breeze sweeps away a patch of mist. Get my first clean look at the decor.

Now I would call it steamy.

The place is decked out like one of those tropical rainforests they used to cry about back in the southern half of the UNSAT territories, back on Earth. It's covered in vines and trees and ferns, and dotted with steaming pools fed by crystal clear waterfalls. Other club-goers enjoy the water. Drinks. Each other. Let's just say it's too hot for dancing. The fog rolls back in and I step into the depths of the ClubZero jungle, trying not to stare.

I brush away a leathery leaf the size of a city block and peek around it. A pair of giggling girls slink past me, but their eyes stay glued to mine until they wade into the water. Their robes float away before the ladies can sink too deep. The friendly one beckons me with a single finger. I have to physically turn my head away with my hands and force my feet to march in the opposite direction.

I search for anything that might be called 'The Grotto.' As far as I'm concerned this whole damned place could go by that handle. I don't know how I'm going to find anything more than what's under my robe in all the fog and plants and rump-thumping music, female distractions aside. Then The Grotto finds me.

A soft hand with a firm grasp wraps my wrist and yanks me through a gap in the stone next to one of the waterfalls. It's a familiar grip. I duck into a rocky alcove with more than a little encouragement. A shallow pool leads out through the backside of the waterfall and back into the main room. The ceiling is low, the torchlight intimate. This must be the place. The Grotto. It's cozy. And empty, except for us. Audrine pulls me in close to her. I can almost feel her hot breath on my neck, even in this clambake. My heart thumps.

"Well hi there, darlin'," I say. "Miss me?"

I attempt to hand her the flowers, previously hidden under my robe and only a little wilted in this sauna. She tosses them aside without a second of hesitation. The bouquet sinks slowly in the pool, along with any hopes I had for romance.

That drunken stupor and needy affection from earlier tonight are both gone, replaced with an impatient confidence. More like the girl that gave me the business between bites. I shouldn't be surprised, she's a hell of an actress. Most broads are. She shoves me onto a seat carved into the rock and begins to pace. I eye her up.

She wears a similar robe to the one I'm sporting. Gives a great view of her gams—and everything else, too. Her face has gone cold sober and her lips twitch like she's trying to figure out where to begin. I give her a hand. "Swell spot for a chat," I say. "Nice and private. You sure know how to woo a fella."

She stops pacing and rolls her eyes at me. "ClubZero is the one place in the resort they don't have Security watching our every move."

"That's funny," I say. "This is the one joint I'd imagine they should want to watch the most."

She shakes her head. "All those guests out there? Most of them aren't with their wives. Some of them are with each other's wives, or worse. JanosCorp doesn't want evidence of that. It's bad for business, and that's bad for everybody."

"What a shame," I say. "I was secretly hoping you had something spicier in mind."

She puts her hands on her hips.

"Maybe next time, Cowboy. We've got bigger fish to fry."

"Says you." I lean back and kick my heels out, throw my hands behind my neck. "I'm on vacation, lady, in case you forgot. All I want to do is relax, and now you've dumped a heap of heartache in my lap. Maybe you want to dump something else there while you're at it? Hell, it's a crying shame to keep things strictly business in a joint like this."

She approaches me, stands over my outstretched feet and bends low to look me in the eyes. Her robe bends lower still and my eyes wander. She snags my chin and drags my face up to hers.

"You finished?" she says.

"Mostly," I say with a frown.

She ignores it and takes the seat to my right.

"They aren't letting the guests leave," she says.

"Don't I know it, doll. As soon as Slick told me *you* were behind my extension, I knew he had to be goldbricking. So what's the hold up?"

She stares at the ground between her painted toes and shakes her head. "They say it's a problem with the SpaceGates. Something about recalibrating the field generators. Maybe something from that pulsar event threw it—"

"But you don't buy what they're selling."

She looks up at me with those big green eyes of hers. They sparkle in the soft light reflected from the water and the wet walls of the cave. Everything sweats in a place like this, even the rocks. "No," she says. "I don't buy it for a second. We've seen plenty of cyclosheets, both here and at the other resorts. There's never been a problem like this before."

"And I'll take a wild guess and say JanosCorp isn't the kind of outfit to go handing out anything for free, especially extended stays to guys like me."

"No," she says. "That contest you won was the exception to the rule. A one-in-a-million marketing stunt. Something must be very wrong here. Half the suites are empty, and they aren't even bringing in new guests to fill them."

"Because that would wreck their alibi about the gates being busted?"

"Technically speaking, no," she says. She chews her lip like yesterday's bubblegum. "The newest generation of wormhole generators create both the departing and arriving gateways. If there were just an issue on our end, we could still accept new guests, we just couldn't get them home again."

"So on the one hand, they're hemorrhaging dough for all the folks they've got to comp. And on the other, they aren't shlumping in any new chumps to pay the bills. Whatever's cramping their style must be pretty ugly for them to shut up shop like that."

She looks up at me and nods.

I continue with my assessment. "And whatever it is, it's serious enough that they won't even clue the staff in on it. Now I'll bet you've been kicking around JanosCorp and old Slick long enough to see them put out a few fires."

Another nod.

"And I'll go double or nothing that they didn't go out of their way to keep you in the dark about any trouble before."

A third.

"They need the staff to stay informed, to run interference. Keep the guests fat and happy and looking the other way."

She stops chewing her lip and perks up a bit. "Whether they tell me or not, I'm going to get to the bottom of this," she says. "All of the corporate orders are coming through Proletti, and I just don't trust him. Not one bit. I'll keep a close eye on the supply inventories. I can almost guarantee that they are still pulling in fresh crates to the depots."

"I don't know about that," I say, stroking my chin. "That piece of meat they brought me tonight had test-tube written all over it. You could call it a steak, if you were feeling generous. And I'm guessing all that RealBeef they fed me earlier in the week didn't come from the CattleRanch simulator."

Her eyes get wide. "But if that's true..."

I get what she's after.

"How long can this place stay afloat without resupply from Earth or one of the offworld ag colonies?"

"Not long," she says. "A week, maybe two. We're not at maximum capacity right now so it's closer to two. But we'll start running out of certain things quicker than that. The guests will not be happy."

"Forget happy!" I stomp a bare foot on the stone floor. "In two weeks the guests'll be eating each other!"

She urges me to quiet down. Her lips get even poutier as she shushes me. I continue in an indoor voice. "Listen," I say. "We need a plan. If they aren't going to let us off this rock, fine. We've got to find our own way out, just you and I."

I put an arm around her. She doesn't shove me off.

She nods slowly, then looks up at me with a start. "What if we're being crazy?" she says. "What if there really is a problem with the WFGs, and they get them back up and running in a few days?"

I give her a good squeeze around the arms.

"Then we've got no reason to worry. We'll laugh about it over drinks. Drinks on you, that is." I look her square in the eye. "But what if we're not crazy?"

She smiles.

"You're right," she says. "We need a plan. If we don't need to use it, all the better. But if we do? If things don't start to look up in three days? We leave. Together. Whether we've gotten to the bottom of all this or not, we find a way off this resort and we go back to Earth."

"What about Slick's journal?" I ask.

"Grab it if you can, Stockton. We may need the evidence. But it won't do us any good if we die here. You've got three days to get it from him. Then—whether we have it or not—we split."

"Agreed," I say, putting my hand out for a shake. She obliges. "Now are you sure you don't want to get to know each other a little better first? Seems we've got the steam room all to ourselves."

She pushes me away and stands up straight.

"What's the matter, doll? Some lucky fella already got his hooks in you?" I think back to her rude friend from the first night in the Garden Dome.

She grabs both my hands and looks me in the eyes.

"There's no man in my life but you, Ames." She blows me a kiss and winks, then throws her hands on her hips. "But now's not the time, Romeo. You need to be careful with that gun," she says. "It may come in handy before too long."

"No doubt about it, beautiful. I've been catching whiffs like somebody's been snooping around for it in my room."

She purses her lips. "Yeah, I'd imagine so," she says. "I'm sure they know you have it. I don't suppose they want to find out if you'd use it." She grabs both my hands again. Looks me square in the eyes. Bats her lashes.

"Would you?" she says. "Would you use it, Stockton? Have you ever shot anyone before?"

I look away and smile.

"Nobody that didn't have it coming, doll."

Our little moment is interrupted by some heavyweight big shot that stumbles in with a pair of floozies on each arm. He's shaped like an uncooked pizza: doughy and round. Exactly the opposite physique of his haughty harem. Real classy-looking dames these ones, with big, bright hair and the dull, dead eyes of the chemically dependent. They've got about one and a quarter robes between the lot of them, and a bowling ball-sized bag of something white and chalky. I'm ready for a big bowl of popcorn, for some live theater, but Audrine has other ideas. We slip out quietly as the last of those robes starts to fly.

She leads me by the wrist through a labyrinth of steamy passageways and steamier clientele. I see things the skinstreams haven't dreamed up yet, until she flashes her MPD against a service slidelock hidden behind a Jurassic-looking shrub. The door glides open and we step through into a plain gray hallway. Very industrial. It's got exactly none of the glitz and glamour of the rest of the resort.

"Where are you dragging me?" I say, rubbing the gooseflesh sprouting on my arms. This hallway has got none of the heat of that steamy jungle, either, and I'm not exactly dressed for the weather.

Audrine stomps down the passage with my wrist in tow.

"I'm bringing you back to your room, Mr. Ames," she says, glancing around. An observation deck blinks menacingly in the corner. They're watching. "It appears you've had too much to drink. Again."

She gives me a sharp elbow to the ribs. I play along, add some sauce to my step. Just a touch though. A guy like me is never so drunk he can't get himself where he needs to go.

"I'm taking you through the service tunnels so as not to *upset* the other guests."

"I don't need a—*hiccough*—babysitter, lady."

The look she flashes me says otherwise.

We stumble through a maze of crisscrossing corridors and twisting tunnels. Stroll past about a hundred thousand slidelocks in the process. Finally we come to the one she's been hunting. I'm amazed that she can nav her way around down here without electronic assistance. These days, most folks couldn't find their way out of a paper bag without an MPD and a recently patched routing protocol.

"Here you are, sir," she says.

The door slides open to reveal the same marble-paneled elevator as the lift for my room.

"This will return you to your suite."

She lowers her voice to a whisper.

"Remember: three days."

"Thanks, doll," I say. "You're the—*hiccough*—best." I bend down to give her a little kiss on the cheek. In my inebriated state, my hands do a little wandering on their own. She shoves me into the elevator. I nearly spill to the floor.

"Nice try," she mouths to me silently.

I give her a wink as the lift door slips shut between us.

NINE

Come morning I decide to sit it out, at least on paper. Nurse a bogus hangover, hope I run into Slick, and catch some zees down at the holobeach while I'm at it. The shore's sporting a Mediterranean drape today, and the gentle breeze and smooth DeepDub rhythms are the perfect accompaniment for a day of lazy surveillance. I try to sell the con that I was stewed to the gills last night, that I'm amongst the walking dead, but the classic smash "Pompom Banana Stand" by the Royal Chubs puts a little pep in my usually lazy gait as I stroll by the bar. The gift shop wants an arm, a leg, and my firstborn child for their cheapest cheaters, so I pinch a pair of mirrored shades from the Tiki Bar lost and found. I toss the sunglasses on and slink into a lonely lounger under the shade of a digital palm and a real umbrella. It's the best stakeout gig I've landed since that shady case at the chophouse strip joint. Or was it a striphouse chop joint?

Unlike the shady case, this gig delivers.

The richos are agitated, right on cue. Bitching up a tropical storm of complaints to a very harried waitstaff.

It's funny the first time it goes down. I drop the specs, take a slug of rye, and watch some done-up dame spit out the first sip of a gold-fish bowl before she dumps the whole fruit fountain on the server's shoes—all because the BotTender switched brands on her.

Hell, it's funny the first few times. But come lunchtime, I grow worried the patrons might go full-tribal on the help. These JanosCorp mooks are hand-picked for their ability to shake off verbal venom, but things are boiling up physical, and fast. The scent of blood is in the water. I gnaw my VatLab burrito and like it, yet you'd think they were serving week old rat-burgers by the way these richos carry on about it. This place is full of beautiful faces, but they sure get ugly fast.

When it finally comes to blows, the first one is oddly appropriate. An ex-ballplayer—at twice his fighting weight, mind you—winds up and unloads his lunch, putting his considerable paunch behind the pitch. A platter of steaming veggies topped with a charbroiled trout sails over my head in a perfect parabola and lands with a splash in the lagoon. Back from whence it came. But that's only strike one. His bratty behavior is catching, and a chain reaction of snack-tossers take their respective mounds. The holographic sky darkens with volley after volley of perfectly edible—if slightly less than luxuri-ous—beach fare. A veritable armada of parsleyed, silver platters sink into the gently rolling turquoise waves, while I wait it out.

The servers scramble for cover and regroup behind overturned lounge chairs and shaggy umbrellas in twos and threes, dodging shrimp cocktail artillery and crab leg grenades. They offer up oversized daiquiris, wave them frantically from behind their makeshift shelters like frozen white flags. I duck and run for the door myself, but take a bowl of chilled chowder to the chest. A Saigon Stinger smashes into the sand before me as I highstep through the culinary bombardment. Things get so hairy I very nearly spill my own beverage.

Snagging a towel on my way out, I wipe clams and corn off my favorite blue and orange tropico and chuckle at the clownishness of it all. At least the lady's little theory is confirmed: the supplies *are* running low and the natives *are* getting restless. Now only if she had the slight-est idea why.

All at once I decide to dig around the resort for another clue or two. My back against the wall beside the entrance to the holobeach, I flick on my ArmPod and open my messages. A quick chuckle escapes my mouth as a team of soaked waiters come spilling out the door, dripping food and drink and stumbling past me. I take a stroll in the other direction and pull up one of those marketing missives from the resortfeed: *Guest's guide to the thousand and one thrills of Seren Luna*. My eyes swim at the sheer number of choices. 'A thousand and one' may be selling this list short. Ballroom breakdancing in seven different styles. Existential cooking classes. Feminist drum lessons. Droptrooper deathmatch gamestreams, complete with fully immersive, next-gen neural interface cradles that "simulate the experience of a real space battle." None for me thanks, that first trip down the slopes was violent enough. I take a swipe through the offerings and let it scroll to a slow stop: the digital equivalent of throwing darts at a map. I groan when the display comes to a rest. Mama Fate just spat in my eye.

A short hike later and I'm staring at a big metal slidelock.

A menacing warning flashes before me, projected three feet in front of the entrance to the Low Gravity Lounge.

WARNING!!! ENTERING EXTREME FUNZONE!!!

The six goddamned exclamation points should be warning enough. I sign off at the podium beside the door: I'm not pregnant, sick and contagious, or especially frail and elderly. A punky-looking JanosCorp crony nods and the door opens before me. I take a deep breath and enter the Degravitization Chamber. Inside, a shiny silver jumpsuit waits for me to put it on.

Three minutes later I'm spinning somersaults through a posh lounge, trying my damnedest not to crash into tables of frowning richo women. If I thought those virtual slopes were tough stuff, I was kidding myself. I sail past a Resistance-free Aerobics class as the uppity, poof-haired instructor throws dirty looks my way. He murmurs into a headset, and no more than three seconds later, no less than four employees shoot out after me: a Rescue Squad, if I've ever seen one. These four young heros chase me through a tray of drinks floating in round, ball-shaped cups, and right out the other side. I'd let 'em catch me, if it were so easy. But there's not much in the way of slowing down once you get your momentum behind you in a zero gee environment. At least those closed-up cups keep the cocktails out of my hair.

Rescue Squad Alpha manages to wrangle me to a halt only moments before I break up a section of bridge-playing old biddies, their rheumy eyes gone wide at the sight of a grown man missiling right for their table.

The wranglers make me promise to take it easy, to move slowly, and to use the foam crash couches planted throughout the place until I get the hang of it. They threaten me with something called a 'nanny tether' if I can't swing it safely on my own. "Thanks," I tell the team, "but I think I'll catch my breath around here for a moment if it's all the same to you."

The Rescue Squad agrees that this is a good course of action. They spin around to go, although I have a suspicion they'll park one or two close by for any emergencies.

"Maybe one of you would be so kind to bring me something to sip on?" I say to the pair of stragglers "That is, unless you want me to go and get it for myself..." I squint at the bar, tucked half-a-world away in a particularly busy corner of the lounge.

The teammates frown, but one fairly lithe little blonde thing agrees to fetch me a whiskey, if I promise to stay put and not to disturb the grannies playing pinochle beside me.

"AstroScout's Honor!" I say.

One of the blue-hairs turns to me with a carefully concealed hand of cards in her grip. "Not much for flying, huh handsome?"

"You said it, grandma."

For the first time I notice the flush in her palm, the pile of chips floating in a staticky, orange ball attached to the center of their table. The lady across the way tosses a few more bits to the pot. "Okay, Helen, you wily skank, I call."

My eyebrows arch.

"Read 'em and weep, bitch!" Helen holds out her flush, King-high diamonds. These grandmas are just full of surprises. The glowing orange pot spits her winnings into Helen's waiting hand, one chip at a time. She deftly palms the stack into her own glowing orange stash, now brimming, and motions for me to take the 'seat' to her left, really more of an empty space for floating. I do so quite carefully.

"Barsoom Barroom Stud," Helen says, shuffling the cards with a sharky grin. "You in? Or don't you have the balls to stick it to a bunch of old ladies?"

"Maybe I'll just watch a hand or two first," I say, struggling to grip the table as my legs float out behind me. "Make sure you aren't sleeving any aces."

She shrugs and doles out another hand to her four ancient friends around the table.

Despite a combined age in the mid-triple digits, each player snatches her cards out of the air like a steel trap. "Ante up, ladies," Helen says, tossing a single shining chip to the orange pile built into the center of the table. The steel disc slips through no problem, but the shimmering orange ball keeps them all safe inside until the hand is won.

"Mind if I ask you a few questions?" I say.

Helen sizes me up from over a pair of leopard-print specs.

"You a cop?" she says, finally.

I shrug and smile a little.

"What gave me away?" I say.

"The bad haircut," Helen says, tapping the table and looking none too happy to have her game held up. "Any normal Joe would have just asked, Mack. Only cops and slimy salesmen ask if they can ask a question before they ask it, and you don't look like you want to sell me a pre-owned ArmPod."

"Fair enough," I say. "I'm off-duty, as it were. Permanently. If it makes any difference to you."

Helen nods for me to continue, as the ladies place their wages.

"You notice anything out of the ordinary around here? Something with the food service? With the guests getting unhappy? With folks not being able to leave?"

Helen laughs and sets her cards, face down on the tethered table.

"This must be your first trip to a TimeResort."

"Yeah, but—"

"Well the first thing you need to know is these kinds of things happen all the time, honeybunches. They never get *all* the kinks worked out at a resort like this, not completely. Abigail, tell the curious kitten here about that last rock old Dick dragged you off to a trip or two ago. You remember the one."

"Ughhh," the lady to my left speaks with a prim and proper New Union twinge. "Do I ever! How could I forget such a shoddy horse-porking excuse for a nine-star facility!"

"What happened?"

"The cosmic radiation drove the synthetics absolutely bonkers, is what happened! The filthy rubbergutted help got worse and worse, until they trapped poor Richard in his room. Wouldn't let him alone for the whole trip!"

The woman across from me chimes in. "Are you sure your lush of a husband didn't have anything to do with it, darling?"

Abigail smiles and tips her drink towards the accuser. "Blow me, Betsy. The synths went mad. They attacked a woman, you blithering old sow. It was all over the 'streams."

Helen smiles and nods towards the woman seated across from her. "Five hundred to you, Maude," she says. "And tell this young man about your little jaunt out to the Miro Cluster."

The sweet old thing spits, and although I don't think the aggression was meant for me, I have to duck out of the way to let the glob float past me all the same. She tosses her cards into the pile in disgust.

"Terrible hand," Maude says. "Didn't anyone teach you to shuffle?"

Helen smiles.

"The Miro Cluster, Maude."

Maude nods and her frown grows bigger. "Those asshats what ran the place claimed they'd found an alien civilization! All very exclusive, all very expensive. I was skeptical, of course, but Stephen couldn't wait to meet this 'new species'. The 'streams were reporting they spoke English and everything. 'Slexicans', they were calling them."

"Stephen has always been terribly gullible, dear," Abigail says.

"But imagine what it's done for her love life!" Helen whispers to me with a playful poke to my ribs.

I shake my head.

"I'd have heard about it if there were actually aliens out there," I say. "What did you find instead?"

"Fucking pigs," Maude says.

"Excuse me?"

I can hardly believe my ears.

"Those fools had toyed around with the genes of some common mud-wallowing hogs. Taught them to stand on two feet, squawk a garbled approximation of 'hello'. They were hideous creatures, hideous. Stephen was terribly dissapointed. 'Last time we trust anyone but the JanosCorp people', I told him."

"Sounds awful," I say.

"Then there was Ethel," Abigal adds, distantly.

The old ladies hold their cards over their hearts and lower their heads for a moment of silence.

"What happened to Ethel?" I ask.

Betsy smiles a sad, longing smile. "It was her heart," Betsy says. "Food poisoning, or so they told us. A bad batch of eel fricasee did her in, up at some gaudy place on the Outer Arm."

"Personally, I always thought it was that young hunk she hustled out there with her," Maude giggles. "That piece of meat worked her poor ticker right up until it popped! Of course you can't tell the family that's what became of dear old Aunt Ethel."

The other ladies nod in agreement, then fiddle with their cards.

Helen turns to me. "Now if you're almost done interrupting our game, maybe you can tell us what this is all about. What's got your panties in a twist, young man?"

I spot the blonde from the rescue squad returning with my drink in the distance. Thank God. I motion for the ladies to lean in close, then cup my hands and whisper.

"It's that prick what runs the place," I say. "Proletti. I've got a hunch he's crooked as they come, and I aim to knock him down a peg or two, drag his sorry ass out into the light."

The four women nod together and back away slowly.

"Well I think he's sexy," Maude says.

"Oh hush up, you hussy," Helen barks. "You'd sleep with one of those mutant pigs so long as it wasn't your own husband!"

"Hey now!" Maude protests. She floats herself out over the table to take a swat at Helen's blue-haired head. A full-fledged grandma fruckus is erupting right before my eyes. I push myself back from the table slowly. Where's that damned girl with my whiskey?

Abigail, the limey, taps me on the shoulder gently, just as her friends start to cause a scene I don't need. "Isn't that the man you're after?" she says, pointing down below us, past a half-dozen other card tables and to a window built right into the floor. "He is rather dashing, isn't he?"

Sure enough, I'll be damned if I don't spy Slick, strutting his stuff in a marble-floored hallway right underneath us—down where the gravity's still good. He's in a hurry, taking big, fast strides and checking the MPD in his wrist. Late for something. And lucky me, he's toting that stupid book the broad has her eyes on. I have just enough time to tail him and find out what's got his oily hide in such a huff. "Thank you, ladies," I say, tipping my hat before it has a chance to float off my head. "It's been a pleasure."

They stop their geriatric cat-fight long enough to say ta-ta. I start to push myself away from the table, but pull up just short. Almost forgot. The blonde arrives with my drink, a glob of golden goo sloshing around inside a glass globe. I snatch it from her and up and away I go, careening through the lounge like a fleshy wrecking ball.

I follow Proletti from fifty feet over his head, so it doesn't make much difference how much commotion I cause up here. I apologize to the other patrons, to the houseplants and waiters I bowl over mid-flight. Slick sticks to a straight line, and I've got a good thing going, bumps and bruises aside. The sailing's smooth, until I reach the edge of the lounge and he keeps on hoofing. A padded, rubber wall stands between me and the path I need to take, while the hallway below cuts onward and Slick doesn't show any signs of slowing down.

Frantically, I scramble up the wall, looking for a passage into the next chamber. I can't let him get too far out of sight or I might not find him again. Finally I find it, a great big circular hole. The way forward. I sigh. Around the edge of the door, the wall is painted up like a great big clown-face. Might as well be a mirror. I swim up through the grinning, jester lips, and the slidelock teeth separate to let me into what surely must be some form of karmic retribution for a long-forgotten past life I must have spent torturing orphans.

The Low Grav Lounge behind me is a serene memory, a pleasant palace of pleasure in my mind, as I float into the screaming Hell of the KiddyLand Zero Gee Jungletorium. It stinks of boogery puke, and the astringent, ammonia stench of the cleaner they pour on top. Half-chewed lumps of cracker fleck against my face as I struggle to pick out Proletti through the haze of crying kids and nearly teared-up employees standing watch. Three or four youngsters bounce off my bad knee. The sound of wailing brats fills my head, just above the rumbling drone of the circus music chirping through the blinking lights and bigtop stripes covering every inch of this evil place.

Yanking my body around the monkey bars, I finally catch sight of Slick again, a couple dozen yards ahead of me, still in the hallway below, the lucky prick. He speaks to a couple of security men, guns on their hips, and although I can't hear a word of it, I can't imagine he has nice things to say. Pointing back towards the way he came, he waves a shiny golden piece of something in their faces. Is that a wrapper from a Snix Bar? It's too far to make out the ooey-gooey chocolatey goodness stuck to the inside. Finally, when he's given them a good thrashing for littering up his hallway—and after he's ordered the tall one to straighten the seam on his shirt—Proletti whips around and disappears into a slidelock behind the guards. I get a glimpse at a large, dark room before the hatch slips shut on his heels.

I've got to get out of this gravity-less abyss and I've got to do it soon if I have any chance of picking up his slimy trail. I'll worry about the guards when I get closer.

I wiggle my way through a web of snotty cargo netting and tangled, screaming children, until I'm up close and personal with the plexisteel window into the hallway underneath. It's some sort of gallery down there, with statues and paintings tucked away to either side. Lush, velvet curtains hang every so often, creating private nooks to enjoy the art. Strange place for a museum, stuck right under this freakshow circus whirlwind. But then again, I never was one to make any sense from richo sensibilities—or lack thereof.

Instead, I try to tackle the practical dilemma before me. How do I get six feet and change of solid Stockton Ames through the three-inch-thick window below me? I give the glass a thump or two, until a tottering toddler begs me to stop with a stone serious scowl smeared across his little face. He'd make a better case if he'd take his knuckle out of his nostril.

I shrug and take a slug from the ball of whiskey in my palm. The hooch slurps down with a little more fight than I'm used to—on account of the missing gravity—but still swallows smooth enough for a bum like me.

"When you're right, you're right, kid. I'm not gonna bully my way through this glass any more than you are." He nods. I gesture towards the whiskey in my hand. He shakes his head again. Then I heave him by the waistband and send him packing back up to his buddies laced into the net overhead.

Johnny Nosedigger was right. The window is out. But how else can I ferret my way into the art show down below? A bright white candy wrapper suddenly wraps itself around my face, blown by some unseen, menacing wind. I smack it away and watch the trash tumble onwards. It floats along the window for a moment, before getting snatched up by an air return already clogged with thoroughly-used tissues and other sundries of the utterly disgusting variety.

I crinkle my nose at the hissing vent and blow out a deep breath. Here goes nothing.

Two minutes and three gut-wrenching retches later, I drop out of a similar, if much cleaner vent in the ceiling of the room below me. The gravity picks right up where it let off and all two hundred twenty pounds of me say hello to the marble floor in the meanest way possible. I pop to my feet and poke my head from behind one of the dark draperies separating the gallery spaces. The two guards are too busy arguing over which one of them left the chocolate bar on the floor to notice my graceless entrance. But they've both got a rotten look about them that says I won't talk my way through. Especially not when the bossman just laid into them for slacking off. I'll need a distraction, and I'll need a good one.

My eyes trace the art around me. A series of enormous, colorless plastic scribbles hang from the rafters in this little nook: not much to work with. Across the way though, I spy a prize worth my time. A huge twirling hunk of stone, in the shape of a very shapely young lady. Miss Marbletits is perfectly naked, and perched on a single toe, arms held high, like she were holding up the sun. She's perched a little precariously from where I'm standing. I doublecheck the guards can't make me, then sneak over beside the statue for a closer look.

The Founder's Muse, the label says. *A likeness of the wife of the first president and founder of the Janos Corporation. On loan from the JanosCorp Executive offices in Rome.*

"I'll be damned," I say. *Missus* Marbletits then. "Sorry, lady."

I give her royal hiney a hefty shove, really put my shoulder into it, and the once balanced ballerina begins to sway on her platform. She rocks back and forth with enough gusto to scare me back to a dark place behind a curtain, and I watch her lean ever closer to the ground. Just when I'm sure she's going to tip, the damned statue rolls back up the way it came and I sneer.

"Just fall you lousy bag!" I shout under my breath.

But Marble Mama just keeps shaking those stony hips. Waving that perfectly carved tail in my face like it's some kind of cosmic joke. I growl. Then wind up and pitch the globe of whiskey at the back of her porcelain head.

The shattering glass sprays spirits all over the curtains behind her, and Doofus and Dopey sprint over from their post to catch the commotion. I drip out from behind my hidey hole and leave them to inspect the wobbly mess I left for them.

I swipe at the panel beside the slidelock Slick disappeared into, but it only beeps angrily at all my efforts. I pound a balled fist into it, trace all manner of obscenities into the touchscreen handscanner. Finally, just when I'm sure the guards are behind me, it flashes green and the door begins to split open.

I peek through the crack, into a huge warehouse of a room, stacked to the roof with bright white shipping crates. The door opens. And right there waiting for me is Proletti's greasy sneer. Smiling at me. He's just finished tucking that damned diary of his into a safe that would make a banker jealous. Eighteen separate latches slam shut, and the whole operation sinks into the floor slowly. In its place emerge a pair of pros packing some serious heat. Not the kind of rent-a-cop stun-sticks the guards outside are toting, these two meanies are palming enough heavy hardware to give me the gulps. Judging by their matching thousand-yard stares and lack of JanosCorp insignia on their flat-black pajamas, these boys look ready to drop me at the drop of a hat. My hands reach for the ceiling all on their own.

"Mr. Ames," Proletti says. "What a pleasant surprise."

My eyes don't leave the holsters of the hooligans behind him.

"Who are your friends, Slick?"

"These men are exterminators, Mr. Ames. It seems we have quite a problem with pests lately."

A lump forms in my throat. Proletti pockets his golden pen and grins some more.

"Maybe you want to call them off?" I say.

"Maybe," he says. "Maybe not."

TEN

Under armed escort, I tuck my tail and head home for classic-stream holos and room service. It's a long, quiet walk back to the StateSuite, to say the least. Proletti's pros threaten to do dirty things to my corpse if I make them have to take a second trip, and I'm inclined to believe they'll keep their word. Seems everybody's a touch eggy after that scene at the holobeach this morning. I order in to avoid a full on revolution at the dinner table.

The beefy waiter winces when I move to swipe him a tip. He's a big boy, but he's been somebody or another's chew toy all night, judging by the quiver in his eye and the dampness of his palms. I slide a few berries extra to the poor guy's cut and get cozy with my dinner and a bottle of midgrade swish.

The next morning I get up early to give it another go. Continue the stakeout. Grab a few more laughs as the galaxy's most important people make asses of themselves in a very public place. I weigh the pros and cons of snapping a few clips for the newstreams. Maybe I'll even chase down some reasoning for the supply shortage and the

SpaceGate blackout—if I find the time between giggles and gulps. I run a laundry list of questions to grill whichever cabana boy is unlucky enough to draw my hammock from a hat. There's just one big hitch in my plans.

The holobeach is closed.

No infocom, nothing. Just a little paper sign tacked up on a great big slidelock where the entrance to my favorite hangout used to be. Handwritten, even.

We're sorry it reads, *this facility is closed for maintenance.*

Not as sorry as I am. The only activity I ever enjoyed in this joint is now off-limits. A whole day's snooping is canned, too. These damned snobs act like brats and now they're getting spanked and me along with 'em. I think about cooling off with a cocktail or two at the ski lodge, but it's not just the lack of liquor in my veins that's got me jazzed. Everything's falling a little too square for a place without any right angles.

This holobeach has been open 24/7 since I got here. Now things slide downhill faster than a hovercycle race and the main attraction is suddenly closed? I want to know why, and I'm not buying an overnight mop-up from yesterday's lunch shift. It's too convenient an excuse, and I don't think JanosCorp has the backbone to take a belt to their guests like that. Not unless they absolutely had to. There's something sinister hiding behind this huge door, and I intend to stare it right in the eye.

I vee up Audrine on the MPD. She answers on the third ring. "Meet me in my room," I say. "Something's up."

I watch her nod in the viewer, a towel wrapped around her presumably wet hair, but she says nothing. She hangs up and I stomp back to the statesuite. When I get there, I pull the magnum out of that gaudy tux and slide it into my waistband. Then I pour myself a stiff one and wait.

I barely have time to finish the drink. Audrine shows up in a flash, sporting heels and a black cocktail dress that sets my midmorning heart aflutter. She's a little out of breath as she steps off the elevator, her curls a little damp after all.

"What's going on?" she says.

I set my empty glass down.

"Pool's closed," I say.

She runs both hands through her soggy locks and glares daggers through my face. "Security is buzzing all over the place this morning, and you drag me up here for this?"

I grab her by the wrist and pull her back towards the door.

"That's a good break," I say. "They'll be too busy to keep an eye on us."

"And just where do you think you're taking me?"

Those eyes of hers get so narrow when she's hot and bothered.

"To find out why the pool's closed," I say, tugging her into the lift. "Where else?"

She starts to hash it out with me one more time but I put a single finger to her lips and ask her to trust me.

"Not the dirty, drunken lout you're familiar with. Not even the guy with the gun standing before you. But the big-city homicide detective with more years on the force than you've had birthdays."

She frowns.

"Well birthday parties, anyway. Trust *him* and we'll get to the bottom of this. Maybe even in one piece."

She rolls her eyes and the rest of her head with them but she doesn't say no. I ask her to poke at her ArmPod and have the lift take us back to the service subfloor, the industrial underbelly buried down below the guest quarters where she hauled me out of that steaming sex-jungle a few nights ago. She wants to know why she should do any such thing. Maybe she thinks I want to revisit the lovetubs, and maybe she's right. But not right now she's not.

"There's food and drink service at the holobeach," I say.

"So what?" She's real smart about it. You'd think I asked her to make me a sandwich.

"So," I say with a smile, "I've never seen a MonkeyBoy come skating through the front door with a tray of potatoes. So there's got to be a service lift in there somewhere. So that's how we're going to get in. So maybe we should both keep our yaps shut and our eyes open."

She stays quiet after that, but I can almost hear the steam sizzle out her ears.

I follow Audrine through a spaghetti bowl of identical corridors once again. Once again, like magic, she leads us right to a slidelock that matches all the others.

"This is it," she says.

She points for me to lead the way. The door opens and I step through—right into the waiting arms of a squad of JanosCorp security goons.

You know the type. Brutes too violent for ordinary police work but too dumb for the military. Big hulking bruisers, these guys. Bursting with muscles and tactical equipment. I wonder if they know how to use either one.

I take a rifle butt to the gut and fold like a bad hand. That's definitely one way to use 'em. Knocks the fight right out of me. I collapse in a heap on the cold concrete and Audrine steps right over me, the two-timing tramp! But boy does she have great stems.

She slithers right up to the silverback rent-a-cop. Pretty rugged, this guy. Six foot and change, and nearly as big around. He scratches at a scarred, shaved head and adjusts a pair of mirrored razor shades. He's got the kind of round figure that defies gravity, like maybe there's a wall of muscle underneath. He's a soft pudgy shell dipped over a powerful core and he's just dying to prove it. Still, I'll bet he's not so bad without all his buddies staring down their psychometer barrels at me.

Audrine actually reaches up and pecks him on the cheek, leaving a perfectly formed pink print that eats at me worse than the pinch I'm in. "This is the man I was telling you about, Sergeant Burke," she says, batting her lashes. "Be careful, he may be armed."

Damn skippy I may be armed. But I don't draw down on these clowns. Not when four or five of them already have a bead on me and then some. I didn't live this long by starting fights I won't win. I play dead as two of them take my heater and toss it to the bossman. He admires it as they stand me up, none too gently. They've got me by the scruff, with one goon to either side and a third with his barrel in my back.

The bossman Burke lowers his shades and stares at me from over the reflective lenses. Smirks. "Don't worry, Ms. DeMarco," he says. "This jerkass won't be bothering you, or anyone else, for quite some time."

That's what he thinks.

"Take him to the interrogation chamber, boys."

The way he says 'interrogation chamber' makes me think they usually call it something else. The goons drag me off through another slidelock as Audrine puts on her phoniest feminine voice.

"Thank you Sergeant Burke. I just don't know—"

The door slips shut.

The room they haul me into looks like a repurposed utility closet. Shelves stacked with cleaning solvents and mop-bots squatting over blinking rechargers. Exposed pipes overhead. Grimy, grease-stained floor below. A flimsy card table flexes under the weight of an industrial strength fusioncell with jumper cables and a chrome tray piled high with archaic dental instruments.

This won't be pretty.

I don't even look for an observation deck. Not in a room like this. What happens in the Interrogation Chamber stays in the Interrogation Chamber. And it looks like I might be staying for quite some time. They fix my wrists to some cuffs hanging from a pipe along the ceiling until I'm all splayed out like a holiday turkey. Ready to be stuffed.

The underling goons start to fiddle with that fusioncell battery. You know, clicking the ends of the jumpers together, showering me with sparks. I start thinking of something to confess to. I'm absolutely positive they don't want to hear my 'I just want to sit by the pool and drink whiskey' stories. One of them rips my shirt open and the buttons drip onto the floor with a series of tiny clinks. It's the quietest, most intimidating sound I've heard in years.

"Thanks fellas," I say. "It was starting to get a little warm in here. All this testosterone really works a guy up, ya know?"

"Shut up!" one of the goonsquad geeks growls at me. He tacks on a nice little suckerpunch, right on the jawbone. I've had worse, but I try not to make a habit of it.

"Just wait until Burkey gets done with your lady friend out there. He'll teach you some manners." I close my eyes and try not to think about Audrine getting chewed on by that ape, or the professional finking she's dropped in my lap. While I'm at it, I'd rather forget taking etiquette lessons from Sergeant Burke, too.

I can feel the curlies rise on my chest, smell them sizzling as Goon #2 holds the jumper terminals a hair from my heart. I squeeze my eyelids tighter and do my best to ignore the horrible crackling the electricity makes. My own smoldering chest hairs slap at my nostrils, and lucky me, if I so much as sneeze my goose is cooked. Looks like this little party is starting early.

I hear the slidelock open.

Guess Ol' Burkey isn't one to miss a bash; he must be a cheap date.

Click. Clack. Hold on now. I know those footsteps.

I open my eyes to find Audrine whiteknuckling one of the psych-rifles, the business-end trained on the whole goonsquad crew.

TZZZaaap. TZap. Tzap. Tzap.

Down goes the goonsquad. All four twitch and tumble on the stained cement as she hops over them to cut off the fusioncell. She pulls out a key from between her…. well she pulls it out anyway. Stands way up on her tippy toes to let me loose. Her hot breath warms my already sweaty neck.

"Goddamn!" I say. "You had me fooled, darlin'."

The tip of her rifle presses into my chest as she fumbles with the maglock. Finally the key clicks into place and I'm free. I snatch the psychometer barrel and push it the other way. "Careful with that thing!" I say. "That bum was half-an-inch from me when you lit him up!" I give Goony #2 a swift kick to the ribs. He keeps on twitching.

"Oh shut up!" she says. "How about 'Thank you, Audrine. You just saved my life'? And besides, a psychometer shot wouldn't have killed you—just left you a drooling slob for a few hours like this miserable lot." She pokes at one fella's face with the pointy toe of her high-heeled pump. "Not that you're much better off as it is."

"Oh shut up yourself," I say. "You can spare me the lectures." I walk over and throw an arm around her waist and one behind her neck. Give her a great big kiss. Right on the lips. She's putty in my arms. Well, putty-ish. "How's that for 'Thanks', 'Driney?"

Now when I was a boy there existed a notion that, in the arms of strong man she desired, a woman was a powerless creature. That she was incapable of resisting her most basic reproductive urges when confronted dead-on with the full brunt of potent masculine prowess. This was obviously a notion of which Audrine had never heard of, let alone believed. I add it to the towering stack of truths I once knew about the world that have since become just plain obsolete.

She slaps me silly and shoves the rifle at my face.

"Don't do that again," she says.

Her muscles look tense on that trigger.

"And don't call me 'Driney."

I take a step back. Put my hands up defensively.

"You got it, doll."

She pushes the barrel towards me again but doesn't pull the trigger. When I'm ninety percent sure she won't shoot me in the face,

I bend over and snatch another psych-rifle from one of the downed goons. Not a bad little model, the Krieger Arms A900. Non-lethal energy weapons were the latest rage back at the precinct before I left; they leave less of a mess. I prefer my museum piece, mess or no, but I've put a few rounds down-range with weapons similar to the one I'm holding. I toss the sling around my neck and prime it. Locked and loaded, I walk out of the interrogation chamber with Audrine close behind.

Burkey lies face down next to an overturned hover-chair, his hairy wrists cuffed to the seat stem. He's not convulsing like the other schmucks in his squad, but he's out colder than a leftover turkey sandwich just the same.

"What happened to him?" I say, plucking my magnum from his battered belt and rubbing at a smudge on the barrel.

She shrugs at me.

"He got fresh," she says, and gives him a kick. "The grabby ape didn't know anything anyway. Maybe you can remember how he looks the next time you try to plant one on me without my permission?"

I tuck the pistol away.

"Consider it remembered."

We walk back out into the service hallway. Audrine takes the lead this time and motions for me to follow. I keep a safe distance and both hands on the psychometer. "This way to the holobeach," she says, pointing down the corridor with her gat.

She's a natural with that rifle in her hands. There's something sexy about a broad in heels and a dress holding an assault weapon. Dangerous women always were a real weakness of mine, but at least I know it. Now if only I were better at keeping away from them.

"Whoa, whoa, whoa," I say. "Hold your horses there, GI Janet. What in the hell was all that about back there? I nearly got deep fried, diced up, and served up hot, and I want to know what for."

She stops and looks back at me. Blinks twice.

"Do you ever speak like a normal human being?" she says.

"Just answer the question, lady. You know what I mean."

She snorts but answers me anyway.

"I needed an excuse to get into a security terminal."

I give her a blank look.

She sighs. "…to splice the feed of the holobeach observation decks. So big men with big guns won't try to stop us the instant we set foot off the lift." She shrugs. "You made for a good excuse. After I incapacitated Sergeant Burke, I replaced the video feed with a loop from yesterday. They'll never even know we're in there. You can snoop around the holobeach to your heart's delight."

Her smile says 'sorry' even if her yap doesn't.

"Didn't we just bump off the big men with big guns?"

She shakes her head at me.

"Just one of the patrol squads. There's about two dozen others running around here somewhere, and we'd do well to avoid them, Mr. Ames. I chose the most inept group for our little stunt. That Sergeant Burke runs a sloppy ship. I checked his records."

"No kidding," I say. "Crummiest torture party I ever got invited to. They didn't even have any chips and dip." I tap my chin. "But why not give me a heads up about your bluff? You scared me halfway-to-Heaven, doll. I would have played along."

Honest I would.

She starts to run again. Impressive in those heels. I jog to keep up. "I didn't tell you," she says over her shoulder, "because you're a terrible actor. I didn't want you to give us away." She smirks back at me, mid-stride.

Everybody's a damned critic.

After a quick jog that's plenty long enough for my bum knee, she skids to a stop before another slidelock. It looks the same as all the others, but this skirt seems to know her way around, even without a computerized compass.

It's my turn to put my hands on my hips.

"If there's a group of guys in there waiting to knock me silly, I'm going to be very unhappy with you."

She feigns offense.

"What's the matter?" she says. "Don't you trust me?"

She flashes me an evil grin as the door slides open.

ELEVEN

A quick lift later and we emerge into the backroom of Senor Tiki's Bar & Grill, or what's left of it anyway. Everything in here is flipped over and smashed twelve ways from Tuesday. Tiptoeing across broken dishes, overturned burners, and busted-out ovens, we stumble to the exit. Years of forensic training tell me this kitchen is definitely closed.

The rattan door to the holobeach outside is still shut, but there's a gash in it large enough to step through. They must have had some pretty hungry customers out there. I kick it off the hinges and we use the door like God intended.

The poolside is in even worse shape than the kitchen, if that's possible. The holoprojector is only half-working, so the place keeps flashing back and forth between a normal indoor pool and a rapidly cycling series of tropical beaches. A bit like taking a leisurely stroll through suburban Glitchville, on your way to goddamned downtown Seizure City. It's enough to make a guy sick. My brain can't decide what's for real and what's just digital spaghetti. Crabs and seagulls and fish and sea turtles slide every which way through the air.

These projected ghosts divebomb my face and everything around it too. The colors and shadows strobe manically until I fumble for an emergency shutoff behind the beer taps. I step in something sticky and wet: some poor fool's spilled drink, left to bake under this madhat electric sun. I throw the lever and immediately wish I had left it on, nevermind the seizures.

This scene is a blood-soaked nightmare. Puddles of people juice are pooled onto the deck and everywhere else, too—including under my feet. I grimace at my ruined shoes, take a step backwards, and take it all in. There are splatters and trails of blood covering the loungers, dripping from thatch umbrellas, soaking into the sides of the Tiki Hut. Absolutely everywhere. A smudged up, sick reflection of the toy carnage from yesterday's food fight. But that was ages ago. A dream. This is here and now and it smacks me right in the gut harder than a goon's gun.

Audrine huddles over the back of a chair, ready to shoot her cookies. I leave her to it and take a look around, a hanky over my mug more for emotional comfort than any sanitary concern. There's no smell other than the sweet stink of plasma and hemoglobin. No bullet holes, shell casings, scorch marks, or blast powder to be found anywhere. Somebody did this the old fashioned way. Manually.

I flip a few cushions but don't find much more than buckets of wet blood. Not enough time for it to dry, especially in these quantities and with the humidity so high in here. The air is sticky with it, and my professional sensibilities go to work. This slaughter couldn't have occurred more than a few hours ago.

A handful of footprints sit scattered across the deck, but not enough for a crime scene of this size. The attack went down fast and it went down dirty. The victims didn't put up much of a fight. At least three dozen dead or dying, from the copious amounts of gore they left behind. If they were around maybe we could ask them for a headcount. But that's the damnedest thing of it all: gallons of blood, but not a single body to be found.

"Who could have done this?" Audrine says, wiping her mouth with the back of her hand. "This isn't right! It's not right!"

I pass her my hanky and shake my head. Shit no it ain't right! I've got another handkerchief in my pocket, but not any answers for her.

"A pack of wolves? A malfunctioning ButcherBot? A gang of highly trained, cyborg commando assassins? Nobody I know and nobody you know either, kid. All my years on the force, I never once saw anything like this. This is a massacre, plain and simple. I'd put my last paycheck this was a professional job, but we can finger the perps later."

I tap my foot, checking first to make sure I'm not standing in another puddle of blood.

"What's got me balled up is the shoddy whitewash. JanosCorp snatched the stiffs and sealed the joint, but they didn't send in the scrub squad. Why not? What am I missing?"

Audrine doesn't have any answers either. She just stares back at me, looking like she might get sick again. I set her down on the cleanest looking lounger I can find and keep talking it out with myself.

"It doesn't add up," I say. "They wouldn't just try to sweep this under the rug. It's a bush league play and the people that hired you have been in the majors too long to swing at garbage like that. Guests will turn up missing. Beautiful, important guests. The murder train has left the station. Unless…"

Unless what? Think Stockton!

Audrine's head pops out of her hands to look up at me. I find what I'm looking for in her glassy green eyes. Maybe I do have at least some of the answers. Twenty some-odd years in the homicide business has to be good for something.

"Unless what?" she says.

She's close to bawling.

"Unless they weren't trying to sweep it under the rug," I say. I pace around, looking for a clue to tell me my hunch is right. "JanosCorp wasn't trying to cover this mess up at all."

Bingo! There's my huckleberry.

"They just wanted to contain it. Keep the killing from spilling out into the rest of the resort. They were afraid of whoever or whatever did this, so they turned tail and raised the drawbridge. Dropped the slidelock and shut the bitch down. But it looks like they didn't do so hot a job of keeping it corked." I point to a pried open grate cover sticking halfway out of the pool. A trail of bloody fingerprints spread right over it.

I lay down on my stomach to get a closer look into the water. Sure enough, there are red streaks smeared across the concrete pool floor as well. Leading right into a dark opening. A dark opening about the size of our busted grate.

"Whoever did this," I say, "took the bodies with them, right through there."

I point into the darkness.

Audrine looks terrified.

"But that means—"

I nod and finish for her. "—that the guilty party is still down there."

She pulls her legs in close and clutches the psychometer wavegun tight into her knees, re-priming it and pointing it at the water. Poor thing. She's not going to like this next part.

I step over to the lifeguard stand and smash a glass box hanging from the viewing platform. Automated SwimWatch scanners hang limp and lifeless beside it as the glass falls to the floor in tiny rounded pellets. Reaching into the box, I pull out a pair of compact rebreathers and try one on. Fits a little snug on a melon like mine, but at least the filter's fresh. Smells like clean plastic sheets. I toss the other mask to Audrine.

She stares at me in disbelief, her eyes like dinner plates.

"You can't possibly mean to go in there alone," she says.

"Not alone," I say, hopping into the pool. "You're coming with me."

"Like hell I am." She crosses her arms.

"Come on, the water's fine," I say, splashing around. "Plus, whatever's down there doesn't have one of these."

I give the psych-rifle a good smack.

"No way." She crosses her arms again. Tighter this time.

I climb back out of the water. It's time to pull out the heavy guns. Play my trump: the hero card. I take a deep breath and try to think what Sheriff Skip McKendrick would say in a spot like this.

"Listen, doll, some of these folks may still be alive down there." She tries to interrupt but I don't let her. "Maybe yes, and maybe no. That's for us to find out. But if they *are* still kicking, they sure as shit need a helping hand right now. And I don't see anybody around but you and me that's going to give it to them. Unless you've got a direct line to the marine corps commandant I don't know about, it's up to us."

I pull her to her feet with a sharp tug. Stare her right in the eye.

"Do you want innocent people to die because you're too scared to help them?"

She shakes her head no.

"Well I need your help too, doll. I need somebody to watch my tail and I'm afraid that somebody's got to be you. So suit up, stop feeling sorry for yourself, and let's get this suicide show on the road, huh kid?"

I give her a friendly little toss into the water.

She lands loud with a big splash. Pops up a split second later with laserbeams in those pretty greens. She smooths out her dress to keep it from floating to the surface, but she doesn't get out of the pool.

I hop in after her and pull the rebreather over my face again. The once balmy water feels icier with her in it. Tame waves lap at our necks. The rebreather mask is cumbersome and covers my whole mug, but hopefully it will keep me wheezing underwater. She tugs hers on too, and I test the voicelink.

"Can you hear me, beautiful?"

Her voice comes back through the built-in speaker, tinny but distinct. "Loud and clear, you asshole."

I dive under first. The grate opening is only big enough for us to swim in single file. It dumps us into a thin channel not much wider than the opening itself and about a hundred yards to the end. A regulation-sized tunnel of love. I swim like a brick, lugging this long-gun. Soaked loafers don't exactly make for good flippers, but I'll be glad to have them if we need to walk across any broken glass or puddles that used to be people in the near future.

I glance back at the broad. Audrine has somehow managed to keep her heels too. She must have the damned things glued to her feet. I wave her forward and against my better judgement, we plunge into the dark passage.

It seems to take forever to swim about ten feet down the tube. Thank God there's emergency mood lighting in here, even if it is just a little glowstrip along the floor. The tunnel is dim. Bright enough to see my arms in front of me but not much else. Good thing too. I'm not sure I could convince these limbs to kick me down a pitch black murderhole any more than the next guy could.

About twenty yards in we swim up to a big fan blocking our path. It's stopped, and thankfully there's just enough play for us to squeeze between the blades. I spot a sparkly-ringed finger wedged into the frame. Severed and leaking red stuff. "Maybe that's a *good* sign," I tell myself. Maybe it means the victims were still alive and struggling recently. And maybe just maybe Audrine won't notice the gore.

We press through the fan and swim about halfway to the end of the tunnel. Forty feet downstream I spot a beam of sweet, sparkling sunshine coming down from on high. Our ticket out. And not a moment too soon. I need to get out of this soggy tube and get a drink into me.

I start to tell Audrine as much but get interrupted when the emergency lights cut out. "Wonderful," I say instead.

The lights kick back on.

Then off.

Then on.

They blink three or four more times, faster with each flash.

Audrine crackles in through the voicelink.

"Swim!" she says. "The power's cycling!"

So what? That's a good thing, right? Besides, we're almost in the clear. Then I hear it.

Or maybe it's more of a feeling than a sound. It starts as a low, vibrating rumble, then becomes a steady hum I can feel in my fillings. The lights switch back on at full strength. *All* the lights. It takes my eyes a second to adjust to the new brightness. Then I steal a glance behind us.

That big, bloody fan is spinning to life.

We both swim as fast as we can but it's no use. The fan drags a powerful current behind us. Circulating the water back into the holo-beach. It sucks us towards the spinning, sword-sharp metal. Slowly at first.

Then faster.

And faster.

Until we're both hurtling right into the whirling blades of death. We're good as fish food.

Audrine manages to catch her feet on the frame of the fan. She must've been an aquatic gymnast in a past life. We're inches away from becoming human sushi when I crash into her. Those slender pins of hers can't possibly keep us both out of the blades. Maybe if I can sneak past her and dive in headfirst, they'll get snagged up on my thick skull, and she can swim to safety.

I lose a shoe. So much for that broken glass. My loafer's confetti coming out the other side. Looks like this kamikaze rescue mission wasn't such a good idea after all.

Her foot slips. The end of her heel gets sliced up like deli pastrami.

Then the next quarter inch.

Then the next.

We're closing in on a whole sandwich here.

Just as the base of the heel gets clipped off cleanly, I unsnap my psych-rifle and cram it butt first into the spinning deathtrap.

The stock slips through.

But a blade catches the fusion core powercell just under the barrel. The gun pops with a nice little bang and a barrage of tiny bubbles. The fan bitches and moans and vibrates horribly. An inky lubricant leaks from the cracked housing like a beautiful, slithering snake. The blades putter to a slow stop and the little severed finger floats up beside us, finally free. I wave goodbye and we race to the opening ahead, then flop out as fast as humanly possible.

Sitting with our feet dangling above the surface of the oily water and our rebreather masks propped up on our foreheads, we both pant for breath. I take off my one remaining shoe and toss it in the water with a little salute. Thanks for the years of service, buddy. Audrine giggles at the gesture.

"Oh my God," she says. "What a rush!" She grabs me by the shoulders and laughs hysterically. "We almost died down there!"

"Don't make a habit of it, dollface," I say.

She smiles at me.

"I'll try not to."

For one moment in time we both forget about the carnage behind us and the mess we're still caught up in. There's no murder, no corporate conspiracies. We're just two people, soaked to the bone in all our clothes and damned happy to be alive. But one moment is all we can afford for now. "I don't want to pickle your dill, darlin', but we've still got a job to do."

I point to the ledge opposite us, where three sets of bloody streaks trail off around a bend into the darkness. We're sitting in some sort of pool maintenance access shaft. There are all kinds of pumps and tubes and barrels of chems stacked neatly at regular intervals. Bright, bluish lighting provides an eerie sheen to the glossy white walls. It's cramped, but squeaky clean. Sterile. The lack of dust and grime just makes the blood on the floor look all that much worse.

We stand up, but not too straight on account of the low-hanging plumbing. Vainly try to wring ourselves out. Audrine examines her now sliced and diced shoes and makes a frown. She kicks them both off and flips on the tactical light on her wavegun. I pull out the magnum and flick the safety free.

We move around the corner side by side. The lights ahead are switched off, burnt out, or otherwise not doing us a lick of good in this part of the shaft. Audrine's taclight reveals the trails of blood leading down a darkened corridor. Of course they lead into the darkness. Where else would they go? In all my years on the force, not one trail of blood ever led me into a well-lit room. In an age where observation decks are hoisted above every corner—and everyone has a camera sewn into their wrist at the age of five—most criminals are vampires. Deathly allergic to daylight. I very much hope we're not dealing with actual vampires down here, but I'm not ready to rule it out.

I hear something.

I signal for Audrine to stop and the noise quits too.

We wait in terrible silence for it to return. A skittering, scratchy noise. It squeaks twice from behind the pipes running along the wall. Audrine flashes the light that way, but there's not enough space between the tubes to see anything more than a flash of movement here and there. Whatever is back there, it scurries each time Audrine highbeams it through the gaps. How did they manage to get a rat problem at a station this far from Earth? We keep moving, but I keep one eye on the wall. If these rodents have brains enough to stowaway to a cushy joint like this, I don't want to turn my back on them. They may be another kind of rat altogether.

There's a big bend up ahead where the passage suddenly jackknifes to the right. I don't hear the skittering anymore and I'm not so sure that's a good thing. We pause just before the turn and count to three silently, with our fingers. Then we pop around the corner with guns drawn and feet wide.

The passage opens up into a larger space here. The crossroads of a pair of maintenance shafts stretches wide at the intersection. It's empty except for a few square chem barrels stacked along the corners. An automated squid-like pump dips a fistful of slender tendrils into each barrel. It kicks on with a hydraulic hiss and gives us both a start. The blood trail slops right into the room but disappears randomly in the middle of an otherwise empty metal floor.

That's no good. Where'd the red stuff get off to? Where I come from, this kind of rainbow usually leads me to a corpse or two. Maybe even a whole potful of golden stiffs. But it looks like our murderous little leprechaun hasn't read the rules.

Suddenly a shadow darts out from behind the pump. It really cranks; all I catch is a blur of something pasty—the color of uncooked turkey with a case of the croup. It's the size of a very large dog or a very small man, and gallops along on all fours with all the grace of a synthetic greyhound hooked on homemade chicken powder. This mystery creature bounds off towards the passageway opening up across the room.

My wrist rises and I toss a few shots his way. Sharp echoes ring out from the curved tunnel walls. Normally I'm a hell of a plinker but today's not so normal. The MagnumRail slugs throw sparks off the pipes behind my target. Audrine squeezes off one psych-rifle beam as the creature rounds a bend about eight yards ahead of us. The psychometer wavegun emits a bassy, hollow thump, and the beast slides into the far wall. It slumps to a dead stop.

Too far to get a good look.

"Where'd you learn to shoot like that?" I ask.

"Not from you, that's for sure." she says.

I shake my head. "If you say so, doll."

"Why don't you stop worrying about me, Ames? Instead, you can tell me what the hell I just shot." She keeps her rifle trained on the creature. Good girl. Hold that bead until we're damned sure it's dead or otherwise not going to gnaw on our noses.

"Search me," I say. "This place got a dog track I don't know about?"

She frowns and shakes her head slowly, then turns back to the game we bagged. It makes a clump about the size of a bag of garbage. Similar shape as well. If we get within sniffing distance, I'll bet lunch it stinks like a sack of crap too. We slink towards the trashman, both of us drawn down on the poor bastard. A single twitch and he's getting a one-way ticket to that great garbage dump in the sky. That is, if Audrine hasn't properly popped his clogs already.

We get close to the end of the original blood trail, eyes fixed on our little friend up ahead. A new set of wet streaks ride out from where he flopped across the floor a few feet ahead of us. The pump kicks on again, its soft hum saddles and mounts the silence like a snorting stallion.

My heart thumps in my ears.

Eyes focused on taking out the trash, we both step right next to the place where the original streak of red stuff stops, and boy oh boy does it feel funny. Our feet crash through a weak panel in the floor with a hearty metallic crunch. Suddenly I'm falling head over heels, and not for some dame either.

We land in a heap a half-second later. The wind flies out of me like a drag-racing RocketSled. I can hear the magnum skid across the metal floor behind us. We've lost the flashlight too. That fall must've gunked up the powercell in Audrine's rifle. Cheap-ass plastic parts. Made by the lowest bidder, I'm sure.

Wherever we've landed, it's pitch black. But then again it's not.

There's a dozen pairs of beady yellow peepers peppering the place, glowing like twenty-four evil little night lights. Giving us a Chicago stare-down. The air is full of mushy, slurping sounds and a smell like the McTasty's compost dumpster. Somebody owes me lunch.

Audrine slams the rifle against the floor and the light shudders back on. Our little friends with the shiny eyes don't like that too much. The nightlights simultaneously slant into angry little slits. The creatures cower back in fear, hiss at us loud enough to hurt my ears and my feelings, too. I finally take a good look at the bastards.

They look like newborn gorilla abortions.

Almost human. Two arms, two legs. A head. But the proportions are all wrong. Legs too short and put on backwards. Arms too long and lean. Little sucker mouths full of shiny, sharp chompers below a stump of a nose. Where those glowing eyes should be though, there's a crusty membrane. They're covered in splotchy, pale-pinkish skin, dripping with goop and almost transparent. Like we could shine the light right through them if we held it close enough.

Nasty little SnotBabies.

Then and there I pray we won't ever get close enough to check the transparency of their gooey hides. Apparently we busted up a buffet. The little buggers hunker down, hunched over a big pile of our missing pool guests. Going to town. Or were, before we crashed the party and ruined their dinner plans.

Big bloody chunks are missing from the corpses. The SnotBabies seem especially fond of the eyes. I watch one pluck a juicy orb from some fat sap's face, then toss it into his round piranha maw like a McTaterPuff. It pops as he bites down, squirting pus-y broth into the dead guy's empty sockets. You'd think the damn thing was gonna lick its lips. If it had lips. Or a tongue.

The SnotBabies have managed to paint the place with blood and shit, to hang leaking entrail garlands from the victims draped over the rafters. If any of these sorry suckers were still alive I'd put a round in their melon for humanity's sake. Lucky for me the whole buffet table has bought the farm already. It's like something out of a late night horrorstream: a low-quality, grainy gorefest with a bad gaffer.

"Oh my God," Audrine says, scanning the light across the tiny bastards.

They hate the beam. Each time it lands on one he takes a small hop back and turns his disgusting little head away. Hissing. Always hissing.

They don't look like they spend much time at the beach, this morning besides.

"What are you waiting for?" I say. "Light them up!"

Audrine pulls the trigger.

Click.

She tries again.

Clickclick.

Damned worthless defense contractors. The biggest bugger gets the hint. He hops the closest corpse and gallops right for us. Are these things smart enough to recognize a bum psych-rifle when they see one? We can't afford to find out. A symphony of curved claws skitters across the metal floor.

If I don't make a play for the magnum now, I'll never get the chance. Sliding across the floor, I snatch it up in a single swoop. "Get down!" I yell to Audrine.

She hugs the deck with just enough time for me to introduce Bugger #1 to his maker. The magnum screams in the confined space as he catches three rounds to the chest. Fat, uranium slugs rip him off his feet and he flops over with a thud on the broad's back. She wriggles around until he tumbles off. Then she wriggles some more.

Still flat on the ground, she cups her hands over her ears and squeezes her eyes tightly shut, but her dropped rifle shines its light onto a whole lot of nothing.

I kick the dead little bastard out of the way and reach down to give her a hand up. "It's alright," I say. "His friends got the message."

She stands up, glassy-eyed, looking a lot like she might retch. She smooths out her dress against her thighs over and over. I've seen this behavior before. It's a crime scene favorite. The witnesses get little tics like this when they're still in shock. She's got a barrelful of monster blood smeared across her cheek and down her neck. It looks like ours, but a little runnier, a little less bright. I'm something of an expert on the subject, especially after today.

I hand her the tropico off my back to wipe her face clean; she's sporting more gore than a little old hanky can handle right about now. I make double-sure to stand with *her* back to the stack of picked-over corpses, and keep a hand on my rod in case something else needs shooting.

"W-w-w-what were those things?" she asks. Her voice quivers like a somnopod in a cheap motel. "W-w-why were they eating those p-p-poor people?"

"I dunno," I say. "And I don't think we oughta hang around to find out. Does your MPD have a map that can get us the hell out of here?"

She nods slowly and starts tapping at the screen. Her eyes are still wide, glossed over, staring through her wrist. I'm not so sure she's in any state to find her way out of a plastiboard box. Her wet fingers slide off the touch surface of the MPD as she frantically paws at it. I put a hand on her shoulder. She stops, breathes deeply and tries again, with purpose. Finally she points at a passageway that opens up behind us.

I silently mouth a prayer that we don't stumble across any more violent surprises, but I don't expect anybody's listening.

TWELVE

Audrine and I sulk back to the employee dorms in silence. Not exactly what I had in mind but it's a start. "I meant out of here like off this damn rock, doll." I stand aside to let her through a small slidelock. "Not back to your place."

She says nothing.

"Don't get me wrong," I say. "A quick brush and tumble would get along with me, but I don't know if now's the time for it."

Audrine sneers at me from over her shoulder. Her room is cute, cramped even. But tidy. Every square inch of surface is clear, and every little lipstick, compact, and unmentionable has a home. Something like a sailor's berth. Exactly the opposite of my living situation up in the Imperial palace.

My eyes are drawn to an industrial chrome briefcase, handcuffed to the post of a basic model somnopod. Wonder what she keeps in there?

I try to peer through the case with x-ray specs I'm not wearing. That is, until Audrine yanks my orbs up towards something much more intriguing. She steps behind a semi-opaque silk dressing screen, painted up pretty with a shiny cityscape. Pulls that sopping wet dress off and drapes it over the only thing standing between me and one hell of a show.

"Listen Stockton." She says it like I'm a kid that should know better. "I'm not going anywhere in a wet, bloody dress." Now that she mentions it that puddle below the screen is a little gorier than it might ought to be. "And neither one of us is wearing shoes! Wherever we're headed, we're going to need something on our feet. Even a brute like you can see the practicality in that."

I shrug. She's got me there. Until she steps back out in a slinky spaghetti-red dress and matching spike heels.

"Real practical footwear, sweetstuff," I say. "You planning on stabbing those SnotBabies to death with your pumps?"

"Oh shut up," she says, giving me a not-so-playful push. "My sneakers are at the gym, clear across the resort. And combat boots aren't exactly in my job description, Sherlock. Besides, I'll bring along my SpektraTek ski gear just in case."

She looks down into her hand, then back up at me. Bats her eyes like a pro chiseler, then tosses me the little autocompression packet. I'm still impressed they can cram such bulky duds inside such a puny package. Although apparently, not small enough for her to find a place to stick it. I tuck the packet away.

"No complaints here, honey," I say, giving her new outfit the old once-over.

"When you stop complaining," she says with a snort, "I'll be sure to check your pulse." She slings the psych-rifle once more and we march out towards the guest quarters. Audrine leads the way with a swing to her step that could put a synth on the stand.

Seren Luna is a ghost town. I don't hear a peep on the long walk back to the Imperial statesuite. Besides, of course, the familiar *click-clack, tip-tap* of Audrine's size seven monster stompers. We don't pass a soul. Living, dead, or dying. No richos. No bratty kids. No walking-mops, or synthos of any kind. No security squads. No mutant alien SnotBabies. I'm starting to feel like we're the last chumps to leave the party. "Guess we didn't get the memo," I say as we step into a lift.

She nods. The door slides shut silently behind us.

The lift lets us out back in my room and I rush over to the wardrobe unit to find some footwear. I ruined the only pair of shoes I brought from home back in that damned swim meet. That leaves me with one pair of rubber flops and the patent leather dandies that came with the origami tux. They've got to be in here somewhere.

Audrine tosses her wavegun onto the bed and makes herself nice and comfortable next to it. Crosses those gorgeous stems and arches her back, resting on her palms behind her. Her flexed triceps are well-toned, but still sleek and feminine.

"What were those things, Stockton? Where did they come from?"

"Beats me, darlin'," I say, rummaging through a wrinkled rainbow of tropicos. "I'm just the guest here, remember? But the way I see it, we've got a couple of crackers that fit the tin." I stop hunting and tap the wardrobe wall as I think aloud. "Maybe your employers picked the wrong moon to build their resort on. Went ahead and made first contact by accident? Those SnotBaby aliens were ETs, cozied up in Fat City on this rock before JanosCorp dropped a mountain of steel and glass and concrete on their heads. Not to mention half of Earth's most spoiled citizens, and one very unlucky homicide detective."

We both contemplate the possibility that Seren Luna was previously inhabited for a moment. It's not much, as far as explanations go, but it's all I can muster on such short notice.

"I'll tell you one thing," I say, shaking my noggin. "Whatever they are, they aren't like anything I've ever seen on Earth. Not even on the latenight cheesestreams."

Audrine nods slowly and stares out the window, caught in the gaze of the twin neutron stars. For the briefest of moments, she lowers her shields. Reveals the soft heart that's hidden underneath her hardened shell. It escapes through her eyes, sad and sweet and dark and vulnerable. It drips out of every word like liquid regret. "I'd always hoped that if there were intelligent life out there, it would be more intelligent than us," she says. "That they could teach us something."

I nod. I'm sure those little bastards could teach us a thing or two about chewing off faces and slurping eyeball goop like it was Gramma's brandy. I catch a snip of sadness slide down her cheek and decide to keep my yap trapped. This whole situation has got her nerves bobbed up like a bad haircut, and a crummy doo is a crying shame for a broad with a face like that. She's going to need to keep up the tough gal act, if she wants to get out of here alive.

Like it or not, I'm going to need her help before all is said and done.

"Of course we're just juggling sky pies here, darlin'. Maybe those things aren't little green men from a far off world," I say. "Hell they're not even green. No one's ever met an alien before, what are the chances they show up now? And that the entire JanosCorp construction crew missed 'em? Slim to none, doll, that's what they are—and I'm a gambling man. For all we know some beaker buff cooked those puppies up in a lab. Spliced some bad genes into SnotBaby stew and shipped them here to settle a score. There's plenty of fat cats aboard asking to get potted by anybody with beef. And from where I stand, beef comes pretty cheap these days."

I look for Audrine's reaction but she's still staring out the window. Seems like a hot ticket to me, but it's starting to smell like the subject needs changing. Besides, I'm getting red-faced with this fruitless search for my shoes. I need to stop jumping guns and concentrate on the primary task at hand—my missing footwear. It's the first law of detective work: one lead at a time.

"Where are those damned shoes?" I say. "I've looked this cave over twice. Where the hell could they possibly have walked off to?"

I toss a wad of trousers over my shoulder.

"Did you try the packbo—" Audrine starts but doesn't finish. What's gotten into her now? Here's to hoping I didn't smack her across the kisser with a faceful of dirty slacks.

I turn around to find her staring into the long, flat barrel of a psych-rifle. It's our old friend Burkey behind the trigger, and boy is he rattled up and ready to pop. A fat vein blares on his shiny dome, and there's a great big purple lump where his left eye used to be.

"Nice shiner, bub," I say. "Where'd you get it?"

"Shut up!"

He primes his gat with a hefty *kuhKLUNK*.

The good sergeant stands before us, flanked by three new security goons. His old crew is probably still stacking zees thanks to Audrine's handiwork with the wavegun. I don't even make a play for the revolver. I'm quick, but nobody's that quick. Once again, they've got beads on me for days. Enough to string up a necklace, even. Burkey motions for Audrine to get up off the bed and come stand beside Mrs. Ames's only son.

"No sudden moves," he says.

She puts her mitts in the air and plays nice.

"Please, listen to me, Sergeant Burke. This man forced me to help him. I had no choice!" She pleads in her best 'I'm so innocent' voice. Bats those lashes and gives him the puppy dog routine.

"Fool me twice, Miss DeMarco…"

He stammers a bit but doesn't lower the rifle. Has us lined up nice like the firing squad scene from *Sonoran Sunrise*.

"…and well, you must think I'm a lot dumber than I look," he finishes, finally.

"I dunno," I say. "You look pretty dumb if you ask me."

He swings his piece over to point in my direction. The beam on that gat is wide enough that any one of them could zap us both with a single shot, but he's made his point. I shut up and rummage through the old 'streams in my mind. What would Sheriff Skip do in a scrape like this? I grit my teeth and scramble the dusty halls in my head for a decent way out.

"Who's dumb now, Ames?" he says with a great big grin. "You won't be causing any more trouble for The Janos Corporation, once we get done with you."

He pulls the trigger.

Just as he squeezes it off, little Rusty darts out from under the bed and clips Sergeant Burke right in the shin. "Good boy!" It's not much, but it's enough to throw Burke's shot high and wide. A familiar bassy *Tzap* buzzes right by my noggin on its way to the ceiling. The static charge it leaves in the air makes my neck hairs stand straighter than a stone cadet.

Close one.

But not close enough. I drop to one knee and pull the magnum. Fire a three round burst, then toss the gun onto the bed and put my hands back in the air before Burke can get his weapon leveled again.

The good sergeant pats his chest with one hand, feeling for holes, while the other hand keeps the psychometer trained on me. His pet monkeys continue to breathe through their open mouths, but they don't do much else. In my experience, apes like these three need explicit instructions to tie their shoes, let alone shoot somebody in the face.

Burke doesn't find any missing parts and belts out a roaring laugh. "Ha!" he says. "I thought they trained you planetside cops better than that! You missed!"

"Did I?" I say.

The whole lot of Security creeps begin to notice a soft snapping sound coming from directly behind them. They turn around slowly; all together, like one of those synchronized space circuses the richos love so much. They have just enough time to see the hairline cracks in the plexisteel behind them come together. All four turn back towards us, eyes wide. They start to scurry.

But it's too late.

I throw an arm around Audrine's waist and toss her into the wardrobe before hopping in myself and pulling it closed behind me. Through the shrinking gap between the doors we catch a sliver of the action outside. The cracks in the glass meet and a section of the dome pops free. The doors come completely shut just as I see Burkey Boy get lifted off his feet, falling out into the cold darkness of space. I pray this cabinet is airtight—and bolted to the floor—or we might be going for a ride ourselves.

Inside it sounds like we're front and center for some kind of space launch as the air pressure in the suite is sucked out to the vacuum on the other side of the dome. There's a loud roar, some crashing and banging like two hovertrucks parking the skin-yacht in Hair Harbor. Then nothing. The pure silence of equilibrium being reached.

Audrine doesn't wait long to shatter it.

"What the hell was that?" she yells from the floor.

The wardrobe lights click on at the sound of her voice. She scrambles up to her feet and smooths out the wrinkles in her dress. Walks over to tell me off to my face. "Now what are we going to do, Ames? Trapped in this damned dresser with no way out? You should have let them take us because we're good as dead now anyway!"

I give her a minute to cool down.

Then I pull her SpektraTek bundle out of my pocket and toss it to her, along with one of the rebreathers from the pool. I don't say a word.

She thumbs the release on the SpektraTek and her ski gear pops to life, the intelligent fabric growing out of itself. Completely wrinkle-free of course. She kicks off her heels and steps into the lower half, turning her back towards me and shimmying out of the dress as she zips up the top. It's nicely form-fitting for a makeshift spacesuit.

"Well I guess you thought of everything, then," she says just before slipping on the rebreather mask and pulling the hood tight around her head.

I raise my eyebrows but keep a straight face.

I throw on my Stockton-sized SpektraTec get-up and don a mask of my own. "Alright," I say through the rebreather's commlink. "Here goes nothing."

I kick open the wardrobe door to the wreck of my former room. It looks like someone is having an intergalactic yard sale. There's a huge hole in the glass dome, large enough to back a cab through. Everything that wasn't bolted down or built into the superstructure of the room is floating out towards eternity. It'll all come down eventually, but not for a long while. I guess there was a gravity amplifier built into the pressurization system. Even the bed is slowly drifting away.

I snatch at the magnum as it wanders up and away, catch it and cram it into a pocket. But what's this? Looks like we missed one particular piece of trash.

Sergeant Burke is still hanging around, his utility belt snagged on a broken segment of the dome frame. I spot his buddies doing somersaults out into the great beyond. He's holding his breath and turning a lovely shade of blue. I can't tell if that's from the lack of oxygen or freezing vacuum or possibly both. He doesn't look too happy about it either way. Still has that damned psych-rifle trained on my face. Persistent bastard.

He pulls the trigger. Nothing.

I walk over briskly and point at his weapon.

"SOUNDWAVES," I mouth to him through the rebreather's clear faceplate.

He looks at me with a sideways glance. The big dumb animal doesn't get much on the first go-round. I snatch the rifle from him and point to the disclaimer stamped into the barrel tube:

For best results operate only in environments > 0.25 ATM. This unit will not function in a vacuum.

I gesture at the airless space around us.

He rolls his eyes at me.

I point at the magnum in my hand: "MAGNETS."

His eyes get wide as I throw a single depleted-uranium slug through his brain. It's fairly clean, all things considered. I leave him staring into empty space, a thin trickle of blood rising out the back of his shiny bald head.

"Oh come on!" Audrine's voice crackles through the commlink. "What did you do that for?"

"I only put the poor bastard out of his misery," I say. "Nobody wants to freeze to death in a vacuum, doll. Don't you watch the 'streams?"

"You're such a humanitarian," she replies.

Audrine steps over Burke's now limp legs. She makes a Mr. Yucko face and tries to avoid the stream of red liquid leaking up from the hole in his skull. It's a little difficult to move with precision in this low gravity, but she manages to make it look easy. Comes to stand next to me, staring down at Seren Luna's rocky pocked surface a couple hundred feet below us.

"The turbolift doors won't open to your room now that the shell integrity has been compromised," she says. "Even with an override."

"I figured as much," I say, staring with a grimace at the long, lonely drop to the gray ground below. It's a hundred yards, if it's five, and I always did have a weak heart for heights. Some bad juju left over from a childhood spent in chintzy high-rise digs. I'd seen what became of my toys when they slipped through the black iron cracks of the rickety, old fire escape.

Clutching the ledge as tight as I can, I get low then brave a peek over the thigh-high wall of my room. Yep, three hundred feet feels about right. Thirty stories is a tall order in Earth gravity, and it looks just as long here, even if it might not feel quite as rough. I wonder if there's enough bedsheets in the whole resort to daisy-chain our way down.

I look up and catch Audrine eyeballing me with a frown and sad brows.

"Why the long fa—"

I don't get the chance to finish.

"Forgive me," she whispers.

She shoves me towards the ledge with everything she's got. Really puts her back into it—a textbook crosscheck if I've ever felt one. My feet catch on the wall as I tumble down towards the surface, end over end.

I've plenty of time for regrets as I fall.

THIRTEEN

An eternity later the surface of Seren Luna rises up to greet me. Weak gravity or no, my momentum builds and builds, then slams me into the dirt face first. I curse the girl, tuck into the best roll I can manage, and pray I don't come apart at the seams.

The SpektraTek coveralls stiffen and flex to absorb the impact as best they can. They spread the shock through the carbon fiber nanotubes strung throughout the suit. Keep the worst of it away from my brittle bones. Still, I reckon even the lousiest skier in the world wouldn't take a dive like this on your average bunny slope. Even the almighty SpektraTek has operational limits and I just cannonballed right over them.

The world blurs by me as my crash landing goes turbulent. Several somersaults later, I lay splayed out on my stomach. Roadkill on the stony, open surface of Seren Luna.

I slowly raise my head. Partly to see where I've landed, but mostly to make sure I'm still capable of moving at all. Apparently I'm not dead, paralyzed, or missing anything important.

Color me surprised.

A cloud of moondust rises up behind me, tracing the ramshackle path I rumbled along the rock-hard, unforgiving surface of this damned planet. Quite a divot I left. Wispy puffs of space-sand drag out for half-a-city-block behind me.

I glance up to the mushroom stalk stateroom but don't see Audrine coming down to shovel me off the pavement. Can't say I blame her. That was a real howler of a landing. Despite the circumstances—and a barely contained, burning desire to scream my lungs out and then scream some more—I'm not ready to rip her a new one just yet. It was the only way down, and one look at my quivering mug would tell her I wasn't taking that plunge on my own volition. And besides, she's a physics wiz. She had to know I'd live to laugh it off, right?

"I'm alive," I cough into the voicelink. "If it makes any difference to you, doll."

There's only static from her end. Maybe she did mean to kill me after all. It takes a big, fat moment to get myself up and on my feet. I dust off my makeshift spacesuit and check it for tears. Thankfully I didn't rip a hole in the damned thing, although I'm not quite sure how. Must be tough stuff, because underneath my protective covering, I feel mashed, smashed, and hammered flat. Like yesterday's piñata.

As I glance around for a service hatch or door or any other way back into the resort, I catch a long look at trouble approaching, and fast. At first it's just another trail of dust weaving between mushroom stalks in the distance. But as the smoke signals get closer, I begin to sketch out the menacing silhouette of a bulky hovercycle. A big, fat combat model by the shape of it. I'd call it a main battle tank, but what's in a name anyway? I can't hear the motor for all the empty vacuum of this atmosphereless rock, but I imagine if I could, it'd rattle my teeth like the dames never did.

She's a real beast of a machine. A shiny chrome fuselage spattered with matte-painted armor plating. Menacing. It's bigger than a cab but smaller than a tram car, though not by much. Three stubby, kettledrum lifts keep it a foot or so off the ground as it rumbles closer.

The driver is somewhere behind a mirrored cockpit. I can almost picture him, sporting a fancy exposuresuit in JanosCorp navy and silver and orange. Helmet painted-up in cartoon violence and bright colors. An armada of tubes and wires have him jacked into the bike's life support and control systems. He's a punk kid, freshly plucked from the latest crop of flight school dropouts. Not good enough to pilot a real bird, so they give him the keys to a knuckledragger like this. He's got a score to settle, and boy oh boy does he know how to compensate. He hotdogs like some two-bit showgirl with spotlight ambitions. This prick pulls a couple of 360s and even a little wheelie or two. He kicks up buckets of dust before sliding to a stop about thirty paces before me. I guess that beast he's driving is more maneuverable than it looks.

The bike sleeps for a moment. The dust starts to settle, rains down between us in fat, flaky sheets. Then the combat mode screams to life. Two gullwing payload modules swing open on either side, revealing hexagonal gridded rocket pods. Armored panels in the undercarriage retract to reveal a pair of twin chaincannons. Four guns in all. Each one large enough to fling uranium fastballs straight through a Commie hovertank's armored strike zone. The barrels start to spin, like a rattle-snake in the old Westerns. Shaking his tail and baring fangs.

I feel ever so slightly outgunned.

The mirrored plexisteel canopy slips backward and disappears into the flat-black armor of the carapace. That showboating driver shows himself, just as I imagined him. Young, cocky, and stupid. He smiles and waves. Gives me the bird. A snarling something is painted on his helmet. Targeting reticules and metered gauges dance on the cockpit glass, lighting up his face like a neon Christmas tree.

Big mistake.

I draw the magnum and bury three rounds between his eyes in one smooth motion. That mirrored canopy would have shut them down, but not the clear heads up display hiding underneath. He bit the big one because he wanted to flip me off.

The dead driver slumps forward against his bike and it begins to roll away slowly. As he dies, a hand reaches out and grabs my shoulder from behind. Did Audrine finally decide to hop down while I was caught up with the combat bike? Leave it to a broad to let me do the heavy lifting.

I turn around to find a big, ugly gorilla face staring back at me. Another squad of hoverbike security goons has gotten the drop on me. Now I'm not one to be stingy with the credit when it's due, but it's pretty easy to be sneaky when you don't make any noise. Gorillaface stabs me in the chest with something hard and zingy. Something that packs a punch. Next thing I know I'm lying on my back, admiring the stars.

The goon puts a thick-soled moonboot on my chest and bares his crooked teeth at me. My toes twitch and the rest of me feels just a little bit souffléed. What is it with these guys and the shock therapy?

Three more goons hop off open-canopy bikes and saunter over to chat with their buddy. They're done up in hard plastic. Navy blue exposure suits with ribbed joints and dayglow accents. Pretty gear for such nasty nosers. One of them snags the magnum from the dirt beside me while I'm still shaking the juice out of my system. Damn. There goes my ticket out of the frying pan.

They stand around for a minute, jawing. Judging by the way they move their mittens and point my way, they're arguing over which one has to ride me back. I guess they have orders to bring me in alive. There's just a thin margin between slightly alive and mostly dead, but it's a swell break and I'm glad to catch it.

One of the Janos goons draws the shortest straw and strolls over to fetch me. He pulls a pair of cuffs from his belt and bends down to sneer at me. I'm still a touch woozy from my bout with the zapper, but I know ugly when I see it, and this guy's got it in spades. He stares at me from behind a clear-paneled mask. Drags his hand across the neck of his puffy, dark exposure suit. Yeah, yeah, I'm dead meat. I get the picture. Let's move on, huh buddy?

But before he can collar me, a freak dust storm rises out of nowhere and swallows us whole. Visibility drops to zero. Then I catch his ugly mug kissing dirt six inches beside me. He's not looking too good. Eyes full of that vacant glaze that says "somebody just socked it to me something fierce."

A hand with a firm grip yanks me to my feet. Or tries to anyways. I'm a bit slow to comply, on account of the recent events that left me free-falling the length of a football field and choking down 10,000 volts for dessert.

"Get up you big lug."

Audrine practically drags me away from my freshly zonked friend. I struggle to put my feet under me. The dust is still thick enough to pass for a nice chocolate malted, but it starts to settle down in little gray flurries that drip onto our heads and shoulders.

"You're like an angel from heaven, doll," I say, only slightly out of breath.

"Might as well be," she says. "That drop was long enough. And quite unnecessary, I might add."

"I'll apologize later, sweetness. Now let's boogie before the rest of these bozos introduce us to some real angels."

"Very cute, Ames," she says. "If only the rest of you was as fast as your mouth. Let's go!"

I'm still scrambling to get upright, and I regain my balance just in time to trip over something big and solid. I lay sprawled out over it sideways, like a bad brat about to get a belting from his old man, when we zoom away.

It's one of the hoverbikes. Not as bulky as the combat model I met earlier. Convertible top. Maybe ten feet long, and most of that motor. It's thin and sleek and not designed for comfort. A lightning rod with a saddle seat, but she's got one hell of a get up and go. I hold on for dear life as Audrine rockets us out into the mushroom stalk forest, spitting a steaming trail of hot moondust just a foot or two from my face.

She must've learned to drive on the JetSled circuit, because we bob and weave between the turbolift tubes like the Gold Cup is on the line. Not the best circumstances for a fella to get situated. I finally get a good grip on the rear fender when I see why she's speeding like a bat out of hell.

Over my shoulder I see one of the other goons as he pulls up beside us on a very familiar looking bike. Pretty similar to our own. Same model even, if I had to guess. He slides in real close and tries to muscle Audrine off the bike, while I dangle helpless on my gut across the seat. I pull in my legs at the knee, to keep them from getting stomped by his hoverlifts, just as he drifts in tighter. He's got one hand on his throttle bars and the other reaches out for our own sticks, grasping for the killswitch.

Maybe I'm not so helpless after all.

I explode into his bike, shoving my soles right into the main thrust manifold running along the length of his ride. It's a hard enough swat to swing him off course just a touch, what with only one hand on his own controls. And at 180 miles an hour, swinging off course—even by just a touch—puts you right into the next mushroom stalk pretty damned quickly. Ouch. I have to shield my eyes as he goes supernova into the concrete tube. When I look up again, chunks of bike and rider rain down around us like flesh and chrome confetti.

I somehow manage to swing a tired, old leg up and over the seat but now I'm facing the wrong way—not that I'd complain about it. Hell, I'm happy just to be upright. My gloved knuckles are white on the rear fender as Audrine tears through the resort grounds like they're her own personal racetrack. She puts her very solid rump into my kidneys, then lifts off the molded vinyl seat to lean into a sharp turn. She nearly bucks me off the back of the bike with every yank of the throttle and each rip of the control sticks. I peer through the cloud behind us as we turn. Two other dust trails crisscross our own, maybe a quarter-click back and gaining.

"Hey doll," I say as casually as I can. "We still got company. Should I set out the silver and china or are you going to shake them?"

"I see them, smartass."

Audrine jerks the controls again and we cut a sharp curve around one of the clear, plexisteel lobby domes popped up over the the rocky surface.

"It's a little hard to outrun them when I've got the same hardware they do," she says. "Not to mention an extra 250 pounds dead weight running its mouth at me while I try to drive."

"Hey now! That's 220 to you, toots," I say. "Less in this gravity."

"Forget it Stockton! We'll never lose them when we kick up a vapor trail forty feet high, no matter how far ahead we get."

I squint into the distance.

"But besides all that it should be a cakewalk, right?"

The goons cut the distance between us with sharp angles and straight lines. These two earned their marks in pursuit school. One of the tails chases us around the big shell. The other guy disappears behind the dome. Where's *he* headed?

Our bike hugs the edge close, and us with it. Audrine leans into the turn something serious. Fully commits. If I could afford to loosen my kung fu grip on the fender—with either hand—I'm sure I could reach out and run my palms along the smooth plexisteel dome. Hell, I could probably lean over and lick it if I didn't have the rebreather over my lips. I have to hand it to her, the broad has immaculate control over this hog, considering the clip we're cruising. One little mistake and we're both bugs on God's great big windshield.

"You're doing fine, kid," I say.

I can't see her face, but I can picture her perfectly—brow knotted, deep in concentration. Chewing her lip like a wad of Raygun Charlie.

Suddenly, the glass in the dome above us shatters. Safety pellets shower our heads as that second goon hops right back into the fight. A maneuver like that takes some serious stones. The crazy asshole tore right through the lobby and caught us with our pants down!

Well, caught *me* anyway. Audrine doesn't miss a beat. She finishes the half-circuit around the dome and cranks the sticks left. Shoots us out at a tangent away from his trajectory. But the bastard spins around quick and nets a nice chunk of distance against us.

We zip away from the stalks and bubbles of the resort proper, out onto the open planet. The buildings get small, then start to disappear. Just as the light from the Calvera II twins begins to fade to a dull, rusty twilight, the other stars twinkle and shine down on us from a thousand and one crazy constellations. For a moment, I'm lost in them. One of those sparkling beauties might even be our own yellow Sun, half-a-universe away. I don't expect I'll ever see it again.

The silent whiz of a huge boulder brings me back to reality. Out here the surface is pockmarked with craters and trenches and other funpark geography. Guess the JanosCorp crew had no reason to steamroll the unused parts of this rock. It's crawling with hills and gullies and other hazards. Truck-sized boulders and craters big as buildings. Might as well be rushhour on the uptown expressway, and look at us, we're running late.

Audrine cuts a razor-sharp right and drops us down into a deep, dry canal with soft walls and plenty of runway. Once she straightens it out, I realize we aren't blazing at the same clip as before. The boulders blur by just a tad slower than I'd like. What is she, rationing gas?

"Hey doll," I say. "Enough with the Sunday driver routine, I've got places to be. Kick this hayburner up a notch or I'm taking the tram."

She hits the sticks with both hands and we start rapidly slowing and accelerating. Lurching. I glance over my shoulder to see Audrine yank back both throttles before throwing them forward together. She's giving it all the juice we've got and it's still not enough for a decent daiquiri.

"Some of that safety glass must have fallen down into the chassis," she says. "I can't get the sticks back up to full power."

Bad news. Ballsy and his buddy are gonna be on us faster than the McTasty's drivethru if we don't get this clunker's Go-Go wands on the mend. I'm ready to flip around and give the damned things a tug myself when an unfamiliar and altogether unwelcome synthvoice kicks in over the commlink.

"Warning! Warning! Rebreather concentrations reaching critical levels. System failure in T-minus ten minutes. Please remove mask and breathe normally to reset levels. Thank you for choosing LeisureTech Industries lifesaving equipment."

Sure. Let me just pop it right off and take a deep breath.

"Hey, darlin'—" I begin.

"I know," Audrine says. "I heard it too."

"Well damn. At least these rebreathers are manufactured consistently. Here I was hoping I had just gotten a dud."

"One thing at a time, Stockton. See if you can't do anything about our tail. We're not going to lose anyone at three-quarters thrust."

It's time to reassess the situation. I'm trapped on the back of a crippled hoverbike in a high-speed chase with bloodthirsty goons hot on our six. I've got nothing to work with but my own two hands and a rapidly dropping oxygen supply. Can't say I've been in much worse scrapes, but hey, the day's not over yet. At the very least, there's got to be something on this bike I can pry off and beat them with. I take a look around the chassis, hoping for a lucky roll.

It's a lot of twisting metal tubes and nylon cable-stays. Not much in the way of weaponry. But what's this? Hidden behind the liftpump?

"Bingo."

I find a little latch on the side of the fender, just above the thrust manifold. I wait for a smooth stretch of road, then give it a tug. It pops open and the lid tumbles away into the dust behind us.

My eyes light up.

Maybe the dice aren't fixed against us after all. I reach in and snatch out a shiny new 3mm Mark VI gaussrifle. She's not the assault model, but beggars can't be choosers. This thing is a pea shooter compared to my magnum, but it's still our best chance at getting off this bike alive.

I squeeze my knees tight and shoulder the weapon. Take aim. It's lighter than it looks. And damned hard to sight from the back of a speeding hoverbike. I take a couple of pot shots.

Nope. Not even close. I'm bouncing around too much back here to hit the broadside of a battleship. If either they, or we, would stop moving, I might have a prayer. Luckily this thing has quite the magazine capacity. Those little 3mm rounds take up no space at all. I can unload all day with ammo to spare, and I intend to do just that.

My targets bob back and forth down a little channel as we cruise through. Most of my shots smack the dirt in front of them or pull way over their heads. I need a plan. Maybe if I start at the ground behind us and slowly inch upwards towards them? I give it a go but even that brilliant strategy is clearly not going to cut it. Too much jostle on our end. The AimTrue® adjustment-dampener on that assault model would sure come in handy right about now. I'm better off just trying to plug me some goon dead on.

Dirt.

Dirt.

Air.

Dirt. Dirt. Dirt.

Clink!

There it is. I was actually aiming at the other guy, but managed to connect with his pal's bike. If dumb luck is all I can get, I'll take it—all the way to the bank. I managed to wing the rear goon's frame. Didn't exactly let the daylight through him, but maybe they'll be less stingy with the breathing room now that they know we've got teeth. The closer they want to get, the more I intend to bite.

"Let's bring it back towards civilization, darling." I say to Audrine through the commlink. "I think I just bought us a little space."

Without a word Audrine swings us up and out of the canal. We catch a little air and my stomach makes a brief visit to my throat, before she slips us into a tight slide. The shock-loaded liftmounts bounce the bike up and down, equalizing the impact on the frame, but not on my sore kiester. We bolt into a field of building-sized boulders and deep basins that crowd the surface like a colony of ballparks. The rims of the craters soaring overhead are the cheap seats. The nosebleeds.

My hunch was right.

The goons have had enough for today. They slowly disengage and split off to hit the showers.

"Yahoo, babydoll!" I say. "Our dinner guests have packed their doggie bags and paid the check. Let's shack up somewhere with some breathable air and celebrate."

"Good shooting, Tex," Audrine replies. "I'll take us back to the service airlo—"

A huge explosion kicks up dust and rocky chunks of moon-cheese fifteen feet ahead of us. Audrine nearly puts the bike down in the dirt. We pick up some serious speed-wobbles as the boulders blaze by, but she manages to level us out again before any of the stone giants can eat us for lunch.

"What the hell was that?" She buzzes us around a knife-edged crag. "I thought you said they left?!"

"They.... did," I say, as I take in just why they decided to split.

A distant dust trail grows bigger by the second, and at the helm, that big combat bike we left back at the resort. I took out the original driver, but one of his goon buddies must've hopped behind the wheel. Maybe even that looker that Audrine cold-clocked. The rocket pods are still deployed, like big hulking shoulder pads on an angry, augmented linebacker. He's blitzing, and our survival chances are about to get sacked.

The shoulder pads light up. Uh oh.

"Incoming!" I scream into the commlink.

I swivel around lightning-quick and throw my arms around Audrine. Manage to grab her right wrist and tug back, straightening us out of a loose turn without a second to spare. Two new craters erupt right where we were headed. Rubble rains down on our heads in finger-sized chunks and sharp shards.

"What the hell is going on, Stockton? It looks like we're on the set of a freaking warstream!"

"Yeah," I reply, "That's about the gist of it. Now make with the fancy wristwork and keep it coming. They've dropped the big guns on us and your skills behind the wheel are the only thing that can call a truce."

"Wonderful," Audrine says, almost absently, as she cranks us back the other way.

She weaves as fast as we can manage, desperately trying not to turn the bike over. At this point, that may be the humane way to get snuffed. Audrine dodges one, two, three more rocket barrages, but each one comes a little bit closer to being too close for comfort. The blast wave from the third is near enough to rock us onto our side. I clench my knees into the seat, ratchet my arms around Audrine's shoulders and watch the ground whizz by my beak until she can straighten us out. I'm not ready to become roadkill just yet, so I call for a change in strategy and flip back around to face the rear.

"Slow us down, doll," I say. "Let him get close, and I'll see if I can't find a weak spot to ping him with the rifle."

Audrine kills both throttles and he rides up on us in a flash.

"At least we'll be too close for missiles," she says.

Right. I thought of that too. Sure I did.

I start scanning the target for vulnerabilities, but I'm staring at a solid wall of armor and engineering. Those eggheads over at Lockheed-Grumman sure have their bases covered. With the mirrored canopy down, the bike on our ass has less soft spots than an overcooked egg. Even the rocket pods use retractable shielding plates. This thing is a fortress, and I'm throwing pebbles.

So much for my plan... but wait, what's this? Two hatches near the nose pop open to reveal... *ahhh shit*. Forgot about those. He's switching to guns. All four chaincannons start to spin as I yell once more into the commlink.

"GO! GO! GO! Step on it!"

A blaze of fist-sized shells chase the dirt behind our bike. Leave four parallel trenches in their wake like a giant invisible paw raking at us with five-foot tiger claws. Audrine lets the sticks fly and we slip out of their way just in time. And right back into Rocketland. Now he's caught us pinballing between the ranges of both weapons systems. Move too far ahead: *KABLOOEY*. Fall back and we're swiss cheese. I guess that plan to bring me in alive was a limited time offer. To sweeten the deal, the crater rims tower around us, boxing us into a series of narrow canyons not unlike cramped downtown streets—the ones with names, not numbers. A stray rocket catches the canyon wall above us, dropping stony slaloms in our path. We're caught between a rock and two or three different hard places.

"Shit! Shit! Shit Stockton! We can't keep this up! We need to do something, now!"

And then it clicks—the ending from *Moonrock Sonata*. StarCaptain Skip McKendrick has a solution for scrapes of all shapes and sizes. Did all his own stunts too.

"Alright, doll," I say, trying my hardest to hide the quiver in my voice. Trying desperately not to sound scared shitless. "I've got a way out, but you're going to have to trust me."

I sling the rifle across my back and kick my legs around to straddle Audrine. "When I count to three, I want you to push off the floorboards as hard as you can."

She turns to eye me as I grab the throttles.

"You're not serious!"

I just smile and cut for the gentle slope of a towering crater rim ahead of us. Here's to Hollywood.

"One."

The chaingun rounds ride our bumper.

"Two."

We mount the slope.

"Three!"

I slam both throttles into full reverse and pull us screaming into Whiplash City. The chaingun rounds rip past our heads on either side, right as we hit the end of our crater-rim runway and catch serious air. Audrine and I both leap for the sky, pulling our legs in tight to our chests. The mirrored canopy of the burly combat model tickles our toes as it shoots under us, tackling our little hovercycle with enough force to draw a roughing flag from even the most nearsighted referee. The collision ruptures a manifold somewhere and the two bikes quickly become one mangled metal omelet. A hot stream of thrust escapes, slicing the air beside us and setting the whole mess spiraling downward. Both machines, now locked in a furious embrace, tumble ass over elbows into the rocky gridiron below.

Audrine and I sail above the empty coliseum of a crater and the rough and tumble wreck heading right for it. I struggle to get my feet under me, not an easy task in this rock's cheap gravity. Never was much for aerobatics. With my body lined up, there's not much to do but wait for a crash landing of my own. It's slow in coming and leaves me with time to kill. I pray that the SpektraTek's mercy isn't all used up from my last skydiving stunt and brace for impact.

Instinctively, I hold my breath.

I land like a gimpy cat, on my feet but not for long. After a couple bounces on my coconut, the tuck and roll trick sets me spinning sideways, very much a human cigar. The torque is enough to help a fella yodel groceries, but I keep it down until I roll to a stop. Audrine lands splayed out next to me, looking like she might download dinner too. The stars swim in the sky above, even with my eyes shut. I sit up straight, watching our twin dust trails sway into the distance. She moves to follow, but I quickly knock her back down and follow suit.

The burning wreckage of both bikes spirals at us, taking little skitters and long hops on its journey. Flat on our backs, we get a great view of the undercarriage as the heap passes inches overhead. Damned things move so slow I almost have time to change the spark plugs. This weak gravity can throw a fella for a loop, that's for sure.

I flip over to watch our rides roll to a stop a good hundred yards behind us. Mountains of dust blow into our backs as we limp to our feet. I want to shake the hand of that shaggy little ski bum, wherever he might be. His damned SpektraTek suit has saved my hide again. I can shake the broad's instead, she was aces back there.

"You alive in there?" I knock on her noggin.

"Ughhh, I almost wish I wasn't."

"Yeah, doll, I can—"

"Warning! Warning! Rebreather status approaching critical. Please refresh air supply immediately."

Uh oh.

"Keep calm," I say. "Keep your breathing slow. There's gotta be something we can hook into on that big bike. Maybe the goon driving it has a backup air tank or two."

We stand up quickly and hobble towards the wreckage. It flickers and glows as small fires pop up from holes in the cracked chassis, then burn out quickly. Not good. Those flames are licking away our only shot at oxygen.

We saunter to it. Not a walk, we're in a hurry. Not a run, we don't want to use too much air.

The wreckage looks even worse up close.

"Critical system failure! Oxygen flow will cease in sixty seconds."

Our little hoverbike is completely wrapped around the front of the combat model, like a slab of burnt metal bacon on a ballpark frank. The mirrored armor visor is still up on the big beast, without so much as a hairline crack. It would take one hell of a haymaker to punch through that thing, and lucky us, what we want is tucked away safe on the other side.

I shrug my shoulders at Audrine.

"It was a good run, doll. Better luck next time, huh?"

I take a seat on the crumpled bumper and start thinking of excuses for Saint Peter.

She ignores me, hoists herself up on the wreck and follows a bright red Rescue arrow painted on the hull to find the canopy release. A quick tug on the latch loop and the mirrored bubble erupts up into the stratosphere with a puff of foggy condensation, revealing a grisly scene underneath. I watch the shimmering canopy get small as it floats up and away, towards the stars, then I scurry up close beside the broad.

Saint Peter can wait.

"Thirty seconds."

The GoonPilot's head is slammed through the cockpit heads-up display. His safety harness is in tatters. His rebreather is tanked too; the mask sits shattered, spouting crimson mist in regular foamy spurts. He must still be alive under there, choking on his own fluids. Not my idea of a good way to go, but I'm staring asphyxiation in the face, same as he is.

Tearing through a mountain of foil-covered debris and loose wires in the remains of the cockpit, we finally locate the life support module.

"5...4...3...2...1. Thank you for using the LeisureTech emergency rebreather system. Oxygen supply will now be cut off. Have a pleasant day!"

I hold my breath and reach for the hose in the cockpit. The damned thing is leaking. I see some dust blowing away from a cracked gasket mount. Hopefully there's still some air getting through to the pipe. I put the nozzle up to a valve on the side of Audrine's mask. She gasps for the air that enters. It might last five, ten minutes the way that seal is spewing pressure. Sure enough, I tap the display on the life support module.

"Seven minutes, darling," I say. "Sorry doll, but that's all the time I can buy you." The rebreather may help, but it's a long lonely walk back to the resort from here.

"Stockton, no!"

She starts fidgeting with the valve. I pull her hand away and put my finger up to her mask, shushing her.

"Nice knowing you, beautiful. I'll... catch you next time, huh?"

My vision goes dark, fuzzy around the edges.

I hop down and sit in the dust with my back to the wreckage. Look up at the universe before me, gasping for a breath that just won't come. I try to find our Sun. Our Earth. But I don't get very far in the vast blanket of light. With all that everything out there, staring right back at me, I fade away.

FOURTEEN

Burning.

My lungs are burning. Twin fusion cores scream inside me, pushed to a meltdown load. Something heavy slams down on my chest. *Thudthud.* Thumping against my ribs. Breaking them. Then, a soft wetness on my lips.

My lids pop open. I gasp like I've never gasped before. I suck the whole world into my aching lungs and exhale hot iron vapor. Audrine hovers over me like a burial shroud. Like a guardian angel. Saving me. She blinks and smiles, carelessly swipes a stray strand of hair behind her ear.

"Welcome back, Mr. Ames."

I struggle to sit up. She lends me an arm for support.

"I told you," my voice is still weak, "call me Stockton."

She laughs and throws her other arm around me, squeezing the life right back out of me.

"Okay, okay, I get it," I say. "You're thrilled to see me. Let me catch my damned breath for Christ's sake."

She backs away and gives me some room. Stands above me. I sit up straight and look around for the first time. We're stowed away in some mighty cramped quarters. A narrow corridor. Very industrial. Orangish emergency lighting illuminates her face. Casts soft shadows in hard colors. This hallway is peppered with random colored blips from indicator panels crawling up the walls every so often. We're caged inside a tight steel skeleton skewered with thick rivets. Exposed insulation and cables drip from every joint in the frame. Bulkheads stenciled with rough paint weigh down on my aching lungs. A series of random characters label the beams. None of it means much of anything to me. I fully expected to wake up dead.

"Where the hell are we?" I say. "I'll be damned if this is part of your gaudy resort."

Audrine shakes her head.

"I'm not quite sure," she says. "I was too busy saving your life to take a tour. There were some footsteps in the dust by the wreck."

Footprints, huh? Like the ones I saw from the ski shuttle?

"I followed them to an alcove with an airlock hatch in the crater wall. Dragging your limp body behind me the whole way, I might add. All it said was *emergency egress*. Oh, and *TimePilot*, with a little logo." She draws her finger in a sideways figure eight pattern in the air.

"And that doesn't mean anything to you?" I ask, struggling to stand.

"No." She makes a half-frown, half-smile. "It doesn't. If this were part of the resort I would like to think I'd know about it. As far as the 'TimePilot' business goes, your guess is as good as mine."

I scratch my chin.

"Maybe this is Slick's big secret? That thing you're so sure he's been looking for."

Audrine shrugs.

"Could be," she says. "We only found it with dumb luck."

I lean against a pipe running against the wall and start to shuffle my way down the corridor. There's another airlock hatch at the far end. We're buttoned up cozy.

"Well, wherever we are," I say, absently knocking on a beam, "thank God somebody left the life support system on."

"Technically speaking, I cut it on," she corrects me. "There was a big, rusty lever, and it was set to *off* when I dragged your sorry butt through the door."

She points to a fat red dial.

"Well I guess I can tell God to shove off then."

I rub my bruised elbows as I totter down the airlock hallway. "And if it was off when we came in, that's good news. Means we don't have to worry about any surprise parties from your JanosCorp friends."

"Or from those horrible monsters," Audrine adds.

"Or from them," I say, twisting open the hatch. "If they even need to breathe at all."

There's a faint rumble and a shrill hiss as the pressure equalizes between the airlock and whatever lies on the other side. Just to be safe, I snatch the Mark VI from my back and get the rifle ready. Edging the heavy steel door open with my foot, I peek through the opening.

It's dark on the other side.

A few of the colored lights blip here and there, but the orange emergency lighting is cut off. I can't make out much. The space opens up wider than the airlock corridor. Good thing too, a guy could get clammy in a can like this. There doesn't appear to be any movement out there, so I take a deep breath and step through.

The lights immediately click on, flashing a few times before staying steady. Must be on a motion sensor. They're bright too, not like the dingy orange glow of the airlock behind us. Firmly in the blue end of the spectrum. Clean looking light, like you'd find in a high class hospital ward. The kind of place they do boobs and butts, but not much else.

"Hello," a female voice says. Real friendly-like.

I spin around, keeping the rifle rump against my shoulder. I don't see a soul but Audrine and me. Hopefully nobody's hiding in the shadows, waiting to do *my* butt next. "Who's there?" I say, priming the rifle. "Be a good little twist and come out where we can see you."

Audrine is right up on me as we step into the center of the room, turning circles, sniffing for trouble. It's a large open octagon, maybe thirty feet across with a central spoke speared through the center. This room has a more finished look to it than the airlock passage, but not by much. Hexagonal white plastic panels are stuck over most of the bare steel walls. White, insulated sheets hang limp from the ceiling. One of these panels has an emblem molded and painted into it, right on the hub at the center. Just like the one Audrine described: a little yellow eight, keeled over on a dark blue shield.

"I am TimePilot," the voice says, seemingly from everywhere. "Who are you?"

Finally I set the rifle stock down against the ground. We're talking to the damned building's AI computer. If there's one thing I like less than chatting up a synth, it's gabbing with an AI. Just a robot without a body, if you ask me. I decide to have a little fun with our digital hostess.

"Howdy, sweetness," I say. "We're Rob and Laura from Earth. We're on our honeymoon. Ain't that swell?"

I begin poking around the joint. Audrine looks at me like I'm crazy but I motion for her to play along.

"Hi," she says, finally.

"Hello Rob and Laura from Earth," the AI says. "It's been a very long time since I've had anyone to talk to. I am glad you are here."

The left side of the place is thrashed, and the right doesn't look much better. There's some serious structural damage that nobody bothered to mend. Girders bent at strange angles, cracks in the paneling. Even the floor has a slope to it. Not so steep it would spill a highball, but maybe enough to shortchange your martini.

"Hey there, TimePilot, was it?" I continue looking around. "Where exactly is here? We got a little lost on our trip out from the resort."

"You are precisely seven billion, three hundred thirty-six million, one hundred fifty-two thousand and seventy-eight kilometers from your home on Earth," the AI responds. "Or if you prefer, twenty-two thousand, six hundred thirty-seven parsecs."

I give Audrine a shrug and a questioning glance. I wouldn't know a kilometer from a parsec if they both bit me in the ass. The metric system died out when I was a kid, a casualty of the T-Wars. Today, it's as meaningless and dead as the doorknob, except to eggheads and history geeks. The broad nods, as if to say, 'yes, this is technically correct.'

"TimePilot," she says. "What are you?"

There's a brief pause.

"I am a near-sentient human computer interface protocol."

"No, no, no," Audrine continues. "We understand that. What we want to know is, what is this structure we are standing inside of right now?" She stomps her foot on the steel floor for emphasis, and maybe to vent just a touch of frustration. A dull clang rings loudly, as if the deck below us were hollow.

"You are standing inside my hull," the AI replies. "I apologize for its condition. I'm afraid there's not much that can be done about it now. The utility synthetic that is responsible for my repairs and general upkeep has been absent without leave for quite some time."

I give the snooping a break and stare into the hub. Is this thing purposely trying to confuse us? Or is it just lousy at its job as a human interface agent?

"Okay," I say. "We're savvy. We're inside your hull. But what are you? I mean, besides an AI."

"Is your question rhetorical, Rob from Earth? I am not equipped to engage in philosophical discussions about the nature of reality, if this is your goal."

I shake my head. "No it's not a damned—"

How can I phrase this so the dipshit computer will give me the business straight? I think it's more than the hull that needs a once-over in here. Audrine beats me to the punch.

"TimePilot, you're a human interface agent, correct?"

"That is correct, Laura from Earth. My primary function is to provide accessibility to complex systems, systems of systems, and sub-routine protocols."

"Okay, that's great," Audrine says. "What are you an interface for? What are these systems you're providing access to?"

"I am an interface for mechanical, navigation, propulsion, and life support systems, as well as hierarchical and associated hardware, soft-ware, and wetware."

"Navigation? Propulsion?" I scratch my head. "So you're not a building at all?"

"That is correct, Rob from Earth. I am an extra-orbital human transport vessel," TimePilot says. "Some would call me 'starship'."

Audrine looks over at me and mouths *starship?*

"TimePilot," she says, "No one has used a starship to get to Seren Luna since the construction vessels left. We don't even have a spacedock. Everyone that's arrived since, including myself and the rest of the staff, arrived by SpaceGate."

It's not a question, so the AI doesn't have an answer. But it cer-tainly begs a query in my book. What is this hunk of junk doing here? Audrine is on it with the follow ups.

"How long have you been here?" she says. "When were you built?"

A single red light flashes behind the logo.

"I'm sorry, Laura," TimePilot says. "My date of manufacture is classified. Is there anything else you would like to know?"

"Classified?" Audrine gives me another look.

"Where is your crew TimePilot?" I ask.

"I do not have a crew," the AI responds. "I am a fully automated pre-programmed vessel capable of interstellar travel without direct human operation."

I'm not buying. Either we're dealing with some scrambled circuits here, or this starship is full of crap. "Come on TP," I say. "You can level with us. You said yourself that you were a human transport vessel. Your primary function is to interface with people, for crying out loud. So where is everybody? Where'd they get off to?"

Because we don't have a better focal point, we both address our questions to the molded panel with the sideways figure eight: the infinity TimePilot logo. Seems as good a spot as any. The voice sings from hidden speakers all around us. What do the etiquette streams say about chatting with somebody when you're standing inside them?

"My human cargo—" TimePilot pauses for a moment. "My human cargo is this way. Please follow the lights Rob and Laura."

Suddenly the overheads cut out.

Small diodes light up along the floor and ceiling. A chasing pattern leads us around the hub. Where the floor seems particularly crooked, a handful of fried electrodes pop sparks as we step over them. Audrine huddles up tight to me, in a tactical sort of way.

I don't like it either, doll.

Sections of panel twist away from the wall, revealing a fancy rounded slidelock behind. A clear viewport in the door shows us a light flickering on in the cabin behind it. The slidelock splits open with a grind and we're slapped with a rush of rank, stale air. We both cover our noses and step up to the door and stare into the room on the other side.

Inside are the bodies of five men and one woman.

Audrine takes one glance and looks away. Each corpse has been near-mummified. Skin leathery and sunken, stretched taut against their bones. Shrunken, beef jerky bodies that seem tiny and childish under their navy blue coveralls, like they're dressed in their old man's work-duds. The mummies are all strapped into little pods, with deflated vinyl airbags hanging limp from the sides and backs. The dead woman is frozen clutching at the webbing locks holding her hostage in the egg-shaped seat.

One pod is empty.

"Who were they?" Audrine asks quietly, almost to herself.

"They are my human cargo, Laura from Earth," TimePilot responds.

"No shit," I say. "Did they have names?"

"Yes," the AI replies.

I roll my eyes.

"Everything is like pulling teeth with you, TP," I say, stepping into the room. I get up close and personal with the nearest body, inspecting his jumpsuit.

"This one says Colonel Parsons." The next one. "First Lieutenant Sobocinski. Were these soldiers, TimePilot? Sailors?"

"That information is classified Rob from Earth."

"Of course it is," I say.

The jumpsuits are unmarked besides the names. Little perforations and stray threads show where other patches were ripped off. Somebody's sanitized the stiffs, and I've got a hunch it's the fella from the empty seat.

"Well I think these guys were military," I say, yanking up the dead lieutenant's sleeve. "And I think Lt. Sobocinski here wants to tell us his side of the story."

I grab the MPD embedded into the corpse's wilted wrist and yank it out. The dried, dusty flesh gives way easily and good thing, this device is massive. It's seated deep down in a thick strip of dried arm meat. I start to stomp towards a terminal on the far side of the room, but Audrine grabs my arm first.

"Stockton, wait." She's firm, in her tone and in her grip.

"TimePilot," she continues, "what happened to these peo—what happened to your human cargo?"

"My human cargo ceased self-sustaining functions shortly after our arrival here," the AI says.

"Why?" Audrine says. "Why did they cease—why did they die, TimePilot? Was it a crash? Did you crash here?"

Silence.

The lights dim, but only for a second.

"There was a collision."

More silence.

"But the collision did not end life functions of the human cargo." The AI's voice doesn't change. It's calm. Polite. Friendly, even.

This is a speech I've heard before. A hundred horrorstreams stole this same plot. I skip to the ending.

"You did," I say. "You ended their life functions, didn't you TimePilot?"

Audrine stares at the molded plastic walls with terror-stricken eyes. Digs her nails into my arm.

"That is correct, Rob from Earth."

There's no remorse. No sorrow. The AI just admitted to killing its crew, but it might as well have told us it's flapjacks for breakfast.

FIFTEEN

Audrine drops my wrist, leaving a couple of fresh claw marks behind. She stares up through some ripped insulation, into the exposed wiring and pipes. Into the heart of this killer machine. "Why? Why did you kill them TimePilot? Or is that classified too?"

"No, Laura from Earth, that information does not require security clearances. The human cargo was liquidated because their mission was no longer viable. My engines were rendered nonfunctional by the collision. We were derelict."

It hesitates.

"I am derelict."

Another pause.

"The human cargo's desire for rescue represented a threat to mission secrecy and multinational security. I could not allow them to broadcast a distress beacon."

I start to move towards the terminal again. Audrine yanks my arm near out of the socket. She silently mouths to me, "Don't piss it off! It could kill *us too*."

The AI speaks up.

"You are correct, Laura from Earth. I have the capability to terminate your life support functions. It is within the authority granted me via my operational jurisdiction."

Apparently TimePilot reads lips.

"Right then," I say with wide eyes and a smile. "Well it sure was swell to meet you TimePilot, but Laura and I will just be getting back to the resort now."

I make a move for the door, pulling 'Laura' behind me. The slide-lock slams shut before I take two steps. A series of claps and clangs tell us we're locked up tighter than a vault full of virgins in a port town.

"I'm sorry, Rob from Earth," TimePilot says. "I cannot allow you to leave."

I throw my hands in the air.

"And just why is that?" I say, spitting with disgust. "Are you lonesome? Maybe you shouldn't have offed your friends if you wanted somebody to shoot the shit with, you lousy machine."

"Your escape could constitute a data leak."

"Could?" Audrine says. "You'll keep us here to die for a possibility?"

"That is correct, Laura from Earth. I am unable to verify this status with operational command. We have not had positive contact in thirty-seven years, one hundred ninety-three days, local time dilation."

"So what?" I say.

"Discrete modelling with precise cognitive event forecasting is outside of my capabilities," TimePilot says. "I cannot discern with acceptable certainty what actions you may or may not take. Therefore, my directive is to treat any potential classified data spill as an absolute certainty. Protocol says all leaked data must be quarantined and sanitized. I am sorry Rob and Laura from Earth. You must be quarantined and sanitized."

I start formulating a plan to bump off this damned machine before it can put us on ice. I'll need a target to start with. Those flashing electrical conduits look promising. With a bit of luck and a couple hundred rounds from the gaussrifle, maybe I can knock this puppy offline. And our air supply with it, no doubt.

Audrine has other ideas.

"Wait, TimePilot," she says. "We haven't been exposed to any classified information. You didn't share any of it with us, remember?"

The AI has an answer for that too.

"Yes, I remember; I am incapable of forgetting. You know my name. You know my location. This constitutes unacceptable risk."

"I don't suppose it would get us anywhere if we crossed our hearts and hoped to die?"

"No," says TimePilot. "It would not."

I take a seat on a white molded bench along the wall. "So how are you gonna do it?" I say. "Cut the O2? Pump in some laughy gas? Or do you have something messier in mind? Well, pipe this you loony bucket of bolts, we'll go down swinging, and hard, if that's how you want to play ball." I clutch the gaussrifle tight, my finger on the boom switch.

"No, Rob from Earth. I will not cause your self-sustaining functions to end."

I loosen my grip some.

"But you just said we must be quarantined and sanitized," Audrine says. "What will you do with us?"

"You will be quarantined. I will inhibit your movements such that you cannot escape my hull. I will monitor and jam any outgoing radio transmissions."

"And the sanitizing part? That sounds like the dance I'd like to sit out," I say.

"Your natural biological processes will ensure you are sanitized in time," the AI says. "Based on my initial scans, Rob will succumb to natural cessation of life functions in—"

"No!" I interrupt. "We don't want to know that. Human cargo doesn't want to know its expiration date, TimePilot." I sigh. "Just leave us here to rot."

"Acknowledged, Rob from Earth," the AI says.

We sit in uncomfortable silence. I bounce the rifle on my knee and look for something to shoot, other than myself and the dame that dragged me into this hot mess.

"TimePilot," Audrine says after a spell, "if we're going to be quarantined and sanitized anyway, can you share your mission with us? Maybe it will help to pass the time."

I glance up at her.

What's she got up her sleeve?

"No, Laura from Earth. I'm afraid I cannot share mission details or any other classified information. It is a violation of my protocol. I am physically unable to do so."

Dead end. Or maybe not. Audrine keeps trying.

"But if we were to find some of this information on our own, say, in a storage device that belonged to some of your human cargo?"

"You are my human cargo now, Rob and Laura from Earth."

I sigh.

"Then in a device that belonged to some of your *previous* human cargo," Audrine continues. "Would that be alright, TimePilot? Or would you need to… terminate our self-sustaining functions?"

Silence.

Once again the lights flicker.

"That action is unrestricted. Classified data discovered independently is not addressed by my protocol. You may proceed."

I tap the ancient MPD against the palm of my hand. "So you're not gonna blow us out the airlocks if we peek at this?"

"No, Rob from Earth," the AI replies.

"Well that's a relief," I say, hopping to my feet and walking over to the terminal. The rifle hangs at my side, cradled by a snug three-point harness. I unclip the sling and lean the gun up against the wall. Really doubt it will do me much good in here anyway.

I slide into a sleek operator's chair and blow forty years of dust off the old MPD. This terminal is an ancient clunker as well. Not even a touchscreen. It's got one of those old type-y keypad interfaces. I thumb the power switch and wait for it to boot. It's a noisy devil, clicking and humming, wheezing and spitting. Damned thing would probably be in a museum back home. After an eternity, it finishes loading and toots a pleasant little startup ditty.

I stare into an array of colored boxes and squiggly symbols that might as well be ancient Oriental calligraphy. And I don't read Gook.

"How the hell do I sync the files from the damned—"

Audrine pushes me away from the terminal. I roll away gently on the chair's track. She hunches over the console and bats her lashes at the screen. Pops open a hidden hatch in the terminal case and feeds the MPD through with a snap. "Let me take care of it," she says with a half-cocked smile.

"Beautiful *and* a master of obsolete computer systems?" I say. "Is there anything you can't do, doll?"

She thinks for a moment.

"Maybe someday you'll find something."

She smiles again and chatters away at the keyboard. A series of cascading menus and submenus are born and die at her command.

Lightning strikes from her fingertips. I'm mesmerized by the rapid-fire rhythm of her tapping. To a cube like me, she's casting spells on this primitive hunk of junk. Snake charming the pants off its moth-munched circuit boards and bending it to her will. In the blink of an eyelash, her typing slows to a steady crawl, then stops.

"Here we are," she says. "Private logs of one First Lieutenant Jamison Sobocinski. This guy had them hidden way down deep. He knew his stuff."

A little video window pops up on the screen. The resolution is awful and the sound ain't much better. It's either a video of our boy Sobocinski spilling his guts or a toonstream of a talking trash heap.

Audrine frowns at the screen.

"I'll see if I can't bring it up on another display." Once again her machine gun fingers go to work. A split second later she's all smiles again.

"There we go."

One of the sections of the white plastic paneling pops out and slides in front of its neighbor, revealing an umbrella-like projection medium and a bulky holodisplay. They sure don't make them like this anymore. In fact, I'm not quite ancient enough to remember a time when they did.

Here's our buddy, in all his low-definition glory. A crackling, float-ing ghost, quietly spilling his guts. The background is bright, but too faint to make out clearly. It could be this same cabin in the starship, or it could be a McTasty's mensroom for all I know. Audrine taps the keys once more and his voice gets louder.

"—can't believe they called my number for this one. I guess some-body had to draw the straw. They tell me that the top brass handpicked me for this mission, that it's an honor. Guess that's the price I pay for being good at my job—"

Audrine scrubs forward a bit. The ghost develops a lethal case of hyperactivity disorder then settles back down.

"Listen, honey. I know you're angry with me. And I know you're even angrier that I can't tell you why I had to leave. But that's the life of an Orbital Defense officer. This mission, it's not like the others. It's…. important. It's going to change everything. Not just for you and Emma. For humanity."

The ghost of First Lieutenant Jamison Sobocinski gets much closer to the camera now.

"That's why I won't be coming back. At least not—well let's just say at least not in time for you and Emma. Not in time for *us*. I can't say too much. This information is all restricted at the highest levels. I'm putting together a log for you in hopes that someday, they'll declassify the mission, and you'll finally get the explanation you deserve. Until then, I love you both."

Audrine fast forwards again, then lets it play. This time the camera seems to be moving, like our boy is holding it as he goes for a stroll. "This guy here, he's the boss. If anything happens to me, you've got him to blame. Say 'hi' Colonel Parsons."

A fit, stately-looking guy with a salt and pepper crewcut salutes the camera with two fingers before turning back to a row of glowing dials. A burly bearded bloke with thick rimmed glasses pushes the captain out of the way with a hand holding some kind of fancy diagnostic scanner. He's dripping electrical leads and chewing on a pencil-thin plasma cutter.

"Don't you have any real work to be doing, Sobo?" the bearded guy says, pulling the penknife from his lips and tapping it on his thigh.

"Not a thing, Scags," Sobo's voice says from behind the camera. "That's why I didn't go to flight engineer school. Too much busy work. You know this bucket of bolts was put together by the lowest bidder, right?"

This Lieutenant's got his head on straight. I like him already.

Scags shakes his noggin and scurries. "Pretty FUBAR if you ask me," he says, disappearing into a duct. He pops his head out to finish. "The damned security officer making home movies of the deepest, darkest mission since forever."

Sobo turns the camera around to face himself.

"Now *that's* my job. Why don't you worry about keeping us from …leaking? Huh, Scags? Besides," he turns the camera to a porthole, showing us a massive nebula in the distance, "who's gonna see it all the way out here?"

Audrine scrubs ahead again. She pulls her hand off the toggle, but I lay mine over hers and keep it pressed.

"This is great drama and all," I say, "but there's not enough action for my taste. Let's find something worth watching, huh doll?"

She rolls her eyes at me.

"What's the matter?" she says. "You have someplace to be?"

I pull my hand away.

"Here ya go," she says. "Some action."

There appears to be some kind of confrontation in the feed. Sobo is arguing with somebody we've never seen before, somebody with his back to the camera. They appear to be in a warehouse of some kind, with endless rows of silver racks towering above them, loaded down with dull metallic crates.

"No way, Doc!" Sobo says. "I don't buy it. That shit won't fly with me."

The other fella turns to face us.

"I don't care if you like it, Lieutenant," he says. He's a stick of a guy, but in decent shape for his age. White hair, wire-rimmed glasses. A crooked beak and weathered brow. Grandpa's seen his share of assignments.

"Don't pull rank with me, *Major*," Sobo says. "If what you've got in there poses a security risk, we all have a right to know. It's my damned job to know!"

The doctor tugs off his glasses and sighs.

"Listen, Jamison, this isn't a personal attack. You just don't have the tickets for this."

Sobo palms his forehead and stares at the ceiling. "What kind of idiot plans a mission where the security officer doesn't have the right clearances to understand the damned payload?"

"Here he comes, you can ask him yourself," Doc replies. The camera pans to reveal the graying colonel from before.

"Is there a problem here, gentlemen?" Colonel Parsons asks. The doctor uses both hands to give the stage to Sobocinski.

"Sir," Sobo says, "if there is anything in the storage bay that poses a threat to the crew or the mission, I need to know about it immediately. According to the manifest we've got a trunkful of flightline and wormhole patches, and nobody's green enough to buy crap like that. Especially not your security officer. What's in there?"

Colonel Parsons blinks once and nods. "Show him, Doc."

The doctor hesitates. "Sir, are you sure? This is against Corps protocol and—"

The colonel cuts him off. "This man gave up his family for the Corps. And for this mission. Just do it. That's an order."

The doctor walks over to a shelving unit and puts his thumb up to a scanner on one of the storage bins. It beeps and whistles. Some latches pop open and the lid rises. A hydraulic lift cranks up a metal cylinder about four-and-a-half feet long.

"What the hell?!" Sobo's eyes get wide, then narrow. Here's a man that knows what he's looking at. It still looks like wormhole patches and flightline to me. "So this mission isn't just about exploration and scientific discovery."

The colonel pats Sobo on the back.

"Fraid not, son."

"It was all bullshit. All that nonsense about bettering humanity and changing the world." Sobo stares at his boots. "We're nothing more than ammo pukes humping munitions and babysitting bombs out here."

The colonel snags Sobo's chin and makes the younger man stare him in the eyes.

"Listen, Lieutenant. There *are* non-military implications for our secondary objectives. But this is the Orbital Defense Marine Corps. Not the Rainbow Friends Philanthropy Club. Thanks to that little non-proliferation mistake President Jackass signed into law last year, we can't keep these bad boys at home anymore. But out here, way out here. We can keep them out of harm's way. Away from little Emma and her friends."

"No," Sobo says, shaking his head. "That's sour too, Colonel. Why come so far out? There are a million isolated places we could stash this stuff in our own neighborhood of the galaxy. Why worry about the relativity and the time dilation? Where's the play in that? It doesn't add up, not all the way it doesn't. What aren't you telling me?"

The colonel glances at the doctor, who apparently has all the answers. Doc sighs and says, "The warheads in the ordinance will experience the time dilation just like you or I would."

Silence.

The doc sighs again. "This means a significant decrease in loss of core mass due to radioactive decay. This poses several benefits in terms of both storage safety and production costs."

The colonel chimes in, "It also means the geeks out in New Mexico can play around with all sorts of new isotopes, now that stability is less of an issue. Higher yields. Smaller packages."

The doctor opens up a second bin. He reaches in and pulls out a much smaller metal cylinder. About the size of a can of beer. Maybe a little longer. A tallboy.

"Now *that* makes sense," Sobo says. "The Corps can save some money and keep the arsenal away from the inspectors and all the bad press.

As a bonus, they can create all sorts of new toys for the black ops boys. And once the mission is complete and that long distance Field Generator is set up offworld, we can have all these PocketNukes back planetside lickity split. The brass just has to snap their fingers and they're back in business."

The doctor carefully replaces the tallboy with both hands and presses another button to activate the closing sequence. "That's about the whole of it, yes," he says.

Audrine pauses the feed.

"The dates in here," she says, "Stockton, this all happened hundreds of years ago."

"Yeah," I say, "I figured as much with all these steam-powered number crunchers lying around. So what if it's old news?"

"So," she says, "this mission was declassified a long time ago. It was all over the 'streams. It is literally old news. Not the specifics, of course, but this all became household knowledge. The Orbital Defense Corps was nearly dechartered for it. Not for the secrecy and deception, *that* was to be expected. It was the mission's failure. The loss of a significant chunk of the UNSAT nuclear arsenal was a huge deal, especially once the war broke out."

I mouth the words, "The war?" That really was ancient history. She looks young enough to be... well, she looks young enough, anyway. She sure as sugar can't be old enough to remember the T-Wars. And I don't recall anything about the ODC getting in hot water during all that mess. Hell, they saved our asses from those godless commie gooks.

What war was *she* talking about?

"Audrine," I say, "how old are you exactly?"

She frowns at me and crosses her arms.

"Mr. Ames, you know that is not a proper question to ask a lady! And now is certainly not the time."

She turns to address the AI before I can keep pressing.

"TimePilot," she says, "your mission is now public knowledge. It was declassified on Earth over one hundred years ago. You don't need to quarantine or sanitize us any longer. If you'll please let us out we will be on our way."

There's silence for a few seconds.

"I'm sorry, Laura from Earth. Public release of information does not constitute declassification. I must receive confirmation from mission control to comply with protocol."

Audrine stomps her foot. We were so close. I walk over and put my arm around her. Then it hits me. The way out.

"TimePilot," I say.

"Yes, Rob from Earth?"

"Do you have the jurisdiction to enlist new recruits? To bring us into ODC service?"

Audrine scratches her head.

"Yes," the AI replies. "Conscription is not specifically disallowed by my protocol. Although such a measure would warrant appropriate cause." The ship's not sold. Not yet.

"What if we could help you complete your mission? Would you let us join up then?"

A slight pause.

"I do not believe you have that capability, Rob and Laura from Earth," TimePilot says.

"What if we could locate that missing utility synth of yours? We could send him back here and he could fix you up, right as rain. Then you could complete your mission. And if I'm lying? Hell, kill us. You already offed your first crew." I run a hand down a mummy's sleeve. "A couple more bodies won't ruin the ambiance in here."

A much longer pause this time.

The lights dim and flicker. TimePilot finally speaks.

"I cannot be assured that you would complete this task as you say. Coarse logic-parsing algorithms return ninety percent probability you would not even attempt completion after leaving my hull. I am also doubtful in your ability to locate the aforementioned synthetic humanoid."

Here's my trump card.

"Don't worry about that, old girl," I say. "I've already met the guy."

Audrine stares at me.

"The SAMM-E unit, right? I know right where to find him. And as far as trust goes? An honest engine like me wouldn't try to slide one past you. I'm good for it, promise. I'll even leave the girl here as collateral until I get back."

"Now wait just a minute!" Audrine says. "If you think for one second that I'm just going to sit here collecting dust while you—"

TimePilot interrupts.

"I accept your terms on one condition."

Audrine and I both look up.

"Laura from Earth will complete this task. My pheromone sensors indicate that she is more likely to honor the agreement."

She sneers at me.

"Well he'll just have to wait here and find out, now won't he?"

I wouldn't really have left the broad high and dry. Well, I would have tried my damnedest not to anyways. I explain to her about bumping into SAMM-E the antique maidbot back at the resort.

"Hmmmm." Audrine purses her lips. "He definitely wasn't in any of the JanosCorp logs." She taps her MPD. "So this won't be of much use."

She smiles at me. I scowl back.

"But if he came from *this* ship, I should know where to find him."

I give her a look that says, "Yeah, right."

"Trust me," she says with a wink.

ONE OF THESE GIRLS IS A SYNTHETIC, BUT JOHNNY CAN'T TELL WHICH ONE. CAN YOU?

AUTOMATED DYNAMICS NEW LEXSYNTH SERIES SYNTHETIC HUMANOIDS
by
AUTODYNE INDUSTRIES

When nothing but the best will do.

SIXTEEN

TimePilot frees us from the tomb. Leads us back through the central hub to a door tucked behind a battery of wheezing air scrubbers. I pat the old purifiers, pray they don't go kaput on us, and follow the broad into a brightly lit supply locker. Dusty gear sits strapped down on a dozen grated shelves all around us, belted in tight with rubber netting and clunky chrome latches. The buckles all pop at once and Audrine gets to shopping. She peers into cabinets, runs her fingers over a river of equipment as it rotates into view. I don't even recognize half the crap in here, but this dame has an armful before I can blink twice. Natural gathering instincts, maybe. She sets her score down on a steel bench and holds a scaly body-stocking up in front of her with both hands. She frowns at it, then nods towards the door.

"Out," she says to me.

I toss a fancy electric pigsticker back into a cubby and park my keister just outside the door. Putting my back and one foot against the bulkhead, I pull a flavorstick and pick my gums.

Ten minutes and two sticks later, Audrine emerges, decked to the nines in a high-tech catsuit. She spins for me and smiles, runways the goods in the cramped white corridor. Boetheon active/reactive combat armor that makes the SpektraTek look like kids' stuff; something long and gun-like on her back; a bandolier bustling with holodecoys and smokeless screens in tiny, metal canisters. She looks like something out of an early warstream, ready to storm the beaches of Wonsan with the boys from the Fighting Fifty-Ninth. I'd half-like to paint her face in dark tiger stripes and tie a red rag around her forehead. The equipment is ancient, but it's solid, military-grade hardware. Plug-and-play death-dealing stuff. It'll get the job done—against the JanosCorp security goons, or those glowy-eyed little freaks, whichever she runs into first.

When she's done twirling, I give her a nice slow clap. She come-hithers me back into the locker room with a single finger, then waits with crossed arms while TimePilot pops another hatch for one last piece of equipment. I glance into the open container. Her final prize is big and dark, and somebody's scrawled *ICARUS* in waxy, white marker across the top of it. Looks heavy, in every sense of the word. Audrine bats her lashes. "Would you be a dear?"

I sigh, then grunt as I tug the sack of bricks out of its snug rubber housing. I heave the black contraption onto the bench beside her and squint. "What the hell is this, doll?"

She turns around and pulls the rifle from her shoulder. "It's my ride back to the resort," she says. "If you'll help me get it on."

I shrug and hoist the beast up to her back. A magnetic harness on the ICARUS clicks to the armor on her shoulders and hips. She dips with the weight of the thing. Nearly tips over face-first into a rackful of rifles, then rights herself with a little help from yours truly. I loosen my grip on the handle at her neck and she eventually stops wobbling.

We walk to the airlock. Well, I walk. She waddles.

When we get there she smiles, testing the controls. A pair of stubby winglets rise out from her sides, nearly poke me in the gut, then retract. I'm just glad she's not ready to burn the boosters inside this shoebox. I step around her and undog the door to the airlock.

"You sure you can handle something like this?" I say, putting my hands below a pair of exhaust ports in the base of the backpack. "You ever hitch your horse to a jetpack before?"

"Maybe not," Audrine smiles. "But I'm a quick study."

I knock on a dark metal bulge beside her waist and frown.

"Yeah, you'd better be. A rocket glued to your rump won't be very forgiving if you're spitting nickels out there, kid. That's a lesson you don't want to learn the hard way."

I tap at a veritable forest of warning labels stenciled below the intake vents. Two dozen reasons she should leave the ICARUS behind. She steps through the hatch into the airlock and ignores each and every last one.

"Don't worry," she says. "I'll take good care of my rump."

I grin half-heartedly, but the frown grows right back.

"Listen," I say. "If you run into any trouble out there, I want you to forget about me. I want you to—"

She puts a finger up to my lips.

"Hush baby don't speak," she says, *almost* mocking me. Then she smacks me across the cheek for good measure.

"I'll be back for you," she says. "Promise."

She clicks her tongue and winks. Then she pulls a helmet on until it clicks into the neck plate. Slides a dark visor down over her face and pushes me away. The door slips shut between us. I can hear the hiss of hydraulics as the airlock depressurizes. She's on her own now.

I toss my toothpick to the deck and stop myself before I stub it out. I'm out of company here, unless you consider this damned hunk of junk I'm trapped inside. In the past, I was never too keen to converse with anything that wasn't human. Hell, plenty of actual people didn't make the cut for conversation either. Whole groups, even. But these are special circumstances, and why the hell not? I've got nothing but time to kill until she gets back, and those slimy SnotBabies have my curiosity piqued.

"TimePilot," I say, "do you know anything about... ETs, errrr, aliens—that is, beings from another planet? You know, strange creatures living this far out in the galaxy?"

"No, Rob from Earth," the AI responds. "There has never been a documented case of human contact with an extraterrestrial life form. My databanks indicate that this should be common knowledge. *You* are the strangest creature I've met in quite some time."

"Yeah, yeah, I, ahh, I know," I say, frowning. I wring my hands together and ignore the insult, for now. "I just thought maybe you had dirt on some sort of top secret spook stuff."

The starship makes a sound like "hmm," only with the boredom dial cranked to max gain. While I'm tooting the wrong ringer I might as well cover all my bases.

"Say TP, there weren't any kind of biological weapons stowed away for your mission, were there? Something that would cause people—or animals maybe—to you know… mutate into monsters?"

"Monsters, Rob?"

"Mutants of any kind, if it sits better that way."

"No," TimePilot says. "My manifest does not contain any genetic mutagens or other biological hazards. Even my warheads and fuel cones are rated E4: safe for macroscopic life forms and other organics."

"Yeah, it was a long shot. Thanks anyway."

I guess the ODC doesn't know any more about those snarling little buggers than I do. Or if they do, this obnoxious ship ain't sharing. But then where in the hell did these SnotBabies come from? We bagged a breeding pair of the slimy bastards under the pool, but how many more are still out there? Out there with the broad, and my only ticket out of this scrape.

I blow out a deep breath.

I need to clear my noodle. Four days ago I was just a guy sipping whiskeys at the beach, working on a crappy tan. A week before that I was nothing but a washed-up cop, on the fast track to nowhere and damned happy to be there. Now I'm tied up with a resortful of dead celebrities, hideous space monsters, brutal corporate thugs, and murderous starships. And I've got one gorgeous gal to blame for all of it. Of all the in-boxes in all the world, she had to leave a message in mine. But if I'm so sore with her, why can't I keep those emerald eyes out of my aching head?

I take a deep breath and then I take a little stroll back to the chamber with the dead marines. Reach down and press start on the holoplayer console. I skip ahead a bit for good measure, then plop myself into the empty crash-couch and kick my heels back, wishing for a tub of buttered popcorn. I settle for a wild cherry chewstick instead.

On the holoscreen, Sobo points the recorder out a porthole and I catch a familiar view. The twin burning globes of Calvera II. Only, a little brighter, and from a greater distance than we're used to seeing up in ResortWorld.

Sobo is just as bewitched as I was the first time I caught a glimpse. He's perfectly silent, watching the two lover-stars waltz. Even as a low-fi, pixelated mess, they make for a beautiful sight. I squint at the screen. Maybe it's just the recording, but I could swear they seem a little further apart. As if they weren't quite comfortable enough to get up close and personal for the dirty dancing I remember from my suite.

Suddenly white streaks shoot past the viewport, and lots of them. Big fat mothers, too. Looks like he's caught up in one of those PolarCycle-whatsits. Still seems scary to me, no matter what the dame says. The recorder shakes off whatever table or ledge Sobo has it resting on and my view smashes to the deck with a static pop. The lieutenant is in frame now, lying on the floor, and enjoying the show about as much as I did.

I feel for the guy. This is a whopper of a storm. The camera quivers like a wino, three days dry in the cold rain. Once or twice Sobo is visibly lifted off the deck and slammed back down. His jaw cracks open on the third and final piledriver, leaving a thin trail of blood on the steel plate and a few fat spatters hanging in the air of the holo, caught on the lens. The audio track is a mixed bag of bassy bangs and screaming crescendos over a wheezy, falsetto drone.

Then, just as suddenly as it started, the solar storm calls it quits. The Lieutenant picks first the camera, then himself up off the floor. It swings down by his side as he sprints towards the chamber I'm parked in now. The mummy crypt.

The holoframe fills up with some familiar faces.

Colonel Parsons shouts for everyone to strap in and shut up. He shoves Sobo into the last chair the man ever sat in. Into the chair he's still sitting in right behind me. The holo's cheap speakers pop with the mad chatter of frightened chaos. Things eventually quiet down as everyone buckles up and harnesses down.

"What the hell is happening Colonel?" Sobo says.

TimePilot's voice squelches in over the holoplayer, as cheerful and polite as ever. "T-minus two minutes to impact."

"We're bracing for an emergency landing, that's what's happening, Lieutenant," Colonel Parsons plays the spitting image of the stoic captain. Throwing his crew into seats and strapping them in. Going down with his ship.

"What the hell happened!?" Sobo asks.

This time the engineer—Scag was it? This time Scag pipes in. He speaks quickly. Forgets to breathe between sentences.

"Don't ask me! We were on target, right on course. All of a sudden we started picking up speed. Breakneck speed. TimePilot burned out the thrusters trying to slow herself down. Damn near broke us up."

He gasps for a breath. "I don't know what could have caused that sudden acceleration. We don't have the drivetech for that kind of velocity.

Shit nobody does! If the logs are right, we were practically a beam of light for a few seconds back there. I've never seen anything like it!"

Doc's turn to talk. He answers with a cool calm that belies their situation. Speaks with a smile on his lips. "That's because *no one* has seen anything like it," he says. "We just witnessed a phenomenon that has been theorized for a very long time—by Einstein himself originally—but never observed firsthand until just now."

The old man is brimming with awe and wonder, like he just watched his boys bring the WarnerBowl trophy over to his place to cool their suds. There's a glint, a glimmer, behind those wire-rimmed specs. This is his Christmas. He's lived his whole life for this moment.

"Well cough it up, damn it! What the hell was it, Doc?" Scag says.

"A wave. It was a gravitational wave."

TimePilot interrupts.

"T-Minus one minute to impact."

"Those two stars we were just passing—" Sobo chimes in.

"Rather remarkable binary neutron stars," the Doc says. "They must have slipped in their orbit. Essentially, the big one is eating away her sister, stealing mass, bit by bit. When she takes a big bite, it causes a flux in the gravitational field—a ripple in spacetime, if you will. And we caught that ripple, that gravitational wave. We are the first beings in all of known existence to experience it."

"Yeah we're all pro spacesurfers now," Scag butts in. "But what are we gonna do about it?"

Colonel Parsons this time.

"Right now we are going to brace for a collision and pray for the best, Sergeant Scaglietti. When we get out of this, SAMM-E can still set up the terrestrial SpaceGate to get us back home. He can set up the gate, then help us clean up the mess. That's what you're going to do, right SAMM-E?"

SAMM-E speaks for the first time. He's sporting a matching blue flightsuit, buckled down and strapped in tight, right in the empty seat where my butt is parked now.

"Affirmative, Colonel. I will do as—"

The holorecorder flies from its perch in Sobo's hand and slams into the far wall. The feed goes static, then dead. Quiet.

"Well I'll be damned," I say to myself. I knew there was something more to those crazy light shows.

I glance up at the ceiling.

"So this is all your fault then, you crusty rustbucket."

"No, Rob from Earth."

"How do you figure, TP? From where I stand, there's one finger to point, and it's a human's to do the pointing with. I'm the only living person around at the moment, so I'm pinning you."

TimePilot doesn't miss a beat, like she's had nothing to do but twiddle her thumbs and practice an alibi for the last forty years. "I was programmed to adjust my velocity against external factors in order to reduce unnecessary strain on my hardware and my human cargo. I performed a correction within two ten-thousandths of a second of the unexpected acceleration event: well within the acceptable limit. As gravitational wave phenomena had never been observed, it could not be accounted for in my adjustment protocol. In the literal sense, I did exactly as I was meant to do. I cannot be blamed."

"So you were just following orders, huh?"

I stand up and pace.

"In a manner of speaking, yes," TimePilot says. "I prefer to think of it as an unfortunate oversight."

"Ah skip it!" I say. "Save the excuses for someone that wants to hear them, you heap. Your words won't bring these boys back to life!" I slam my fist down onto one of the dead marine's outstretched hands. It crumbles like expensive cheese, showering the air with flaky dust.

I'm done talking. Motes of mummy stuff drift to the crinkled steel deck. I watch it fall. To my surprise, the AI attempts to clear the air. "These were not the first martyrs for the march of human progress, Rob from Earth. They will not be the last."

TimePilot's feminine voice is pleasant as ever, but I can read between the lines. I stare up at the ceiling, eyes burning.

"Don't threaten me, you leaky tub!"

"I can assure you I meant no hostility by my statement," the AI says. "My human cargo knew the risks when they left Earth."

I look away.

"Yeah, well I didn't."

"I'm sorry to hear that, Rob," TimePilot says. "Would you like to share your story with me?"

I sigh.

"Maybe some other time."

"Yes, perhaps that would be best, Rob from Earth. Your bio-rhythms indicate that you are near exhaustion. Would you care to rest in my living quarters? I am to understand that they are quite comfortable for human cargo."

"Why?" I say. "So you can ice me in my sleep?"

Nothing, for a moment.

"If I wished to terminate your life functions, Rob from Earth, I would not require you to be in a resting state."

"So says you." I sigh. "Well go ahead then, lead on. Whisk me away to these luxurious quarters."

TimePilot does.

And before I know it, I'm stacking Zs three at a time.

SEVENTEEN

I'm home. *Really* home.

PeoplesBank Stadium, a Knights' game. I *must* be dreaming, these seats are great. Tucked into one of those cushy, corporate fieldboxes. Two dozen two-faced JanosCorp logos stare out at me from the walls, from the backs of the massive recliners in front of me, but I steer my eyes towards the gridiron. From this close, I can almost make out the players' faces under their battle-scarred helmets. Angry and flushed and dripping sweat. Only their mirrored visors block my view.

It's a tight game but the Knights just can't pull ahead of the other guys. The Bombers, maybe, judging by their navy blue unis and Boetheon logos. Both squads knock on the door, but manage to screw the pooch at each end. A giveaway here. A missed opportunity there. A series of brilliant hooks and ladders marches the bogies right down our throats before a big blitz and fumble leaves them with nothing to show for the bruises. Our boys are carted off the field like it's some kind of warzone out there. The friendly signal caller goes down in a twisted, broken heap near our own end zone.

A whistle sounds. Timeout.

Two teams of syntho medics start to scrape what's left of our QB from the turf. Then the coach—not the current coach, or that bum from when I left town anyway—but *the* coach. Mr. Calvin Wallace. The Big Chief himself. Winner of four consecutive WarnerBowl trophies and the hearts and minds of a whole generation of blue-blooded sports fans. This man is Jesus, the UNSAT President, and the old man we never had, all rolled into one. A living legend. He hops the wall and marches up into the stands, billowing pungent clouds from the fat cigar he never seems to put down. Never seems to need a light, either. Big Chief Wallace climbs into *my* box. Personally grabs me by the hand and pokes me in the chest with a hairy-knuckled sausage of a finger. A whole hand's-worth of championship gemstones sparkle. The smoke from his stogie stings my eyes, but I don't look away.

"Time to man up, son," he says between puffs. "You're our only hope. Get down there and win it for us. Win one for all of us, Ames."

The bleachers erupt in a roar as I take the field.

Equipment crawls over me. Assembles itself on the fly. Shoulder pads, a helmet, a jersey with the full complement of corporate sponsors. Freshly geared, I slip into the center of the huddle and draw up a play in my palm. My helmet display flashes a splash of red warnings.

It'll never work. Give up now. Take a knee and save yourself the trouble.

My teammates' faces are gone, hidden behind the chrome visors bolted to their battered helmets. I stare into twelve distorted reflections of my own ugly mug and spit at the playcalling computer's lack of faith.

"Halo gold!" I shout to my men. "Halo gold Lincoln left forty-five basin, on one, on one!"

I split my flankers out wide. Send the T-back up to the line of scrimmage. The A and B backs too. I'm alone in the backfield. It all sits square on my shoulders: the game, a whole stadium full of hopes and dreams. Nine figures worth of Vegas action, plus countless back alley bets and other friendly wagers. The cheers pound a deafening heartbeat I can feel in my own chest. Defenders snort like caged apes across the trench, tearing up chunks of turf as they paw at the sloppy field. Their eyes are crusty membranes above the eyeblack. Frothy blood and foam dribbles from their round, sucker mouths.

Somewhere, a million miles away, a whistle blows.

My lungs erupt, barking a cadence that could chew the craters off an asteroid. I take the snap, and it nearly takes me off my feet. The ball weighs a hundred ninety-five pounds. My feet weigh even more.

I fake a flip to my right and shoot the left gap. Pulling linemen explode into the defense like laser-guided bowling bowls. Mountains of men crumble and fall in an avalanche of sweaty, bruised flesh. I highstep over body after body, contort my torso to avoid a forest of razor-sharp claws reaching out from the mangled pile. The pigskin is tucked away safely in my arms, like a swaddled infant child. It coos softly as I sprint into the open field, leaving a trail of crumpled men and monsters in my wake. I shake first one, then another 'backer with ankle-snapping jukes. But my trick knee buckles and the third linebacker doesn't bite. He's the largest man I've ever seen and he trucks into me like a freight tram, knocking my helmet into the stratosphere. It lands somewhere in the upper decks, in the hands of a happy fan with his feet in a fresh puddle of cold domestic. Somehow, I manage to keep my feet under me and stagger forward, an inch at a time. The huge linebacker rips at the ball-baby, draped over my back like a steel shadow.

My ears bleed with the sound of the crowd's chant.

"Stock-ton! Stock-ton!"

Each step is an earthquake. I drag the massive beast along. Swarms of defenders hop back on their feet and get hot on my tail. Just a little further and I'm in. The goal line calls to me. Teases me. Each blade of grass bends and waves, beckons me onward. That white stripe is impossibly close and incredibly clear. The clock ticks down to zero. There are no second chances now. I stumble. Reach the sobbing ball out for the end zone with everything I've got. Only an inch to go.

"Stockton! Stockton!"

Audrine, shaking me. Gone are the defenders, the crowd, Big Chief Wallace and his cloud of smoke. My dream.

"Stockton," she says. "Wake up!"

"No, babydoll, not yet. I was just about to score," I say. I attempt to roll away from her in the propped-open somnopod.

"Now I know you were dreaming." She shakes me some more. This isn't a battle I'm going to win.

"Alright, alright," I say. "I'm up. Where's the fire?"

I yawn and stretch.

"Right here," Audrine says. "Look who I found."

She's got my old packbot, holding it to her chest like it's some kind of oversized puppy. I have to say, I'm a bit jazzed to see him myself. I don't want to be that guy that talks to his damn suitcase, but the little bastard did save my neck a few hours ago. I give him a friendly pat.

"Swell," I say.

"He was out on the surface, all by himself, coming to find you," she says. "Poor little guy, to be stuck with such a brute for an owner."

"Yeah," I say, "I'm lucky to have such loyal luggage." I give Audrine a quick once-over. "You look to be in one piece. No missing appendages. All major organs where they belong, I hope."

"It was a piece of cake." She winks at me. "The resort was empty. No security squads. No SnotBabies. Not even any guests or staff. They must have gotten the Field Generator back online and shipped everyone home. And you and I will be right behind them! We can figure out Proletti's plan from a safe distance."

I nod and pull a toothpick from my pocket. Tart mango zest bites at the tip of my tongue, along with the notion that this broad has an awfully optimistic view of our once-dire sitch.

"If TP will let us leave," I add. "Did you find the synth?"

She smiles.

"Sure did. He was right where I knew he'd be, up on the solarium deck."

I flip the pick with my tongue and wince at the sour taste.

"And how did you know he'd be up there?" I point the pick in her direction. "If you've got secrets, let's hear 'em doll. Secrets will get us dead in a hurry in a spot like this."

She tosses a hand to her hip, but only one.

"I knew right where he'd be because synth models from his era needed to recharge their fuel cells with a photovoltaic module." I frown. She sighs. "A solar panel, Stockton. He has a solar panel. And the best place to catch good, UV spectrum light is up on the solarium deck." She flips the hair away from her eyes and stares me down.

"Any more questions, Inspector?"

"You can be a real smart ass when you want to, honey. Anybody ever tell you that?"

She stands with her hands on her hips but says nothing.

"Lucky for you that's just my type." I wink. "For a kid, you're a regular wiz when it comes to the outdated tech. Were you a console jockey in a past life or what?"

She just rolls her eyes at me.

"When we get home," I say, "remind me to bring you for Trivia Tuesdays at the Wellton." I sit up and stretch. I haven't slept like that in ages. A good old-fashioned somnopod was absolutely aces after all those nights in that screwy, open-air bed. I'm not a fella that's accustomed to change. "So where's the synth now?" I ask, standing and stifling another yawn.

She points out to the main chamber behind her with a thumb. "Out there catching up with the ship," she says. "Are you eager to join them?"

"In a tick," I say. "I want to take care of some business while they're too tied up to pay us any mind."

I lead Audrine through the main hub. We tiptoe around the back of the center post. Sure enough, we catch the two machines chattering away at each other like a couple of old hens. Sounds a bit heated. Well, as heated as two AIs programmed for polite discourse can get. They fail to notice us sneaking past, or I fail to notice their noticing.

We pop into the supply closet so I can secure some of that same gear that Audrine snatched earlier—minus the jet pack, of course. Just because she found calm waters doesn't mean we'll always sail so smooth. If we've got another date with danger tonight, I'd like to come with a covered dish.

I start to strip and the broad gets red, turns around fast. This combat armor is a bit of a squeeze, but lucky me it's made to stretch. I zap, strap, and latch myself into the full fighting rig. Haven't suited up like this since my days back at the academy. It feels good, even if the zips are a touch tight. Audrine hands me a weapon as I spin to face her. Maybe she likes what she sees after all.

Decked down and fully strapped, we slink up a long, crinkled corridor to the cargo hold. The door is crunched twelve ways from Tuesday, so we shimmy through a gap in the slidelock one at a time. The hold looks just like it did in the holotape. Row after row of massive shelves stacked high with locked metal boxes. Audrine taps a toe. "And just what could you possibly want in here?"

I give her a great big grin for an answer.

She walks over to the nearest chest and tries to pry the lid.

"Locked tighter than a nun's knees?" I ask quietly.

"What do you think?" she says.

I shush her and whisper a reply.

"Let's keep it down, huh doll? I'd rather that rather-violent AI out there not watch us get rude in here."

I tap on the locked box before us with both palms.

"Just how do you expect to get inside?" she says.

I smile again and pull something out of my pocket.

"I found a skeleton key," I say. "Open sesame!"

I press something up to the lock interface and it beeps and whistles in acknowledgement. The hydraulics kick on and the box whips open. Audrine frowns, then reaches down to snatch the 'key' from my closed fist. "What is that? What do you have?" she says, tugging at my fingers.

I let her pry them apart.

The good doctor's mummified thumb spills out onto the floor. Audrine starts to scream but I throw a mitt over her mouth. I put a finger to my lips and make the intergalactic sign for *shove a sock in it*. There may be some slim chance that TimePilot is too damaged—or otherwise tied up with the synth—to pay us any mind. I'd prefer to keep it that way while we play space pirate in here.

"How in God's name did you—you know what? Nevermind. I don't even want to know."

I reach into the now open container and fish out one of those tallboy BabyNukes. I smile at Audrine again, bouncing the cylinder up and down in my palm. Like a doctored boxing glove, it's heavier than it looks. An unassuming flat metal canister with a couple of buttons built in, to the guys and gals that don't know what three gigatons looks like. A heaping helping of whoop-ass pie to those of us that do.

She grabs my arm and presses the tallboy into my hand, squeezing my fingers around it with her little mitts. Her eyes scream at me—*it's not a toy*. Her mouth only whispers. "What do you plan to do with that thing anyway?"

I flip open a patch on my hip, tuck my treasure inside, and snap it shut. "What does anybody do with a handheld nuclear device, doll?"

She gives me a blank look.

"Whatever the hell he wants to, that's what."

We creep back towards the main hub but stroll inside nonchalant-like. TimePilot and SAMM-E are still knee-deep in stage-nine manic chatter-mode. They don't pay us a lick of attention. Apparently they have quite the score to settle. SAMM-E whips up an important point. "—the only way to c-c-c-confirm that theory is to send the humans back th-th-through the gate."

I butt in.

"Send who where now, rubberguts?"

SAMM-E turns to face me. Seems he has the same predisposition for yakking at the TimePilot logo in the central shaft of the hub. Must be a design feature.

"We would l-l-l-like for the t-t-t-two of you to t-t-travel back to Orbital Defense Corps headq-q-q-q—"

I cut him off again. The last thing I need is these two circuitbreakers making plans for me and my special lady friend. "Yeah, yeah," I say. "You want us to return to mission control. I get it. What for?"

Now it's TimePilot's turn to lay it on me.

"Command must be informed of the coordinates of the terrestrial field generator so that a rescue mission may be sent to repair me and collect my data. My bipedal colleague took it upon himself to activate the gate, despite the fact that mission control had no way of ascertaining our current location."

SAMM-E bursts in. "Which would not have been a p-p-problem if someone hadn't liqui-d-d-dated our human agents!"

TimePilot fires back a retort but I stop the madness.

"Hey! Can it! Both of you! I'm all busted on listening to you two machines bicker like a couple of boozy birds! Were you programmed to do this?" They start to answer but I don't give them the chance. "You know what, I don't care," I say. "It's a rhetorical question. Didn't they teach you about those in the factory?" Once again, I don't leave time to reply. "Did either of you ever consider that nobody *wants* to rescue you?"

The synth starts to mumble and the ship gets dim for a moment.

"Stockton..." Audrine frowns at me.

"Hold on now. I think I might be on to something here. Do you think Proletti found this rock by tossing darts at a star chart? Who's to say he didn't buy the coordinates wholesale from the ODC archives?"

"But why?" Audrine asks.

"So far, this ship sounds like exactly the kind of thing Slick might be looking for. Who knows what a creep like that wants with a big batch of bombs, but I'll bet he wants 'em just the same."

"Sure," Audrine says, "But h—"

"Forget it," I say. I throw a thumb SAMM-E's way. "Tell me why Johnny Stutters over here can't make the trip back to HQ? I'd rather head straight home if it's all the same to you. I'll ring up the commandant from my favorite booth in the back at Shakey's. AstroScout's honor, I will."

SAMM-E looks somewhat hurt by the 'Johnny Stutters' jab—or maybe by the fact that the Corps hung him out to dry—not that it's any skin off my hump. I can't quite read the emotions on his plasticy, pseudo-human face. I'm not even positive he has feelings to hurt; he is an ancient hunk of junk after all. Might predate the psychological simulator chip, for all I know. Either way, I'll be good so long as he doesn't start leaking lubricant tears onto my new shoes.

"I c-c-c-cannot travel through the s-s-s-s-spacegate for t-t-t-technical reasons," the synth says.

I throw my hands up in the air. An explanation from motormouth here will take longer than I care to listen. "TimePilot," I say, "shake it up and spill the beans. Why won't your buddy here make a housecall?"

"That's simple Rob from Earth. SAMM-E's storage modules hold data using a non-quantum, solid-state drive," TimePilot says.

I shake my head. "Give it to me in English," I say.

Audrine handles the translation. "It means that using the SpaceGate will wipe his memory, Stockton."

I mull it over for a moment. On the one hand, this is not what I signed on for when I agreed to help her in that damned ski simulator. This ain't my fight, and I'm not the hero type. None of this nonsense is my idea of a good time. On the other paw, though, I've had enough missiles and mutants and corporate conspiracies for one week. I'm in over my head and a SpaceGate is a SpaceGate at this point. I'd be happy to hand the investigation over to the first person that will take it from me. If he happens to be a good with a gun, that's swell for him.

"Alright, then," I say, "It's got to be us. Let's hit the bricks before I change my mind. Could use a man in uniform around here. If they can spare a whole company it's all the better."

As hesitant as I am to show up uninvited at some top secret military lab, I'm even more anxious to get out of this homicidal rocketship, get off this damned rock, and get back to Earth. I step towards the airlock but nobody follows.

"Unless there's something else we need to know?" I say.

Audrine stands at the hub, icy still, staring at something on the wall. She lifts my left arm up to the interface.

A panel flips open, revealing a familiar sight. It reads *Relativity*, and sure enough, there's the little clock right below. But this timepiece is glitchier than homemade spaghetti-code cooked up by a simian Jet junky; it's gone bananas.

Counts up very quickly, peaks just before the digits read out all nines. Slows as it comes to a stop. Then it rapidly slides back down the scale. When it crosses the last 0, the little + becomes a − and it keeps on cruising.

We stare in silence for a moment.

After it cycles twice my curiosity gets the best of me.

"So we're travelling back in time now?"

"T-T-T-T-Travel to the past is not a p-p-possibility," SAMM-E says. "All current th-th-th-theories and models of the universe prohibit travel to any p-p-p-prior point in a given timeline."

"Well that minus sign isn't just for looks," I say. "Maybe we hopped over to another timeline?" Audrine gives me an eyeful that says 'you ought to know better than that.' I sneer. "Pardon me for not having an advanced degree in particle physics, professor."

"TimePilot," she says, "was this display damaged in the crash? Do your internal logs come up with anything different?"

"No, Laura from Earth," the AI replies. "I detect no malfunction within this system. The display is consistent with my calculations and backup arrays. My logs indicate that the irregularities began shortly *before* the collision that disabled me."

Audrine bites her lip.

"The wave," she says. "The wave threw off your instruments. You can't calculate the dilation because your internal clock system doesn't know how to interpret the effects of the gravitational wave. It's throwing a fault, just like the propulsion system that made you crash."

"This is the most likely scenario, Laura," TimePilot says. "Of course, it is not possible for me to subjectively understand the error within my system—because I am the system and the system is me. I am too close to the problem, so to speak."

Heady talk for a hunk of busted steel and sparking circuits.

"Yeah, yeah," I say, "It's a crying shame. Things are hard all over. What are some of the other possibilities?"

"There are many other possibilities Rob from Earth," TimePilot says. "Because this gravitational wave phenomenon is not fully understood, any number of factors could be at play."

"Well let's hear 'em then." I've had about enough cryptic answers from this murderous wreck of a ship for one lifetime.

"In one scenario, these readings are correct," TimePilot explains. "The gravitational wave may have broken the previously accepted model of relativity. We may be traveling to the past, then to the future. We may be caught in a spacetime vortex—frozen in time, relative to the rest of the universe. We may be any number of things. There can be no certainties when dealing with the unknown."

I grab Audrine's wrist and drag her towards the airlock. "You're wrong about that last bit, TP. We are certainly *wasting* time talking about all this crap. There's not a lot we can do about it now, right? We'll see where we are when we get there. In the meantime, let's scoot."

"Okay. Okay," Audrine says, pulling her arm free.

We pop helmets on and step through the hatch into the airlock chamber. Just as I'm about to pull the lever and shut the slide, the StutterBot steps through with my suitcase in his arms. He brushes Rusty softly, like the suitcase is some kind of tetanus-inducing pet.

"And just where do you think you're going?" I ask.

"I am c-c-c-coming with you," SAMM-E says. "You will need me to f-f-find the original f-f-f-field generator. And to p-p-put in the coordinates. And to s-s-s-send you through."

"J-J-J-Jesus Christ!" I say. "Alright, alright, tag along if you've got to. Just stay out of my way, or I'll take you out of it. Can you squeeze that into your tiny rubber brains?"

The big dumb syntho grins down at me with a face that's just organic enough to dangle somewhere between terrifying and hilarious. I throw the switch. The door slides shut and the airlock steams up as the precious oxygen is recycled back into the life support system. It whistles for a few seconds before Audrine undogs the hatch to the open surface of Seren Luna.

The hovercycle wreckage lies mangled on the front lawn. It smolders from a handful of fissures in the hull, randomly belching fat carrots of thin, white smoke. I guess the tow service ain't so good out here. This statue of twisted metal will probably be frozen here for the rest of time, however short that may be.

Parked behind the wreck is an enormous metal cylinder, floating a few feet above the rocky surface on stubby stilts. "Is that the shuttle? From the AlpineSim complex? Wow honey," I say. "Couldn't find anything less conspicuous?"

Audrine shrugs it off.

"A lady's got to travel in style," she says. "And besides, I checked the security voicecom channels. They were all dead." She yanks an emergency release on the hovershuttle hatch.

"The voice channels were dead? Or the security goons were?" I say, stepping up into the wide, ritzy cabin. "That's a big difference to a guy like me, doll."

"Take your pick," Audrine says. "Like I said before, the resort is empty. If anyone is still around, I think they've got plenty of problems to deal with, without worrying about us."

"I hope you're right, kid."

She takes Rusty from the synth and plops him down on the polished marble floor. The shuttle awakens with a soft rumble.

"So long, TimePilot," I say, with a salute. "See you never."

181

EIGHTEEN

Compared to the stark utility of the crash-landed starship, this hovershuttle is a plush dreamboat. Painted up pretty in contrasting woodgrains and exotic leathers. I sink into an enormous, overstuffed bench. This ride is like the mobile version of some fancy richo parlor. The only accoutrements I can't find are a big roaring fire, a bearskin rug, and a roomful of snoots clinking brandy-snifters with their pinkies out. Although, they might be in here somewhere, I haven't checked under the seats.

SAMM-E hops in, the door winks shut, and we rumble off the landing struts.

Audrine punches the life support toggle and the cabin pumps in some fresh oxygen. When the air is good to breathe, she tosses her helmet aside and switches the shuttle to manual override. The broad throws the big beast into gear with a tap of her thumb, then pilots us along with her ArmPod. It's not an ideal steering wheel, but then again this yacht doesn't exactly come with the sports package. We putter back into the mushroom stalk kingdom at a leisurely stroll.

As we roll through, it's no secret that the resort is experiencing issues with the power grid. Lights from the rooms above us flicker and pulse wildly, like a bargain basement fireworks finale popping off over our heads. Most of the big lobby bubbles lie dark and empty, and the twinkling starlight throws long, reddish shadows off the metal frames and fancy furniture inside. I keep an eye out for any human activity, but I come up empty-handed. Just one day ago this joint was a bustling beehive of luxury, but that's ancient history now. Today's Seren Luna is abandoned. Dim and dangerous. And as much as I'd like to know who turned off the lights, I'd rather see us get back home alive.

Audrine glides us up to the docking station at the ski lodge and backs the shuttle in square. We pair up with the resort. Two fat, robotic mooring arms reach out and hug us tight as the hatchport slips open in the back of the bus. We're lucky it goes down smooth; the juice is wonky here too. The lights in the shuttlebay flicker like one of those expensive dining room candles. I poke around.

Bent ski poles and cold, half-full mugs of ChocoHot lie littered all over the wood floors. The fireplace sits empty; holoflames burnt down to virtual ashes while the emitters spit very real sparks onto the floor. A red ski patrol jacket lays draped over a softly swaying chairlift. It's the only sign of life in the whole place.

Audrine and I draw down matching multiphase RemChester Z3650 model plasmacasters. I'm happy to have the firepower. These rifles are heavy. Solid. Each one has enough gas in the tank to bury an entire Rooskie platoon under a firehose of white-hot stop-it—or so a childhood stacked with classic warstreams wants me to believe. We click on the underbarrel light rigs and lead the way down the ramp together. SAMM-E has the suitcase in his arms again, following us close. He's gonna spoil the damned thing if I let him keep this up. We pause again at the bottom of the slope to survey the scene.

"Be careful with this bad boy," I say, tapping Audrine's weapon. "We don't want to put any holes in the wall, doll—crack a nut and depressurize the joint."

She gives me that old familiar *you oughta know better* sidelong glance. It's getting to be a regular crowd favorite with this broad, or so she'd like to believe. She tucks the look into a pocket, ready to snatch it out again at a moment's notice.

Then she reaches over and flips a switch on the stock of *my* rifle.

"Phase II," she says. "It'll knock your socks off but won't punch through the hull. That's the 'multi' in multiphase plasmacaster, Private Ames. These weapons were designed for a variety of combat scenarios, including intraship firefights. Marine Corps boarding parties don't want to 'crack a nut' any more than you do, *doll*." She smiles. "The selector switch is right here beside the trigger."

She points to the toggle and winks at me.

I shake my head and smile back at her, snatching another flavor-stick from the box on my belt. "You're quite the history buff, doll."

"Something like that," she says with a frown. "Just remember; the higher the phase you're set to, the more bite you'll get out of each shot. Phase I is non-lethal, at least on paper. Phase III will chew through a mountain. But don't forget, the higher phases also burn through the plasma reserves faster. We didn't bring any spare cells, so show a little self-control, will you?"

I nod, bite down on the salty stick in my mouth, and walk out into the rest of the resort. We take soft, short steps, scanning the hall with wide sweeps of the halogens strapped to our gun barrels. The beams bounce off the polished floor but not much else. Trouble's out there, I can practically taste it. It sounds like melted plastic wires, schizophrenic lights, and slidelocks that pop open and shut all by their lonesome. It smells like silence.

There's a quick pop overhead and we're showered with chunky, stinging sparks. The lady squeals and I don't blame her. The ceiling continues to rain electricity in random fits as we step aside.

"Damn," I say. "This place went to Pittsburgh quick. All fried up on the outside but still raw in the center. Come on Stutters, lead the way. Take us to this extra-special SpaceGate before I change my mind and hoof it the whole way home."

SAMM-E takes a few shuffled steps before pausing to glance back at us. He furiously pets Mr. Wobbles. Going to put a polish on that packbot if he doesn't take a break. The poor syntho must be pretty shaken. Not quite what you'd expect from an Orbital Defense Corps android, but then again, I've never met a brave 'bot before.

Audrine motions him forward gently and the chase is on, slow and steady as it were. He leads us through one empty hallway. Then another and another. Most of the corridors we walk look as trashed as the first one, if not worse. We dig ourselves down a deep hole of mounting repair bills, and I'm glad I'm not the one paying.

This twist wasn't kidding about the place being lonely, either. If I hadn't hung a hat here yesterday, I'd swear it would take a month to wreck and empty a dive this size. But all the shenanigans that cleared this place out went down in less than twenty-four hours' time, and that's a fact worth jotting. I toss it in the old cranial casebook and stay on my toes. It would be nice to have some answers before we bounce back Earthside.

I keep my eyes open for clues until I find a fresh one: a slidelock what needs a closer look. A track of four deep gouges rips across the door's surface and hangs at the edge, like somebody awful strong man-handled a stick of wet butter. Impressive. I'm sure JanosCorp didn't cut any corners on the alloy in these things. Those SnotBabies must come with some seriously sharp can-openers, if they're the ones that did the dice job. And if they aren't, I don't want to hear who did. We've got enough problems on our plate right now.

Audrine starts to comment on the scratched-up door, but I quickly shush her. I expect a vocal protest from her pretty lips, but none's coming. She roasts me silently with hate-filled eyes instead. Good on her. I'm glad I don't need to spell it out. Silence isn't easy on the nerves in a spot like this, but neither is having your face serve as supper for a pack of savages. Audrine understands. Most broads like to babble or giggle when the going gets tight. It's easier to distract yourself than to ignore what's eating you quietly. Either this dame is different, or she's damned good at hiding it.

I pick at the scratches in the door. From a distance they're smooth as good scotch, but up close they're pitted with bubbly little dimples. Apparently those monsters' claws pour like champagne. The pock-marked metal points to some kind of chemical reaction. I file it under *Things We Know about SpaceApes but Wish We Didn't*. I'm sure it's the first of many entries. With a nod of my noggin, I motion us onward.

I keep my peepers peeled. There's not a chance those glowy-eyed little bastards packed up and split. Wherever they've disappeared to, they snatched the guests and staff with them. I'm not so sure I buy Audrine's 'They patched the Gate and everyone got home safe and sound and shared hot fudge sundaes when they got there' routine. Hell, I doubt she really believes it. It's a nice story, but in my line of work, the fairytale endings are few and far between.

The only sign of life I spot is a stray white sweater parked in the crack of a malfunctioning door. The slide opens and shuts on a striped sleeve, until SAMM-E absently brushes it aside as he staggers by. I count the cost of rehabbing the wreckage, and add up damages for a lawsuit of my own to tack on top while we walk.

After we pass the eighteenth ruined painting, I start to critique the synth instead. He's got a wandering lull to his step, zig-zagging down the hallway with a hesitation I've never seen from his kind. Most robots are programmed for efficiency, but this one's got a bolt loose. And here I am without a wrench.

Eventually SAMM-E stops walking and points to an unmarked slidelock. It's a big one, a servicelift from the looks of it. There's a flashing call button and a ragtag army of wrecked luggage piled around it, nearly destroyed. Most of the packbots are fried-to-the-hat and lying in scattered heaps. Shirts and slacks, toiletries and underthings, all the contents are strewn about like the guts from a stuck pig. A couple of the high-end TravelStar cases still have their maglevs engaged. They hover silently next to their fallen comrades. I'm not happy to see the suitcases, to say the least.

I kick one out of the way and round on the synth.

"Say SAMM-E, looks like we weren't the only ones looking for that top secret SpaceGate," I say. "You know, the one only you could lead us to?"

SAMM-E and Audrine exchange a glance.

"What's the catch?" I give him a hard poke in the chest. His fake plastic eyes go wide. This twitchy synth will spill his rubber guts before the dame ever will. He's caught in my headlights, shoots another looksy to the girl. They're giving me the runaround, and now I'm the guy that knows it. What kind of rube do they take me for?

"Never mind her!" I say, giving him another little love tap. "I'm the one that you'll need to worry about if I don't get some answers and I don't get them soon! What's up your slimy syntho sleeve, Stutters? What have you two signed me up for?"

Audrine screams for me to leave him be but I've already snagged him by the shoulders and started to shake. Rusty slips free and clatters to the ground and I hardly notice. Finally, the broad open-hands me right across the kisser. The slap rings out like a clap of thunder in the silence that follows.

I let SAMM-E go and take a step back, too proud to check my lip for blood—although it sure stings like I might ought to.

"I put him up to it," she says meekly, eyes to the floor.

"Up to what?" I say. "Where is he leading us?"

She tosses her tresses aside and looks up at me with those gorgeous greens. Bites down on her lip and squints. "We can't just leave them here, Stockton!"

"Leave who here?" I say. Then I take a look around. The piles of clothes and luggage, the missing guests. It starts adding up. A mangled BuddyBear stares up at me from under a torn yellow dress. It's clear as this broad's complexion. I slap my forehead, sick with myself for missing the obvious motivation lying all around me.

"Oh hell no!" I say.

"Stockton, please just trust me. It's the right thing to do." She puts her paws on my chest. Pleads. The synth tries his damnedest to mirror her puppy dog eyes. With his primitive facial servos, he manages to look only one-half batty, and all the rest just plain slow.

"You haven't given me a lot of reasons to trust you, darling."

She sighs like a hurricane. Heartbroken.

She knows I'm too stubborn to change my mind. She knows what kind of man I am. Where my priorities lie. Here's a guy that looks out for himself and nobody else. Not if he can help it. A sad, lonely old man set in his ways. Her puppy dogs have gone glossy. They shine in the flickering, feeble light of a chandelier on the fritz. Here's *my* shot to pull a fast one.

"But if there are kids down there," I kick over the robobear, "we can't just leave them to croak. Now, there's no promise that anyone's still alive, but we might as well find out for sure—if it helps you sleep at night."

Her mouth hangs, slightly ajar.

I tuck her chin up and smile.

"All you had to do was ask, doll. I'm no monster."

I expect some lip but she lights up instead. Wraps her arms around me and squeezes hard. Like a good handshake that lasts too long. Our rifles rub against each other awkwardly. We're not exactly dressed for an intimate moment. "Besides," I say. "If we find any survivors, they may have some idea just what the hell happened here."

She nods and moves to open the slidelock, but I grab her wrist before she can finger the touchpad.

"Not so fast," I say, looking around. "Whoever is hiding down there, they weren't alone." I point to the luggage. "These clothes didn't rip themselves to ribbons."

Audrine fishes a shredded bikini-top out of the mess with the toe of her boot. Her expression tells me the makeshift fringe isn't just the latest fall fashion. She nods and drops the top back into the pile. I bend over to examine the door closely. It's smooth as can be. "No SnotBaby can-openers touched this thing. There's not a single blemish. Why not?"

"Maybe those monsters decided to move on?" Audrine says. Her tone suggests she doesn't have a lot of faith in that particular diagnosis.

I'd like to offer a second opinion.

"Or maybe it's a setup," I say. "We don't know how smart they are, how many of them there are. Hell we don't even know *what* they are! What we *do* know about these creeps wouldn't pour a shot, and I like my drinks a lot stiffer than just a dash and a splash. That goes double when it comes to mutant alien monsters."

I pop one of the taclights off my rifle barrel and sling the weapon onto my back. Dropping to one knee, I sweep a beam and begin to examine the walls around the doorway. So far it's all vanilla pudding. Maybe the broad is onto something after all. The bogeymen really did turn tail. But wait now. "What's this?"

I find some faint scratching around the edge of a smooth panel, then motion for Audrine to back up and cover me. She pulls her rifle and slides into position a few paces behind me. Checks her toggles and gives me the thumbs-up.

I'm careful to keep the noise down, just in case we're still clinging to any element of surprise. But pressing gently against the panel with my palm gets me nowhere. It's solid, cold and metallic. Just like it looks. I pass on the silent treatment and give it a good knock. A dull clang tells me there's a hollow space behind it. A perfect hidey-hole for a pack of snarling SpaceApes.

"Alright," I say. "I'm going to pop this sucker free. If there's something in there, I want you to zap it and I want you to zap it good. You got it?"

Audrine nods.

I crack my knuckles and take a deep breath.

"On three. One…two…three!"

I throw the panel open and Audrine lets one fly. The wad of burning hot plasma passes maybe an inch from the tip of my sniffer. It makes a woozy whistle as it screams past me and a plopping thud when it wallops whatever's in there. The chemical stench makes my head swim laps.

"Goddamn!" I say.

I fall backwards and let the panel go, lucky to escape with a few singed nose hairs. The metal plate swings back into place with a creak, making a few passes before it slows to a full and complete stop. The hot wad inside crackles and fizzes like bacon in an atomic oven. Pungent tendrils of white smoke stream out of some hidden vents in the wall.

"Whatever it was, I think you got it," I say, waving the acrid stink away from my face. "Did you bag us a big one?"

Audrine shrugs her shoulders.

"Well what in the hell was in there?"

She shrugs again and bites her lip.

"I didn't get a good look at it," she says with a frown.

I glare at her.

"Hey, you said if I see something in there, I should zap it. That's just what I did. I didn't exactly have time for an interview, Detective."

I turn my palms upward.

"Fair enough," I say. "Looks like we've got time for one now. Let's take a peek." I move back in place and put my hand up on the panel's edge. "This time though, let's wait and see what it is before you decide to vaporize it." I pause for a second. "But if it starts to move this way, waste it, okay doll?"

Audrine rolls her eyes at me.

"Would you just open the grate already?"

She doesn't have to tell me twice.

I re-adjust my feet and slowly slide the plate off its hidden latch. This time I give the opening plenty of leeway. My arm is fully extended, on the off-chance Audrine gets trigger happy in spells. She shines her rifle's lamp into the hole for a few seconds, then points the barrel down at the floor. She approaches and leans in, studying the contents.

"Well what was it?" I say.

"Hmmmm." She frowns, reaching into the darkness.

Her arm disappears into the cavity.

"Looks like I bagged a—" she yanks her arm out and tosses a smoldering *something* right into my grill. I drop the panel and bat at my face, lose my footing and spill over backwards onto the floor.

"—sock!" she finishes.

It takes me a moment to catch up. Maybe two or three seconds, tops. But it's plenty of time for Audrine to fall onto the floor next to me, laughing her ass off. She wheezes in tiny breaths between great big witch cackles. Practically choking at her own joke.

Yeah, yeah. She got me good.

I sit up. Pinch the smoking stocking off my chest with two fingers and toss it over a shoulder. The air is filled with the unholy stink of cooling chemical goo and scorched synthetic fibers.

"Not exactly a great time for practical jokes," I mutter.

Her guffaws fade into a series of manic chuckles, bracketed with gasps for air. Finally the giggle train rolls to a slow stop.

"Oh come on," she says. "You're just upset that I scared you. Don't play this off like some kind of security issue. Mean old Mister Sock didn't bite you, did he?" She pokes at my ribs playfully.

Suddenly SAMM-E is above me, both arms outstretched to help us up. "I don't mean to in-t-t-t-trude," he says, "but what exactly are you afraid of?"

Audrine can't resist.

"You mean besides the sock?" she says.

"SAMM-E," I say, ignoring her, "You didn't spot a lick out of the ordinary before this shrew dragged you back to the TimePilot?" Audrine's eyes narrow at the word 'shrew'. Serves her right.

"Well I d-d-did notice that there were luh-less guests about. There were some s-s-s-strange stains in some of the hallways as well, but nothing that posed a th-th-threat," he says. His rubbery lips purse into a perfect O as the rest of his face goes stretchy. It takes me a shake to realize that this is his pre-programmed pondering expression. He's curious. Doesn't know about the SnotBabies.

Not yet he doesn't.

That makes him the perfect sap to run point for our little outfit.

"Oh, okay," I say, pushing the call button for the turbolift repeatedly. Audrine is back to chewing lip and looking antsy. I give her the old 'quiet' eyes. "Well then buddy, why don't you scoot downstairs and make certain there's no new trouble brewing. We'll work on our tans until you get back."

The lift pops open with a friendly ding and I give him a good hard shove inside. He's more solid than he looks. Got some bulk under that butler suit. Heavy, even, I'd say. I'm no robo-connoisseur, but they sure as hell don't make 'em like they used to. He starts to voice a protest but the door slips shut on him. There's a slight rumble as the lift engages, taking SAMM-E for a ride.

When I look back Audrine has Rusty in her crossed arms. She bores into me with angry eyes. "You didn't have to do that. He's just a simple synth."

I shrug.

"Better him than you or me," I say. "Besides, maybe those SnotBabies don't like the taste of synthflesh anymore than I do."

She's still staring.

"Listen doll, he'll be fine," I say. "He's an Orbital Defense Marine, remember?" This last line adjusts her attitude a touch in the right direction. The smile slowly returns to her face.

"In the meantime," I say, "we need to be ready to barbecue whatever comes back up that lift."

I prime my plasmacaster and her grin flies the coop.

"For crying out loud lady! It's just a precaution!" I take Rusty from her and set him down at our feet. We both ready rifles and take a few healthy steps back.

The floor begins to hum once more.

Here comes our man. Hopefully he's got good news and not a liftful of hungry SnotBabies. That was a mighty quick trip, so I'm leaning towards a clear coast in our near future. A turbulence-free trip to snatch some brats and maybe even a dame or two and haul 'em all back to Earth. The ready light flashes on the slidelock as the door slides open.

"So SAMM-E boy," I say. "What did you find down there?"

The lift is empty.

191

NINETEEN

"SAMM-E?! *SAMM-E?!*"

Audrine rushes into the gaping maw of the turbolift.

Not quite ready to commit to the idea that this box is entirely safe, I poke my head around first. The soft mood-lighting inside is a sharp contrast to the flickering harshness behind me. I cut off my taclight. There's no sign of the synth, or anything else for that matter.

"Any chance of this thing kicking on without our say-so?" I ask, glancing at the control unit. It flashes ominously, taunting me with a rhythmic blue glare.

"No," Audrine says. "A pressure plate in the floor prevents outside overrides when the units are occupied and—"

"Outside overrides?" I frown.

"Standard fare, Stockton. Housekeeping's automated systems dispatch cleaning crews through the empty lifts. But like I said, there are failsafes built in. This lift is ours once we step into it."

"Well then explain to me how in the hell it rode back up empty," I say. "I didn't press the call switch, and I don't see any maidbots lined up behind us. Somebody, or something, must have sent it."

"Now that's quite the mystery, isn't it?" she says in her best impression of the wisest of wise guys. "Maybe it was just a glitch, Stockton. The whole electrical grid is shot, in case you hadn't noticed. You don't really think those creatures are smart enough to reprogram the resort utility protocols, do you?"

I shake my head and keep on shaking.

It's a nice story but I'm just window shopping. I've got a nose for trouble and this servicelift smells like last week's sturgeon. I glance up at the roof, check for an escape hatch. Nothing. The inside is smoother than oak-aged rye. There's nowhere for any potential threats to hide. So why don't I feel any better about crawling inside?

"Just so we're clear, you want me to get into the possibly malfunctioning elevator with you?"

The broad beckons me in with a single finger. I sigh and make the sign of the cross. Then I do it again. Finally, against my better judgement, I step inside the lift.

Audrine folds her arms in front of her.

"See?" she says. "Perfectly safe."

"Well maybe you're right, Prince—"

I don't get a chance to finish.

The lights dim, then brighten, then cut out completely. Suddenly the floor is gone. We're falling. Fast. This is no controlled descent. I see the flickering lights of several floors flash past the still-open door. My mind flashes to something my neighbor, a professional liftjockey, used to tell me when I was a kid. "When these things give out," he'd say, tapping a greasy wrench along a busted panel. "It's not the fall that gets you. It's that sudden stop at the end."

The lights cut on and a horrible screech ruins the hearing in my good ear. This is what he was warning me about.

WHAM!

Audrine and I both move from floating three feet above the floor to right smack into it, all in about a split second. I catch the worst of the fall on my chin and my left knee. Practically crack myself in two. My jaw fills with the warm copper flavor of fresh blood. I spit it out, hoping to keep all my molars in my mouth. As I pry my torso off the rifle underneath me, it feels a little like bench-pressing a taxi with the maglevs switched off. I grunt and groan and steal a glance over at Audrine. She got the better end of the landing and don't I know it. Square on the old caboose: nature's air bag.

She stands up. Rubs her rear and frowns.

"I think the ribbing in these suits just saved our lives, Stockton," she says, fingering the honeycombed veins of the reactive armor. An orangey fiber-optic glow flashes along her suit, as if acknowledging her unspoken gratitude.

"I think I'd rather be dead," I moan. "And that screeching noise? That was the emergency brakes cutting on. Let's not forget to send them a card."

I grab my chin and try to wrench my mandible back into place. I'm fairly certain this is what it feels like to get thwomped by a freight tram. Perfectly safe, my foot! I start to tell the broad what we both already know but think better of it. *I Told You So*s are not going to get me anywhere right now.

Audrine helps me to my feet and I let her. I take a quick survey of the scene. Even the lift is whooped. Our view resembles the inside of a tallboy somebody stomped on the sidewalk. The metal around the floor and ceiling is folded up and smushed over itself, ready for the recycling chute.

Speaking of tallboys... I double check the BabyNuke clipped to my waist. Looks to be in one piece, but I don't have the stones to shake it and find out for sure. Instead I stash it away again and take another look around.

The door to the lift is still open, but there ain't much of a view. There's a section of flickering light coming in from the top of the car, maybe ten feet above the soles of our shoes. Below that is nothing but unremarkable smooth alloy: the lift tube sleeve. The empty pipe highway that all the lift cars flow through. There's a decent gap between the car and the sleeve shaft, but that's how it's designed to work. Something about preventing air pressure from building up in the tube as the lifts race through.

I glance up at the light coming from above.

Looks like we missed our stop. A sliver of unremarkable ceiling panel is all I can see through the gap. There's some kind of open room up there, but that's all I can make of it from down here in smooshed-can-land. We've got about twelve inches of clearance to the sleeve from the lift platform. I take a peek down below us and quickly wish I hadn't. The light disappears into a deep darkness that extends to forever for all I know. My stomach goes queasy. I hug the lift car with all my might and try peeking into the abyss again.

194

There's a single large canister pressed between the lift and the tube: one of the emergency brakes.

"Thanks little buddy."

Below that is a lot of nothing.

"Ugh," I say, "I never thought I'd know what it was like to be some piece of vatlab beef, all stuffed up in a can."

"A dented can at that," Audrine says, running her hand over a section of accordioned alloy. She eyes that opening at the top of the door.

"If you can get me up there," she says, "I think I might be able to squeeze through." I give it another glance, then look down at her. Start doing some rough estimates with my fingers.

"I dunno, honey," I say, "Maybe if you lay off the McTasty's for the next couple of years."

"Shut up and pick me up already," she says. She turns to lean over the darkness and places her hands along the smooth side of the exposed tube sleeve. I glance at the abyss under her.

"Better you than me, doll." I place my hands along her smooth sides, and on the count of three, hoist her up to where she can grasp the ledge. She surprises me by pulling her chin up to the floor above us pretty much unaided. Nice guns on this one. I wouldn't have pinned her for a gym rat.

"What's the lowdown, sugar?" I ask.

"I can't see much!" she says. But she says it with a voice that's far too excited for those words. She pulls herself higher until she's almost out of my mitts.

"Well why the hell not?" I ask.

She strains her neck, hauls herself higher still.

"Because… there's a bunch… of luggage… in the way," she says.

"Well that's the first good sign we've seen in miles!"

Audrine yanks completely away from my help now, but it's slim pickings between the top of the lift car and the floor of the stop we missed. She struggles to get her elbows high and find the leverage to slide through the narrow opening of the room above us.

All the extra weight she's packing from the combat gear doesn't help. Neither do the slick metal walls of the lift tube. Her boots slide down and leave rubber streaks as she fights for traction. I debate whether to give her a hand on the only real target I can reach: her well-toned rump.

I very quickly decide against it. Those are some serious boots she's rocking and they are godawful close to my kisser.

"Here… comes… another… good sign," she huffs.

Survivors? A tow truck? I'm swimming in positive possibilities when our old pal Stuttering Samuel pokes his head into the lift. Not exactly the help I was hoping for, but I'm glad to have it just the same.

"W-w-what happened to the lift?" he says, his head cocked sideways.

"Nevermind that, bub," I say. "Give the lady a damned hand, huh?"

"Yes of c-c-c-course," he says.

He disappears from my view once more. Audrine reaches first one, then the other hand up to him. Her breathing returns to normal as the synth reels her in. She looks down at me. Catches me staring. What can I say? She's just poured into that active/reactive get-up.

"Enjoying the view?" she asks, half-angry.

"Best one yet," I say with a wink.

She turns her attention back up to SAMM-E. It's a delicate maneuver. If she turns her head sideways and shimmies exactly right, there's *just* enough clearance for her to slide her chassis under. I can't fathom how the hell they're gonna wrangle me up and out that skinny gap. I might be stuck here waiting for the local LiftDoctor. I might be waiting a while.

Eyeballing the floor, I count tiles and ponder my options until I'm interrupted by a commotion from above. Audrine shouts a string of expletives that would make a longshoreman blush. She's about halfway through the hole. Looks like she was just about ready to squeeze that marvelous keister out of the can.

Was trying. Past tense.

She scurries in reverse now. Tries to get herself back inside the lift. And in a hurry. She sticks both palms to the lift tube and shoves with all her strength, throwing herself back into the elevator. What's gotten into her? Nothing's changed from where I stand, and yet she's crawling back to me about as fast as she can. Guess there's a first time for everything.

Next thing I know she pops out above me.

I move to make the catch but she pummels me like a sack of stones. I do manage to catch the stock of her plasmacaster in my chest. It knocks me into the wall on the far side of the lift and knocks the wind right out of me. We both land splayed out on the floor and we're very quickly back to where we started: falling.

The sudden jolt of her impact shakes the lift loose. We only slide about a foot down the tube track, but that was an important twelve inches. Our exit is gone. That little glimmer of light is gone. We're trapped now. And in the dark.

Audrine crawls up off of me and I growl.

"What the hell was that about?"

She says nothing, but instead flips on her tactights, panning the floor with her plasmacaster. And there it is, her sense of urgency all wrapped up with a bow on top. The head of a particularly globular SnotBaby, spewing gooey mucous out of his severed neckpipes. Stinking like hot garbage. The damned thing bites at us, even without a body. I scoot away from the teeth, my butt on the deck.

"Jesus Load-bearing Christ!" I say, shuffling to my feet. I press my back up against the far wall of the lift. "Were there more of them up there?"

"Oh yes," she says. "Plenty more."

She walks over to the severed head. Raises one of those badass boots high above it, ready to introduce the severed SnotFace to the floor. But she thinks twice, and good thing she does. I'm not so sure the brakes could handle another jolt. Audrine puts a finger to her lips, then boots the little bastard out of the lift like a game-winning field goal. He ricochets off the tube sleeve before dropping through the gap and into the darkness below.

But apparently the elevator has an agenda all its own. It ignores her restraint and breaks anyway. There's a loud *pop-crackle* from beneath me and my feet fly out from under me for a third time. The car jerks sideways, towards the wall behind my back. Audrine tumbles into me, her balance swallowed up by the now-tilted floor. Her outstretched palms slam into the wall above me as she braces herself. I catch a knee to the chin and count stars.

I'm vaguely aware of her impact tilting the lift even further. Our little tin can is rattling around inside this lift tube, or maybe that's just my brains inside my skull. A second, then a third popping noise clangs out from around the circumference of the floor. Each crack jolts us down a little further towards the side under my ass. I shake my head and squeeze my sphincter. Pucker-factor reaches an all-time high.

The floor rises above me like a ramp and a little crack of daylight peeks down once more from the floor we missed. Only I'm not so happy to see it.

That crack of light gets lousy with SnotBaby claws in a hurry. They reach down through the gap and tear at the wall, leaving long scratches in the tube sleeve that are the better part of a half-inch deep. The shrieking claws compete with the groan of metal fatigue roaring out from under my ass. I watch the claws chew up the wall and wonder if our active/reactive armor is harder than the alloy JanosCorp uses for its elevators.

Better than even money says I don't really want to find out.

"Oh my God, poor SAMM-E!" Audrine says, her eyes glued to the SnotBaby octopus reaching down at us.

"SAMM-E?!" I yell over the horrible symphony of screechy scratching and grinding metal. "Forget SAMM-E! Three more E-brakes and this lift is nicked. And you and I right along with it!"

And right on cue, another brake bites the dust, slamming us forward and raining down a confetti of severed SnotBaby arms into our personal space. The claws mostly fall harmlessly into the abyss. Mostly. A lone ranger manages to get a hold of Audrine's shoulder on his way down. Three paper-thin slashes slice right into her armor, as if Boetheon's best work was nothing but a greasy sack of cheap take out. The severed arm finally lets loose, and it tumbles out the open door with its disembodied buddies.

It's all I can do to keep myself from sliding down into the darkness after it. The lift leans hard towards the open shaft, like somebody's trying to shake us out.

"Two more brakes!" I say it as calmly as I can, boot-heels dug into the floor. "We need a can-opener and fast!"

Audrine grabs at the cut in her shoulder but says nothing. Thin tendrils of red liquid leak out slowly from between her fingers. She takes her hand off the wound and gushes puddles.

My basic trauma training kicks in. She's suddenly in danger of bleeding out, and I press my palm into her arm with all I've got. This broad's got other ideas though. She reaches for my rifle with a trembling hand, flicks the phase selector from II to III, and collapses into my lap, unconscious. Damn! Why didn't I think of that earlier? "Phase II packs a punch but Phase III will cut clear through a mountain," I whisper to myself, remembering her words. Let's hope this lift tube isn't too much tougher than your average mountain then.

Struggling to maintain a good grip with my bloody paws, I hold Audrine's limp body against me with one hand and unload the plasmacaster into the exposed tube sleeve with the other. I aim for a body-sized section of the wall, but it's mostly a spray-and-pray affair. I can't watch myself work. The plasma sparks and spits in blinding flashes as it contacts the alloy. The lift quickly fills up with a toxic-scented white smoke that smells and tastes like burning batteries. My eyes and lungs agree. Definitely burning batteries.

I pull the trigger until it clicks. I've used up the damned fuel cell, and even after she warned me! I toss the empty rifle aside and reach for Audrine's. I finally find it in the smoke, still strapped to her back.

I flip her selector to Phase III and put a couple more rounds in the wall for good measure, then drop it back to the webbing cradled around her neck. I need both hands to hold her, just underneath her arms. Can't afford to lose my grip, not where we're going. I hunch over and haul her limp body backwards through the hole I *hope* I just made. My adrenaline pops and fizzes as I make the big, blind step backwards across the black gap.

To my great surprise, my feet find solid ground behind me.

"So far so good." We collapse in a jumble in the darkness on the other side. I hear an orchestra of SnotBaby claws warming up on the floor above us, but they're all playing second fiddle.

A very unpleasant sensation screams across most of my upper body. I peel a lamp from the rifle still slung across Audrine's back and shine it down my arm. Thick smoke pours from bubbling patches across my armor. Some of that melting alloy and plasma must have dripped onto me as we escaped the lift. It looks like I was splashed with a bucket of burning-hot armor-eating amoebas. I'm going to be a puddle on the floor if I don't get this stuff off me, and soon.

I unzip and strip off the top part of my armor in a highway hurry. It hangs below my waist like a half-shed snakeskin. Damned suit doesn't separate into two pieces. There are a handful of palm-sized burn holes in it, still smoldering. I guess it wasn't made to act or react to this kind of abuse.

I take a drink at Audrine.

She's out like a light, despite the scorch marks seething smoke signals onto her torso, too. Given the circumstances, I don't think she'd mind if I helped her get undressed. I unsnap, unlatch and unzip her faster than a kid with a curfew. Luckily she has an undershirt on, although it's drenched with sweat and pockmarked with tiny, crispy-crusted perforations. With her armor peeled, I get a better look at that gash in her shoulder.

"You don't look so hot, doll."

The gash is still gushing like a hose. I rip off a strip of my own undershirt and tie it on tight. The chintzy white fabric quickly soaks through with blood. I need to find some more medical supplies, if she wants a chance in ten of making it to dinner tonight.

I look around for anything I can use to stop the bleeding. The smoke from the hole I punched in the wall is just starting to clear and I finally get a clean view of my handiwork. Not bad. That tube sleeve was a solid six inches thick. And there on the other side is that rotten lift. Doesn't it know how this hero stuff works? It was supposed to plummet right as we leaped to freedom. I hock a juicy one through the hole to show my appreciation.

And wouldn't you know that's the loog that broke the turbolift's back? There's one more pop, and the loose lift bangs its way down the tube into the darkness below. Guess there were only five brakes on this particular model.

The clanging echo of the rogue lift carries up the shaft for a solid minute or two, as I put pressure on Audrine's wound. The sound doesn't end abruptly either. It just kind of fades into a soft mechanical hum as the runaway car falls further down the drop. This service shaft must have a bottom floor somewhere in the seventh circle of Hell.

I drag the girl away from the hole a ways, then turn back around to assess the situation. Audrine and I are huddled in some sort of sub-floor tucked under the room above us. The walls are covered in duct-work, wiring, and pipes of different diameters, but there's not a single first aid kit to be found. This place is not so different from where we first ran into the SnotBabies, behind the HoloBeach. Apparently we've all got a thing for making double dates in maintenance access areas.

Audrine breathes steadily, but only in shallow, wet gasps. She's not in good shape. Something else is off too. A vague, itchy feeling crawls all over my skin like the sheets at an hourly motel, but I grasp at straws to tell myself why.

Then I finger it.

The skitter-skattering of the SnotBabies above us has stopped. I turn around just in time to see the first bastard crawling in through the hole I just hauled us through a moment ago.

That godawful lift was the only thing between the SpaceApe Orchestra and us. Our slimy new friend lets out a terrible hiss as I snatch Audrine's plasmacaster from the padded strap around her neck.

He wastes no time in giving us the bum's rush. I give him first the rifle butt, then a boot to the face, and then a one-way trip down Plasma Slag Lane. He's not done twitching before four more of his buddies join the fiesta.

My caster spits hot death into the fray and the SnotBabies melt like big tubs of McDippinSauce. They dot the floor, each one his own tombstone. A single claw reaches out at me from the nearest puddle of sizzling goo.

The carnage is bathed by only a faint glow coming from the lift tube and the room above. And just like that, the light is blotted out as a swarm of dark shapes slither through the hole. "Alright, round two, you slimy bastards!" I show them my war face before lacing into the second wave.

Click.

"What the hell?"

They're still coming. I pull the trigger once more.

Click.

Clickclickclickclickclick.

Aw, shit! I didn't remember to flip the selector switch back down to Phase I or II. The damned magazine is empty. I burned through the plasma cell! Again! She warned me and I didn't listen and now we're both going to die because of my stupid, thick skull!

I drop the rifle and hunker down in front of her quivering body. I bare my teeth and pull a six-inch vibraknife from the carbonized sheath on my leg.

"Bring it on suckers, I'm not going down without a fight!"

TWENTY

I crouch low like a linebacker, ready to break up the next play, the vibrating knife stiff in my outstretched arm. The SnotBabies scamper at full gallop, an army of little shadows skittering down the short corridor, coming right for me. I can't quite count them because of the mood lighting, but let's just say there's a lot more of them than there are of me. I hope to even those odds a touch.

T-minus two seconds to impact.

I grit my teeth and brandish the electric blade out in front of me. It buzzes angrily in my bloody, sweaty palm. My knuckles are white against the rubber-webbed grip.

Here they come.

The lead bastard takes a flying leap for my throat.

But comes to a screaming stop an inch from my face.

I slowly recognize a gloved hand, wrapped around the SpaceApe's throat. Someone reaches over my shoulder and has caught the damned SnotBaby like a fastball. The glove clamps shut into a tight fist and covers me in snotty monster discharge. The lifeless mutant falls

202

harmlessly to my feet, defeated. Wheezing short gasps that spray a thin goop in jagged spatters from its crushed gullet.

Suddenly I'm shoved aside as whoever just saved my hide takes control of the situation. A tall, dark figure struts past me and dispatches each oncoming enemy as surgically as the first.

Number two gets stomped into the steel deck.

A fierce backhand smashes three and four through a standpipe outlet. The ductwork snaps and hot steam cuts through their gaping guts. They scream like sizzling sausages.

Our savior moves delicately but determinedly. With an efficient grace. Three calm strides to the next target, then he explodes into a vicious strike. Like the human equivalent of my magnum, his limbs are lightning. He floats like a butterfly and stings like a sledgehammer. It's a live-action kung fu flick and I am the lone member of an extremely impressed audience.

Five, six, seven. All drop like pins.

The stranger mops snot down the hallway until he stands alone, beside the still-smoldering hole to the lift tube. He's silhouetted by the light peeking in from above. A proud warrior, posed crane-like amongst a heap of fallen mutant foes.

But he didn't get them all.

Looks like one of the little bastards slipped through his extermination routine. Lucky number eight hisses between the shadowy stranger and me, scampering like a four legged StockRocket for yours truly. I guess this creep knows how to pick his fights. He slips and slides over the pulpy, liquefied remains of his bastard brothers.

I brandish the vibraknife again, feeling more than a little shaky with my hand-to-hand techniques. It's been a few years since I brought a knife to a gunfight and that's how I like to keep it. The monster makes a flying bite at my face. Sticky gruel pours from his round sucker mouth as he takes to the air.

I slice out in front of me with the buzzing blade.

But instead of SnotBaby soufflé, the only thing I manage to carve up is the empty space in front of me. Butter me up, I'm toast. I'm sprayed with a rank wetness as the last remaining monster comes to a screeching halt in midair, not unlike his first friend did a few short seconds ago. Some kind of shiny mechanical squid rips through his slimy chest. Metallic tentacles pop open and catch his pasty torso about a hair's width from my outstretched arm. I nearly drop the knife.

SnotBaby #8 goes down with a mushy thud.

The tentacles curl back up and the entire robosquid retracts itself down a cable snaked along the floor. Right back into the waiting wrist of my guardian angel. Still silhouetted by the light coming in from the tube, my new best friend begins to walk towards me.

I sheath the vibraknife and wipe the sweat, slime and viscera from my brow. Have to stop myself from applauding his performance.

"Gee, thanks pal!" I extend my arm out for a shake. "I'd be lunch without you."

"D-d-d-don't mention it, Mr. Ames," the stranger replies.

"SAMM-E?"

I accidently say it out loud.

"You'd p-p-prefer I was Skip McKendrick?" He shuffles past me and my still outstretched hand. "Let's get a look at M-M-Miss DeMarco," he says, blowing by me. I stand there like a damned fool, my jaw hanging open.

SAMM-E bends down by Audrine's side. The tips of his fingers peel apart to reveal a cabinetful of surgical instruments. Miniature pincers and pliers and scissors and scalpels and tubes erupt from tiny orifices. I watch them dance around on his fingertips until SAMM-E smiles, satisfied with the selection. He pats her head gently, then jabs her jugular with a short needle from one thumb while running a gridded scanning-laser over her sliced-up shoulder with the other.

"Where the hell did you learn to fight like that?" I ask.

He doesn't take his eyes from Audrine's wounds. "P-please Mr. Ames, I need to concentrate. These creatures produce a very p-p-powerful neurotoxin in addition to the f-f-f-flouric acid that coats their m-m-manuum."

Three more needles protrude from his fingers and pierce her sweating, slender neck in rapid succession. She lies motionless.

"Yeah, sure, SAMM-E," I say. "Whatever you say." I should have paid more attention to the sciencestreams back at the academy.

SAMM-E brushes the hair from her face and Audrine quivers softly, her eyes still shut. He yanks the needles free and she starts to convulse violently. The synth holds her shoulders to the floor and motions for me to lend a hand.

I kneel down across from him and cradle her head, staring into his plastic face with terror in my eyes, but SAMM-E's too busy playing DocBot to pay me any mind.

A nozzle in the pad of his index finger showers a fine mist into the three gashes in her shoulder, coating them perfectly without so much as a drop of overspray. The mist fizzes like tonic when it touches her skin. It smells clean and bleachy, like the annual steribath you give your ArmPod.

She continues to seize as the sizzle in her wound dies down after a second or two. SAMM-E swaps out the misting-gun for a new toy. Three braided cables emerge from his ring finger and begin to spin around themselves, their tips glowing white hot. He strokes the twirling tubes down the length of each slash mark exactly once, cauterizing the whole wound in three passes. He doesn't color outside the lines with this tool either.

I'm amazed he can do such delicate work with her flopping around like a sick fish. Her boots make pathetic little thumps on the floor as both of her legs kick out in spastic seizures. Her back arches and falls in a rhythmic beat. Her lips quiver, stretching a half-snarl across her beautiful face. I keep a gentle hold on the back of her neck and stroke her hair softly.

The cauterizer tubes slip back into the synth's finger and one last instrument emerges. A long, evil-looking needle slides out of his pinky knuckle. With the same slow grace he used to dispatch the SnotBabies, he punches that sucker right into the center of her sternum with a thump. Audrine's eyes shoot open as she pops upright, gasping loudly. Every muscle in her body goes tense for a split second before releasing all at once. She falls completely limp just as quickly and collapses back into my lap. Her lips flutter to a stop.

"This is the moment of truth," SAMM-E says. "If I d-d-dosed her correctly, Miss DeMarco's b-body should be metabolizing the antivenin now."

She lies still, breathless. The air is deathly quiet.

An eternity passes.

Finally she erupts into a desperate, wheezy gasp. Her back rises from the floor as she wolfs down a sackful of air. SAMM-E glances at me with a plastic smile plastered across his rubber mug.

"She sh-sh-should be g-g-good as new now," he says, wiping his hands together and standing upright. His half-humanoid face looks almost smug. "I included some nice endorphins to p-p-p-perk her up." He pauses and stares down at me with his arms crossed. "And M-M-Mister Ames?"

I stare up at him, speechless.

"I *am* an Orbital D-D-Defense Marine," he says with a wink. "I w-wouldn't be much of one if I didn't know how to f-f-f-fight."

Well I'll be damned. I guess even the DocBots have to earn their stripes in the Corps.

Audrine comes around, and much sooner than I'd have thought. I hunch over her, still cradling her neck. Her eyes flutter open and look right through me.

"SAMM-E," she says, her voice still a little weak. "I thought you were a goner!"

"Th-th-those things walked right p-p-past me to get down here to you t-t-two," he says. "I'd imagine I d-d-don't smell like dinner t-t-to them."

"They didn't put up much of a fight," I say.

SAMM-E raises an eyebrow. Must have something stuck in his ocular module. "Oh I assure y-y-y-you they are quite d-dangerous to your organic bodies," he says. "Th-these things were designed to k-k-kill. Very highly-developed w-w-weapon systems."

Audrine rises to her elbows. She bends first one, then the other leg. When she's satisfied they both work, she climbs to her feet with some assistance from the synth. She rubs her temples, blinks a few times, and gets right down to business. "So these creatures were engineered, SAMM-E? Were they some kind of ODC experiment?"

He shakes his head. "N-n-not necessarily engineered," he says, "but d-definitely deadly. Whether they were designed by n-natural evolution, or by something else entirely, these creatures were born to k-k-k-kill human beings. The mechanism of t-t-t-toxicity is very s-specific to your human biology and b-brain structure."

"Where did they come from?" Audrine asks.

He walks past us deeper into the dark corridor.

"I a-a-a-assure you, I have n-no earthly idea." He disappears into the darkness. Apparently the lecture is over.

I hear a high-pitched whine, then a sharp clang, and a bright light shines down on him. A flurry of dust motes dance in the beams. Looks like SAMM-E found an access panel to the floor above us.

Thank the Lord. I don't think I could handle having to scurry back through that open lift shaft. The synth pulls himself through the ceiling in a single fluid motion. A second later he drops down two open arms and yanks the broad up.

"What makes you so sure they were made to snack on us, SAMM-E?" I ask, pushing his arms aside. I can pull my own weight. A bead of sweat obscures my vision as I crawl up onto the floor. When I get there, I almost slide back down.

At one time, this must have been some kind of waste processing facility. Right now it's got more in common with a bootleg butchershop. Against one wall, a tram-sized bin is filled with raw trash. Crumpled wrappers, discarded clothes—including quite a few silky robes—large platters of half-eaten food. Typical richo resort stuff. Inside the bin, an automated sifter pulls handfuls of junk onto a conveyor that disappears into the wall. On the other side, a second conveyor hauls the finished product back in. Piles of compressed recycling cubes spill off of the overloaded hover cart onto the floor—a new cube every five seconds or so. This is where it starts to look like a cheap scene from a late night horrorstream.

Many of the cubes lie filled with the bloody husks of human beings in addition to the usual recyclables. There is gore splattered everywhere. The floor. The walls. The ceiling. 'Shredded' is the first word that comes to mind. Suitcases lie strewn about everywhere. I can't keep from imagining this place as a room-sized blendomatic, making TimeTourist-flavored McTastySlurp syrup, and then processing it into little bouillon cubes for distribution.

The majority of the packbots in the room are gashed and smashed, too. A large pile of them fills a doorway and spills back into the room with the servicelift. They're stacked higher than my head so that I can't see through to the other side.

"These poor bastards tried to barricade themselves in with their luggage," I say.

Audrine walks over to a slidelock on the wall between the conveyors, stepping gingerly to avoid the puddles of blood pooling out of the machinery. She tries the release but gets no response. "This door is locked down," she says.

"How's that?"

She reads the error code on the release interface.

"It's a security protocol."

"But then that means—" I say, climbing over the packbot pile into the next room. I emerge in an empty foyer. The only exit is the gaping turbolift tube. "—that those slimy little bastards came down here on the lift." I finish in a near whisper.

Audrine crawls over the luggage heap to see for herself. "How intelligent are these monsters?" she says, after she summits and descends Mount Packmore. We both stare out into the blackness of the lift shaft. It gives my willies the jeebies and my jeebies the creeps.

Before there's time to answer, the luggage pile starts to wake up. One of the packbots at the peak takes a tumble down to Audrine's feet. My head snaps towards the rustle instinctively. My hand finds the knife.

But it's just SAMM-E, coming to join the party.

Apparently he knocked one suitcase loose on his way over. Audrine and I share a short chuckle. Seems she spooked too. But wait. A bag at the bottom is still moving. Now two. The whole pile shakes.

Something *is* under there.

I jump in front of the broad, grab the nearest suitcase and raise it high over my head, ready to crush whatever crawls out right into a paper-thin pancake. Then I plan to smash it some more. I can just make out a skinny little stick of an arm pushing its way out of the stack. I swing for the fences.

But come up short. My arms hit the brakes as something grips both wrists with vice-like pressure.

"N-N-No, Mr. Ames!"

It's that damned synth! I give him a death stare but he doesn't release me. "What's the big idea, budd—" I stop speaking. The packbots fall away to reveal a shivering little creature underneath the pile. However this is no SnotBaby space monster.

It's a little girl.

Chunky plastic specs sit crooked across her cherub face. She's got quite the shiner under her left eye and a whole mess of matching black and blue down her arms and legs. A nest of curly brown locks falls into a pair of disheveled ponytails. Her yellow princess dress is surprisingly clean, if a bit rumpled. She stares up at me with big brown eyes that are filled to the brim with tears and fear. Glancing around the room, the little girl's gaze passes Audrine and sticks there.

Audrine's mood switches gears faster than a RocketSled's digital engine-shifter. From femme fatale to manic mama in the blink of a tiny, bruised eye. The broad's biological instincts overwhelm her all at once and she rushes to our newfound charge. Great. Just what I need. One more female to look after. And a kid at that. Audrine immediately makes with the motherly stuff, wiping grime from the brat's face and cooing sweet nothings into her dirty little ears.

I roll my eyes and turn away.

"What's your name sweetheart?" Audrine asks in a voice she wouldn't dream of using with me. There's silence for a moment. "It's all right, you can tell us," Audrine says. "We're your friends."

I turn back around. The little girl is shaking her head and looking at the ground. She's maybe six or seven, but what the hell do I know about kids?

"It's okay, honey. Everything is going to be just fine. Why don't you tell us your name?" Audrine is still trying to coax an answer from this little burden.

"M-m-mommy?" the little girl says with a tiny, squeak-filled whine. And she talks like the damned robot to boot. Wonderful. This trip just keeps getting better.

"I don't know where your mother is." Audrine pats her on the back. "But we can help you find her! Mr. Ames over there is a police officer, a detective."

I put my hands up defensively. "Oh no. Don't drag me into this."

The little girl takes a long hard look at me through her comically crooked eyeglasses.

"Gee, Mister," she squeaks. "What happened to your clothes?"

"I, uhhh, ummmm, well, you see, there were these horrible little muta—"

Audrine cuts me off.

"Someone messed up our spacesuits!" she practically shouts, stepping between the brat and I. "It's a mystery! We need you to help us solve the case! Can you do that, sweetie?"

The girl peeks around Audrine's leg, summing me up once more. I give her a slanted smile. She looks back at Audrine and gives her a big nod. I guess I pass the stranger-danger litmus after all.

Audrine smiles.

"Wonderful!" she says, in a tone that speaks volumes about her history with kids. "It's a deal then. You help us solve the case of the Great Spacesuit Caper, and we'll help you find your mother. Dealsies?"

Audrine puts out her hand to shake on it.

The little girl reaches up and accepts the offer with a grin and a nod. I turn back around to examine the open lift shaft. I've had just about enough of this nurserystream nonsense.

"There's just one more thing we need to know, sweetie," Audrine says. "What's your name?"

"My name is Bekka. Bekka-Ann Iris D—"

"Wonderful," I say, cutting her short. "Damned glad to meet ya, Becky. Now that we're all old friends let's find a way out of this god-forsaken hellhole."

I can feel Audrine frowning into my back.

"How about we go this way?" a squeaky voice says. I turn around to see Audrine snatch the little monster before she can get a glimpse over the crumbled luggage mound and into the blood-soaked dumpster behind it. Audrine grabs her tiny shoulders and turns Bekka back my way.

"No, no, Bekka," she says firmly. "We already came from that way, it's not sa—" she stops. She's hunched over with her arm around the girl but her sassy greens are glued to something behind me. I spin around quick to see what all the fuss is about.

It's the lift.

The indicator light flashes green above the open lift tube. I shake my head. "It's gotta just be a damned—"

A new lift drops into the open doorway from above.

"—glitch," I say.

This cab has the inner slidelock in place. A fresh, undented tin can. The indicator light cuts to a steady *ON*. SAMM-E and I hurry to make a wall between the ladyfolk and the lift, ready to protect them from whatever comes pouring out.

There's a pleasant DING as the door slides open.

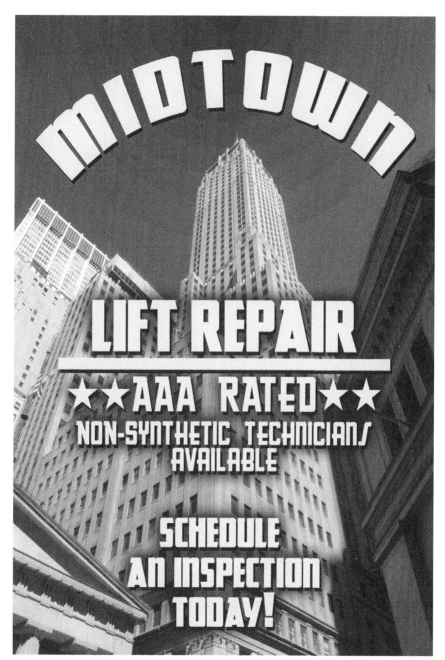

TWENTY-ONE

Except nothing pours out. Nobody steps off the lift.

I stare into the gaping doors, looking for a healthy heap of old-fashioned trouble—the last licks of my daily recommended dose—but I come up hungry. Just when I know the damned thing's empty, a familiar hunk-a-junk hovers out the door. Old Rusty wobbles out with a little gloat in his float. And what the hell is that hanging off his back?

"Could that be a...?"

The suitcase brought a damned BuddyBear! How in the hell did *that* get in there? Rusty rolls right past me to Audrine and Bekka. So much for the loyal luggage routine. The brat bends down to say hello and a blind man can see she's got an eye for the stuffed animal crammed halfway between his clamshell case. Even Audrine looks happy to see the little guy. And why shouldn't she? The rusty bag of bolts did save our hides back there in the StateSuite just a few hours earlier. SAMM-E walks over to join the fun. It's a regular family reunion.

Bekka puts both hands on the bear, tries to tug his fuzzy pelt out from between Rusty's crusty clasps. It's a useless act, of course.

As hard as she yanks, she just tugs the floating packbot along too. SAMM-E looks either constipated or concerned. Audrine chuckles softly to herself as she shakes her head.

I eye them under an angry neanderthal brow.

Finally the synth steps in.

"If y-y-you'll excuse me, young miss," he says, "I can assist you with this t-t-t-task." She looks up at him with big brown eyes as he bends down to free her prize. It should take just one good yank from the syntho's metal mitts.

But before he can separate bear from 'bot, a pang of panic blind-sides me like a case of the trots after a bad burrito. Cold sweat drips down my back and clams my hands. That BuddyBear has no business being in that suitcase. That suitcase has no business riding the lift all by his lonesome. None of this adds up a single-freaking-lick, and I've got a horrible hunch why. I dive for the dames. A panicked shout jumps from of my lungs.

I scoop up the kid in one arm and Audrine in the other, then toss the two skirts at the wall of luggage between the rooms and leap after them. Together, we crash into the top of the pile and tumble down the other side, an avalanche of limbs and torsos and packbots and frightened cries. I wince when we reach the bottom, bracing for the blast of bad news I know is coming.

But nothing happens.

We pop our heads up together to rubberneck. SAMM-E stands with the bear in his hands, holding it out towards the girl. He has a cheesy smile three miles wide glued across his stupid rubber mug. Maybe I was wrong about—

BOOM! SAMM-E's smile goes supernova. Slagged. An explosive roar pinballs off the cramped metal walls and rings around inside my empty skull. I can hear the echoes in my teeth. The pile of luggage beneath us rattles, absorbs a good bit of the impact even, but the blast still knocks us all on our asses. It feels a lot like playing catch with a cannonball.

Rusty must have been packed with charges. The bear? Some kind of plush proximity detonator. A pull-fuse packbot pipebomb.

I peel myself off the floor and quickly take inventory. My face, my legs, both arms. Nothing missing. I scan the twists too. Slightly concussed maybe, but still alive. Shaken, but still stirring. Time to check the synth, or at least what's left of him.

Short licks of flame lap at my ass as I hurdle Mount Packmore once again. An automated dry-sprinkler hisses on and douses us all with a powdery white chemical that tastes like mothball chalkdust and has me sneezing fits. Most of the suitcases lie ripped open and fused together from the terrible heat of the explosion. A technicolor waterfall of melted plastic linings leaks through the shattered-metal shells and pools on the floor. It rains a rainbow of smoldering cloth crumbs, and a thin gray haze fills the air. When the sneezing settles and the dust clears, I spy the synth, alone in the corner.

He sits up, propped against the wall beside the empty elevator shaft, a good six yards from where the blast knocked him off his feet. Both his arms look a lot like the luggage. What's left of them paints matching stains on the steel deck. Loose wires and stringy strands of melted rubber synthskin trail out of his stumps and flirt with the twin puddles parked beside his aluminum keister.

Judging from the frantic animal noises coming from behind me, Bekka is in the process of discovering the blender mess in the other room. I just hope that there's not enough left of her mother for her to make a positive ID.

Altogether, things have turned sour very quickly.

I try to help SAMM-E up without getting his dripping robo-entrails all over my bare arms. I'm mostly successful and get him to his feet with only minor char to the backs of my hands.

"I-I-I-I'm v-v-very sorry, Muh-muh-mEE *EEE bzzz hrkkk*—Mr. Ames-s-s-s," he says. His voice gets hollow, distant. His vocal modulator is on its way out, following the rest of his broken, robotic body.

"Don't sweat it, pal," I say. I give him a pat on the back and he shudders at the impact. I trace a tremor from his neck down to his toes. "We'll get you some new arms, a new suit too. Get you patched up good as new, huh buddy?"

Maybe I believe it's the truth. And maybe I believe that offering comfort for the dying is more important than the truth at a time like this. Even for a stupid synth that nearly got us all blasted to bits.

Audrine climbs back to us with the bleary-eyed little girl in her soot-stained arms. She sets Bekka down. They both look like ghosts, soaked in the fine, white, firefighting powder. The little one's tantrum fades into pure traumatic shock. She just stands there. Silently shivering. Staring into space. Twin trails of tears slice through the chalkdust on her cheeks as she whimpers softly to herself.

I scan for Rusty. It takes me a moment to recognize the smoking heap of metal he's become as my own suitcase. He ain't wobbling any more, that's for sure. The top half of his casing is blown to smithereens. Shredded—like everything else on this Hell-blasted rock. He leaks watery, green coolant along the floor, as his one remaining maglev attempts to drag his metal carcass across the floor. Back to his master. Back to me.

Still faithful, even in death.

I look away. I can't bear to watch. This suitcase has been the best damned friend I've ever known, sad as it sounds. Had him all my life, since I was just a lonely little boy. Even if he wasn't fancy and smart like all the newest models the other kids paraded around town, he was always there to listen to all my hopes and fears and dreams, without judgement. But not anymore he won't be.

I walk to him, scoop him up in both arms. He's still hot from the blast, and he bleeds oily robo-juices all over me. His lift-drive wheezes and sputters against my grip, weak as a baby's breath. I pat him on the casing, tell him it'll be alright. That he's been a good friend.

I take a deep breath.

Then I reach in and yank at his battery leads, one by one, pulling them out. Putting him out of his misery. His one remaining maglev slowly disengages, letting out the last little breath of life in him. I set him back down on the floor where he lay still. Quiet. Dead.

Poor fella. God rest his robo-bones.

I run my grease-stained hands through my hair, trying to think of a plan. Any plan. But I'm too late. There's a tap on my shoulder.

I turn to find that Proletti creep flanked by a squad of JanosCorp security goons, grinning like a twisted sicko and still clutching that goddamned notebook. They must've slithered in through the locked-down slidelock in the other room, a rat-pack of six-foot snakes. They put guns to the broad, and to the little bim, too. One of the goons thwacks me upside the chin with a pistol. My lights go dim, but not all the way out.

SAMM-E starts to make a move. Even without arms, I'd imagine he can hold his own in a tussle. But that slick prick Proletti draws a gilded, silver pistol and puts the whole clip in the synth's chest. *Bangbangbang.*

Audrine screams. The girl covers her eyes.

The synth's facial servos slump to a screaming stop. His mouth moves but no sounds come out. He stumbles, spewing six matching spouts of brownish lube in a perfect fountain arc from the fresh holes in his vest. Finally SAMM-E teeters and falls forward like a domino, splashing into a puddle of his own juices. Slick walks over and gives his lifeless body a kick. I hope that jerk gets pneumatic fluid all over his snobby, designer shoes.

The bastard turns to me and smiles as he blows imaginary smoke from the tip of his ivory-inlaid piece. "Hello, Detective," he says. "Still looking for this?"

He waves the notebook at me before tucking it away.

I want to wipe that shit-eating grin off his face but the goons have got me by the guns something good. I struggle anyway, manage to rip one arm free and use it to pummel the chump on my left's beak. Then I go straight for the craw of the guy that has my other arm. I snatch his neck like an errant endzone pass.

"*Tsk. Tsk. Tsk,*" Proletti clicks at me, reloading. He raises the million-dollar pistol to Audrine's temple. Another of his tamed apes has her in a stranglehold. Her green eyes go wide, blank. "Let's be civil now, Mr. Ames," he says to me in his signature nasally, richo tone. The prancing pronunciations scrape like nails across my eardrums.

"C'mon Proletti," I say, tightening my grip on the goon's throat. "We both know you aren't going to shoot the girl."

A twisted smirk crawls across his face. "No, no. I suppose you're right," he says. He snaps his fingers and one of his lackeys decks Audrine in the mouth. She cries out, but only a little peep escapes. Doesn't want to give him the satisfaction. My gut says this is a broad that's taken a punch before, although I wouldn't have guessed it until just now. A little dribble of blood pools in the corner of her lip.

I glare at him.

"What's the matter, Slick? Can't do the dirty work yourself?" I don't release my iron grip on the goonthroat in my grasp.

But Proletti raises his hand to snap once more and calls my bluff. I drop the arm to my side and sigh, defeated. The freshly freed security slug wheezes in chunky, broken breaths.

"I'm ready to play nice." I show them palms. "Let's just leave the ladies out of this, huh fellas?"

New goons grab me again and old SlickSuit stalks towards me. He runs a matching inlaid ivory comb through his greasy, black pompadour. "That's the privilege of power, Mr. Ames. I don't have to do the dirty work." He tucks the comb away and cracks me in the jaw with the butt of his gun. "Unless of course I feel so inclined."

Proletti pulls a small device from his breast pocket, an MPD remote on a short, silver leash. All of the snotty banker-types use them, what since their ArmPod panels are always covered in imported silk suitsleeves. Slick makes a few selections on the device before returning it to his jacket.

Suddenly there's a new car in the lift tube.

It all comes together, just like that. King Bastard here set the whole thing up. Pulled all the strings for our little misadventure in the lift. Slagged the synth and Rusty too. That stunt with the bear bomb, the SnotBabies and the shredded guests—this creep is behind it all. Proletti nods his greasy head towards the lift. The goons herd us in like livestock and he follows at a leisurely pace. We're not in any hurry. When we're all cozy, the ride rumbles to life. We're going up. I want to know how come. "Where are you taking us, you bastard? Why not just shoot us where we stand and be done with it?"

He laughs. "No, no, that wouldn't do at all, Detective. Not now. It simply wouldn't do. Wouldn't *fit the bill*, to put it in your very common vernacular. Besides, I think I've had a change of heart. You'll get to live after all."

Audrine absently licks the blood from her lip and joins the conversation as the lift slows to a stop. "What bill you creep? What are you talking about, Stephon?"

The slidelock pops open and we step off the elevator into a bright hallway. JanosCorp technicians buzz around us with plasmatorches, sealing slidelocks and welding plexisteel over open ductwork. Hunkering down and shoring-up the perimeter. Keeping those SpaceApes out, but only for themselves. There are no guests to be seen. Besides our little prison detail, I can't find a single soul that's not sporting a navy and orange JanosCorp jumpsuit. These jerks are taking measures to protect their own people, but leaving the paying customers out in the cold.

"Miss DeMarco, I'm disappointed in your familiarity," Proletti says. He leads us, strutting coolly down the hallway. "And I'm sure the details of my plans for you and your friends would only ruin the surprise."

He stops mid-stride and grabs Bekka by the chin, staring into her tiny bruised face with hateful, beady eyes. Audrine and I hold our breath. The girl's chin quivers. But Slick just pats her on the head and moves on.

"Everyone loves a good surprise."

He snickers at his own foul excuse for a joke, just as a guttural growl rumbles in my throat.

We pass into a large atrium. Wait a minute now, I recognize this spot. We're back at the main lobby, back where I first met this prick. We don't stop for a holo-opportunity. He passes right through and turns us into a darkish tunnel. I remember it just fine: the one that leads down to the SpaceGate. We leave a whole mess of armed goons behind us, guarding the entrance. Only Proletti and his handpicked pack of housebroken thugs accompany us down the corridor. Looks like they're marching us someplace private, and I somehow doubt we're headed for the ClubZero grotto.

Unless I'm denser than I think, we're in one hell of a scrape here. I'd like to get our captor chatting, and the best way I know is to run my own mouth, and run it like a racehorse.

"You're not so slick, Proletti," I say. "I catch your grift."

This snags his attention alright. He raises an eyebrow and looks over a shiny shoulder at me. "Enlighten us," he says, spreading his hands and frowning, but only ever so slightly.

"You need a fall guy," I say. "A patsy. To take the blame for the shit-show you made of your resort. We're handy and that's good enough for you. You plan to sell us down the river to cover your own ass." I stop to smile. "How'd I do?"

We come to a halt in the SpaceGate lounge, but mostly because we've run out of hallway. The lux lounge looks about the same as the last time we were here. Fancy and dim. No sign that the SpaceApes have done any vacationing around this way. There's a small crowd of yellow-suited technicians huddled around the departure station machines, tinkering with some of the interface nodes. A fat stack of big white shipping containers stand, hatches agape, in the far corner. I spy crates of tactical equipment and body armor half-unpacked inside them. The same crates Slick had stacked in that vault beside the art gallery, I'd wager. He was prepared for violence all along.

"*Well color me surprised, Mack!*" Proletti says, mocking me. "Although I suppose I should have expected it. You were an investigator in your previous occupation, were you not?" He grins so big it shuts his eyes. "Nevertheless, the cat's out of the bag now, as they say. I'm sure you'll be hearing all about it from the Grand Inquisition panel soon enough."

"Hearing about what?" Audrine asks. Her voice is defiant and proud, her eyes like suns.

"Well you should know better than anyone, Miss DeMarco!" The falsity drips from his words. I recognize the salty smell of pure, unadulterated bullshit, like only a city cop force fed a lifetime of lame excuses can appreciate. I feel compelled to strangle him with his tie until his head pops off, and then strangle him some more. Proletti continues, despite my deepest desires for him to swallow his own tongue in a choking fit.

"It's a timeless tale, really. This cunning caper stars a beautiful raven-haired corpo-terrorist, hired to infiltrate JanosCorp ranks by one of our bitterest rivals, let's say… YangtzeSystems." He grins at her. "This temptress tampers with the sweepstakes so that a rogue contractor—a former homicide detective, absolutely cracked, mind you, and not a terribly gifted investigator to begin with—so that this man can gain access to the resort and go on a horrendous killing spree, thereby ruining Seren Luna's reputation and JanosCorps' credibility. Next thing's next, the Yangtze corporate board moves in on the luxury TimeResort sector, our marketshare becomes their marketshare, and Yangtze stockholders become very wealthy indeed."

"Yada, yada, yada, you're an asshole." I hiss at him. "What kind of chumps would believe a whopper like that?"

"Oh everyone will believe it!" He grins. "My people are absolute experts at this sort of thing. *That* you can count on." He clicks his tongue twice. "I dare venture to say Miss DeMarco may even believe a good portion of it already."

I glance over at Audrine. She has her head down, staring at her toes. Guilty. But why? What's her play in all this? I know his story is a big bowl of pork chop fooey, so why doesn't she? Audrine speaks into her shoes. "They'll make sure that no one is left alive to contradict their story."

"Those people locked up and parfaited down below?" I say.

"An unfortunate necessity." Proletti doesn't bat a lash. He's a rare breed of scum. The kind of criminal that can't spare a single drop of remorse. Not for anyone, anything. In my experience these types of cons are dumb as dirt and frothing mad. Certified bat-shit bonkers. But Slick here is cool, calm. Calculating. A real villain from the comic-streams. It's a bad combination, even on a good day, even for a super-hero. And I've never been much of the hero type.

What kind of rotten tree dropped an apple as bad as Proletti? What rank, golden sewer vomited him up, twisted and broken under that glossy sheen and million-dollar smile? Here's a man that's evil in all the right ways. A social-climbing corporate stooge that's not afraid to kill his way to the top. First he offed this resort full of richos. Next on his list? Us.

"What about the girl?" Audrine wants to know. Jesus, I'd nearly forgotten all about little Bekka in all this commotion. She's been quiet as an ArmPod with a busted battery feed. I look her over. Those big brown eyes stare lifelessly into empty space. Tiny hands tremble at her side. Mouth all a-quiver. The Southside Smile, we used to call it down at the station. Grade-A shellshock.

"She may prove useful," Proletti says. He walks over and pets her gingerly on the head. "The young ones are always so impressionable at this age. I'm sure she'd love to corroborate our side of the story, with a little encouragement, of course."

"You bastard!" I say, flexing against my captors. Struggling to get near enough to bite his pretty little nose clean off and spit it in his eye.

Proletti fakes a yawn.

"Enough of this drudgery, let's get the two of you home so you can stand trial for your *heinous* crimes." He turns to the technicians. "Gentlemen are we ready to send our guests away?"

The jumpsuits argue amongst themselves for a moment. There's a brief eruption of hushed shouts and rapid-fire finger pointing.

"Well?!" Stephon Proletti is a man used to snappy answers.

One of the WrenchMonkeys speaks up. "Almost ready sir," the stooge says, rubbing sweaty palms on his golden coveralls.

Proletti stomps over to them. "What do you mean, *almost ready*? How long can it take you to turn one blasted machine back on!"

The outspoken tech suddenly finds the floor very interesting. "Well, ah, you see, we lost the homing transmission loop when you requested we cut the system offline." Proletti stares at him in angry silence. "And we *are* back online now, fully functional... on our end."

On our end. I don't like the sound of that.

Proletti practically foams.

"Then. What. Are. You. Waiting for?"

Another technician speaks up.

"We aren't getting a response signal from the target, sir," he says. "The station back on Earth isn't broadcasting. At least not to us... it could be any sort of interfer—"

Proletti interrupts.

"Send them anyway," he says.

"Sir?" the technician says.

Proletti repeats himself.

"Send. Them. Anyway."

"Sir if the attenuator needs recalibrating they may never reach the station on Earth. Even a narrow margin of err—"

Proletti stabs the man in the chest with a pair of pointed fingers. "Perhaps you'd like to go first AND SEE IF I GIVE A DAMN!" He raises his silver pistol to this WrenchMonkey's golden gut.

The man backs away slowly. "No, sir," he says, snapping to attention. "Ready for departure. At your mark." These JanosCorp cronies *oughta* be accustomed to abusive bosses by now. This fella must be new on the job. Fresh meat from the henchman temp agency.

Proletti snaps his fingers and they push the three of us towards the deepscan machines.

"Do try to stay still," Slick says. "We'd hate for you to come out the other side with... imperfections."

We receive our scans like good little dogs. Three passes of the bright red laser grid inside a big glass tube and the machine dings completion. Three Security goons haul over a trio of floating maglev restraint tables. There's not enough goon to go around, to strap each one of us in and keep a weapon trained on all of us at once, so we take turns.

Someone shoves me towards the table. They latch me down, ignoring my bared teeth. I don't know what they make these tables for, but it's definitely not for comfort. I feel like a stiff on a slab and I'm sure I will be soon enough.

I can just barely lift my head up to glance around as they push me into the transmission chamber. I must look a lot like a frozen dinner getting tossed into the EasyNuke. The goons grab Audrine by the forearm and twist her wrist into one of the magnetic restraints.

From my vantage point, I've got a great view of the ceiling. The crystal danglies from a godawful-fancy chandelier shimmy and shake.

Something is crawling around up there.

A lump forms in my throat.

One of the oval-shaped overhead panels drops out and crashes to the floor with a clang. A big ball of snarling mucus pours out the fresh hole into the center of the room. Guess those selfish engineers hadn't gotten around to sealing up the SpaceGate terminal yet.

A dozen snarling SnotBabies rip right into the heart of the JanosCorp gang. The technicians try to run for it, but they're on the wrong side of the room for an escape. They sprint right into the fruckus. Three golden jumpsuits come out the other side with a new friend or two ripping them to pieces.

The others don't come out at all.

The goons put up more of a fight response, although it goes just about as well for them. The element of surprise hangs a heavy advantage for these snarling SpaceApes. They're ambush predators, through and through.

Audrine manages to wrangle the situation to her advantage as fast as she can. She quickly swings the table—still attached to her wrist—out in front of her to clear some space. Knocks the closest two goons right into the twisting tornado of teeth and claws and rotten, venomous slobber. Rotating herself around the transmission chamber entrance, Audrine finds the interface console and gets to tapping on the glass. She finishes swiping her last command and snatches something up from a little cubby in the console. Lickety split, she spins back around, swooping Bekka up in the process. She keeps the table between herself and the fray the whole time.

I'm impressed, to say the least.

Audrine takes her free hand and pops something into Bekka's, then mine, then her own mouth. "Hurry up and swallow," she says. "We don't have much time. The wormhole generator will kick on any second now. You want to be asleep when it takes you apart, trust me."

Sure enough, what started as a quiet hum from the equipment behind us very quickly grows into a thunderous roar. The floor begins to vibrate.

"Jesus, you're beautiful," I say, my words all but lost in the bloody chaos and the sweet rumble of the machinery. I get one last glimpse of Proletti, backed into a corner and bleeding, surrounded by snarling SnotBabies, before the transmission chamber clamps shut and the pill takes hold. My lids get heavy.

Then darkness.

TWENTY-TWO

Dear sweet Lord, that technician was right!

We've missed the mark. That lousy planetside SpaceGate station whiffed. Dropped the ball, and us along with it. My sleeping pill wears off much too quickly, and I'm either awake or dead. Floating through the empty vacuum of space, a swirling cloud of teensy smileycon particles. There was no resonance restabilizer to put my body back together. I don't feel anything at all like a smileycon. It's pitch black. Freezing. So cold, I can't feel anything beyond a nightmarish sense of dread and desperation. A deafening silence, like thunder, weighs down on me.

This is what the absolute zero, dead cold of the universe feels like. This is what all of existence will return to, someday. When all the stars burn out, all the planets stop spinning. Long after the last wisps of sentient life have gone poof, and disappeared into the endless night. When entropy plays out its final hand, this is all that will be left. The cold. The darkness. The silence. Pure emptiness. Everything that ever was returned to the nothingness from which it was born.

All our animal instinct, keenly honed senses, and carefully constructed logic, evolved over billions of years of dog-eat-dog survival, none of it counts a lick when we square up against the inevitable. I'm sitting on a ticket to the limited engagement sneak peek preview of the end of the world.

Time passes, but how much? Who's to say? Centuries or seconds. Minutes or millenia. My mind races. It could be ages. Mountains of sand down the hourglass of my existence.

Or even worse, it could be no time at all.

There's no frame of reference. No stimulation. No sensory input. Just the darkness and the bitter cold and my own terrible thoughts to keep me company. I can literally feel the sanity seeping out of my mind, like a slow drip. A leaky gasket at the intersection of every tired neuron, firing all at once. Spilling my consciousness into the ether. How long before I crack? How long before I lose even that leak?

And then it hits me.

If I'm shooting the void as a nebula of disjointed particles, why am I able to form thoughts at all? How can my brain function in a billion little pieces? I am already dead. I must be. My last living second stretches out for an eternity of self-reflection and remorse. Is this the purgatory the priests promised us if we didn't behave? One last chance to review the worthlessness of our sad, short lives?

I reach back, far as I can, searching for the good times, for the memories I don't want to lose. My mother's laughter, tucking me into a child-sized somnopod on a cold February night. My first Knights' WarnerBowl victory parade, twirling a pennant at Coach Wallace himself, from high atop Ma's bony shoulders. There aren't many more moments worth holding onto. In fact, I may as well—

Wait. What was that?

I hear something. A drip. A single drop of something. Was it real? Or just the sound of my consciousness coming apart at the seams? If I hear it again, I'll know it was real. Know that *I'm* real.

An eternity creeps by.

Nothing.

I wonder where in the universe I might be, if I'm actually anywhere at all. I know the wormhole field generators work by digging holes through the fabric of space and time, but I don't know enough about them to place myself anywhere on a map. Am I trapped in some subspace tunnel? Somewhere outside the realm of physical existence, deep in the heart of the dark beyond? Riding a rail of light straight into the Great Big Nowhere? Maybe the rest of the world is going on like normal, just as if I had never been born at all. Maybe we've erased ourselves from the map altogether.

No. There it is again. A gentle, heavenly *plop*. It *must* be real. Am I telling myself this because I believe it, or because I need to believe it? There! A third time! Whatever it is, it's dripping faster now. I must be *somewhere* if there's something to drip, something for it to drip onto. Somewhere with gravity and everything. I've never been so happy to hear a leaky pipe in all my life.

It weeps louder. Quicker. A steady stream of *plips* and *plops* keeps an off-time rhythm that's music to my fragile psyche. A new noise joins the band. "Ughhhhh." It comes from below me. Audrine!

"Audrine!" I say, a little too loudly.

"Unnghhhhhh." There she is again!

"Audrine," I say, this time with the volume down. "Where the hell are we? Get up and get me out of these damned restraints."

"Ughhh. S-S-S-Stockton?" she says, finally coming to. She scuffles below me. "Stockton is that you?"

"Hey lady, that's Detective Ames to you! Now get your sweet ass up and cut me loose."

I consciously decide to keep my doubts about our existence to myself. No need to spill the beans on just how easy it is to rattle my cage. The last thing I need is some amateur headshrinking, especially from *this* broad.

There are scurrying sounds beside me, to the right. Then there are hands on my wrists. Wet hands. I guess Miss DeMarco must have been on the receiving end of those drips.

"Alright, alright you big lug." She finishes unlatching my wrists, my torso, and my legs from the cart. "How about a 'Thank you for saving my life, Audrine'?"

I'll give it to her.

"Thank you for saving my life, Audrine," I say. Then I shake off a shiver that chills me to the spine. "Now where the hell did you save it to? The McTasty's meat locker? Why is it so damned dark and so damned cold in here?"

She clasps my hands and pulls me up to a seated position. My muscles cry out in spastic fits, but I'm glad to find them able to work at all.

"I have no idea," she says.

I touch my temple and shake my skull, even though there's no one to see it in the dark. "You have no idea where you saved us to? Did you just start dialing random contacts on the targeting console?"

I tap for the floor with outstretched toes.

"No," she says. "I have no idea why it's so dark and cold. We *should* be deep in the heart of Orbital Defense Corps Special Operations Command right now. ODC SOCOM."

"Try saying that ten times fast."

She ignores me.

"There *should* be some ugly Gunnery Sergeant demanding to know who we are and where we came from and why he shouldn't shoot us dead right where we stand."

I nod. She's done us solid so far. I'm wrong to quibble. Fat chance I'll swallow my pride and say I'm sorry, though. Her skin's thick enough to cope. She'll live without an authentic apology, but we may still freeze to death in here all the same. We're in a tight fix, and I'd very much like to get out of it.

"Well maybe those JanosCorp engineers were right," I say. "Maybe we missed our mark. Maybe we got lucky and landed at the next terminal. Some Hink-drenched colony-rock way out in the deep stuff. Maybe we're mining comet-tail ice cubes for rocketship cocktail shakers?" I take a shaky step forward. The ground is slick and I can't see a lick, but I manage to stay mostly upright. I hold my arms out for balance.

"Not a chance," Audrine says. "If we didn't hit the target SpaceGate, it's statistically impossible for us to make it anywhere at all. At these distances, the margin for error is slim to none. We're talking hundreds of trillionths of arcseconds here. Picoarcseconds. Almost femtoarcseconds. Remember Stockton, the universe is 99.99% empty space. The quantum attenuation alone would make sure we never got anywhere but where we intended to go."

"I'll take your word for it." I reach out to feel a hard, smooth surface in front of me. "I'm starting to feel like a fish in a bowl here, doll. If this is a Marine base, how do we get them to turn the lights on and let us out?"

"Like this," Audrine says. She takes a deep breath before speaking loudly. Carefully enunciating each syllable. "Oscar Delta X-ray Echo Charlie Uniform Hotel Bloodhound, reporting condition gold. Repeat: condition gold. Requesting security override authorization:

Whiskey Tango Golf Sierra Sierra Tango Foxtrot Three One Four Oh Niner."

"Where in God's Great Uncle Charlie's name did you pull a line like that from?" I ask.

She quickly shushes me. There's no response from outside our fishtank. The soft, steady dripping rings through my head.

Then a low rumble roars to life from above and below us. That steady drip goes quiet, then louder, as a whole bucket of water pours down onto my outstretched hand. I yank it away and shake it like a shaved labrador. The four walls boxing us in fold out and away, and a piercing light beams in through the angular cracks where they split. My eyes, accustomed to the darkness, don't adjust fast enough.

"Damn!" My arm flies up to shield my scorched retinas. A minute later I lower it and open my lids. The chamber lies totally open now, all four walls folded flat into the wet floor. The dripping water slithers into regular, rectangular drains. It slurps and gargles on its way into the pipes. Audrine bends gracefully, at the knees, to collect the limp body of little Bekka. I keep forgetting about the girl. Guess I'd make for a lousy babysitter, but I won't let it ruin my day.

"Is she... okay?" I say.

Audrine stands up cradling the little girl in her arms.

"Just sleeping," she says. "She should be fine. Her little liver can't process the pill as fast as yours or mine. The bigger you are the better your body can metabolize the drugs." She heaves the girl to a shoulder and presses a single finger to her lips, then whispers at me for the girl's sake. "Were you awake for long before I woke up, Stockton?"

I step into the brightness outside the transmission chamber.

"Ages, doll. Absolutely ages."

I have to squint as I scan my surroundings. I stare into the inside of a blurry eggshell, apparently from the wrong side of a half-dozen pints of the strong stuff. Everything's fuzzy and white. Those knock-out pharmies really get my vision zotzed. I smile through the beer goggles anyway. I'm just happy I can see anything at all, blurry or no. It wasn't such a sure bet just a few short minutes ago. And besides, something else is eating me.

"I *do* want to have a little chat about how you knew the coordinates for some top secret Orbital Defense joint, not to mention the access codes to sneak us through the security routine. That's a lot of spook stuff for one skirt to dig up on her day off, doll."

Audrine steps out to join me, still carrying the girl.

"That's because I didn't have to dig them up, Ames. SAMM-E shared them with me. He knew that we'd need the coordinates and the codes, so we practiced memorizing both sets on the ride back to free your sorry butt from TimePilot."

The logic is square, but I can't help but figure this twist's got a bad case of DC amnesia. Maybe she's feeding me the truth. And maybe I'll even buy it for the time being. But I'll be damned if she's giving me the whole burrito. I sit on the slab and wait for my vision to come back.

My eyes finally adjust and I get a good look around. This place *is* a freezer. An icy overcoat swirls over every last detail. Icicle stalactites droop from the ceiling. White stalagmites reach up along conduits on the walls. It explains the dripping water and the goosebumps on my goosebumps, but not much else.

"Guess the ODC is trying to save a little loot on the heating bill, huh?" I give Audrine a friendly poke to the shoulder, but she bends away to avoid my teasing. Bekka sways peacefully in her arms.

"This shouldn't be," she says. She turns to face me and dumps the little sack of rocks into my unwilling arms. I nearly drop the kid a dozen or so times before I finally figure out a decent way to tote the brat. She's not heavy, just the teensiest, tiniest bit cumbersome, what with all her floppy cherub mop and short, ragdoll limbs.

Free from her sleepy burden, Audrine examines the structure around us. It's your standard-issue industrial digs, from the bits and pieces poking through the ice. Dark, unpainted steel beams and severe angles. Spacious. All of it draped in thick, frozen water. A milky white sheen eats at the harsh geometry, coats our world in slick soft curves.

Audrine bends over to brush some frost from a panel. "The life support systems in a facility like this shouldn't be capable of this kind of failure," she says. "Where are the redundant failsafes? The emergency overrides? Even if the fusion core went down, the compressor banks would feed from solar-powered capacitors."

I shrug. "Maybe we can call up the Marine Corps Commandant and ask him who turned out the sun?"

She shakes her head at my joke.

"That's even stranger!" she says. "There's nobody here to talk to! We should have been greeted by a half-dozen security details by now, or at least the freaking SpaceGate operators. So where are they? Where is everyone? Where is *anyone*? Why would the ODC abandon a facility like this?"

She manages to pry a huge sheet of ice from an interface node. It shatters into a thousand jagged pieces at her feet. In small doses, the ice is fragile and translucent. But taken as a whole, it's heavy. Threatening and beautiful. Just like the broad.

"Maybe they had some kind of mechanical problem in this part of the base," I say. "Outdated widgets, chintzy wiring, all that jazz. Maybe some private contractor convinced the ODC brass that it would be cheaper to build a new joint rather than repair the old one. We've been away for a while. It would only make sense that they've upgraded facilities since SAMM-E's time."

"Yeah," she says, fiddling with the interface panel. "Maybe you're right. There's only one way to find out."

She presses one final finger on the screen. A frozen wall in front of us begins to crackle and fuss. The permafrost crumbles away in fat slabs. Cascades of powdery ice-dust—snowflakes even—spill down to cover our feet. A slidelock, previously encrusted shut, groans open before us.

We step through a shower of flakes into the blustery unknown.

TWENTY-THREE

Turns out the unknown ain't all it's cracked up to be. Me? I'm just happy somebody's left the lights on out here.

We walk out into a frozen landscape just as barren as the SpaceGate transmission chamber behind us. Bigger, sure. But decorated in the same monochrome, industrial-tundra design. Audrine and I stand together at the ass-end of a massive corridor. We squint into an ice tunnel wide enough for two magtrams to pass each other comfortably. Damned thing is so long it makes me dizzy just to glimpse for the far side. A frosty sheen blankets everything. It's all ice, all the way down. Feels a lot like stepping into someone's long neglected freezer unit, and we're the leftovers.

I hug Bekka's tiny body close. She doesn't make for a bad little blanket, but we're all three going to turn into ice sculptures if we don't find something warm to wear, and soon. This tactical number might have provided decent insulation if it wasn't torn to tatters around my waist. Audrine's get-up looks just as bad. The thin fabric of my under-shirt gets stiff with frost. Bekka's little legs begin to quiver in my arms, although, thank the Lord, her eyes and yap stay shut.

"The kid's starting to shake, doll. And I ain't far behind her."

"Okay," Audrine says. "First we find warmer clothes. Then we locate the command center and see if we can't track down where all the marines have disappeared to."

I shake my head. "I don't even know where *we've* disappeared to, darlin'. You skirted me earlier, and I'd like to see my questions answered before I start shlepping sleeping beauty here anywhere." I pat Bekka's backside gently. "No holding out now honey: where are we?"

"Skirted you?! I did no such thing!" she says. "Like I most certainly told you earlier, we are in the Orbital Defense Corps Special Operations Command facility. Guess what, *darling?* We're still there!"

I let out a monstrous sigh that flitters through Bekka's banged-up braids before it comes to rest in Audrine's ears. "And where on God's green Earth might that be, beautiful? By the looks of it they stuck this joint somewhere just inside the Arctic Circle!"

"Oh," she said. "I hadn't thought of it that way."

"In my experience your sex seldom does."

She scoffs. "I, uhhhh, well I have no idea where the facility is located, Stockton, geographically speaking. SAMM-E never shared that little detail with me."

"And you didn't think to ask. Go figure."

"No I didn't, Mr. Ames. I didn't think we'd need to stop and ask for directions, now did I?" She flips her hair and snorts. "Although logically speaking, I suppose it would make sense that they would want to build their base someplace remote, this being a top secret military installation and all."

I sigh. "I suppose it would. They did such a swell job of hiding this place, you and I are the only two to find it yet."

"Stockton," she says, pleading. "I know as much as you about it."

"Sure, doll. Whatever you say."

She huffs and spins on her heel. Nearly slips as she stomps away from me, the brat getting heavy in my arms.

We continue our way down the endless ice tube in silence. An hour later we approach the first break in the featureless, snow-capped landscape. An intersection. A welcome break from the snowblind boredom of the last few miles. This new, smaller passageway bisects our tunnel at a perfectly perpendicular ninety-degree angle. I glance down it, unimpressed. It looks just as long and empty as the one we've been walking already, stretching out to forever-and-a-half in both directions.

There's no signage, no identifying markings of any kind, at least none that aren't buried under six inches of snowpack. In other words, there's no reason to change course. But Audrine pulls up and waits. She bites her lip and stares into the long, empty space of the smaller tunnel.

"Tootsies getting tired?" I say, hefting Bekka to my other shoulder.

"Maybe we should take this passage," Audrine says. She cranes her neck to look first down one side, then the other. Then she picks at the icy wall nervously. It's all the same tundra from where I stand.

"Why's that?" I say. "Both sides look just as empty and frozen as the last twenty minutes of this one." I'm very conscious of the fog escaping from my mouth as I speak. "For your sake though, I'll take another peek." There's nothing of note. No one has been here in a long while. I find precisely zero reasons to expect any more out of this passage than the last one. "Well would you look at that? Absolutely nothing new to see!" I shake my head. "Sorry, doll. I say we stick to our guns and stick it out on this main path."

"Listen, *Detective*." I just love it when she puts that vinegar in her voice. "This is the first branch we've found. It's narrower, which means it was probably intended for foot traffic. That first hallway you're so fond of looks like a classic-case equipment transport tunnel." I motion for her to get on with it. She rolls her eyes and continues. "Last time I checked, dearest, we didn't have any equipment to ride besides our own feet. So unless you plan to start carrying me too, I'm going this way!"

She grabs me by the arm and drags me along behind her.

It *is* significantly narrower than the other corridor, but still large enough to make me feel small in comparison. We march for a while, in stony silence. The only sound is the dull electric hum of anemic, orangish floodlights and the raspy crunch of snow under our boots.

After twenty more minutes of monotonous marching, the ice begins to weigh down on me. There's no getting away from it. Everywhere I look, there it is. Little stalactite tentacles tease me from their frozen perches high above us. They taunt me. Tell me, "You'll be ours soon enough, Ames."

I prop Bekka over a shoulder, holding her tight with my right arm. I glare at Audrine from a few paces behind and whisper to myself. "Why do all the worst dames happen to have all the best curves in all the right places? Who can say no to an ass like that?"

"What's that?" Audrine asks.

"Not a thing, doll."

Growling softly, I take a swing at some of the frozen tendrils along the wall. A sheet breaks free. Then another. I feel mildly better. Until ragged chunks of ice cascade down around my ankles in vicious waves. The bastards very nearly tie my boots together.

I pitch forward. The sleeping girl swings out in front of me. Wild, chestnut pigtails flop around and smack me in the face. I attempt to blow loose hairs out of my mouth while using my one free hand as some last-ditch leverage to remain upright.

Audrine puts a hand to her lips, trying to muffle her laughter as I slip and slide across the icy mess I just made. Suddenly, her eyes narrow. She stops walking, turns back, and rushes right past me. "Don't mind us," I say. "Just falling all over ourselves here. No need for you to bother."

When I finally regain my footing, I find Audrine with her nose to a small section of recently pounded wall. Either she's lost her marbles, or this particular patch of white stuff has a secret to hide. I saunter over carefully, still clutching the sleeping kiddie tight. Sure enough, there's something stenciled there, right under the snow. Audrine brushes at it enough to find the serifed corner of what might be a letter, stenciled in heavy type.

Audrine looks up at me with a fresh light in her eyes, and only the faintest hint of "I told you so." It's the first sign we've found that there's even anything worth seeing under all this permafrost. I smile. I don't care who finds it, I just want a ticket out of here. She scrapes away another three feet of wall to reveal the rest of the infographic. *BARRACKS*, it says. I smile wide, then help her blow snow with my free hand.

We peel at the ice together until I can just make out the edge of an enormous slidelock next to the letters. "Bingo," she says. I hand the sleeping child off to Audrine and begin to tear at the wall with both hands, searching for the door controls like some kind of snow-crazed maniac. I clear away what feels like acres of ice before we finally find the damned control panel. It's a beautiful sight, tiny buttons glowing softly green. I poke at the interface with numb, trembling fingers.

"Come on now, Bell Pepper!" I say. "Open sesame!"

Audrine nods eagerly, but this slidelock is somehow even groggier than the last one. I hear the pneumatics yawning inside the gigantic doorframe. The mechanical guts cough snowy flem from steel tubes in an arc around us. We tap frozen toes as the door bitches and moans, then rumbles and tumbles from deep inside. Finally the fat metal slide lurches upward with a wheezy sputter. I close my eyes, blow out a deep breath, and rub my hands together.

But when I open them, the damned thing has stopped. This stupid, dog-dirt door has only climbed about twenty inches off the floor plate.

"Wonderful," I say. "We finally find a way out, and it's guarded by the laziest damned door I ever saw."

It struggles to open the rest of the way, grinding and groaning and sounding altogether unpleasant, but it doesn't make much vertical progress. Gains an inch one second then loses it the next. I give the worthless slab of steel a swift kick to help the process.

"Unghhhh," I say, falling on all fours to peek under the pathetic gap we've gained. I find nothing but darkness on the other side. "Why do they have to make them open up and down? I'd feel so much better shimmying through a nice gap standing upright, like a man oughta."

Audrine eyes the fluctuating space under the slidelock with a finger in her teeth. "Security feature," she says. "They figure it's harder to pry open a five-ton hunk of alloy against the force of gravity." Now she eyes me, both eyebrows arched. She taps me on the chest. "And I imagine they think you'd have to be an idiot to attempt to slide under 10,000 pounds of broken door."

"Aww come on! You serious?"

She nods and points to the gap. "Would you rather make the lady go first?"

I growl and crouch, then spin around on my ass and lay down flat. "*One…. Two…. Three!*" I throw all my weight behind me and scurry under the door as fast as humanly possible. When I stop, I half expect to look down and find a shut slidelock where my legs used to be. Thankfully that's not the case. I mumble an appreciative prayer. Turning over onto my knees, I bend low to peer back under the door, but I'm careful not to put anything other than words underneath the damned thing. "Coming?"

But instead of Audrine's sexy stalks, I get a faceful of kiddy legs as she stuffs Bekka under the door.

"Alright, alright!" I say. Cradling the kid close to my body, I rotate her lifeless lump away from the finicky gap in one smooth-ish motion. Just as quickly, something snaps above us. I glance up and a flurry of flakes powder my nose.

"Brrrr!" I shake my head and spit snow. Looks like those crummy slidelock servos finally decided to plow the tracks. The door starts to creep open, like it should have three minutes ago.

"Ain't that perfect," I mumble angrily. "I crawl under this death trap and Miss *You'd-Hafta-Be-an-Idiot* gets to walk right in."

The slab rises, revealing twenty more inches of Audrine's lovely legs. It climbs higher. Another loud crack sounds. A shower—of sparks this time—plummets from the door jamb. Something inside the door calls it quits and all five tons of metal comes barreling down to the floor. There's a boom that sounds like, well, like someone's just dropped five tons of alloy at my feet. My teeth rattle and my trick knee buckles. I fall forward and smash my skull against the steel of the now shut door. I'm showered with snowflakes as the heavy metal door vibrates like a crash cymbal. And it's not the only thing moving.

There's an explosion of activity in my arms. This damned door woke up the kid! And not in a nice way. She's screaming, we're in the dark, and I am utterly and absolutely hosed here!

"Damnit Audrine!"

I pound on the panel, but there's no response from the other side. If I didn't know any better—and I'm not so sure I don't—I'd say the broad half-planned it this way. Ditched me and the little darling, too. I carefully set Bekka down. She continues to wail like a sabretooth banshee with a broken fang. I flip on my MPD screen to illuminate my face and wrench the friendliest smile I can muster across my frostbitten mug. I'd do just about anything to calm this kid right about now.

"Shhhhh. Shhhh." I pat her head.

Still she sobs.

"You're alright. Everything is alright."

I might as well be shaking her and screaming in her face, for all the good it's doing me. Onward she wails.

"Come on now, kiddo, please? Let's tone it done, huh?"

I grimace, as her shrieks reach world-record volumes and pitch. I can feel my fingernails digging ditches into my palms, but I am somehow powerless to stop them. My patience breaks, all at once.

"For crying out loud would you shove a damned sock in it, pip-squeak?!" The kid shushes up, whimpers softly to herself. Stares at me with big, wet, doe eyes. "Listen ShortStack," I say. The heat dissipates from my voice. "If you and I's gonna be friends, I'm gonna need you to take a chill pill, and I'm gonna need you to take it now."

She pauses for a moment, between sniffles, and pushes her glasses back up her nose. "I dunno Mister Stockton," she says. "It's pretty cold in here already."

I can't read the little twerp any more than I could read a Hink prayer book. Children ain't exactly my cup of DunkRoast, no kidding. I stare into her tiny, blank face with one crinkled brow for a moment. Then I stare some more. Finally I shrug and smirk. "Right-O, kid. Cold as a can of snow pea frogurt. I'm going to scrounge us up some warmer duds fast as I can, but I need you to hang tight and stay tough. You catch me?"

I put out my hand for a shake. She grabs it but doesn't let go.

"Okay," she says. "I can be tough." Those tears are all but dried up, just like that. I smile and nod, then turn to go, but she tugs at my hand before I can take a step. "Can I ask you something, Mister Stockton?"

"Sure, kid."

"Why do you talk so funny?" she says.

My smile turns over. "Because it's the way I talk, kid, that's why. What kind of question is that anyway, Pipsqueak?" I mumble angrily under my breath. A truckload of things about this kid's crappy lineage almost pours out, right into her tiny, pug-nosed mug. But I stop just short. She doesn't need to hear it. She's only a kid, Stockton. She doesn't know any better. Cut her a little slack, huh? I squeeze her shoulder. "Maybe I was born a decade or two too late is all, kid."

She turns her head to the side and scratches at her noggin. "But what does that mean 'you were born too late'?"

I sigh. "It means I watched a lot of moldy 'streams when I was your age, kiddo. Didn't have many friends or an old man to gab with, so I chatted up the stars on our ancient holo—not that they did much chatting back mind you. This was before the interactive 'streams, see?"

She still looks confused.

"It means I learned to speak from all the golden age greats in the classic pictures. Dames and dudes long since gone, Junior. Back when men were men, and women knew their place, especially the teeny tiny ones! Jeezel Petes you're a regular interrogator, aren't you? Got any more questions while we're at it?"

She nods and rubs her bare arms below the poofy sleeves of her princess dress. "Why's it so cold in here anyway?"

Wish I knew the answer to that myself, but that's not what the kid needs to hear. "Somebody must be trying to turn us into

McTastyFreezes," I say. "But don't you worry, LittleBritches, I won't let 'em." She smiles and wraps a second hand around mine as we head off into the darkness.

I swipe on my MPD's flashlight app to blaze a trail before us. It's no DayMaker, but the bank of built-in LEDs keeps us from bumping into each other. I can't quite figure what size room we're breezing into. My ArmPod lamps don't reach all that far and besides, there's a maze of skinny, frozen boxes blocking the view.

The room is laid out in a grid of these narrow igloos: fifteen feet high, about the same long ways. Little more than shoulder width across. Somnobunks would be my guess. Looks about the same size and shape as what we had at the academy, but the details are all buried under a three-foot-thick blanket of snow. Every little thing in these barracks is as frozen-over as the rest of this damned meatlocker.

Could be crates of mink coats under all that ice, and fashion aside, we could use the help. I'm shivering where I stand, and I can't imagine the kiddo's faring much better. But experience tells me the somnobunk stashpods will only open for their owners' pawprints. Handscanner locks, if they're anything like what we used back at the academy. That is, if they'd open at all in this frosted nightmare.

I stop to kick at some ice until I find what's underneath. Sure enough, here lie the personal effects of one Private Björkson. Locked up tight with no key in sight. I growl in frustration before leading us onward through the frozen labyrinth. Maybe we'll luck out and find some first class screw-up that's up and left his pod ajar.

Bekka looks up at me and smiles. I have to hand it to her, she's been a real trooper since our little chat. Not one complaint. Not about the chill, not about the hike. I can feel her tiny hands tremble from the cold, but she's put on a brave face, just like I asked her to. Maybe this kid ain't such bad news after all. She tugs on my hand.

"Hey Mister Stockton?" she says.

"What's up, Tiny?" I shine the light down on her face.

"Where is Miss Audrine?"

"She's… ahhh, she's looking for warmer clothes too," I say. Not exactly a lie. "She wants you and I to find some duds of our own and catch up with her in a bit."

Bekka nods slowly and crinkles her nose, gives her glasses a little ride back up her button. "Maybe *that* man can give us some clothes."

She points into the darkness.

I instinctively reach for a magnum that's not there. Weaponless, I swallow hard and shine my MPD in the direction Bekka gestures.

I let out a little sigh of relief when I see him. Bekka's friend is a frozen stiff. A tiny trail of crystallized blood droplets lead right up to him. Short splatter pattern. Staggered. Somebody, or something, snuck up on this guy. He only got a few steps away before he went down hard. But all this is yesterday's news. From the thickness of the ice covering his corpse, this snowman's been checked in at the Dirtnap Motel for days. Maybe since before the kid was born for all I know.

I approach cautiously anyways. Can never be too careful when it comes to a murder scene. It's like the old saying goes: *What doesn't kill you can still leave you looking awful ugly.* I take a knee and examine the evidence, but Bekka keeps her distance. Our little ice sculpture has one fatal defect. He's headless. "Here's your cause of death, Mr. Coroner." All those years of night school forensics classes have really paid off.

Where his dome should be, a puny puddle of frozen red stuff shines in the low light. My MPD beam reflects across the slick surface of the frozen blood. Now I've seen my share of gore, but something's slightly off about this batch. There's not much of it, for starters. I bend down to take a closer sniff of the scene.

Something pierces the surface of the iceblood. Little spiral towers, rising from the slickness. A couple dozen miniature nodules, raised less than a quarter inch from the flat crimson puddle below. Funnier still, these bumps are clear. Clearer than the ice covering the rest of his body.

I click my tongue and take it in from a few different angles. In all my years as a cop, I never saw anything like these ice spirals. The headless corpse, on the other hand, he was a regular customer. Then again, I never investigated a murder in a meat locker before. It could be any manner of drugs or other impurities that freeze out faster than the rest of the blood collecting in those little spirals. I was always more of a question-the-witness kind of cop—and this chump's not talking. I like to leave the molecular chem-nalysis for the pinheads down in the basement, God bless their pasty, pimpled souls.

I hold my arm closer to shed some more light on the curious frozen nobs. It almost looks like there's something circulating up the spirals. Air bubbles, maybe? It *could* be the saline content of the blood being leached by the cold atmosphere, and then again I could be next in line for pope. "What else would—"

The munchkin breaks my train of thought. "Wow! What happened to him?" she says, giving the stiff a little poke with the soft tip of her ballet slipper. Some of the ice cracks and crumbles away from somewhere near the dead guy's hip. Guess ShortStuff's not so shy after all.

"Somebody turned him into a McTastyFreeze," I say. I'm a little surprised she's taking this so well, what after her reaction to the blood-soaked blend-o-matic back at the resort. Maybe all the cold air has gotten to her head? I eyeball her for a moment, until I'm absolutely sure she's not going to run off screaming.

"Let's see what he's wearing, huh kiddo?"

I begin to drag the corpse away from the blotchy stain where his head used to be. I don't know what those little ice towers are, and I'm not too keen to find out if they bite. Until somebody smarter than me says otherwise, I'm not ready to rule them out as the cause of death. A healthy distance would make me a happy man.

Bekka helps me break the glaze off the body. Kind of a sick game for a kid, but she might as well get used to it if she's gonna hang with a guy like me. Our investigation turns up two crucial pieces of evidence. First, turns out "he" is a "she." And second, she's got a nice set of cold weather duds that she just plain doesn't find fashionable any longer. I begin unfastening the magstraps on her lovely purple parka.

There's a tiny tap on my shoulder.

"What are you doing, Mister Stockton?!" The munchkin's gone mad on me. Hands on her little hips. Scowling like a rabid savage. Is this something she learned from her mother? Picked up from Audrine? Or are all women just born with the innate ability to bust my chops?

"I'm snagging us some warmer clothes, Squirt. I don't know that she needs them any longer."

I get back to working the lady's latches with numb, frozen thumbs.

Bekka shakes a finger at me. "But you can't just *take* them Mister Stockton!" She stomps her foot. Literally puts her foot down, right on my right paw.

"And why is that?" I say, shaking my hand free with a grunt and a grimace.

"Because it's stealing!" she says. "And stealing is wrong." She nods at me with a deadpan stare stuck to her tiny moon-faced mug.

Oh boy. We got a pint-sized samaritan here.

"So you don't want me to steal from the nice headless lady?"

She nods and grins. A big smile. Eyes shut.

"For the love of God! Who raised you, kid? Saint Arnie, heavenly advocate for the dense? Patron saint of suckers and chumps?"

She frowns at me. Her lip begins to quiver.

"Okay, geeze," I say, trying to think my way out of this one. The last thing I want is for her to start bawling again. "What if, uhhh… what if we tossed her a couple of clams for her clothes?"

Bekka scratches her head. "Clams?" she says, frowning.

"Pay her for them, kid. A business transaction."

ShortStuff's face lights up.

"Yeah?" I say. "That works for you?"

She shrugs and nods.

"Alright then." I pretend to fiddle with my MPD for a moment. "How much should we give her? 5,000?"

Another frown.

"10,000 bucks?! Are you nuts, kid?"

She smiles again and nods furiously.

"Okay if you say so, but holy hell you drive a hard bargain!" I pretend to swipe the stiff's forearm. The Ice Lady's ArmPod is frozen solid, if she even has one under there. But it's enough of a show for the kid. Bekka's a happy camper and I can pry the damned gear from this corpse without a full-blown conniption on my hands. We strip the corpse down like a hot ride in a bad part of town.

I give the underlayers to the twerp. She's absolutely swimming in sweaters, but it should be enough to keep her as toasty warm as a stack of hotcakes. Her little hands lose a little of their shiver. She rubs her covered arms and laughs.

I keep the outer shell. It's a woman's parka, but I'll be damned if our frozen friend wasn't a large lady. It fits me pretty nicely, all things considered. I don't quite have the hips to fill it out, but at least I won't be someone's second helping of meat popsicle.

Bekka examines our outfits. She looks ridiculous in her getup—and I can't imagine I'm doing much better—but the smile on her face says that suits her just fine. Her sleeves hang down to the ground and the thick sweaters are nearly ankle-length smocks on her pygmy frame. I'd love to grab an extra layer for Audrine, but we've stripped this snowman down to her skivvies. If we ever see the broad again, I'll gladly give her the coat off my back, so long as she takes the kid with it.

"Well, now what?" I say, waving my MPD lantern and gazing out at the endless maze of somnobunks.

We won't freeze for a while, but I haven't given much thought to our next move. Honestly, I never expected to make it this far.

"We should find Miss Audrine," Bekka says, fidgeting with her droopy sleeves.

"What's the matter kid? You don't like hanging with old Uncle Stockton?"

She stares at me with an angry frown. Taps her foot.

How can something so small give me such a big pain in my ass?

"Alright! Alright!" I say.

"Let's just find her, okay?" the kid says. I don't know how she can be so vulnerable and so bossy at the same time. A teensy bit like a tiny Audrine, even. Or maybe I just bring out the best in the female spirit wherever I find it.

"Right-O, Pipsqueak," I say, shining the beam back the way we came. At least I think that's the way we came. All these rows of ice cubes are starting to look identical. I'm a touch discombobulated, to say the least. I flash my arm the other direction. Eh? Good enough for me.

"This way," I say.

TWENTY-FOUR

I plan to head in one direction until we reach a wall with a door in it. This room is huge, and yet it must have an edge to it somewhere. It can't go on forever, but tell that to my aching legs. If I wasn't positive we weren't crossing our own tracks, I'd think we had traced ten circles through the joint. I set a quick pace and the kid keeps up. "We don't want to be in the icebox any longer than the next guy," I tell her between pants.

She swallows hard and nods.

We pass a cluster of four dull gray pipes, each one about four feet across. Personal transport tubes: single-serving lifts. One hombre per ride. I guess the soldiers stationed here had an easier way to get around, and don't I know why. My sore soles are jealous, but there's no way I'm going to trust a lift when the slidelocks won't even open like they should. One faulty pneumatic pump and we'd be red jelly, smeared across a slice of ice-toast. Little Bekka gazes longingly at the tubes as we lumber past them. I just shake my head and keep moving.

"Not in this lifetime, honey."

I've learned my lesson, walked away from too much trouble to get taken out by a second helping of glitchy lift.

We stomp past several other tube clusters, spaced at regular intervals amongst the frozen bunks. By the time the third one comes and goes, Bekka doesn't even raise her head. She just stares at her toes as they peek out from under her enormous sweaterdress, her dangling sleeves snaking twin trails through the frosty floor behind us.

We walk in silence for an eternity. Bekka grows up. Gets married. Has kids of her own. *Then* we reach the edge of the room. I pat the wall with both hands first to make sure it's not a mirage. The two of us simultaneously slump against the ice, blowing steam. Each breath billows a foggy cloud of vapor like we're a couple of regular chainsmokers. I pop a toothpick between my chompers and eyeball the endless row we just walked. Savoring the fresh cinnamon burn, I watch the beam from my MPD fade into darkness. Next I check on Bekka, impressed the pipsqueak kept pace. How many miles did we hoof? Why would anyone need a room this large? How many damned marines were garrisoned here?

"Twelve thousand, two hundred and seventy-three," Bekka says.

I sit up straight. The hair on the back of my neck does too. Is she reading my mind? "What?" I say, turning to examine her face. I don't spot any signs of mental powers, but then again I don't know what to look for.

"That's how many steps we took," she says, once more tweaking her crooked specs. "I like to count things." She gives me a big toothy grin with a couple of missing members. The kind of smile you'd expect from a pro pug that tends to forget his mouthpiece.

"No kidding?" I stand up and stretch. "Well let's get the hell out of this freezer so you can count something nice like sunbeams or puppydogs or empty bottles of beer."

She takes my hand and rises to her feet.

"Which way, Mister Stockton?" she says, peering first one way down the frozen wall, then the other.

"This way," I say.

I kick in a sheet of ice that looks softer than it isn't. It sits slightly shallower than the rest of the wall. A good place to hide a door. The ice sheet falls in a magnificent shower of snowflakes. Bekka dances in the flurries and manages to wrangle a few stragglers on the tip of her tongue. She grins, smugly satisfied with her catch.

It's amazing, after all we've been through, this little girl still has an appreciation for the little things. She hasn't let tragedy take its toll. Hasn't let life take the kid out of her, least not yet she hasn't. Maybe I could learn a little something, huh? Bekka dances, laughing in the dim light of my ArmPod. I can't stop a smile from sprouting across my own frosty mug, no matter how hard I bite down on the spiced stick clenched between my teeth.

Together we find a slidelock hiding underneath the former ice shelf. With a big, beautiful emergency release lever built right in. Bekka points up at a glorious, softly glowing sign that reads *EXIT*, recently freed from its snowy embrace. A pale red light shines down on our happy faces.

I give the release latch a good tug and the door panel slowly slides down into the floor. I have to chuckle.

"Why couldn't the first door open like this?"

When the door drops below us entirely, something clicks in the wall. I wince, expecting the worst. A shrill klaxon screams, and a previously hidden light emerges above the portway, switches on, and begins to strobe once every few seconds. The alarm startles a jump into me, like sudden, screaming noises often do, but it's painfully obvious no one is coming to investigate our emergency.

I glance down along the wall. Identical lights flash in time with the one above our heads. Other beacons light up at regular intervals along the interior rows, highlighting the transport tube clusters. The emergency lighting illuminates each and every exit for the thousands of ghost soldiers stationed here, one ex-cop, and a little girl.

The immensity of the facility flashes around us and slowly sinks in. The blinking lights form a grid way out into the dark distance, dropping off the horizon before hitting the far wall. It feels like the runway for the world's largest low-orbit shuttle. We wave goodbye and step through the doorway together. A motion sensor catches us trespassing and flips on a bank of cascading light panels built into the floor below our feet. The lights chase each other along our path, glowing faintly through the ice, showing us the way out.

I groan.

The way out involves following the lights up a steep stairwell. I glance upward. The panels rise up as far as I can see, then they go up some more. It must be nice to be an electrical impulse, speeding through a wire. Less legwork. I take a deep breath and mount step numero uno. Before we climb three floors, I've got Bekka on my back once more. I carry her—heavier now than she was an hour ago—and my own weary bones upward and onward.

I climb halfway to heaven with this monkey on my back. The numbers stenciled at each landing fill me with both hope and dread. They count backwards, and I can only hope they show some mercy when we reach sublevel zero. Forty-two becomes twenty-four, then twelve. My calves become angry.

I have to tell Bekka several times that I do not need or want to know how many individual stairs we've climbed. Doesn't stop her from keeping count though. The blaring alarm and the ice slowly disappear with each step, and both are completely gone before I break a second sweat. The stairwell feels a bit warmer as we move up, but it's probably just all this exercise.

"It's good for me," I tell myself between urges to ralph.

Sublevel zero comes and goes with no exit to speak of. I swear under my breath and keep on climbing. Level one. Level two. Now we're counting up, and that's enough counting for me. Each new number stabs daggers into my heart as I see it stenciled on a wall without a doorway. At least when we were counting down I knew how far away we were from zero. We could climb another forty-two flights for all I know.

Thankfully, we don't go quite that far.

Just as my knees start to buckle, we find a bright shiny exit illuminated at level six. I've never been so happy to see a door in all my life. I want to give it a big hug and buy it a drink. Stumbling up to the slidelock with the kid in my arms, I pray aloud that the damned thing will let us through.

"Please open," I say, exhausted. "Dear sweet Lord in heaven, dear Hinky heathen god of doorways and dirt, please don't let this door be locked or I don't know what I'll do."

Just like that it glides ajar. Welcomes us with open arms. No prying off ice sheets, no emergency release latches. Just a good old-fashioned slidelock doing its job and letting people traipse through without a care.

"Thank you, Mr. Door, sir. Excellent performance. Top notch service."

I set the kid down to scope out the scene on the other side. I step out into an unremarkable feeder hallway and poke my head around. I've seen my share of spots just like it. Long empty spaces that hardly get used except for emergencies—or crimes. It's the kind of place dead bodies like to turn up back in the big city. Thankfully, I don't spot any stiffs here. This hallway's cleaner than a politico's doctored rap sheet, and emptier than his promises. It stretches out before us in a gentle curve. Quiet. Peaceful. Delightfully free of ice. I give the kid a quick whistle and we follow the blinking lights down the curve to our left.

It's immediately obvious that the whistling was a poor choice of summons. I awakened something evil in the little monster beside me, and now she won't stuff a sock in it. My once quiet hallway quickly becomes a mad clatter of racket. A little ditty here. Another one there. All strung together-like. First with the whistling. Then with the humming. Then out and out singing. And now all three at once. She rapid-fire switches up the tracks too. Nothing in her crummy, toddler songbook lasts any longer than twelve seconds, and it drives me up the wall and back down the other side.

I let her keep at it for a few minutes, on account of her being so small. On account of me needing to work on my temper if she and I's gonna be pals. "Maybe she'll wear herself out?" I think to myself. Finally though, I've had enough of the ADHDJ act.

"Hey!" I say, maybe a bit too harshly. I turn the burn down a touch. "Why don't you finish one?"

She stops singing. "Finish one of what?" she wants to know.

And here I thought she was a bright kid.

I do some micro-whistling of my own, as an example.

"One of your songs, SmallFry. Don't you know the ending to any of those tunes?"

She's quiet again for a sec. Purses her lips and wiggles her glasses around her nose by scrunching up her face. "But I *am* finishing them. Those *are* the endings."

"Well maybe you ought to write 'em a bit longer then, kiddo. You're making me nuts."

She's quick on the draw.

"Oh I didn't make these up," she says. "I learned them from the 'streams. Mommy says I'm good at learning songs!"

"Is that right?" I say. "Aren't any of the 'streams playing anything longer than ten seconds?"

She thinks for a moment.

"No," she says. She's silent for a while. Thinking. "How long are the songs from your time, Mister Stockton?"

Her answer wallops me like a Newyville slugger.

She's not just some dumb kid singing the first few measures of every song she's ever heard. She's a normal kid from a stupid future. One where nobody has an attention span longer than—well, longer than some spazzy kid's. I start to wonder what the future will hold for a dinosaur like me, if we ever make it back home. I had my issues with the culture from my time, but at least it was mine. I shake my head.

"They were loooooooooooong," I say with a smile.

The kid giggles. We keep strolling around the always-bending, never-ending feeder hallway. Her songs bother me less now that I have an explanation for them, and I take the time to teach her some classics. The moldy oldies, even from my day. Her mother was right; she *is* a quick learner. Good taste too. Really digs the stuff I had to dust off from way back. Groups like Big Boosh and the Banditos, or BögYächter. She can't get enough of "No Time for Love", an early Dust Bunnies single from the *Homemade Cocaine* EP. Just when I start to run short on kid-friendly material, the guidelights blink to a halt up ahead. The end of the line. There's only darkness beyond.

As we approach, Bekka reaches out for my hand once more. I take it and pull her in closer. There's no telling what may be out there. We stand for a moment at the end of the hallway, gazing out into the blackness of the chamber beyond it. The dancing lights glide to a dead stop right under our toes.

I move forward but she's glued to the floor. She tugs at my hand, pulling me back into the light.

"What's the matter, Squirt? Afraid of the dark?"

She shakes her head.

"There's someone out there, Mister Stockton. I can hear them talking."

I get still and take a listen.

"I don't hear anything. Come on Bekka, hitch 'em up and scramble. There's nobody out there."

She shakes her head again and pulls me down close so she can whisper in my ear. "I can hear them talking... in here." She points to her temple.

I nod slowly and give her hand a good squeeze.

"I won't let anything happen to you, ShortStuff. Promise."

She smiles, but with worry in her eyes.

"Come on, kid. It's too late to go back now."

"Are you sure Mister Stockton?" she says.

"Trust me, kid. It's not my first rodeo."

We walk into the pitch black room. Bekka takes a glance back at our happy, musical corridor, but she moves with me. It's dark in here, but our vision will adjust in time. We move slowly. Together. With purpose. Each step is a statement. *We're gonna keep going. We won't stop until we find Audrine and go home.*

It's a slow process, even though the room isn't huge. I'd almost call it another hallway, running perpendicular to the one we popped out of. The guidelights blinking behind us only throw the faintest perspective on things. My ArmPod does the rest, but it doesn't do it well.

This new passage was ransacked at some point in the past. Hard to say how long ago. Plastic wall panels lay ripped-out and bashed-in on either side of us. We tiptoe carefully to avoid tripping over the fiber-wraps, conduits, and other building guts strewn out across the floor. Somebody ripped this place to shreds, but why? Were they looking for something? For someone? Or did they trash the place just to trash it? It's hard to imagine a group of punk kids vandalizing a top secret military base, but that's exactly what it looks like to me.

ShortStack and I step through the corridor and ease out the other side. It dumps us into another much wider corridor that curls around in a great lazy curve, like the architect had a thing for snacking on snails. The wall panels have been picked apart here too, but there's more room for us to maneuver through the entrails. The ceiling wraps around to the far wall in another gentle arc before sloping back to the floor. It's almost like the track for a RocketTube race. A great big frosted donut, and we're the creamy filling. A dim, peachy glow seeps out from around the corner, where the bend disappears behind itself. We move towards it on soft feet. Step toe-to-heel to keep the noise down. The glow gets brighter as we approach. Brighter, but not blinding. It's a dull shine at best. Eventually we round the bend and catch a glimpse of the source.

It's a window. A clear plexisteel porthole carved into the side of our metal snail shell. Bekka and I both stop in our tracks when it comes into view. Our first look at the outside world. A first chance to really get our bearings. Frankly, there's not that much to see. That faint shine is all there is to it. A muddy haze fills the window, the color of rusty, government cheese. I almost second guess myself. Maybe it's not a window at all, just some kind of busted-up holodisplay. But no, there's a real depth behind the haze. It shimmers like a fruity phantom.

A series of terminals sit laid out in front of the window, with a half-dozen big-backed command pods serving them. Looks to me like some kind of fancy flight control deck. We move in for a closer look and a second opinion.

As we approach, the view doesn't change much. This porthole is all kinds of fogged up. Only one significant feature appears: a marking drawn in the fog, like somebody left a note for their sweetie on the bathroom mirror after a steamy shower. It's a symbol. A fancy lower-case "h" with a little crossbar at the top of the straight part, and a little squiggle at the end of the curvy bit.

"What in the hell do you think that means?" I ask the kid. "And who in the hell wrote it?"

She shrugs.

Suddenly one of the big bucket command seats whips into motion. It's a monstrous thing, more chariot than chair. The servos grind and groan like arthritic wrists as it twists around to face us. Like everything else in this joint, it's missed at least the last half-dozen service appointments. The side panels are peppered with a series of stripped, silent projectors, and all the other high-tech bells and whistles pried loose and dangling dead. A modern luxury model with its guts gone to the hock house. The high back of the chair's interface panel blocks the light from the window. Whoever, or whatever, is in the chair is shrouded in darkness. Blacked out.

A heavily modulated, synthetic voice crackles in the stillness.

"It's the symbol for Saturn."

Holy potatoes! This robot wonk really got the drop on us! I'm twice as startled as I am scared, but I toss my dukes up anyway, on the off chance this fella's looking to scrap. The smart money says if he wanted us dead, we'd already be that way. But with the munchkin on my watch, I'm not afraid to hedge our bets and live to tell about it.

"Show yourself!" I say.

He climbs down out of the chair. A fairly little guy, but tell that to the massive machine-pistol in his mitt. The business end smiles squarely into my chest. He's got a dark exposure suit on. ODC Marine

Corps issue. The kind with the articulated rubber joints and the creepy, reflective bug-eyed helmet. The helmet explains the modulated voice, but not much else. I've got questions that still need answering. "Who are you? Where did you come from?"

Slowly, he raises his free hand to unlatch the faceplate on his helmet. First the respiration hose swings down and then the mirrored visor shield flips up. Some very familiar emerald eyes stare back at me.

"Goddamnit Audrine," I say. "You scared the shit out of us!"

"Hey," she says, slapping my face. "Watch your language in front of Bekka!" She holsters her sidearm and I'm glad to see her do it.

Bekka pops out from behind me and gives the lady a big hug. "It's true, Miss Audrine," the kid says. "You scared the shit out of us."

Audrine glares up at me but doesn't reach for the gun.

"These are some interesting clothes you've got on, Bekka," Audrine says. "Let me guess, Mister Stockton dressed you?" Audrine lifts up one of the kid's arms and inspects a dangling, frost-coated sleeve. She uses a practiced, calm falsetto. Her *I'm-freaking-out-but-I-don't-want-you-to-know-it* voice.

Bekka smiles, oblivious.

"Mister Stockton bought them for me from a dead lady!"

Audrine frowns. "Was she dead before you found her? Or did Mister Stockton help her get that way?"

I step between them. "Listen doll, if you're done pointing pistols at us, do you want to explain that symbol you scribbled on the window? Are we on Saturn or are you just doodling?"

Audrine says nothing. She walks over to the porthole and wipes away the moisture, symbol and all, with a gloved hand. A thick, mustardy mist rolls by outside. Droplets of golden liquid race down the exterior of the six-inch-thick glass, like God himself is taking a leak on our little viewport. Wherever we are, it's raining urine, and somebody had asparagus for lunch.

"Nice day," I say, "but you're not answering my question."

"Wait for it," she says.

Just as a blustery gust really gets that mustardy mist whipping, Audrine raises an arm and points out the window. The yellow droplets run horizontal for a moment. As the fog clears, it reveals an industrial wasteland outside. Squat metal cylinders—or what's left of them—dot a wide, wet plain. Scant reminders of the mist hug the surface outside in patches, like soiled bed sheets. Where it's exposed, the rocky ground is pockmarked with little bodies of liquid in a variety of sizes: some PissPuddles, some PissPonds. Here and there an out and out PissLake, but nothing I'd call a Sea of Pee. The metal cylinders poke through the wet and dry parts alike. Their skeletal frames and rust-streaked paneling form a grid that stretches out to our left and right. As the fog bank rolls away into the distance, I can see that this grid extends towards the horizon as well. Side to side and front to back, these moth-eaten silos dominate the landscape.

Soon enough the fog clears completely and the horizon itself comes into view. Beyond it is my answer. Sitting fat in the ruddy-tinted sky is a striped yellow ball surrounded by a sliver of lineated disc. Saturn. I'd recognize the old bitch anywhere. The 'verts for the Yangtze intrasolar cruise lines are always hyping *the beautiful views of our nearest neighbors.* Well, were always hyping. I don't see any pleasure vessels out there now. Just a big creamy planet, a bunch of rings, and a few scattered moons.

"So if that's Saturn," I say, turning to face Audrine, "where the hell are *we?*"

She looks away.

"Oh Stockton, it's just not right," she says. She drops the pretense for now. That tough gal act flutters away with the mist, as she looks out into the rings. Her eyes run watery and red, like she's been bawling. "We must be on Titan, Saturn's largest moon, only—"

I grab her by the shoulders, *make* her look me in the eye. "Spare me the lecture, toots, I know what Titan is. I want to know what's soured up that pretty puss of yours. What's the trouble here? Tell me simple so I'll understand."

"Stockton, if this is Titan, something terrible has happened," she says, wiping her eyes. "It shouldn't look like this. The rust… the rain… the empty station… the colors! They're all wrong." She starts to sob. "Stockton, I wanted to tell you, believe me, I did. But I couldn't, and now I'm afraid it's too late. Now I'm afraid—"

She quits speaking.

"Listen doll," I jump in. "I don't care if Titan puts on a wig and a dress and starts singing showtunes with Jupiter. I just want to get all three of us back to Earth while our heads are still attached to our necks."

She stops me right there. Shoves me so hard I spin around backwards. So I can see what she sees. Her eyes go owly staring past my shoulder.

There are three—no four—big lugs standing no more than twenty feet from us. And I mean big. Tall drinks of water, all four of them.

Decked out head-to-toe in white suits. Maybe contamination gear, maybe pressure suits. Masked. Booted. Gloved. Like the DoomTrooper baddies from a StarCaptain Skip McKendrick flick, or some other classicstream space opera with a half-decent wardrobe budget.

Bekka covers her ears, shuts her eyes and begins screaming the words to that Dust Bunnies track she loved so much. It sounds vile now, erupting from her wheezy little lungs out of fear and madness.

Time slows to a crawl as one of the intruders raises an arm and points something at us. Something long and cylindrical. Something sinister. Audrine reaches for her holster but it's too late. The hair stands up on the back of my neck. I smell ozone. The floor rises to greet me, right on the chin.

Then nothing.

HOMEMADE COCAINE

ONLY FROM

CAPSCOPE RECORDS

The **New EP** *from*

THE

DUSTBUNNIES

FEATURING THE HIT TRACK
"NO TIME FOR LOVE"

TWENTY-FIVE

I'm warm.

It's nice to feel some heat in my bones. No. Scratch that. I'm *too* hot. Goddamned burning up in here. Someone's drained out my blood and replaced it with a big bowl of boiling soup. I pop into a sitting position and my eyes rocket open.

A SnotBaby dives for my face.

He slams into a clear barrier a few inches from the tip of my nose. I wipe a bead of sweat from my brow and pan around.

Hot damn! I'm surrounded by the bastards. A whole freaking colony of the greasy little monsters sits stewing not four feet away from me. Like so many loose women, they claw over each other to get at my tasty, tender man-flesh. Scratching like dopefiends at the glass between us. I stare them down and hope it holds.

The burning sensation slowly fades from my veins.

I ignore the apes best I can and survey the scene. Audrine is still out, sleeping peacefully on the floor beside me. I place a palm over her lips to make sure she's still wheezing. No sign of the kid.

We're cooped up in some kind of clear, plexisteel cube: a cage if I've ever seen one. Measures about eight feet to a side. Smaller than a cheap motel room back home, but not by much.

Thick-ribbed white tubing feeds into the top and out of the bottom of our little cell. Food delivery and, uh, waste collection, would be my guess. The tubes disappear into a river of similar cables swimming around the cage in a torso-thick twist.

These are the only accoutrements.

The area outside our cell is full of hundreds—if not thousands—of identical clear boxes. All the same size, same shape. Piled on top of each other in a perfect grid. It's cages all the way up, all the way down, and all the way around. I don't see any solid structure to the room at all, just neatly racked stacks of clear cubes and a smooth tangle of white tubes tying them all together.

Inside these other cubes it's a goddamned menagerie.

Half of the cells are empty. Most of the occupied cages are brimming with SnotBabies, chewing on each other and blocking the views behind them. I spy a few other creatures here and there. Some smallish songbirds I don't recognize. Across the way I catch a glimpse of furry hooves. There's a single, ginger tomcat in the cube behind us. Puss is not too crazy about the SnotBaby neighbors. He seems to like me well enough though. Stops his hissing and rubs his orange ass up against the glass between us.

"Trust me, Mack," I say to him, "You don't want to get involved."

"Awwww, he likes you."

Audrine's awake.

"Where is—holy shit!" She sees the SpaceApes, then breathes a deep sigh of relief when the plexisteel keeps them out. Holds a flat hand over her chest as countless generations of relieved women have done before her. "Where is Bekka?"

"Oh I told her to take a walk," I say with a shrug.

"Stockton!"

"Listen doll, I know about as much as you. Less even," I say. "You ought to expect that by now. But here's my take: we've been scooped up by the intergalactic dog catchers. We're stuck in a clear kennel and the kid is gone. Any more than that and your guess is as good as mine—and likely better."

She sits cross-legged on the floor and takes in our surroundings.

"Maybe we can find a way out," she says.

"Yeah, I'll ask the SnotBabies next door if they'll have us over for cheese and crackers."

Audrine snorts and begins examining the sides and edges of the cube. She gives the floor a good stomping, then snoops around the corners some more.

"No offense, dollface, but if these guys can't get out," I thumb the SpaceApes behind me, "I don't think we'll have much luck of it."

She stops. Here come the hands on the hips.

"I never took you for a quitter, Stockton," she says. "I thought you were a fighter." She sounds more disappointed than angry.

I have to hand it to her. She's got an insatiable will to survive. She's a real steel daisy, this one, sprouted up through the cracks of some gilded glass garden into something more than just a pretty bloom, waiting to be plucked. This broad knows another kind of hunger. Not the pointed prick of an empty belly, or the raw, animal magnetism of a life of crime, or even the murky gleam of that one last fix. No, she knows the lung-crushing, endless weight of uptown expectations. Of rejected promises that look oh-so sweet in the rearview. She's tough, even by my standards, but here and now she's just plain wrong.

"Being a good fighter means knowing when to take your licks and when to put on your gloves, kid. But if you really want to bust out of here, pry open that drain in the floor and I'll pop this bad boy down there." I pull out the tallboy nuke from my pocket and wave it at her. She raises a finger, but before she can scold me, the air in our little cell turns solid. We're both lifted off the floor. Floating in midair, we can't move a muscle. There's a faint stink of ozone, but nothing looks any different. I can still breathe, which is nice.

"Looks like I struck a nerve."

Apparently I can still speak as well.

Suddenly the cubes around ours begin to boogie. They rearrange themselves as if by magic, clearing a passage for our cage to pop through. It reminds me of a single-player gamestream I used to love as a kid: *CubeIt*.

The boxes slide around smoothly, and our cage zips forward with no delay. Someone's played this game before. Each move is perfect and brilliant. We quickly pick up speed until we are literally flying through a sea of blurry glass. We pass all manner of creatures, great and small, but we're moving too quick to take them in. Some of the cubes get bigger, but only one or two cellmates inside are large enough to recognize in the bumrush.

The front of our cage presses up against a plain white wall and comes to a screeching stop. Normally we'd be kneedeep in Whiplash City, but the solid air cushions our braking bodies perfectly. I don't feel a thing. Beside us, a great gray whale stares us down with an eyeball the size of a coconut pie. He's all alone, floating happily in an enormous clear cube without so much as a drop of water to keep him company. I wink at him then steer my eyes forward.

The wall we've smacked into is perfectly flat, with a thin, milky film to it. Looks like albino toadskin. Little shimmery pulses of light fleck the surface and dance, as if the wall is trying to communicate with us. Like it wants to say "Hi."

"Great. We've been kidnapped by intelligent architecture."

The blinking intensifies until the twinkles come to a point at the front of our cage. Then the wall parts like the Red Sea, or a bad toupee. It grows from a tiny hole to an exact silhouette of our cube faster than I can say "So long, Moby Dick!" The milky sheen is still there, but the solid white mass behind it is gone. The whale waves a massive flipper at us as we're sucked in and spit out from the kennel room, like so much chopped liver.

We pass right through the waxy, blinking membrane into a large open chamber. It takes me a moment to realize that the gravity has changed. Although we were pushed *forward* out of the menagerie, we actually came *up* from the floor of this room. Suspended like grapes in a brick of flavorless Jiggle-Oh gelatin, we hang tight, arms and legs frozen stiff.

Audrine and I face up towards the ceiling of a large dome. It's made of that same milky white material, but there are six sprawling chrome arches that come together above us. They meet at the top and form a ring, surrounding a disk of the toadskin stuff about forty feet directly overhead. This room, like the last one, is bright, but with some trick lighting that seems to come from everywhere and nowhere all at once. I don't spot a single lamp anywhere. Don't see any shadows for that matter either.

The magic lights dim a bit and a booming voice shatters the silence. It's deep. Male, I'd wager. "Greetings, humans." It speaks Universal with the slightest hint of an accent. Not like a voicecom simulator exactly, more like someone that hasn't spoken at all in a very long time. Hesitant. An alien monk breaking his vow of silence to have a chat with yours truly and my special lady friend. I'm flattered.

"Howdy, Chief," I say. "How ya doin'?"

"Stockton!" Audrine gasps.

Maybe it was a bit flippant considering the circumstances. Someday this conversation may be rebroadcast in the historystreams. What with this being Mankind's first encounter with an alien life form and all. I suppose I have it in me to act a touch more refined, like an ambassador for my species oughta, if only for the school kids' sake.

"If released," the voice thunders, "will weapon discharge?"

It takes me a second to translate: If *I'm* released, will I blow this place sky high? That's what I'd want to know if I were in his loafers anyway.

"Nah, I'll play nice," I say. "Promise."

There's a brief silence. The walls sparkle a bit faster than before and then the broad and I are gently lowered to the floor and released. It feels a little like being manhandled by marshmallow bunnies. Firm and soft, all at once. There's no fighting it, not one ounce, but it ain't exactly uncomfortable.

With my feet back on the ground and my muscles free to move again, I get a better lay of the land. Our cage rests on a little platform similar to the chrome ring directly overhead. Then I see them. Those same suited-up lugs that got the drop on us in the freezer station on Titan. The DoomTroopers. Or whoever they might be under those generic white masks. They watch us from a little silver booth built into the base of one of the great chrome arches. I wave, friendly-like, but they stand still, silent. Maybe they don't know the gesture. I can think of a few others I'd like to teach them while I'm at it.

"Place canister on floor," the voice says. There's five of 'em watching. I wonder which one is doing the talking, who's calling the shots. Each one looks exactly identical in those hazmat get-ups. In the meantime, I do as I'm told.

As soon as the nuke hits the floor, the clear walls of the cube unfold around us. A smooth, mirrored walkway rises up through the milky floor, leading us towards the booth. We take a walk, leaving the bomb behind. I wave goodbye to it over my shoulder. As Audrine and I approach, the voice speaks again.

"Please accept apology for confinement. Be aware that release is expedient as containment protocol allows."

The chrome path leads us around to the side of the booth. Right into that white wall. A door-sized gap opens up to allow us through, but that pearly translucent layer is still there: a gauzy curtain that's sure to leave a sticky sap all over us. Audrine and I both stop walking.

"Please enter," the voice says. "Membrane allows passage."

I cautiously put a foot forward. Just like he said, the membrane gives, like nothing were there at all. As I step the rest of me through, I get a taste of it on my bare skin. It's warm and wet and forms to my features with a little elastic bounce. But true to his word, I walk cleanly through to the other side. No residue, no dampness. No acid goo dissolving my eyeballs or parasitic brain worms crawling into my ears to dine on what's left of my mind.

Audrine follows behind me and I notice the blinking lights as they radiate out from the door, shooting around the walls in every direction. When she's walked through, the wall closes up behind her, as if the gap had never been there to begin with.

We stand in a short, empty hallway with our captors. The only visible architecture is the bank of windows that make up the booth. No decorative touches, no filigree or fancy trim. Just smooth, solid shapes in milky white and polished silver. Our hosts tower over us. For crying out loud! Each one must be nine feet tall! My hasty plan to overpower them goes right out the bank of windows beside us. I'll have to hatch from scratch if we want to wriggle free.

"Please follow—" the voice begins, but Audrine cuts him off.

It's my turn to look surprised.

"Where's the girl?" she demands. Good question.

"Young one suffers tissue damage. Requires treatment."

"Take us to her," Audrine says. "Now."

There's a brief pause. I get the feeling they are talking amongst themselves but no words are exchanged, at least none that I can hear with human ears. "Delivery assured at completion of sanitation and reconstructive procedure," our captor says. "Please follow." He turns to the door.

"Like hell," I say and make a break for it. A beeline right to the end of the hallway behind us. I pray my instincts are correct and the doorway will magically open for me when I get there. Or, if these guys are in control of everything—and it sure looks like they might be—I'll be getting a faceful of solid wall, like the cartoon dog on the short end of Kraft E. Rabbit's fake tunnel prank. But for all I know, this may be my one and only shot at escape, so I cross my fingers, lower a shoulder, and sprint for freedom.

Lucky me, the wall opens up with ten feet to go and I pass right through the membrane, lickety split. I book it right through into another white passage, but with no windows this time. Glancing over a shoulder, I continue my dash to freedom. The doorway slurps shut behind me and shuts out Audrine and the tall, white aliens. They don't give chase, so I slow my roll a touch. No telling how long it'll take me to escape, plus it's been awhile since I took some laps on a treadmill. My bum knee starts to give me grief, and I continue, slower still, and with a cautious hitch to my step. Huffing and puffing, I approach the far end of the hallway, maybe forty yards from the side I came in. It opens and I pop through once more.

Right back into the same room I just left.

"How in the hell?!" My maw hangs slack.

Audrine and those ETs are all standing at the end of the corridor, right where I left them. Did I get turned around somehow in the hallway? Am I losing my damned mind? I flip back around and run the other way, the way I *thought* I went the first time. The door swallows me.

Same hallway. Same result. Coming out the other end puts me right back where I started. What the hell kind of trick is this? How can a straight hallway bring me in a full circle? I must be dreaming. This all must be some crazy, crackpot delusion. Some shellshock-induced nightmare. I've finally snapped my bean. I give myself a good slap, then do it all again.

Nothing.

Still here. Same giant alien zookeepers in white hazmat gear. Same sexy broad with her hands on her hips, shaking her head.

"Escape is futile, human," the alien voice says.

"I was just coming to that same conclusion, fellas," I say, stumbling back to them with my head down and my tail between my legs.

"Please be aware, harm not intended," he continues. "Compliance with protocol ensures well-being."

Tell that to my screaming lungs and stiff shins. "Roger that," I say. "But just so we're on the same page, you say it was in our own best interest that you slugged us out cold and dragged us back to your zoological funhouse?"

Silence. The floor around them blinks faster as they stop to think, or discuss, or whatever it is they do before they speak. Translate, maybe. My guess says they're having a rough time with the sarcasm. Or the pronouns.

"Time reveals all," the voice says. "Must implement decontamination procedure. Please follow."

We do. They lead us down a different hallway in the opposite direction, but only one of our hosts steps through the door. The others wait to either side and don't follow us inside. If this passage opens back up to the same room with the window booths, I'm gonna sock somebody in the eye, nine feet high or no.

Thankfully that's not the case. We step into a similar windowless passage, and then, on the far end of that one, into a small chamber. In the center of the room are two octagonal glass structures, similar to the clear cages but skinnier. Made for one. The rest of the room is almost bare. A pair of low protrusions simmer up from the floor as we walk in: benches. I'm happy to have a place to park it, after all the exercise I've had lately. Another of the silver rings surrounds some white toadskin on a short pedestal in front of the solo cages.

"Remove garments and enter decontamination tanks," the voice says. He pivots and stalks back out the way we came in.

Leaves us alone.

I give Audrine a wink.

"Well doll, we best do as the man says."

TWENTY-SIX

Audrine rolls her eyes at me. "Turn around," she says. "No peeking! And for the love of god would you stop calling me 'doll'?"

I comply, for a few seconds at least. When I turn back, she's already in the tank, with a thick orange liquid racing up to the nape of her neck. The soupy stuff doesn't exactly provide a clear picture, but I can make out her silhouette perfectly. That's one hourglass I wouldn't mind turning over. The tank tops off, coming to a quick stop just a sliver shy of full. The orange stuff sloshes around well over her head.

I watch for a moment—not because of the view, which is great just the same—but to make sure she doesn't drown in the stuff. The slow and steady rise and fall of her chest tells me she's still breathing. Must be some magic soup she's swimming in.

I strip down and hop in the other tank. A door swings up from the floor and seals me in. The orange goo seeps up from my feet, warm and syrupy. They must have a hell of a flow going to pump it in here so fast. It rises around me, like helium into a balloon.

Before I know it I'm swimming in soup, too. It's uncanny, breathing in something that looks and feels like a hot McCarrot smoothie. But it comes easy, once I get the hang of it. The liquid warmth fills my nose, my throat, my lungs with an earthy sweet scent, yet I'm sucking air all the same. In fact, breathing's never felt better. My whole body tingles with electricity as the soup scrubs me down from the inside out. I'm slightly buoyant in the stuff. Floating, both mind and body.

Time passes, but I can't say how much. Bathing in the goo-soup is the most relaxing thing I've ever known. Every single cell in my body is getting its back rubbed. I feel simultaneously at ease and energized. I feel like a kid again. Even the tightness in my gimp knee fades away to a dull ache. I grin and giggle, then laugh some more as a string of sticky bubbles pour out my nostrils.

When the orange stuff starts to drain, I shake a pang of regret. Throw on the sportstream and a burger or two and I could soak like this for another twenty-four hours. The goo pours out as fast as it filled and leaves me standing naked in the tank with two handfuls of Stockton. Audrine is already out and lurking in front of my tank. She's wearing some kind of gray, smock-y, robe-like thing and a curious expression.

"Nice duds," I say. "Now where do I get mine?"

She tosses me a bundle as I step out and throws a pair of bedroom eyes in my direction.

"They popped up through that silver ring when I was done," she says. I catch the robe with one hand and pull it over my head quickly. It's soft, and starts out way too big, then quickly shrinks itself down to match the proportions of Audrine's. A one-size-fits-all, colorless dress.

I start to laugh.

"What's so funny?" Audrine asks. I can tell by the relaxed look on her face that she enjoyed the soup bath as much as I did. Even her posture seems better. There's no trace of the carrot soup shampoo on her skin or in her hair. It must come off clean, like a master thief. Or a lipstick stain on your favorite shirt.

"What are the odds?" I say. "We travel halfway around the damned galaxy, but the ETs don't find us until we're nearly back home. Right in our own backyard. Just a few planets down, a few moons over. Too bad they didn't swoop us up back at Seren Luna, would've been a smoother ride I'm sure."

She laughs nervously.

"Yeah," she says. "Funny."

"Now what was it you wanted to tell me back in that meatlocker, honey? You were sorry about something?"

She winces. Swallows hard and exhales a long lungful.

"I'm... I'm sorry I got you mixed up in all this trouble," she says. She bats those baby greens like they were last year's model. "If it weren't for me, you'd be back at home, enjoying your life. I know it's not much—and it seems so trivial now—but that's what I wanted to tell you on Titan. I'm sorry."

My eyes narrow.

She does look genuinely guilty, but if that's the whole truth I'll eat a hatful of soggy boot stew. I've played this game before, cracked cons twice as tough as this broad. Not that she's a pushover. In fact, she's got a knack for covering her tracks. A trained liar, tried and true. But for whatever reason, she trips up trying to trick yours truly. A moment's hesitation gives her away. A forced tone to her sorrowful sighs that only a trained ear could pick out.

I look her in the eye.

"Don't sweat it, doll." She looks relieved. "But just for laughs, why don't you tell me what you planned to say back there instead?"

She turns away. Bites her lip, but says nothing. I hang tight. Offer only a perfectly silent, thousand-yard stare, right through her. Right into that hidden place deep inside her that she keeps tucked away. Soft and vulnerable, I drag it out into the light with a steady, unblinking gaze and a wordless accusation. It's torture on a perp, but only one that cares what you think of her.

She glances back at me. Once. Twice. Then the dam breaks and it all comes out. "Oh Stockton, I wanted to tell you, I promise I did! But everything moved so fast, and I couldn't find the right time and then it came and went and we were already in over our heads."

I grab her above the elbows and pull her in close. Continue to stare down into those big green eyes.

"Spill it, kid! You've teased me enough already."

She breaks my gaze.

"Stockton there was some truth to what Proletti said, before he... well, before we got away."

It's like I thought, then.

"How much truth?"

I let her go and sit down on the bench, wishing I had a flavorstick to mangle, or even better a full-flavor Benton Blue, with a whiskey chaser.

"I *was* embedded in JanosCorp, as an agent for an outside interest, just like Proletti claimed."

"Right, YangtzeSystems."

"No," she says, "that was just conjecture on his part. It would make sense on paper, but it wasn't true. I wasn't sent on any corporate espionage mission."

"Help me out here, beautiful. If you weren't working for one of JanosCorp's competitors, who was it signing your paystubs? What kind of gig were you on? I'd love to meet the man with a knack for recruiting talent like yours."

She looks down at her bare feet before taking a seat on the bench across from me. "I'm sure you would," she says, "But who says my boss was a man?" She sits up straight, back pert, and points her chest cannons my way.

I raise an eyebrow.

"Let's just say it was an investigation for an interested party. It doesn't matter who I was working for, Stockton, not now anyway. Now I'm working for myself, and I'm working for you, too. More than you know, I'm working for you."

"Let's pretend I believe you. What kind of investigation are we talking about? What were you up to up at that resort?"

"My job was to keep an eye on Seren Luna. On the whole facility really, but specifically on Proletti."

"Yeah?" I say. "What did you have on him that needed watching? I'll admit he was a piece of shit, but that's not usually enough to get a surveillance team on your tail. Trust me, I would know."

She gives me half a smile.

"Originally we were tipped off by the way he left the academic world and came to JanosCorp."

"And how did he do that?" I say.

"With a bang," she says. "His entire research team at MITT disappeared. *Poof.* Everyone on his project was there one day and gone the next. A team of two professors, six graduate students, and one unlucky janitor—they all just vanished. There was some evidence of a lab accident, a cover-up by the university, but no formal charges were ever filed."

"Hmmm," I say. "It makes sense. A stuffy school like that wouldn't want too many pairs of outside eyes on their dirty laundry. What kind of goods was Proletti's team working on?"

"In Universal? Applied relativity. The kind of research that a company like JanosCorp absolutely drools over. The kind of research that gets a longshot project like Seren Luna greenlit by the board of trustees. Honestly, the details I was able to dig up were spotty at best. Most of his work was lost in the 'accident'. Networks wiped, an extensive whitewash over the whole thing. There wasn't much to go on when the team never turned up. Proletti himself was MIA for a few days, that is, until he turned up at JanosCorp HQ with a resume in hand. The natural assumption was that the corporation had something to do with the disappearance of the researchers."

I nod. "But now you don't think so?"

Audrine brushes her hair behind an ear and shakes her head at me. "I don't know what to think anymore," she says. "I'm lost."

I nod again, chew it over for a second. There's just one important piece she's failed to mention. "So I take it the JanosCorp marketing team didn't just magically draw my name out of a hat then?" I say. "You were looking for another investigator to help you break the case. Maybe you pulled some strings? Gave them a nudge my way?"

She moves her lips but no sound escapes. Her guilty eyes say it all.

"I'll be damned," I say. The weight of her silent confession settles on my shoulders like a lead overcoat. "That JanosCorp holoboard back in the alley, before any of this started... The observation decks eyeing me like so much fresh meat... Tell the truth now, Doll; did you have anything to do with those dead kids in the back of that cab?"

"Of course not!" she says, a little too quickly.

"But you know the stiffs I mean."

It's not a question and she doesn't answer it.

How far back does it stretch? What's her play in this? I'd like to know, but I'm far too smart to think she'll outright admit to murder. Besides, she can't even look me in the eye anymore. She watches me from under a haphazard strand of hair. Waiting for my move. For a violent outburst and waiting for what she deserves. I stand up and grab her by the shoulders, pull her chin up until I stare square into those emerald greens, all shiny and wet.

"Look, doll. You don't have to be sorry. I'm not sore. I'd rather be in trouble with you than safe at home without you. For all I know those kids had it coming." I bend down and press my lips to hers. She only fights it for a second. "Besides," I say with a wink, "who'd have gotten you out of all those tight spots if I weren't around?"

She laughs, a little for my weak joke but more out of relief. Relief that I'm not boiling over and swinging fists at the news that this is all her fault. That she dragged me into a gory mess and didn't have the decency to let me know it. That she still won't feed me the whole story, even after all we've been through.

She smiles softly but there's a lick of burning fury hidden in the back of her eyes. This is a broad that very much doesn't like to be kissed without her permission, hot water or no.

"There's just one little thing you left out," I say.

"What's that?" she asks.

"If you needed help solving a case, why on earth would you pick a sap like me? There must have been plenty of pro snoops out there with better service records than I could offer. Guys that didn't have so many big ugly red marks in their past."

"You mean men that still cared about the work?" she says. "Cops that never lost a partner on the job?"

I shut my eyes.

"Yeah," I say. "Guys like that."

"Your records mentioned a name, over and over. 'Mendoza'. But anything much more than that was wiped clean. Someone must have been looking out for you, Stockton."

"Yeah," I say. "Or sweeping me under a rug. With the rest of the mistakes."

"What happened?" she asks. "What happened to your partner?"

I sigh, and the story falls out of my mouth like a half-chewed flavorstick. "This was ages ago, doll, before I earned that life sentence in homicide. 'Jay' Mendoza and I ran a desk out of the Special Investigations Unit. Vice. A two-man takedown squad. We were tasked with stopping a wave of counterfeiting and smuggling for finished goods. Faulty ArmPods, stolen handbags. EasyNuke dinners and new shoes. Nothing that mattered much, except to the corporationals hemorrhaging profits. It must have made someone important upset.

"Anyways, we uncover a mountain under this molehill. A sophisticated smuggling ring that went all the way to the top. Guns, drugs, unlicensed synthetics. Powerful people in political places making sure it all went off without any official interference. And of course, just the two of us to take it down, two pairs of cuffs at a time.

"So one day we get a tip, a couple of mid-level mooks are making moves without the bosses' consent. Being careless about a deal on the side. It wasn't much, but it was more than we'd had in weeks. I convinced Mendoza to ride.

"We tail these jokers down to the docks. Follow them onto one of those massive cargo crawlers down at the southside LIFT. That's the space elevator kid, you ever had a close look?"

She shakes her head no.

"Big mother... four city blocks big. A wide open, open-air platform stacked tall with shipping crates. The LIFT ferries freight up and down the gravity well. Carries raw materials down from the transport liners up in orbit. Humps the finished products back up so they can ship it out to all those faraway colony worlds.

"Long story short, the LIFT starts to climb, piled high with potentially pirated goods, and me and Mendoza to bag the boys responsible. We split up to look it over, find our guys and whatever bootleg booty they had onboard. We have to hurry, this thing will be sky high and out of the atmosphere before too long. Mendoza goes one way. I go the other. I get lucky, duck into the right storage container just before the air gets too thin to breathe. We ride all the way up, don't have a choice; the damned thing's automated. I hide out in the backseat of a late model magcab for the better part of four days, until we reach the orbital station."

Audrine nods. "What happened then?"

"I came back down with one of the crooks in cuffs."

"And Mendoza?"

"Jay never came down at all," I say.

She swallows. "Were you friends?"

"Jaxon Mendoza was a good cop, had a nose for numbers. He could tell at a glance when the alibis didn't add up. But he wasn't the type to share a beer with. No, we weren't pals. In fact I could barely stomach the guy sometimes. Made me feel all the worse when I didn't have to stomach him anymore. He was dead and gone, because I had convinced him it was good idea to chase a couple crooks up the space elevator."

I take a long rub at my temples. Shut my eyes again and breathe in deep. "Of all the cops on all the planets in all the world, you called me. You must've had your pick of a thousand better choices than a washed-up hack like me."

She smiles with sad eyes and pats me on the back.

"Oh there were plenty more than that," she says. "And not just cops, either. Believe me, I looked them all over, up and down. The multinational agencies, private concerns, the military. Everyone."

She chews her lip and stares into space. Counts her words before she speaks. "It wasn't a logical decision, that's for sure. Just looking at the numbers wasn't enough for me. I took meticulous handwritten notes, piles of them. I couldn't afford to leave an electronic trail behind me. Backgrounds, personalities, strengths and weaknesses, I jotted it all down in an antique notebook. One day I find a page torn out, with your name scrawled across it. In my own handwriting. I didn't remember writing it. Still don't. I worked a lot of sleepless nights in those days, after my normal shifts at the resort. Your name wasn't familiar to me when I found it, but I looked you up anyway."

She sighs and looks up at me.

"It was no wonder I hadn't found you before. Your measurables were very much outside of my search filters. But when I saw your holo, your history, I got the feeling like I knew you already, even though I was sure we'd never met. Like I could trust you. There were plenty of better choices, but I knew you were right for the job. I knew, just absolutely knew—without any rational explanation—that fate wanted you and me together on this one."

Superstition doesn't get you very far in a cop's world, but somehow I think she already knows that, so I keep it to myself.

"Well," I say, smiling, "I hope you were right."

She straightens her smock over her thighs. "Me too," she says.

"When we get back home, I'll buy the first round at Shakey's and you can fill in the gaps. Tell me all about your boss, and why he was so interested in that damned resort and the sack of nuts who run it aground. But for now, we've got better gossip to gab about." I throw a thumb towards the door. "What do you make of these lugs that nabbed us?"

"I make that they can hear everything we're saying."

She tops it off with a look that says 'behave.'

"Noted," I say, tapping my temple. "What else you got?"

"They don't mean to hurt us."

"Yeah, so they say. But why not? What makes you so sure we can trust them? Wasn't an hour ago they cold-clocked us and stuck us in a cage. Took the girl God-knows-where."

She shakes her head. "Women's intuition?" she says.

I frown.

"And logic," she adds. "If they have bad intentions, why let us out of the cage at all? Why allow you to run away like that? It's painfully obvious they've been in perfect control of the situation since we got here. Nothing is going to get by them that they don't want to, including me and including you. So why let us exercise our free will? They can make us do whatever they want, at any time, but instead they're *asking* us to do it."

"And in your book that makes them real nice guys," I say. "So if they don't want to hurt us, what do they want?"

She shrugs.

"I don't know. Maybe they want to study us. Maybe they want to help us. Maybe they just want to get rid of us. Maybe they don't know what they want. Maybe we just fell in their laps and they're just playing it by ear."

I nod. "I can relate to that, doll, but I say we go find out for sure." I grab Audrine by the hand and march towards the door. We step through it into another plain white hallway, identical to the first two.

"Do you have any idea at all where you're going?" she asks.

"No," I say. "But I don't think it matters." We approach the far membrane and it slips open for us. "I don't think it matters because *they* know where we're going."

Once more we step through.

This time we emerge not back in the passage with the booth—not where we came from when we last stepped through this door—but in a totally new place. Well, relatively new. Same white walls. Same chrome arches. But this room has one big difference: an enormous viewport. A bubble of perfectly clear plexisteel opens up to the great vacuum beyond.

Titan is below us, a rust-colored, rocky thing with thick yellow clouds and those familiar pools of piss. Saturn looms large behind the moon, a proud mama, with all her shiny rings out for display. A couple of sister moons dot the ringscape. The port is positioned so that we can't see the rest of the ship. At least, I'm assuming we're on a ship. Who knows with these goofs and their funhouse hallways. For all I know this may be an intergalactic truckstop and we've just dropped in to top off the tank and grab a bag of McChipperCrisps.

I pry my eyes from the viewport and catch all five zookeepers standing watch quietly. They're stretched out in a perfect line at the bottom of the windowwall. Five identical masks stare blankly at the two of us.

I walk towards them, dragging Audrine along by the arm.

"How's it shaking?" I say.

We skid to a stop a good ten feet from the lineup.

"Appreciate compliance," their voice says. "Sanitation successful."

"Yeah it was a nice soak. Hell of a tub, fellas. But is this the best you could do in the wardrobe department?"

I grab at the dress draped over me.

Audrine shoves me out of the way and steps between us. "Shut up, Stockton," she says. "You promised to bring the girl. Where is she?"

She shakes her finger at them like a weapon. If it scares them, they don't know how to show it.

"Reconstructive process incomplete. Delivery assured at completion." ShortStuff didn't seem all that bad off last I saw her. Either these guys found something we missed, or they're stalling. Not that we're in much of a position to call their bluff. I decide to wait for a better draw and let this hand play out.

Audrine makes that squinty-eyed, determined look of hers. Her hands are—of course—glued to her hips. This seems to be her natural state when dealing with males of any species. "What do you want with us? What are your intentions?"

"Primary objective requires genetic cataloging. Status: complete. Chronicle updated. Tertiary objective requires compliance with sentient beings' requests. Status: incomplete," they say.

I chime in. "So all you wanted was to take a little scan of our DNA and then send us on our merry little way?" I highly doubt that's their plan, if I'm understanding these goobs correctly.

A pause.

"Affirmative."

Well I'll be. "I'll take a rye then," I say. "Neat."

Audrine glares me down, but just like clockwork, a little clear cube rises up out of the floor next to me. Inside it is a ball-shaped vessel filled with an amber liquid. I'll be damned. They've even got the drinks in cages! I take it out and take a taste, half-expecting to keel over gagging or worse. But it's good stuff. Nice and smooth. I swish it around my mouth as the cube sinks back down and disappears from sight.

"We want to know more about you," Audrine says. She approaches them carefully, quietly. Half-stalking, but with both hands out, to show she means no harm. She raises a finger to her lip, fidgeting.

In contrast, our hosts stand perfectly still. No chest movements. No scratching, no twitching. They might as well be inanimate.

"Request acknowledged," they say. "Initiate inquiry."

Audrine is right up on them now, studying them like bugs. She runs a hand over a long, smooth forearm, wrapped in that white pressure-suit material. Now that I see their clothes up close, they look like they're made out of the same stuff as the floors and walls of this place. Shares that same mucusy, toadskin quality. Very fashion forward of them. Straight from the runways of Planet X, I'm sure.

"What do you look like under there?" she says, stretching up on her tippy toes to brush the bottom of a face mask.

She's brave, for a bim.

Who knows what kind of plug-ugly mugs those helmets are hiding?

There's a long silence. The floor underneath them lights up, shooting sparkles back and forth below their boots. When it stops, the suits come off. I'd almost say they melt away, but it's more mechanical than that. Cascade apart, maybe. They fold up into themselves in ways that my SpektraTek gear can only dream of. Each alien creature ends up with a button-sized disc in an outstretched palm.

Creature doesn't quite cut it, either. These guys don't look all that strange. More like funhouse-mirror reflections of normal human beings. Long and lean. Impossibly thin, like pasty string beans. Their skin is a chalky, colorless plastic, completely devoid of pigmentation. They are hairless, sexless. Living action figures.

Their faces are the worst part. All of them are identically featureless. There are no mouths, no ears. Everything is smooth angles and rounded edges. Like all of their mugs were half-erased, or never fully formed in the first place. They almost remind me of the ETs from early era horrorstream: the little green men that rode around in silver saucers shooting ray guns and abducting people.

The only way to tell the quintuplets apart is their peepers. They're brilliant slits in an otherwise empty palette. Each zookeeper can claim his own color eyes: red, blue, yellow, green, and purple.

Audrine and I stand and stare.

They speak, shattering the silence. I'm thrown off. There are no mouths to move. No voiceholes to make the words.

"Request fulfilled. Initiate additional request." There's no indication in the eyes or the face to give away the speaker as the sound hits our ears. Each one is a perfect statue.

"How do we know which one of you is speaking?" I say. "You all sound the same. To us, anyways."

There's no response. None of them turn to face each other, but I know that they're chatting it over all the same.

I swig my whiskey and wait.

"Communications en masse," the voice says. "No individuals, only The Collective."

"I see," I say, having another sip. "So what does The Collective want?"

"Primary objective requires genetic cataloging. Status: complete. Chronicle updated. Tertiary objective requires compliance with sentient beings' requests. Status: incomplete."

"At least they're consistent." I turn to Audrine. "I think what they mean is 'Your wish is our command'." I use my best monkeysuit voice.

She's still studying them. Ignoring me.

Finally, when she's satisfied, she crosses her arms and speaks, soft yet firm. "Take us home," she says.

"Why didn't I think of that?"

Here I've been so caught up in trying to stay alive, I almost forgot that there was anything to go back to. As hesitant as I am to live in a world where the longest songs are twenty seconds short, at least there'll be music in my life again.

In fact, home sounds better than it ever has.

They respond immediately. "Destination recognition affirmed. Intrastellar travel required. Engage?"

She just repeats herself, quietly. It's hardly more than a whisper.

"Take us home."

"Acknowledged."

I take a peek over The Collective's heads, at the scene outside the window. I don't know what I'm expecting. A grand flash of light? Some kind of explosive lift off? I certainly don't get one. I don't even get a lurch. The view just starts to slowly shift. And I mean slowly. I'll have plenty of time to tell Titan and Saturn adios as they drip away at a lazy snail's pace. Apparently we're not in any rush.

"Travel initiated," they say.

"Say fellas," I say with a slug of hooch, "How do you know where to take us anyway? You didn't ask for an address and I don't want to stop for directions."

"Subjects' genetic constitution and linguistic profile compliant with Chronicle entries tagged Homeworld: Earth."

These guys know their stuff. Was it a lucky guess?

I polish off the whiskey.

"So this Chronicle of yours," I say, "you've got an entry in it for Earthlings then?"

"Affirmative," they say.

I tap on my dry glass. Another cube pops up and I switch out my empty for a freshy and the whole kit and kaboodle disappears back into the floor. The service is swell.

I take a swill and continue my interrogation. "So that means you've picked up our kind before? Humans?"

There's a pause. The floor sparkles tell me they're chatting again. "Affirmative," they say after a moment. "Human genetic constitution defines Chronicle prime objective."

I glance out the window. Saturn and her kids are gone. Just empty black space now, a blanket of stars winking in the distance. They must have kicked up the go-juice when I wasn't looking.

"Prime objective, huh? So you've got a hankering for humans?" I say, remembering the classicstream martians and their fondness for abducting young couples from the backseats of big-body convertibles. "A real jonesing for the Joneses? Is that why you try to look like us? With your two arms and two legs and ten fingers and—" I stop to count. "—ten toes?"

Audrine gives me a concerned look. "Stockton, where are you going with this?" is what her lips say. Her eyes tell another tale: *stop antagonizing them!*

"No, dollface," I reply. "We've got a right to know. There's no way in hell that the first two alien species we run into happen to look this much like we do. First the SnotBabies and now these lugs. It's just too big a coincidence. I'd accept some mutant squid monsters, or intelligent slime, or something so wild and wacky it blew my mind to bits. Hell, even talking pigs would be better. But these guys may as well be my long lost cousins from Topeka Prime."

I take a big pull from the whiskey and turn to face her.

"Not to mention the fact that they've got a whole warehouse crawling with those other bastards downstairs! The ones with the claws and the fangs. And those assholes look like us too! In a roundabout sort of way. At least more than you'd expect from the product of alien evolution; from creatures born billions of miles from Earth and all the conditions that shaped us from the smartest monkeys in the jungle. Why are these guys keeping those assholes around? What's the obsession with this form? Why the hard-on for humanity?"

But Audrine has stopped paying me any mind.

She's got her peepers fixed out the viewport. Have we arrived already? I turn to check it out.

We've definitely stopped, but I wouldn't say we've arrived. We're parked above a burnt-out husk of a planet. Like a McTastyTot left in the fryer too long, this is one crispy potato. It's charcoal black, with glowing red seams criss-crossing the surface. There's no atmosphere, no oceans, no clouds, no life. Just a big hunk of charred rock with some lava rivers thrown in for good measure.

I chuckle.

"Whats the matter boys?" I say. "Engine trouble?"

The statues don't laugh.

"Destination achieved: Homeworld Earth. Sensors indicate surface unsuitable for landing party. Define secondary destination."

The situation is quickly losing its humor. "Very funny fellas," I say. I drain the rest of my glass in one long gulp. "Now stop messing around and take us home."

I look at Audrine.

She's crying. Tears stream down her cheeks but she doesn't lift her gaze from that blistery ball we used to call Earth.

"Aw shit."

TWENTY-SEVEN

We've been staring out the window for the better part of an hour. Not that the view's changed any. The zookeepers haven't moved an inch. They continue to stand like statues at attention. No one says a word. You could hang a hat on this awful silence. Everything we've ever known is still a smoldering ruin thousands of miles below us.

Audrine finally breaks the silence with a wave of wailing cries.

"It's... it's all gone," she says between sniffles.

I wrap an arm around her. I don't know how much comfort I can offer at a time like this, but the least I can do is offer it. I give her a gentle squeeze and hold her tight.

Me? I learned a long time ago that I was broken. Emotionally malformed. News like this is tragic, sure. But it's still just news to me. I don't have names and faces to stick the hurt to. My world died without ever being born, a long time ago, and I went right on living, whether I had reason to or not. The end of the world is old hat for a guy with no friends, no family, and no feelings.

Or so I keep telling myself.

"Everything… Everyone… There's nothing left," she says. "What's the point of going on? What's the point of anything?"

I step in front of her and put my hands on her shoulders. It's a question I don't go a day without asking myself, but I don't want to hear it from her lips. She's stronger than she knows. There's hope for her yet.

"Don't say that, doll. What about you and me? We're still here, and that's got to count for something."

She stops sniffling for a second, looks up at me with those big green puppy dog eyes. "Count for something?" she parrots.

The tears gush again.

"Hey!" I give her a shake. "Cut it out! It does count for something! But only if we stand up and take our lumps."

I point out the window.

"All of that down there? That's all gone. Caput. Crossed-out. Donezo. Deceased. And no amount of boohooing is gonna bring it back."

I point at my chest, then stab a finger into hers.

"But all this is still here, and there's plenty of time for us to make a difference. But only if we don't give up. Only if we keep fighting."

She repeats me again. "…keep fighting?"

Her eyes are glassed over. It's a hard pill to swallow. More of a suppository, really. I embrace her, then turn to face the alien chorus line.

"So what was it?" I say. "A supervolcano? An asteroid? Thermonuclear global warfare? What? Guys like you? Some other alien scumbags? I'm not pointing any fingers here, fellas, but something wiped our planet off the map, and—if it's not too much trouble—I'd very much like to know what it was."

I realize that I am pointing fingers. I've been pounding on Purple's chest as I grill the suspects. He's as still and silent as ever. Neither acknowledging nor denying my half-assed accusations.

There's a hand on my shoulder now. Audrine. Her violent weeping trickles to a steady whimper. "There's… only… one thing that could have done it," she says.

"Yeah? What's that?"

"Time."

"I don't follow," I say. "How could time do that?"

I wave towards the dead shell of our planet. The oceans and air sucked away. A cross-stitched hash of molten magma canals left in their stead. It doesn't square up. This place has been thoroughly thrashed.

I've seen a hundred disasterstreams play out the scenario, starring a hundred different villains. Alien overlords harvest the planet for resources, suck it dry. Earth herself has had enough and flames out in one last geothermal kamikaze mission. Ecological hara-kiri. Or my favorite, the culprits we all knew would be responsible when the apocalypse finally arrived: us. Mankind finally blows ourselves to bits. Warfare, overpopulation, playing God with robots and genetics, energy science gone wrong… it doesn't matter. I've seen the Earth go quiet in countless different ways—but never once because of time. And never once for keeps. Never for real.

I need an answer.

And lucky me, The Collective has one for me. "Stellar mass core stability deteriorates over time. Post main sequence evolution in progress. Solar radial expansion responsible for sterilization of inner terrestrial bodies including Homeworld Earth."

I shake my head and turn to Audrine.

"What in the hell are they babbling about?"

"The sun," she says. "The sun grew larger and the heat from it burned up the atmosphere and evaporated the oceans. The goddamned sun. The very same star that gave us energy, light, *life*—for billions of years. The sun cooked the Earth until nothing was left but hot rock and ashes."

This all sounds a little too fantastical to me. "Well what would make it do that?" I say. "It never cooked us alive before. Why should it start up now? Who flipped on the fryer?"

Audrine shakes her head. "Like I said before, the only thing that could have done it is time." She walks between Collective Red and Collective Green to get up close to the viewport. I follow her.

"We always knew it would happen," she continues, tracing her finger around the outline of our dead planet. "As the sun gets older, it burns up more of the hydrogen fuel in its core and loses mass. As it loses mass, there is less gravity pulling it into itself. Eventually, it loses its ability to hold itself together."

"A lot of that going around," I say, with a half-hearted attempt at a smile.

She ignores me. "It grows larger, gets closer, things heat up—until it's too close." She hangs her head and drops her finger from the window glass. "But how did it happen so quickly? Our best scientists estimated it wouldn't be an issue for almost six-and-a-half billion years. They all agreed—" She stops for a moment. "Oh God," she says.

I'm putting the pieces together.

"We're six point five billion years late to the party." It's a swell theory but a little confirmation would be nice. "Hey fellas," I turn to The Collective. They rotate to face us, all together like. "Is there any truth to this? We on the right path?"

"Query confirmed," they say. "Chronicle archives associate subjects' genetic composition with epoch six billion nine hundred fifty-three million solar orbit completions prior to present."

"Goddamn," I say. "Remind me to sue the shit out of The Janos Corporation if they're still around." Blank stares from the chorus line. Nobody's in the mood for jokes.

Audrine brushes past me and gets cozy with Collective Red. "If we've been gone that long, Stockton," she says, examining the alien closely, "then these creatures... they might not be extraterrestrials at all. They could be our descendants. Our evolutionary great, great grandchildren."

"Yeah right," I say, taking a look. "With a mug like that? Next you'll tell me those little bastards with the teeth are all my nephews."

I was only joshing but the look she sends me says otherwise.

"Oh hell no," I say. "I know I said they look like us but I didn't really mean it—not like that! Boys, tell her that she's nuts. There's no way humanity evolved into this."

I stare up into one of those expressionless faces.

They talk it over for a bit. "Query incorrect," they say. "Entry: Collective lineage traceable through entry: Homo sapiens."

"Get out of town," I say. "And the SnotBabies? The nasty bastards you've got by the dozens down in those cages?"

"Query confirmed. Entry: Homonanos deinohypodus lineage traceable through entry: Homo sapiens."

"Of course!" I say, throwing my hands into the air. "We're responsible for all the freakshow specimens in the whole goddamned galaxy! At least tell me there are some real ugly ET bastards out there. Some deepspace sludgesuckers that make you guys look like so much leftover casserole."

"Query false. All extant Chronicle entries' lineage traceable through entries marked: Homeworld Earth."

Audrine speaks up. "So you never found any life that didn't have an ancestor from Earth? Not a single extra-terrestrial cell in the whole galaxy? After almost seven billion years? We really were unique? Alone? There was no one else out there?"

"Query correct."

Audrine takes a seat on the floor. This is big potatoes in her book. She's more shaken up by this newsbreak than by the destruction of our home planet. I never did meet a dame that had her priorities straight and this one's no exception.

"It's a goddamned lonely universe out there," I say. "But at least we'll have plenty of company to cry with," I say. "Seems to me everybody lost their homeworld."

It's the kind of comfort that blows over in a stiff wind, but it's all I can find for the moment. My brain wants to keep flapping my jaw, but my heart says I don't need to tell Audrine what she already knows. She stares at the ground between her bare legs, her head in her hands. Can't say I understand it, but then again she's frayed pretty thin right about now, and I never was much for a funeral.

I turn to The Collective.

"What about us?" I say. "You have an entry for human beings, so there must be other folks like us around. What about some of the offworld colonies? Any of them still kicking?"

Audrine mumbles something into the floor. I listen close.

"Stockton, six billion years is a very long time. Our sun wasn't the only one that changed. If there are any habitable colony worlds left, they'd be full of people that look like this." She clumsily gestures at the zookeepers without looking up. "Or worse."

I think of all those caged SpaceApes. Her logic's sound, but I'm not ready to call it quits just yet.

"We weren't the only ones on that time resort, doll. Somebody else must have made it out alive. Can you fellas find some other humans? Somebody from our time? Maybe give us a lift to wherever-the-hell they might be? That is, if you don't have other plans for us already?"

They talk it over for a moment, in perfect silence. A mighty long moment. This must be the question of the century. Finally they speak.

"Request acknowledged," The Collective says. "Estimated transit duration: 148 hours. Engage?"

"Please," Audrine says, "get us the hell away from here."

Keeps Ticking Until the End of Time.

ROLOTAG
The Galaxy's Finest Timepieces.
(now available in women's styles)

TWENTY-EIGHT

According to our handlers' estimation, we've got about a week to kill. I don't anticipate a pleasure cruise, in fact I half expect to be put back in the cage with the cat, but the accommodations are surprisingly plush. Not Seren Luna swanky, but good enough for a guy like me. They set Audrine and I up with a little cabin all our own. Decked out with furniture and everything. Somnopods, loungers, the whole nine yards. These brutes aren't huge on comfort for themselves—I have yet to see one so much as sit down—so this comes as a pleasant surprise. The decor's all minimalist as it gets, but I'm not complaining. They offer up some additional togs, too. Plain gray trousers and a featureless white shirt. Something slightly more feminine for the lady. Not the height of fashion, but at least I can get out of this damned dress. I'm a happy camper, all things considered.

What can I say? My highball is half-full.

We pass the time in what The Collective calls the 'Human Quarters.' There's a nice little viewport next to a blocky, white lounger. Audrine spends her days gazing out the window, tracing invisible constellations between the slowly fading points of light. If she were keeping her calendar up to date, there'd only be that one entry.

After a few days of it, I offer an alternative.

"Say doll, that's a swell view and all, but wouldn't you like to stretch your legs every once in a while?"

She glances towards me briefly, then returns to the window without saying a word.

"Maybe you want me to stretch 'em for you?"

She ignores me again, continues tracing patterns into the glass.

I take a seat next to her.

"That's a lot of twinkle out there," I say. "Who cranked up the starshine while we were away?"

She drops her hands to her lap. "They aren't any brighter," she says. "There are more of them. Almost twice as many."

Her voice is soft. Robotic.

"Well how'd they get there? They been knocking star-boots and making star-babies?"

She takes her eyes from the window long enough to look at me like I'm an idiot. "The Andromeda galaxy has slowly merged into our own Milky Way, Stockton. Brought a half-a-trillion stars into our sky. It took billions of years, but now both galaxies are almost right on top of each other."

I scoot closer, throw an arm around her. "Not a bad place to be."

"Yeah," she says. "Just another perk of living six billion years in the future." She gestures flippantly out the window. "It's beautiful now," she says. "Right up until the black holes at the center of both galaxies slip into each other. Right up until everything that's left is engulfed in cosmic fire."

I shrug. "Well maybe I ought to grab us a couple drinks, so we can toast to the end of the universe, honey. Should be some show, huh? Let's you and I get cozy and we can kiss tomorrow goodbye." I brush her hair behind her ear.

She looks deep into my eyes. Opens her mouth, but nothing comes out. She shuts her eyes instead, and her fingers wander to the buttons on her blouse. She loosens the top.

"Is this what you want Stockton?"

I shrug. "It's a start."

A glisten forms in the corner of her eye. "Is this *all* you want? To get drunk and *knock boots*?"

Her fingers halt on the next fastener, just as the view's getting good. When she looks up, she glares into me. "Well here I am, big man. Come and take me, if that's all I mean to you."

I stand and rub my temples.

"I don't get you, doll. One minute you're hot to trot, or pretending to be anyway. So long as you get what you want, you can string me along, halfway through history, halfway across the damned galaxy, bleeding and bruised, drooling over every shred of affection you toss to me like so many scraps from the dinner table. You're not afraid to use sex as a weapon so long as it suits you, and then you get all bent out of shape when it backfires. You're a real piece of work, kid."

"Don't call me 'kid', you dirty old man. Maybe if you didn't have a junior high hard-on half the time I could find another way to reach you!"

I round on her, fast and angry. My fingers fly apart as I gesture at the empty space between us.

"Reach me? You've been dragging me around in the dark, doll. I've had to pull teeth to get what little you've shared with me already, and half of that I'd have to be an idiot to take at face value. You've been as straight with me as a plate of spaghetti, and frankly, I'm getting more than a little sick of the same old dish. What's any of this for? What do you want from me?"

She snorts once, and the stiffness drops from her bones. "I want you to trust me," she says. "I want you to believe me when I tell you I've got your best interest at heart, and that I've already given up more for you than you could ever know, Stockton."

I pat her on the back.

"Yeah well, let me know if you need anything else, darlin'."

She collapses into her own arms, and turns away so I won't see the waterworks streaming from her face. Her body quakes, but she fights to keep even the faintest sniffle out of the air and out of my ears.

"Just leave me alone," she says.

I head for the door.

Looks like I'm drinking alone. I won't judge her for feeling sorry for herself, not even after the way she's treated me. But she could at least do something to take the edge off. After a career of sniffing out stiffs, a bottle of Jensen's is still the only therapy I can stomach. I leave her buttoned up and sobbing silently in the cabin to search for a barkeep. Shouldn't take more than a gallon-and-a-half of the good stuff to get her crying eyes out of my mind.

I'm starting to get the gist of navigating the hallways in this heap. A few quick saunters to the head were primer enough. It's a simple gig really, one even a soggy frank like yours truly can get his noodle around. All the doors lead to a hallway. And all the hallways lead to wherever you want to go. How's that for square? All I need to do is think of something, and I'll be damned if that door in front of me doesn't open right up to it. And right now, I'm thinking about a nice tall cup of corn juice.

But that thought alone won't cut it. I need a rumslinger to fetch the hooch for me, and the zookeeps are the only olive-stuffers on staff. So I make a brainful of old Yellow Eyes and take a stroll and let the magic hallways do the rest.

I pop out in a room I haven't seen before. A big storage bay lies spread out below me, packed tight with row after row of floating chrome spheres, each one about five feet across. They're bright and shiny. Perfectly smooth mirrorballs. A single ball swims effortlessly through the grid like our cube boogied through the cage room. It eventually maneuvers its way right out of a shiny metal ring in the wall. An overhead window displays the handiwork: a line of silver spheres falling up towards a swirly, bright blue planet above us. The next ball in line makes a go for it. Then another. I'm mesmerized. It's a beautifully orchestrated dance number that leaves a perfectly formed trail of space marble breadcrumbs, snaking through the sea of stars into a big sapphire pool. Just gorgeous.

Yellow walks the rows, examining the spheres as they rush by. Like a well-prepped tango partner, he steps out of the way just in time, every time. Each sphere looks identical to me, but he eyes them closely as they float past, like he's gunning for a certain flavor gumball under all that candy-coated chrome sheen.

I call out to him from the viewing platform.

"Hey Chief, how about a couple of stiff ones?"

I ask for two and why not? Despite herself, Audrine would be better off with a big bowl of loudmouth soup. If she doesn't want it, well then that's just another serving for me.

"On second thought, better gentle up the lady's, pal. She's soft when it comes to the sauce."

His head whips around to spot me. Bad move. With his concentration broken, Yellow Eyes falls out of sync with the spheres. Like a drunk on the dancefloor, he starts to miss the beat.

First one ball brushes against him from behind, nudging him forward with just enough gumption to smack the next one in front of him. He bounces back into another.

Then another.

And another. Within a matter of seconds he's pinballing around down there, at the mercy of the sliding spheres. I watch through gritted teeth as he's mashed and mangled, his head spinning around on a wet spaghetti neck. Each thwomp puts him a little closer to that ring portal. A little closer to the cold vacuum outside.

Panic overcomes me.

I search for some sort of emergency release, a life preserver, anything! But there's nothing to find. This damned ship doesn't have any sort of manual controls anywhere. The observation deck is empty. Maybe if I tried to command it like the doors? With my mind? I concentrate as hard as I can, forming a perfect mental picture of the orbs all coming to a screeching stop, of the zookeeper walking away safely, if a little bit battered. He's even got a gimpy limp in my head.

But my head is as far as the fantasy gets. The dance eventually slows down and comes to a stop, but not before Yellow gets kicked out the portal, spiraling away with the rest of the marbles. Spaced. His body spins wildly, arms stuck at his side. A kitten in a twister. I can't look away. There's no panic in his eyes. He's perfectly still, his frozen mug just as expressionless as always. It's eerie, to see someone so incredibly hosed look as if they couldn't care less about it.

I watch him get smaller and smaller, until he's swallowed into the immensity of the big blue planet behind him. Even when he's gone, I continue staring into the space where he dropped out of sight. Staring with my eyes and my mind. Eventually I shake my head and make for the door. I concentrate on his pal Red and tear down the hallway doubletime.

I'm there in seconds.

I skid to a halt beside Red, frantically shouting between gasps.

"Your buddy...with...the yellow...he's gone...out the...airlock."

He just stares at me with that big, dumb, blank face.

"Report acknowledged," he says. Or they say. I haven't quite figured that part out yet. They only use 'The Collective' to refer to themselves, even when they aren't all together. Come to think of it—shit, this isn't news to him. If they can talk to each other from room to room, he's already aware that his buddy is on a long hike to nowhere, and he's not doing a damned thing to help out.

Red looks away and goes back to studying some foggy brown liquid in a little glass jar. Just like nothing happened at all. I back away slowly, unable to fathom his lack of concern. Granted these guys aren't much for emotional responses, but he didn't even lift a finger. I don't care how evolved you are, you watch your buddies' backs. That's the prime objective where I come from.

I shuffle back to the broad and our little cabin, wishing I had that drink right about now. Should have asked Red for it, seeing as he wasn't too tied up saving his friend. Audrine still stares aimlessly out the window like some gutter-punk with an arm full of dope.

I fill her in.

"Maybe they've given up too," she says. She turns to face me. Her eyes are red and glassy and puffy, but she makes double-sure her cheeks are dry before I can get a peek at them.

"I dunno," I say. "I get the feeling these freaks are keeping something from us." She turns away and shrugs. It's obvious she could care less but I keep blabbing anyway. Maybe it's the only thing I *can* do at a time like this. "I'm gonna do some snooping, see if I can dig up any dirt."

She doesn't react.

"Do you want to talk about it?" I say, sitting next to her.

"Talk about what?" She doesn't peel her gaze from the window. "Is this your way of saying sorry?"

"Shit, Audrine. Sure I'm sorry." I shake my head. "The Earth is gone. The whole damned planet. You must have lost somebody. I just figured you might feel better chatting about it, but don't let me twist your arm off."

She turns to face me. Her face is blank. Empty. The starlight twinkles like a hundred million diamonds reflected in her shiny, wet eyes, but her own light has died down so low I can't picture it ever coming back full strength.

"I lost everybody that I loved a long time ago, Stockton. Even before all of this. But thanks. For trying, anyways."

I leave it at that.

Audrine stares out the viewport once more as I stand to go. I catch the hint of a whimper on my way out. At least she's saving the water-works for when I'm not around. It's all I can do to hold myself together without hearing her bawl. My emotional armor might be thicker than hers on account of the testosterone in my veins, but it's not impenetrable. Keeping busy is the only tonic I've got for the biting, bitter despair of knowing that everything I've ever known is just a memory now. Would do Audrine some good to get out too, if I could jimmy her from that sofa and the weepy stars outside.

I stop in the hallway, wracking my brains. I need a plan. I know I can't keep popping in on The Collective. I don't care what secrets they've got stashed away, I don't want to see any more of them bounced on my account. But what else can I try? Where else can I look?

I retrace my steps, visiting all of the spots I've already been to: the cage room, the tub room, I even go back to the hangar with the spheres. That beautiful marble dance has stopped and the blue planet is gone. The viewport displays a cold, empty vacuum. Might as well be a mirror, for as good as I feel right now. I'm quickly running out of places to check for clues. Clues to what, I couldn't say. I just know they're all I've got to cling to.

Then it hits me. Why hadn't I thought of it earlier?

I rush back to the corridor and dial up an image of Bekka. Her smiling freckly face, those crooked little glasses. I can picture her perfectly, standing with her paws up on a windowpane, counting the stars as they blur by. All eight-and-a-half billion of them.

Stepping through the membrane, I emerge in a truly huge facility. It's one perfectly straight tube stretching out for the long haul before me. The round ceiling towers overhead, dotted with chrome arches at regular intervals along its length. But the most prominent features are the spheres. Thousands of them line the walls, clear up to the ceiling. They appear identical to the ones in the room where Yellow bit the big one. Reflective chrome surface, about five, maybe six feet across. Perfectly round and smooth. But these orbs don't float. Each one is hooked into the wall with an arm-thick, grooved tube.

I approach the closest one to get a better look and the detective in me goes to work. What the hell are these things for anyway? Why were they ejecting them into that planet? Are these even the same spheres? It's not what I came here for, but sometimes the ugliest clues are the ones that crack the case. Until I find Bekka, I'm not ready to leave any stones unturned with these freakshow zookeeps. Could she be hidden away in one of these silver balls, like a miniature version of the orange goo-soup?

I lay a hand on the surface of the sphere and am surprised to feel warmth. I would have expected a cold metallic quality, like dinner at the in-laws', but it's a long drive from that.

Soft. Tingly. Almost organic. Pleasant.

Even stranger, the ball grows toastier as I leave my hand on it. A faint red glow bleeds out along the surface from my palm, creeping larger at a geriatric sloth-crawl. After a minute or so, the glow covers the sphere and it begins to change color, fading from rosy-cheeks pink to a sheer white sheen, then melting away into a translucent haze. I put my other hand to the surface and peer inside.

The orb is filled with a murky amber liquid. Some flickering source of light shines through from the back, where the sphere is attached to the grooved tube. Silhouetted against this beacon though, there's a dark little humanoid embryo curled up in the fetal position. Maybe three feet long, on a good day. About the right size, but not human enough to be the girl.

So these spheres are what, mechanical eggs? The little shadow puppet inside is a huddled hunk of frail-looking limbs with spindly digits, a tiny body, and a massive noggin. A tadpole scarecrow. With my free hand, I give the guy a little tap tap. "Sleeping in there, pal?"

He steers that massive head to look me over, impossibly slow, but I can't make out any details on account of the backlighting.

The fetus reaches out a gangly shadow arm and touches the inside of the egg below my palm with slender fingertips. Instantly I'm filled with an intense feeling of sadness. Emptiness. Worthlessness. Hopelessness. But it's not a lonely feeling. It's as if I'm sharing in a great grief with the whole wide world. As if we've *all* lost something very important, and we might never get it back.

All the feelings I've buried inside me bubble up to the surface. My eyes start to water and my body quivers. From the edge of my vision, I catch other eggs start to light up and glow. My bad knee goes weak. I shake violently, anchored to the floor and the egg in front of me. Tears stream down my face and I feel a strong magnetic pull, urging my body in towards the egg. Tugging at every fiber of my soul. With every ounce of will I've got, I tear my hand away and stumble backwards. The orb regains its shiny luster quickly and I lose sight of the little fella inside.

What in the hell are these things? And why did thinking of Bekka bring me here? Do they have her locked up in one of those eggs? If they do, I've got my work cut out for me. The spheres stretch down the corridor as far as I can see. Thousands of them, stacked from floor to ceiling, around the arc above me and back down to the floor again.

Surrounding me. I race down the row, randomly checking the spheres. Using two hands causes them to melt open faster, although I'm careful not to linger too long. They all turn up like the first one. Sad little fetus creeps. No regular humans. No Bekka.

The orbs go on forever and I stop checking them. I'm sprinting. Dripping sweat. Hoping there will be an answer waiting for me somewhere down the line. This tunnel must be ten miles long, but the exercise is good for me and I'd run it twice if I had to. My cloudy head clears a touch. Finally I reach a break in the orbs. The end of the line. On both sides of the hall are windows. A glance through them shows me just how hopeless my search is. Identical tubes on either side. Chock full of spheres. More tubes on the other sides of those. Who knows how many spheres there are. Even little Bekka couldn't count them all.

Ahead of me, in the terminus of the hallway, is a flat wall. I walk towards it and a doorway opens up, but the thin, milky membrane remains. As I move to step through, the membrane rejects me. It sends a jolt of electricity through my body and just plain refuses to let me pass. I growl and try again. No dice. I take a running start. Sprint into the damned door. The membrane bends in like elastic before spitting me back out the way I came. I fly away, flopping across the deck for a few feet. I lie like a pile of sad, worthless rags, my face to the floorboards.

Why won't it let me in? I pound the deck with both fists. None of the other doors were shut on this damned ship. I didn't even know they had locks. Why now? What's behind there that I can't see?

I feel a presence above me and I get my answer.

My eyes trace skinny white leg-stalks. It's one of the zookeepers. It's… Yellow. How do you like that? He's back! Maybe they did rescue him after all.

And he's not alone.

"Bekka!"

I jump to my feet and give her a great big bear hug. She's a little slow to the draw but she squeezes me back, sleepily. I'm all smiles.

"How ya doin, kiddo?" I ask.

She doesn't say a word. Just keeps on squeezing.

"I'm happy to see you too," I say.

I turn to Yellow.

"Thanks pal," I say.

He just stares down at me, his clock as clean as the cold vacuum he disappeared into a few hours ago. "And sorry," I continue. "You know, about... earlier today. I didn't mean to—" I can't find the words to finish.

"Sorry, anyways."

There's no reply.

TWENTY-NINE

I burst into the cabin, kid in tow.

"Look who I found."

Audrine is lying in the lounger by the window, but not for long. She flies over to us and showers Bekka with kisses. Looks like this was just what the DocBot ordered. The glaze over her eyes is gone. She moves with more pep than I've seen from her in days. She's alive again. Resurrected by her love for a little girl. I start to tell Audrine about Yellow being back from the dead, but then I don't. Now's not the time. I kick back against the wall and grin, and I don't say a thing. I just let the scene play out without me. Audrine gives me a glance that says 'thank you', even if her pride won't let her lips speak those words aloud.

We pass a few more days on The Collective cruiser. Well, 'days' doesn't quite cut it, now does it? There aren't any days or nights when you're not orbiting a star on a rotating object, or so Audrine informs me.

Just cycles of waking and resting. I take her word for it. It's always dark outside and light inside. We do a good bit of sleeping just the same. Recharge our engines, and whenever we feel like it too.

The Collective doesn't keep any clocks around and our ArmPods can't tell time without a network to nanny them. The onboard tech is too cool to interface with the six-billion-year-old fossils embedded in our forearms. Me? I never needed anyone to tell me it was past my bedtime. I nab my share of zees and then I nab some more. ShortStack's not far behind me.

Audrine is happy to have someone to look after. It keeps her busy on a ship without much in the way of entertainment. The Collective's idea of dinner and a show is standing around silently while we shovel up bowls of clear nutrient pebbles. If they need anything to eat to keep from keeling over, they don't show it while we're around.

With the girl back, the tensions between Audrine and I have lightened. She might be sore with me, but she won't show it while the little one's about. Lucky for the lady—and maybe for me, too—watching after Bekka has turned into a full-time job. The kid loves to run around, explore the ship, watch The Collective work. Like a good cop, Bekka's keen to snoop but doesn't ask too many questions. She just giggles to herself and mutters under her breath, like she's figuring things out on her own.

Audrine is coping well, and I'm thrilled. But she's starting to hover. Chasing Bekka around like a busted NannyBot. After a couple days of it, I try to convince her otherwise, tell her that the ship is perfectly safe. Tell her the adults could use some 'alone time' to talk it out, clear the air. I send Bekka out to play so we can discuss our need for privacy in private. Audrine tells ShortStack to wait in the hallway. As soon as Bekka disappears out the door, the broad hops right on my back.

There's an anger brewing inside her. Those fists are clinched tight, knuckles white. I can almost see her nails digging trails into her palms. Wishing ever so slightly they were digging into my neck instead. "Do you want her to get sucked out the airlock like your friend with the yellow eyes?" Audrine asks.

I shrug, but make sure I'm at least an arm's length away first. "Don't sweat it, doll. He eventually made it back in one piece… somehow," I say. "And that little girl knows her onions when it comes to this ship, no kidding. She's safer out there than you or me would be."

"And that's good enough for you?"

Suddenly the rage collapses into despair. She's been putting on a brave face for the kid—for me even—but deep down, Audrine is still a full-on fiery wreck. I had my suspicions, but since the kid's been back we've avoided any kind of blowout breakdown, and *that* was good enough for me. Since I brought Bekka back it's been sunshine and mint juleps, at least on the surface.

"Stockton," she says through a wall of tears, "I just couldn't bear to lose her. Not her too. Not again. Not after everything else."

She collapses into a shower of sobs, for the first time failing to hide it from me. Forgetting to act tough.

I hold Audrine in my arms and squeeze her tight. I want to squeeze the sad right out of her, but her shivers start to send tremors through me instead. I cough to cover the quivers wracking me at the core. I play the stoic, all day everyday. Ignore my own pain. My own grief. Try to pretend like I didn't lose anything. Like I didn't lose everything. I'm on the verge of buckling.

The doorway opens.

ShortStuff steps through the membrane. I immediately pull myself together. Sit up straight. Wrench a smile across my kisser and toss a glance the kid's way.

"Why is Miss Audrine crying?" Bekka says.

I don't know how to answer.

We haven't broken the news to the kid yet. *Sorry Charlie, the entire planet has been cooked to a crisp! But at least you won't have homework!* That's not something they cover in the parenting books—not that we've read any. I never signed up for any of this, but Bekka's at least half my burden now, whether I like it or not. Audrine and I both stammer for a moment, packing a lot of "umm"s and "ahh"s into a three second gap.

"Is it because everyone is gone?"

This is one sharp little girl. I nod.

"Yes, Bekka," I say. "Miss Audrine is sad that everyone is gone."

Bekka nods too, then walks over to join us. She tugs at Audrine's arm and gives her a great big squeeze like only a little girl can. Throws all her weight into it. Audrine stops sobbing and looks down at our little friend.

"Miss Audrine," Bekka says, "my friends want you to know that you don't have to be sad." She reaches up on her tippy toes and wipes some tears from Audrine's cheek. "They say that it only seems like everyone is gone to you. But everyone all lived for a really, really long time. Just like normal. Better even! And for them, they were the sad ones. They were sad because you were the one that was gone."

Deep stuff for a munchkin. This is one *very* sharp little girl. And who are these friends putting such clever ideas into her tiny head? The Collective? What are they, chatting over cards and stogies when I look the other way?

Audrine thanks Bekka with a kiss on the forehead.

"Listen LittleBritches," I say. "Why don't you run along so Miss Audrine and I can finish talking?"

She looks up at the lady for approval. Audrine nods and Bekka scampers away. We wait for her to make it out the door before continuing the conversation.

"Where did that come from?" I ask.

"She's a very sweet little girl," Audrine says, wiping her eyes. "It was like poetry."

"Yeah," I say. "Where'd she cop it from? That line was a little too deep for such a tiny tomato to put together all on her lonesome. Has she been jawing with our gracious hosts while I'm in the can, or what?"

"Not that I've noticed," Audrine says. "She's probably just a scared little girl that happens to be very in touch with her feelings—not that a brute like you could relate to anything of the sort. She misses her mother and wants to imagine that her mother misses her as well."

"Alright," I say. "I'll buy it for now. But who are these friends of hers? You've seen her talking to herself. Carrying on with ghosts and laughing at empty rooms and silence. What gives?"

Audrine shakes her head at me.

"Stockton, you are paranoid! She's seven years old! There aren't any other kids around. She has no one to play with except you and me and her imagination. And we both know how much fun the two of us have been lately. Of course she's going to make up imaginary friends. I'd be concerned if she didn't!"

I take Audrine's word for it. Kids aren't anything close to my deck of cards. But I promise myself to keep a close eye on the pipsqueak just the same.

∞

The zookeepers don't have much dope on these other folks they're taking us to meet. Audrine wants to know if there will be any children for Bekka to play with. I want to know numbers, situations, locations. Food supplies and bar stocks. Logistics. ShortStack isn't much interested one way or another and she's got the right idea for as much as the boys in white are sharing. The Collective only have a destination and a vague genetic profile. "The other humans are at these coordinates. The other humans are just like you." Or that's all the freaks are willing to spill. I have a hard enough time deciphering their goofy way of speaking when they have something simple to say. Regardless, this lack of intel's a scary prospect. It's a real blind date scenario and I don't want to take one for the team.

The Collective let us run a tab for their hospitality and I'm grateful, but I still don't trust these faceless mugs with their rainbow eyes and ten-foot-tall foreheads. They're too quiet, with too many secrets. Where I come from, having something to hide can go two ways. It can get you killed or it can get me killed—and I don't want to get me killed.

Finally, the big day comes. We get prettied up in our finest rags. Nothing too rich, they're not hiding a BergdorfMarcus up here. Matching multi-zip gray utilities for the adults, courtesy of The Collective. I finger some embroidery stitched into the sleeve. *ORIGINS*, it says. It's curious, the first time I've seen anything resembling letters or language on the zookeepers' ride. I imagine they picked the stuff up wholesale, as salvage, seeing as they couldn't squeeze into any of the jumpsuits if they tried. Fits us just fine though.

Bekka curtsies in a nice yellow sundress and matching hair ribbons, thanks to Audrine's skill with a needle and thread. And here I am, telling her embroidery is an archaic skill. The girls pace nervously as we wait for our hosts. I'm a little hot to trot too, to tell the truth. It's a landmark event. Our little family is going to make its glorious reunion with the human race. An intergalactic homecoming.

A happy ending for everybody.

Mostly though, it's a great day to celebrate. All five zookeepers show up at our door to tell us we've dropped anchor and it's time to split. Even the statues are done up for the occasion; each wears a long flowing white robe with flashy swirling accents that match his eyes.

Like the wisemen before them, they've come bearing gifts: a big box of flavorsticks, and an even bigger cube of corn mash for me;

a well-loved, if slightly ratty BuddyBear for Bekka; and, in a hilariously misguided attempt, a fat stack of needles and pinchushions for Audrine. She thanks them gracefully just the same.

The Collective lead us in a little procession through the ship. It's all very ceremonial, like a parade honoring some late, great politico. We march silently in single file, passing through most of the other rooms we've visited before. This must be the first time I've gone around my elbow to get to my ass on this heap, and I chalk it up to showmanship. Some kind of grand finale farewell tour. We say goodbye to the silver spheres, the glass cubes with the menagerie denizens of Snot Baby City, and the healthy heaping of endless identical hallways in between. It's perfectly boring and incredibly fitting for our statuesque hosts.

Finally, we come to the reception chamber. Like so many of the other rooms, this one has a large viewport cut into the wall. But it's what's outside this window that catches our eyes.

Our new home. Our future.

In the distance, a sprawling station looms over a strange sight. A pair of perfectly smooth, enormous silver spheres sit in the distance behind the settlement. Not unlike the trunkful of fetus eggs the Collective has in storage, only super-sized, and only the two of them. They dwarf the station crawling around in front of them. I'd wager each one was at least ten miles wide, but I forgot my ruler.

"What in the hell are those?" I ask no one in particular.

"Those are stars, Stockton," Audrine says. "At least, I think so."

"Stars?" I say. "Those big shiny balls out there? What kind of stars look like that? More like a pair of metal melons if you ask me."

Audrine shakes her head and squints.

"They're neutron stars," she says. "Or at least, what's left of them."

"Neutron stars, huh? What gives with the chrome finish? I thought stars were just big balls of fire."

"Neutron stars are some of the densest objects in the universe, Stockton. Just a pinch of neutron star would weigh more than a mountain back on Earth. And a big mountain at that. These stars are so heavy that all of their protons and electrons get crushed in on themselves, until there's only neutrons rema—"

"Maybe tell me so I'll understand it, huh doll?"

"Put it this way: the gravity is so strong, that if you got close enough to one of those things, it would pull you in with so much force that your atoms would be destroyed."

"Destroyed, huh? Is that all?"

She smirks and mashes a fist into her palm.

"All of the matter in your body would be crushed into the same type of material as the star before you even had a chance to think about burning up, big boy. You'd be assimilated. Absorbed."

"Sounds lovely," I say. "I'm glad we'll have such nice neighbors at our new digs. How do you know so much about all this anyway? I guess I should hardly be surprised by anything you have to say by now, but this all sounds a little too technical for a pretty twist like you. No offense, doll."

Audrine gives me one of those looks that could strip paint.

"I know all about neutron stars, smart ass, because the Calvera II system that Seren Luna orbited was just like this one, only younger in its sequence. Not quite so collapsed, orbits less decayed. It was the intense gravity of those stars that made Seren Luna so progressively relative. They're what made it a good place to put a TimeResort."

"Sure," I say. "But those babies were sparkling and pretty. Bright red diamonds. Not like God's lost marbles out there. Not at all."

"Well, technically, the windows and domes at the resort made those particular stars much prettier, at least to our eyes. They displayed some false-color interpretations of the X-ray end of the spectrum, so the guests would find them more pleasant to look at."

"I'll say." I give a crooked look at the pinballs outside.

"In fact, given six billion years, without the help of the smart glass from the resort, those two stars would in all honesty look a lot like these two... you don't think—"

"Hey doll, I'm not ready to rule anything out." I scan the field for anything even faintly familiar. "But I don't see anything that looks like a resort out there."

The station itself looms huge, but without any frame of reference it's hard to tell meters from miles. The structure is certainly rambling, snaking around itself like a big bowl of dull, gray noodles. There's a large lumpy mass in the center, with veiny tendrils crawling out to the left and right. The whole thing has a haphazard feel to it. Different colors, different shapes, stacked together with no rhyme or reason. Like it was strung together by scavenging HoboBots, one ground-score at a time. Piecemeal StarCity, low-rent stellar tenements, last refuge of humanity.

Good enough for me.

We're still a good haul away, so it's hard to make out any fine details. Even when I squint, I don't spy any 'verts flashing *Live Girls* or holos hawking cheap hooch from this distance.

"Couldn't pull us in any closer?" I ask the zookeepers.

"Query denied," they say. "Presence of large unstable mass prevents advance."

Maybe those shiny space marbles have *them* scared, too.

"Well how do you expect us to get over there?" I say with a frown. "Should we start swimming?"

"Intermediary transport requested," they reply.

I peek out the window once more and spot a little pinpoint of light leaving the sprawl. Sure enough, it grows from a single pixel, to a toy shuttle, to a full-sized ride. Looks like tech from our time, too. Thank God. I wasn't quite sure what The Collective freakshow would consider "acceptable genetic variance." For all we knew they were sending us home to a station full of talking swine. It'll be good to have something in common with our new friends, even if it's just our idea of a smooth ride.

Audrine gathers us in close, straightening Bekka's glasses and wiping away a smudge on her cheek. She smooths my doo, too, before futzing with her own. She wants us to be the prettiest belles at the ball. I get it. First impressions are a one-shot show. I clutch the whiskey close under my arm as the shuttle docks below the viewport. Pull on my best quizstream smile and straighten my collar.

The doorway opens.

Four grungy-looking guys step through the membrane. My flat-foot-trained eyes are instinctively drawn to their hips. They're packing heat. A hodge podge of hacked-up long guns. It rubs me funny, but I try to stick myself in their size tens. If I were swooping strangers from some future freakshow tub, I'd hang a little hinky too. One of them straggles back behind the others, a rag-tagged, taped-up rifle slung over his shoulder. Pokey lugs one of those clear cubes that The Collective love so much. A big one. It's packed with racks and racks of tiny vials. Some of the test tubes are topped off with red liquid, others a milky white. Whatever they might have inside them, that's a lot of samples. A couple hundred doses from where I stand.

The other three humans assess us carefully, at a distance. Their peepers are glued to yours truly for the most part, as they circle slow, heads low. On the prowl. Like a pack of wolves. Or vultures.

Eyes dart to Audrine and stick around a touch too long for my fancy. I catch one licking his grimy lips. When they start to notice Bekka, I decide to break the tension.

"Howdy," I say, extending my arm for a handshake. "Stockton Ames, damned glad to meet ya!"

Wrong move. Hands flash to holsters. I take one rifle butt to the gut, then another to the back of the neck. The whiskey cube jumps out of my mitts and skitters across the floor. Next thing I know, I'm face down on the deck with a boot on my back and a rifle muzzle to my brainstem. What, do I have a sign on my back asking strangers to smack me with their guns and knock me to the dirt?

Despite the false start, there's still a slim shake to diffuse this mess.

"A little jumpy, huh fellas?" I grunt from my perch on the floor. "Can't say I blame ya. Listen, no hard feelings."

"No harm, no foul," Audrine adds in cheerfully.

"Tell that to the lump growing on my neck."

They ignore me, except to stomp harder on my stern side. I get a swollen hunch that this rude introduction is only the beginning of a very abusive relationship.

"Nice work, FutureBoys," one of the new guys says. The Collective?! They were in on this? "Why didn't you tell us there were *two* females?"

Those bastards!

"You sold us out!" I get the business end of a steel-capped boot. If this keeps up, I'll be gargling my own incisors before the day is over.

"That's enough out of you," the goon on my back says. They are officially deputized 'goon' status now. Card-carrying scumbags.

The other two lowlifes round on Audrine and Bekka. The broad takes a defensive stance, hips low, arms wide. Tries to stick Bekka behind her. But the little one is slick. Bekka dips out, weaving between the statue-esque members of The Collective. The guy with the vials has to set down his package to join in the chase. He snakes around the zookeepers too, finally nabs ShortStuff by the wrist and twists, until a tiny cry escapes her little lips.

Bekka's yelp seems to really upset Greenie, the nearest zookeep. Like lightning, the statue comes to life. Zaps his string bean arm out and gets a lanky paw around the weasel's neck. Lifts him right off his feet. The goon drops his weapon, using both hands to jimmy himself from the zookeeper's mammoth mitts. His legs flail around like he's practicing for an AirSprint marathon.

We've got a bit of a Plutonian standoff developing. Audrine is still managing to elude the two guys after her, backing away slowly. Her caboose is close to cooked, though. There's only so much room for the queen to maneuver on a board this small. Bekka's back on the lam. I'm well out of commission, a well-packed monkey on my back. And the last remaining goon is about to be snuffed out by a nine-foot-tall monster mannequin. If only these other statues would spring to life, we might have a fighting chance to come out of this scrape on top.

That course of action quickly becomes a cadaver. One of Audrine's chasers has had enough. He racks his rummage-sale rifle and opens up on The Collective. Must be some kind of non-kinetic model. A beam job. The rounds don't bounce, there's no ricochet. Just a brassy roar and a flash of light. But it gets the job done. All five of our former hosts are down for the long count. Cut to ribbons.

A golden, viscous fluid glazes everything and pools up beneath The Collective's shredded corpsepile. Poor Bekka cries out again, crouched behind a heap of bodies, her face splattered with CollectiveJuice greasepaint and streaked with fresh tears.

These goons are done messing around.

Another readies his rifle with an audible *CLA-CLACK* and points it squarely at Audrine.

"Forget it lady," he growls. "It's over."

She hangs her head in defeat.

THIRTY

The scumlords lock us down in bulky maglock shackles: wrists and ankles. Just like the ones we used to have back at the precinct, the kind of cuffs we only brought out for the real sickos. For guys like these. One of them kicks the vial cube as they line us up. The clear crate sloshes right into the french-fried bodies of The Collective, slip-sliding through a golden puddle on the floor. Looks like the statues were just a series of pneumatic tubes. Each slice of zookeeper is nothing but a cross-sectioned bundle of fiber optic cable, thoroughly shredded and lazily leaking sparkling amber fluid. No other organs or bones poke out from the mess.

There's a bit of red-blooded human viscera mixed in for good measure. Apparently, Goon #1 carved up his buddy along with his intended targets. He showed no hesitation. No remorse. What kind of cold-blooded Hell have we stumbled into?

One at a time, they march us through the exit membrane and into the airlock of a squalid shuttle. More of a dinghy really.

I'm surprised this wreck holds air at all.

One of the goons cradles my whiskey. Bekka still has her bear, clutched tight to her chest with chained little arms. Their dilapidated puddlejumper smells like sweat and fear, and not just the fresh kind. It's an old stench. Stagnant. Baked-in.

The shuttle airlock grinds shut with a groan. It could use a good lubing. As a matter of fact, this whole vessel could use a once-over with a couple cans of something strong. Electrical conduits are taped together carelessly. A rusty fuzz blankets the bulkheads and some unknown funk is caked onto the grates of the deck. Cheese-crusted McTasty's wrappers and other bits of litter lie stuffed behind pipes and crammed in crevices. Small armies of cockroaches scurry away at our approach.

Mister Lead Captor pounds three times on the cabin hatch. He looks up at an observation deck above the door, smiles and flips the camera the bird. The hatch hisses open with a puff of dust and he walks through. Audrine, Bekka and I move to follow.

The two goons behind us give us kidney sticks with their rifle barrels. "Nuh uh uhhhh," #1 says. He turns as he steps around us to keep the business-end of his weapon trained on our tender-bits.

"The trash rides back here," the other says, following his friend. He taps the holo recorder as he steps through the airlock. "We'll be watching," he says. "No screwing around, or—" He makes his hands into an opening slidelock. "—whooosh!" he finishes with a grin. The door slams shut behind him. I'll bet these plugs really would flush us out the hatch if we gave them half-a-reason to. We might be better off.

Audrine holds Bekka close as we rumble out of our dock with The Collective's ship, her chained arms draped over the little girl's chest like living armor. As we pull away, I peer through the cracked gash of a rear viewport and get my first good look at the exterior of the zookeeps' ride. It's a massive ship, easily dwarfing our dirty dinghy. Like a flea on a dead doberman, we're hopping off.

The Collective's tub is a manic maze. Constantly shifting, rotating, rearranging. It's made of ten thousand shiny white bubbles of various sizes and shapes, each one larger than our little boat. Altogether it would dwarf my building back home. Hell, it would dwarf any of the buildings back home, even those massive arcology towers out in the 'burbs. The bubbles roll around each other in a random but orchestrated waltz, much like the silver spheres or the clear cage cubes. There's a pattern to the madness.

"So that's how they did it," I say, mostly to myself.

The movement explains why you could walk out the same door and end up in a million different places. Those rooms were on the shove so you didn't have to be. The entire tub flip-flopped the floorplan at your beck and call. I like it. Simple. Effective. Sure saved me some long hikes and sore soles. I only wish we were still there to enjoy it.

Bekka looks up from her bear and waves goodbye. As she does, the bubbleship gets fuzzy at the far end, like the stream feed's gone bad. The vibration thickens slowly down the hull towards us and the bow begins reaching out towards infinity, like a piece of gum stretched between your shoe and the sidewalk. The gum-string snaps and the rest of the ship follows suit. In seconds, the whole thing is gone, sling-shotted to some distant star. To someplace safe.

"Cowards," Audrine says. She looks away, disgusted.

Bekka continues staring out the window, towards the little point of light they've disappeared into. I wonder who's flying the damn thing and start futzing with my shackles absently. I know it's not going to do me any good, these cuffs are solid as they come, but I'd feel like a shmuck if I didn't try.

The view doesn't change much for a while. A dark canvas splashed with stars. Below us, they're bunched so tightly they flow into a river of light. I'd call it pretty if I weren't watching it out the back of this shitheap paddywagon.

After a few minutes of flying straight, we boogie into a wide, sweeping bank. It's sudden enough to catch us all off guard, but not extreme enough to warrant more than a few short stumbles from our chained legs. Guess the inertial dampener is busted in this heap. Hell, I'm just glad the artificial gravity is working at all. I'd hate to be floating around in here with all this garbage and grime and God-knows-what-else. Audrine lefts her leg to make way for a particularly unprepared insect as it somersaults by.

As we roll out of the turn, we get a change of scenery, sliding right up beside that noodle station. Only it doesn't look like any station I've ever seen before. More like a graveyard. A refugee camp for wayward vessels. A salvage lot. There's a huge variety of spaceships, docked up to one another in a massive mound, like a mechanical orgy. Mostly personal craft: pleasure liners, staryachts, that sort of thing. A few military or cargo vessels thrown in for good measure. Many of these ships are in bad shape. Hull breaches, exposed skeletal ribbing. Serious structural damage.

I'm no freight jockey, but I know a clunker when I see one and I see a lot of them right now. This pile of rides extends for miles in both directions. Long, tubular corridors snake their way from cluster to cluster, like worms through a soggy stiff. At one point we pass a team of sorry saps in clunky EVO suits, assembling a new section of tubage. The tiny points of their torches burn an afterimage into my retinas that's still there when I shut my eyes and look away.

We zoom along next to the exterior wall of the 'station' for a few minutes before slowing down. I grab a standpipe assembly and brace myself for a rough docking procedure. This pilot isn't exactly Mr. McGentleflutters up there, and this ain't the Rainbow Friends' Cloudship from the Saturday morning toonstream, neither. But the docking doesn't come. Instead we pull a hard left, diving face first into the rusty heart of the junkyard. It's not a smooth ride and I can only imagine why. We bob and weave through the tangled mess of ships and copper-clad capillaries connecting them all together.

It's unnerving, only being able to watch out the back window. You can't anticipate any of the maneuvers, only see their justification once you've made them. You don't catch a 'why' until after the fact. A bit like life really.

I don't figure we'll make it through in one piece.

Not at the clip we're cruising. Not in this tight a squeeze. But we do make it. Without so much as a single bump and good thing. A little bump goes a long way when we're talking spaceships. Of course there's no accounting for near misses when you can't see where you're going.

We finally drop down to what I'd consider a safe pace, this time pulling up alongside the middle decks of a massive beast of a vessel. She's a dull, faded beige, and easily the size of a couple hundred of the smaller crafts. Might even give that Collective bubbleship a run for its money.

"Wow!" Bekka says with wide eyes, "This one is really big!"

I'd have to agree with her. We continue to roll alongside it.

"It's a Heavy Transport Vessel," Audrine says. "A materials tanker. People use these to build new homes on faraway worlds. They used one like this to build the resort at Seren Luna."

"Are we going to build a new home?" Bekka asks.

"I hope so," Audrine says, squeezing the little girl tight. She repeats herself softly. "I hope so."

We slow to a stop as our shuttle turns away from the monstrosity. Looks like we're backing in. We lurch in reverse into the big boy, approaching the hull through a huge set of hangar doors. Somebody's scrawled the words *FORGET IT* across them in sloppy, uneven capitals. The doors creak apart before us as we wait to enter. They move molasses slow and they're maintained about as well as our shuttle, showering our glass hatch with thin, stringy sparks.

Finally the doors slide away, revealing streaks of rust and a patchwork quilt of hull repairs inside. We putter in and wait for the airlock doors to do their thing. The first set clangs together, shutting out the unforgiving emptiness of the vacuum outside. Our ride shakes a bit as the hangar airlock is pressurized. A loud groaning rattles the shuttle as the interior doors breach. One more short hop and the pilot puts us down on the deck.

The goons emerge from the forward cabin, rifles in hand, engaged in some mindless banter. They're quick with the gun butts, prodding us out the rear hatch as it folds open. There's a low deck height on this particular model, so Audrine and I hop down, before turning around to help Bekka.

We emerge into a large, darkened hangar. Only a few glowing spots beam down from the high ceiling at random intervals. Looks like nobody here knows how to change a bulb. I catch a whiff of that slaggy, scorched-metal welding aroma. Sure enough, my eyes are assaulted by a bright flash of plasma arc torches. A crew is lazily patching the skin of another bird in the next stall. There are a half-dozen other small craft in here, parked crooked in the bays along the main runway like the rotten teeth in a junky's gums. Most are in worse shape than that hunk of bunk we ferried in on. We're herded past them by the goons, who acknowledge the hoots, hollers and catcalls of the maintenance monkeys with sly nods and big smiles.

I try to walk tough. Stand tall. Stare down the creeps making eyes at Audrine and Bekka. Let them know we won't go down without a fight, but it's a little difficult to look tough in leg irons.

We make it to the ass-end of the hangar. The stink of pneumatic fluid and hot plasma singes my nostrils and makes me woozy. I could sure go for a rye right about now. The giant cargo slidelock at the back of the hangar is mostly ajar, the door panel hanging open at an awkward angle with enough room to walk right under.

What a shithole.

We step through the broken door into a lobby of sorts, a bank of lift tubes splayed around us in a semicircle. And I do mean tubes—only one of the lifts is actually parked here. The rest are just doorways opening into dark, dead drops. I contemplate hip-checking one of the goons down a shaft, but think better of it. I've had enough fun with elevators for one lifetime.

One of the goons hocks a loog down an empty tube as we're ushered into the adjacent lift. It's a big mother. The lift, that is. Not the loog. For unloading cargo originally, would be my guess. You could comfortably fit a couple magcabs inside if you needed to.

They step in behind us, gunsights never leaving our torsos. The slidelock closes behind us as Goon #2 hits the bottom option on the terminal. Looks like we're going all the way down. The lift lurches a bit, dropping a few inches before the pneumatics cut in and begin our controlled descent. Audrine and I share a nervous glance.

They sneer at our reaction and Goon #3 reaches down to pinch Bekka's cheek. "Whatsamatta sweetie?" he says with a sneer. "There's nothing to be scared about."

He flashes blackish teeth.

"Don't you touch her!" Audrine says, giving him a hard shove with manacled hands.

Here we go.

"Aww lady, you shouldn'ta done that," he says, shouldering his rifle and cracking his knuckles.

THIRTY-TWO

The lift cranks to a stop five minutes later.

I'm sporting quite the shiner and a badly busted lip, but you should see the other guy. He's gonna be slurping his McTasty's Brand meatpatties through a straw after the hurt I laid on him. Maybe next time he'll learn to keep his hands to himself.

Frankly, I'm a little surprised they didn't just off me outright. I know they have it in them—I watched them slice up one of their own not thirty minutes ago—but I guess I'm worth a lot more alive than I am dead. It's good to know, but I don't intend to press my luck about it. Then again, I don't *intend* to do lots of things.

I definitely didn't make life any easier on myself. The jerks are much less hesitant to use the rifle rumps as we exit, and they weren't exactly stingy with them before. Goon #3 is left to nurse his limp jaw in the lift while they herd us out. I give him a wink as I step by. He pretends not to notice. First smart thing he's done all day.

A rush of cold, wet air greets me as I step out of the lift. My eyes search for the ceiling in a cavern of a space that would make the Knight's

PeoplesBank Stadium feel quaint. Must be the ship's hold. Big black girders frame a rack system that towers above us in all directions, holding, well, more girders. Sheets of plexisteel are piled in rolled stacks around us. Like the rest of the tanker, it ain't exactly bright in here. They've got the lamps on where they need them, mostly, and not anywhere else.

We follow a barely lit path as it winds between soaring rows of hastily placed building materials. I try not to trip, but I have to glance up from time to time to doublecheck that the half-assed stacks aren't going to come crashing down on our heads. The creaks and groans leaking out don't help me to feel any better about the shoddy stack-job.

Once again the stench of molten metal fills the air. Some grease-monkeys are baking steel banana pie in here, or I'll have the first slice. Stepping lightly, we approach a little kiosk dipped into the teetering, towering racks. More like a cubby really, tucked under a mountain of flexible conduit and thin, dented sheet metal. Looks like the kind of joint that slings bootleg McTastyFreezes by the bay, and boy am I parched. A pair of thick-armed thugs lounge outside, sawed-off dustguns holstered on their hips.

The thugs stop jawing and flash us the old once-over. They've got the look of two mooks that are paid to be concerned, sporting ratty neon tanks and dark, baggy dungarees, taped into their chunky moon-boots. I smile and shake my head at the Dust Bunnies logo stenciled onto one of their shirts. These fellas glance at us through slanted, colorless eyes as we approach. A tubby little ball of flesh squats behind a counter built into the kiosk, stabbing a smoking soldering iron into a BuddyBear's exposed circuit board. He's an older guy, not much pepper to his salt. A once-white wife-beater fights a losing battle with his bulky frame, and his tufted face lights up when he sees us.

Bekka clutches her own bear even tighter and covers its eyes.

One of the goons gives me a particularly nasty 'stop' command with his boot. Right in the side of the knee. It buckles faster than a bluenose's belt and I make a little pile of my own in front of the cubby.

"Now, now," the fatman says, setting down his circuit-burner. "Is that anyway to treat our new guests?"

He lifts up a section of counter, and loose tools and trash pour to the floor. The fat man waddles over to us. Like everyone else we've met here, he's grimy. Smeared with grease and stained with crusty perspiration. Must be a full-time job to stay clean in a place like this, and they've only hired part-time help.

He wipes his paws on the front of his sweats, not that it helps any. At this point, he's just pushing the dirt around.

"Shove off, Smitty," Goon #1 says from behind me. "You didn't see what the big guy did to Marv. Just give us the chits and fade." He hocks another one onto my back.

Poor guy must have a sinus infection.

Smitty bends down with some effort, helps me to my feet. Even brushes the goob off my back. What a saint. He stares into my face, a huge grin poking through the scraggly mess he must think is a beard.

"Well I'm sure Marv had it coming," he says with a wink for me. "Maybe you'd like me to inform the man upstairs that you've been abusing our new friends?"

This Smitty sounds nice enough. Maybe we just got off to a slow start here. Bad luck brought us a couple of errand boys with no manners and mean streaks to match. Smitty reaches into his pocket and pulls out a handful of something. Silently sprinkles a dash of color into each of the goons outstretched palms. Something light. Plasticy.

The two goons count out their score in calloused palms before pocketing it. "He's your problem now."

They walk out the way we came in and Smitty leads us in the opposite direction. The thugs with the dusters and tank tops follow behind us, chatting again at a healthy distance. Each one keeps a single eye on us, and judging by the size of their guns, that's enough for them.

Smitty puts a flabby arm around my shoulder. It's damp, but I pretend not to care. "I trust our colleagues weren't too rough with you back there?"

"Nothing I couldn't handle," I say.

"That's good, that's good!" he says. "The Tartarus can be a great place to live, so long as you follow the rules. Our Captain, he's a great man. Really a top notch human being. He tries to keep things like this to a minimum." Smitty gestures to my swollen face.

"Is that so?" I say, feigning disinterest. We duck our heads to pass under a section of thick pipe skewered across the path before us. It's good to hear, if he means it. My mouth has gotten me into hot water before, but in a place like this it just might get me boiled, and fast.

"Oh, yes, yes, yes, yes," he says. All those 'yesses' come out at once, like he poured them from a bucket. "Surely you've heard of our Captain Nyxo." It's not a question. "Tell, me," he says, "which quadrant did you come from?"

"Quadrant?" I say.

"You know," he says. "Which part of The Heap? We're right smack in the middle of the Forward Central Core here on the Tartarus."

"The Heap?"

His face lights up. The beard drips crumbs at the stretch of his smile. "Don't tell me we've got a bunch of first timers here today!" he says. He pulls the collar of my coveralls back and peers at my neck. "Oh don't mind me!" he says. I know better than to 'mind him' in front of his buddies behind us. He gets a good look and lets go. "Why, you weren't jerking me around!" he says.

"Now why would I want to go and do that?" I say.

"Some honest to goodness newbies!" he yells back to the two guys tailing us. They each nod once then return to their chat. "Oh this is exciting!" He claps his hands together like a schoolgirl. "We haven't seen any fresh faces around here in such a long time!"

He pats me on the back and leads us along the pathway, which has only gotten less walkable since we started down it. The building supplies hang at sharp, stupid angles, choking the trail. A stray strand of stiff wire reaches out and snags my shirt, ripping a tiny tear and scratching into my shoulder as I shuffle by on chained legs. Glancing around, I notice a definite lack of action going on around here. Where are all the worker bees that should be tacking up tar-paper with all these materials? I hear some faint clangs and bangs in the distance, but this joint is mostly blown.

"So where did you come from? *When* did you come from? How did you get here? Were there others with you?" Smitty blabbers on. He doesn't really pause to breathe as he speaks. I don't know when he expects us to slip an answer in.

"Uhhhh," I say, until he cuts me short.

"Oh, we'll have time for all that chitter-chatter later on. I'm sure the Captain will want to meet you. He always likes to greet the new folks personally! In the meantime let's get you over to orientation."

'Orientation' comes out funny. Drawn out, like it's some kind of inside joke. Like it means something different to him than it does to me.

We make a sharp right at a wide pile of compressed air tanks, then a left under a roll of dangling fiberwrap strands that tickle my nose, then three straight rights, a couple more lefts. I'm not so sure I could nav my way out of this junkyard if someone drew me a map. The path gets narrower and narrower, as the effort to clear the materials out of the way got lazier and lazier. A bundle of waist-thick cable leans precariously against a net of frayed webbing. Our little chain gang shimmies past it, sideways and single file. We reach a dead end, with just a single shoulder-width culvert stabbing through the wall of junk ahead. Thankfully, Smitty calls an all-stop before I drop to my knees and belly-crawl.

Beside us, a shadowy shack of a structure pulses with a dull, red glow. *Oryntayshon* is scrawled on a piece of rusty scrap panel above the entrance. Smitty ducks through the door-hole and waves us in.

"You'll have to excuse the dust," he says. "We're in the middle of a very large project at the moment and haven't had much time to focus on our internal facilities. Come, come, come. It's quite all right."

We step into the shack, although from inside it's really more of a closet with a ramshackle roof. That winking red glow pours out of a plexisteel panel in the back. There's a low rumbling noise and a slight vibration from the floor, like we're parked one deck above a snoring dragon-mech.

The thugs move to block the door. Audrine glances nervously in their direction. "No need to worry," Smitty says. "Here let me get these maglocks off of you. Just a safety precaution, I'm sure you understand. We can't be too careful."

He bends down and releases the shackles on my legs. I stretch each ankle out individually and shake. Maybe things'll work out after all. I extend my wrists to our tubby friend so he can bag those bracelets as well. In one swift motion he pulls something from a pocket and slaps it on the back of my neck. Didn't think the old bowl of jelly had it in him.

"What the hell?" I say.

It's cold. Tingly. Slimy. Buzzing needle-thin tendrils spiderweb into my flesh. An icy chill vines its way around my spinal cord, tap dances into my brainstem. "Is this some kind of transderma medipatch or what?"

I instinctively reach up to peel it off. But I don't get that far.

My arm takes a timeout mid-reach. My biceps quiver under tension, but try as hard as I can, they won't move a hair. And it's not just my arms. My head, my legs, my eyes, it's like somebody hit the pause button on my whole damned body. Smitty waves a black rectangular gadget in front of me.

"Don't try to fight it," he says. "The SI chip is 100% effective at blocking neuromuscular synapses from your somatic nervous system. Of course your spinal reflexes and smooth muscle groups will still function normally." He knocks on my funny bone with the remote to prove his point. My arm waves slightly with each tap. "We wouldn't want that old ticker of yours to stop tocking, now would we?"

He cackles at his own wisecrack.

In all the commotion, Audrine gathers Bekka into the far corner of the shack, and tries to back away through a mess of tangled wire fence. "*Tsk, tsk, tsk,*" Smitty says, turning to face them. He snaps and the two thugs have their guns drawn in an instant.

"Be good little girls and come get your chips from Ol' Smitsies."

One of the thugs racks a shell with a loud *CLA-chick-chock* to show us all he means business. Audrine and Bekka comply. They stand in front of me, and each one shivers when Smitty sticks her with the chip.

"Look straight ahead now, yes that's right," he says. He adjusts the position of their heads manually. When he's satisfied, he locks them down and pops the joints in his fingers.

"I am terribly sorry about this," he says, walking down the line and staring into each of our eyes. I can feel his hot breath on my face like last week's garbage. "It most certainly is for *your* benefit. I assure you, the alternative is much worse. This next part is… unpleasant, to say the least. Please try to stay perfectly still."

He walks away now, waddling over to the glowing red panel in the back. I can only catch him out of the corner of my eye, but it looks like he's putting his arm into some kind of big oven mitt, all the way to the shoulder. He turns around and steps out of view.

There's a little creaky whining sound, like a magcab with bad brakes backing over a basset hound, then the shack gets toasty. A blast of bone dry, boiling hot air erupts from the back, along with a deafening roar. Smitty pokes that sleeping dragon. Another creak. The gust and the noise die down and Smitty is back in front of me, holding something long and dark, with a glowing tip. He slides it close to my cheek, lets me feel the heat.

I'm sweating alright.

He puts his lips to my ear. "So sorry, frienddddd," he whispers softly, drawing out the last syllable like a sigh. Then he backs away and sticks the brand right into the side of my neck. I want to scream. I want to run, to fight, to grab it away from him and beat him to death with the damned poker until he's a pulpy puddle of slop on the floor beneath me. But I can't do a damned thing.

The brand burns so hot that it feels cold. He stabs it into my flesh harder. My nostrils fill with a smell like burning hair, except I know it's not hair. It's skin. My skin. My muscle. Smoking. Burning. Cooking.

I gag on a wisp of black smoke and Smitty pulls the brand away.

"Don't want to ruin the mark," he says with a giggle.

The fat bastard returns to the furnace vent in the back, recharges the iron and steps up to do Audrine next. I don't want to watch but my eyes won't shut. This damned chip holds my lids open, forces me to see. It's worse than having my own neck seared, but not by much.

Smitty takes great pride in his work. He's happy to be doing it. He smiles as he buries the prod into her slender neck. When he finishes with Audrine he gives her smoldering wound a little lick. Smacks his lips. "Tastes a smidge like bacon," he says. "Remember bacon, boys?"

I'm going to kill this Smitty, one way or another. He's a dead man, even if it calls for all the marbles in my sack.

Audrine's charred flesh is raised in the shape of the brand. A smileycon, of all things, with a vertical line drawn down through the center.

He goes back to the furnace a third time. So help me God if he harms one hair on that little girl's head, I'll go straight for his throat as soon as he releases me. He returns to Bekka, the steaming poker in hand. Brushes her hair aside, gets a closer look. Her eyes don't move. She's frozen, unable to express the terror that's tearing her apart inside. He holds the brand up next to her tiny neck. Tries another angle. Then another. Finally he pulls it away.

"You'll have to grow some before we can mark you, little one," he says with a shrug. He turns to the thugs. "I told them we needed some child-sized tools, but no one ever listens to old Smitty, now do they?"

Thank God. He turns back to Audrine and I.

"Apologies, friends," his voice is a hiss in my ears. Serpent-like. "We must make sure that ship property is properly marked. We can't have Captain Nyxo's belongings wandering off on him, can we?"

I try to growl but all that comes out is a wheezing cough.

"Now if I let you loose, will you promise to be good little pets?"

Smitty drinks in our faces closely, pressing his fat, rotten smile up to my beeze in the process. The stink pouring out his lips would choke a goat.

"Yes, yes, yes," he says. "I think perhaps we will behave."

He totters away to a safe distance outside the shack just to be sure, then tugs out the remote.

He clicks us free with a single finger and I move straight for him. Paws out, ready to crush his weaselly little windpipe. There are no thoughts in my brain, just a burning rage. A reptile instinct to kill. To bag this bastard with my bare hams.

I make it two or three steps before the thugs unload both dust-guns square into my babybacks from near point blank. The force yanks me off my feet as the blast powder burrows into my back muscles. I'm thrown wide of the doorway and slam headfirst into a stack of thick steel beams. My brain smacks the inside of my skull so hard I can hear it ring.

The last thing I see is Smitty's gap-toothed grin, looking me over.

THIRTY-THREE

I come around slowly.

The first thing I recognize is pain: a soggy, lead blanket that covers everything else in stinging needles and bone-deep bruises. Then a gentle rocking motion, like I'm hitching a ride in a hovering baby buggy. Then some voices. That slaggy, scorched-iron stench that permeates everything and wallops my already wincing nostrils. But mostly, all I know is the pain. My vision returns last.

I've got a lovely view of the floor grates, swaying back and forth, tying my guts in knots. They're dragging me somewhere. My char-broiled neck burns so bad it's practically numb. My back is blazing, pounded. Like a hundred lemons squeezed into a thousand papercuts. Like I've been marinated and tenderized by a heavyweight prizefighter. There's blood slipping down my sleeves, falling off my hands onto the grates below, but not so much I should cry about it.

Why am I not dead? Those dustguns should have cut me in half.

I want to ask, but all that comes out is a wet "unnnghhh" sound. We stop moving for a moment and my esophagus plays double-dutch with my tonsils. Smitty's matted beard pops into my field of view.

318

Hunks of pale, congealed fat are burrowed in the gray, hairy mess.

"So we're awake now, are we?" he says. "Welcome back to the land of the living, friend." He disappears once more, and makes a nasally clucking noise with what's left of his teeth.

The swaying starts up again.

"You're right on time," he says. "We've almost got you back to your new quarters. I'm sure you'll just love them!" He claps me on the back. A network of nerves cry uncle, sizzling across my skin and down into my ribs. For a moment it even drowns out the screams from my pan-seared neck. "And aren't you a lucky one! If those first two dummy rounds didn't take you down, Germayne and JJ here had real shells in the chamber next. We'd be mopping you out of the deck right about now."

So that's why I'm still kicking. Less-than-lethal ammo. Would explain the stinging chorus of needles in my back, too. Pointed little pellets of vaporized chemical salts to maximize the burn. A dollop of knock-out drops in the powder to make me blackout. That, or the blunt force trauma of headbutting a pile of plexisteel pipes. I make a mental note to ask my neurologist.

We arrive at our destination and I'm heaved in like a sack of canned potatoes. Small cell, smooth cement floor, iron bars all around, a single rusty bucket in the corner. Not exactly the Ritz. It could use a once-over with a paint roller. Or a slamdozer.

"Please enjoy your stay," Smitty says with a sickening smile. "Someone will be with you shortly I'm sure." He turns to Bekka and Audrine, ushering them into an adjacent cage with a surprising tenderness. "And I will certainly be back to visit you two lovelies." He turns to go.

"Hey Smitty." I say. He turns to face me. "Eat shit."

His grin sours. "Now, now. After all the kindness I've showed you? Germayne, JJ? Let's teach our guest here some manners."

Here it comes. I'm good as ground beef. I can't even manage to sit up, let alone broil these bruisers off. I close my eyes, hoping to take my beating with some dignity.

I feel a pair of mitts on each arm. They pick me up. Guess it's no fun to kick a dog while he's down. My new pals lift me off my feet and shove my shoulders up against the cement wall in the back. Hot damn! The chem pellets grind up into my hide like black peppercorn buckshot, currying my nerve endings. I wince through clenched teeth and squeeze my eyes shut to bear it.

The thugs get me into a wall-sit position, like we used to do for PT at the academy. They put me propped against the wall, an invisible chair under my ass. And then, well, that's it. They leave me there. I try to open my eyes.

Shit! They've switched on the puppet chip again. I'm stuck like this until they release me. Footsteps head out. The cell door creaks shut with a clang. "Now you just sit here and think about what you've done for a few hours," Smitty says.

Hours!? Ten minutes was a good record for us at the academy, and that was back when I was a few years younger, a few sizes smaller. My legs are going to break off at the knee before these fellas get back to free me. Not to mention the salty, stinging crumbs slowly digesting my bleeding back muscles. I hear three sets of boots fade down the hallway and disappear.

Silence for a few seconds, then some scuffling moves towards me. "Stockton! Stockton! Can you hear me?" It's Audrine. "Are you okay?"

I can't respond. The blood slides down my back in a network of itchy channels and drips to the floor with a series of tiny *plip-plops*.

"I'm absolutely sure he can hear you."

Another voice. A stranger. From the left. Female. New Union accent. Prim and proper, just like the Queen Mother's Auntie Alice. Sounds like we have some company. "As far as if he's alright or otherwise, I wouldn't worry much about it either way."

Audrine backs away, startled by our new friend too. "Why... why shouldn't I worry about it?"

"Hmmmm," the stranger says. "How to put it gently? It's best if you just forget him now. Doesn't matter what your relationship was before—" A pause. "—and I don't see any rings, dear. You should certainly give him up. They won't let you stay together, not here. If anything they'll just use him against you."

Audrine approaches my cell again.

"*They*? Who is they? This Captain Nyxo guy?"

The stranger laughs, a tinny, empty sound.

"This captain? That captain? It doesn't matter. The station chiefs and quadrant warlords are much the same all over The Heap. They have a saying: 'Flesh is flesh.' Nyxo is only different because he's important. A big shot. Personally I'd rather belong to someone powerful than some 8-bit bandit commanding a hedgehopper like he's king of the forest. Less chance of getting zapped by a stray raiding party."

There's silence again. "I'm sorry," Audrine says finally, "but I have no idea what you're talking about. The Heap? Station chiefs? Raiding parties? This is all very new to us."

The stranger gets closer.

"Oh, darling," she says. "I'm so sorry! It's been so long since I've seen any new arrivals. I was nearly positive there weren't any left to find." She sighs. "My name is Zee." There's another brief pause, some rattling near the bars. A handshake maybe.

"So," Zee continues, "When and where did you come from?"

Audrine tells her.

"Mmhhmm," Zee says. "Many of us have similar stories. Those gravitational wave events occurred at most of the TimeResorts eventually, even affected some of the deeper plotted StarLiners. Seren Luna just happened to be one of the first to make the leap. To nosedive a few billion years into the future.

"Back on Earth, they didn't know what happened, of course. The resorts just started dropping off the map. We stopped getting response calls from the remote Generators. There were all kinds of theories of course. Supernovas. Terrorist attacks. Revolts by the guests. Alien invasion. The Rapture." Zee sighs again.

"But if you knew all that, how did you end up stuck here?" Audrine says. There's a shuffling sound, closely followed by a third sigh. Our new friend Zee gets comfortable in the next cell.

"I worked for a JanosCorp research and recovery team," she says. "Corporate salvage. We were sent to investigate the 'abandoned' TimeResorts. Of course we didn't figure out what had happened until it was too late. My team and I all ended up riding a gravity wave six point something billion years into the future, just like you and everyone else here, with all of our notes and findings in tow. It's too bad, really. We had the data. Could have shut those places down, saved so many poor souls from… well, from this."

"And what about The Collective?" Audrine says.

"First I've heard of them," Zee answers. "Though I'm not surprised. Humanity made all kinds of interesting evolutionary branches while we were in transit. All of them our direct descendants. There are rumors, even, that our genetic offspring have evolved beyond our familiar four dimensions, into beings we cannot possibly comprehend with our simple, biochemical brains. Not that there's any way to prove something so absurd, of course.

"As a species, Homo sapiens are relics now. Living fossils of a time long since passed, paying the price for stepping beyond our bounds. The universe doesn't belong to us anymore, inasmuch as it ever did." She sighs. "I'm sure you've met the Hags? Nasty little buggers. Sharp teeth? Big claws? Pale, slimy skin?"

"Yes, we're familiar," Audrine says. I picture her absently rubbing the three tender scars slashed through her shoulder.

"Those fiends are everywhere," Zee continues. "My team and I ran into them time and again at the empty resorts. We never figured out where they came from—or *when*, for that matter—just that they were incredibly successful, biologically speaking. You'll have a hard time finding anyone here that hasn't had a bloody run with them."

"And where is here?" Audrine asks. "We keep hearing about this Heap…"

"Ahh, yes," Zee says, "The Heap." She takes a deep breath. "The bloody, good-for-nothing Heap. The Heap is humanity's last stand, sad as it were. Well at least Homo sapiens' last stand: humanity as you and I know it, anyway. Unless there are some lost pockets of human civilization out there somewhere, and I certainly haven't seen any signs of them, this is it. Home-sweet-home."

"But what is it?" Audrine says. "Where did it come from?"

"It's an interstellar refugee camp. A collection of starships, frozen comet cores, asteroids, space junk, orbital stations, and, well, human flesh," Zee explains. "I don't know the how or why of the origin. My team found it much the way you did. They say someone arrived first, and after some beacons went up, everyone else started to drop anchor here as well."

"Drop anchor where?" Audrine asks. "Where are we exactly? In the galaxy, I mean."

"Don't you know then, dearie?"

"Know what?"

"Well I rather assumed you recognized the twins out there."

"You don't mean…"

"I'm afraid so. You're right back where you started: the Calvera II system. Of course there's nothing left of your resort. Some sort of massive explosion tore Seren Luna to tiny pieces a long time ago, likely not long after you left. It was to be the last stop on our investigatory tour. Little did we know how true that would be."

"TimePilot…" Audrine says. "The payload…"

"What's that, dearie?"

"Nothing. Nothing important, anyway. Why here? What's so special about Calvera II? I apologize for asking so many questions, but I don't really have anyone else to ask."

"Oh no, it's quite alright. You're lucky you found me. Most of the dullards around here wouldn't know a gravitational wave from their own filthy arses." Zee taps the bars. "My assumption was that the survivors wanted to ride out the rest of their time at a highly progressive relativity—just like the guests at your resort did. They hope that someone out there will swoop in and save them. Rescue them from this horrible future. Maybe someone like those friends that dropped you off."

"Fat chance," Audrine says. "Isn't anyone worried about the neutron stars collapsing even further? Isn't it terribly dangerous?"

My legs start to cramp up something fierce, but I'm very much on board with Audrine's line of questioning. She'd have made a fine detective. I'll have to congratulate her later.

"I suppose it's marginally dangerous," Zee says. "When those two stars finally slip into each other, there will be quite the violent display. Hot plasma. Gamma ray burst. Bad news. A brand new black hole will be waiting to eat up anything that wasn't vaporized in the fire. But that shouldn't be for millions of years yet, relative time."

"You know, we didn't expect to end up billions of years in the future either," Audrine says. "And yet here we are."

"Yes, but we're talking relativity. As long as we orbit the Calvera II twins, we'll experience the same dilation they will. We're safe enough here, I suppose. You have more to worry about the men inside this station than anything outside it, far as I know. Long as the hulls hold air, we'll get by.

"Personally I'd have plopped down on a habitable planet—something with some nice, sunny beaches, perhaps, a bloody breathable atmosphere, even—but nobody asked me, now did they? It's not a terrible location we have here, for a frigid, empty void I suppose. Plenty of room for everyone. There may be some other merit to the place. Something I haven't thought of. Some use for the large gravitational forces. Frankly though, I have my own problems to fret over, dear."

Silence again as Audrine soaks it in. "How did you find the Heap" Audrine asks. "What brought you here?"

"When we tried to report in halfway through our mission and got no response, we knew something had happened. So we made a return trip and had much the same realization that you did. We very quickly realized Earth was no longer a viable location for life, so we searched the old home system for other survivors. There weren't any survivors to be found, of course. Just a swollen sun, a few scorched stones and a bunch of empty orbital stations. We came here when we received radio signals—the only signals mind you—that had the look of intelligent life."

She laughs.

"*Intelligent*. We didn't realize until it was too late that this place is more like a zoo. A step backward for mankind. *Pffft*. We'd have been better off out there in open space. On our own."

"What happened to the rest of your team?" Audrine asks.

"Enslaved, dead, or otherwise preoccupied. As a general rule, most of the captured men are put on extra-vehicular operations: EVO duty. Any kind of dangerous work requiring vacuum exposure is done with slaves: facility maintenance, patching hulls, welding new tunnels, scrapping old ships, salvaging what they can from vessels without working life support systems."

"Seems like kind of important work for forced labor," Audrine says. "Aren't they worried about sabotage? Plain-old poor workmanship?"

My thoughts exactly.

"No," Zee says. "The overseers have a bit of a harsh hand when it comes to any kind of failure, deliberate or otherwise. 'One and done.' A single, teensy mistake and they cut your cord. Severe your tether to The Heap. Leave you to float off into the void and think about what you've done until your oxygen runs out. It's a great deterrent against mutinous behavior, although it doesn't do much for morale.

"Lately, they've been working on something enormous, something difficult. A lot of the crews aren't coming back at all. I don't know what it is they're building out there, only that it must be a truly massive undertaking. They've been coordinating across quadrants—and these savages never do that! The men in charge are not very good at sharing, responsibilities or anything else. Hence the branding."

"And what about the women?" Audrine says.

"Ahh!" Zee laughs. "That we'll find out soon enough won't we?" She pauses, takes a deep, longing breath. "It's not so bad, once you grow accustomed to it. Some cleaning, some cooking. Some more 'adult' activities. Most of the free men will treat you well enough, as long as you keep your head down and don't stick your neck out. Like, well..." She clears her throat. "Like for the wee one here."

Audrine gasps.

"You can't expect me to just throw her to the wolves!"

"I know it's difficult, darling," Zee says, "but the wolves will have her whether you throw her to them or not. Better to have you alive and able to care for her. There are similar punishment policies for the female slaves. They might hesitate with a pretty face like yours, but I can assure you, they aren't above putting you out the airlock. Or worse."

My legs quake. A steady stream of sweat pours from my head.

My back and neck are one big bowl of dragon-chili fire. But it's my conscience with the biggest gripe. I can't let anything happen to Bekka and Audrine. Anything more than they've already been through. If I could just find some way to let them fly the coop, I'd pay their way.

I hear something slide over towards me. Bekka's squeaky little voice pierces my veil. "Don't worry, Mister Stockton," she says softly. "My friends say everything is going to be alright." This kid's got some mighty optimistic invisible friends. I want to tell her thanks, that she's spot on. But of course, I can't say a damned thing. She scampers back to the other side of her cell in a highway hurry, and then I hear them too.

Footsteps.

Somebody's coming. Heavy boots, several pairs. A gaggle, even. This might be my ticket. I need to take my time, play it cool. Wait for the right moment to strike.

There's a clattering at the gate.

"Alright, big guy!" A male voice says. "On your feet! Work detail's kicking off and you're on the docket."

THIRTY-FOUR

They release me from the SI chip's grasp. My legs turn to butter and I melt to the floor. I'm a pile of limbs on the concrete before I even know they've cut me loose. If I ever hit the gym again, it'll be too soon.

Someone puts hands on me chop-chop, sliding my head into a rough burlap sack. I don't even get a chance to sprinkle the scene, check on Audrine and the kid, eyeball our awfully informative new friend. They pull me up to my feet but don't bother with the leg irons this time. No need. I can just barely walk as it is. My muscles are rubber, still trembling from my time on the invisible chair. On the positive side, I think I set a new world record. Some cuffs clamp down on my wrists and they begin to drag me away.

"Where are you taking hi—" Audrine is interrupted by the hot buzz of a high-voltage stunstick. I hear the goon running it up and down the bars of her cage, laughing. The stunner pops and screams as the electrodes clip the cold, metal rods. I know I'm scratching a hard buck here, but I call out to her anyway, goons be damned.

"Nevermind me," I shout through the hood. "Look out for the kid."

The goon with the wand turns his prod on me. Zaps me hard, right in the crank. The shock knocks me to my knees and gives me the heaves, but not any time to feel sorry for myself.

"One more peep and it's curtains for you, Stretch," he says, mocking me and yanking me to my feet. "Are we crystal?"

I nod in my sack-hat, unable to make words even if I wanted to.

"Bullion," he says.

They half-kick, half-march me through another maze of twists and turns and I'm good to my word, a perfectly silent little lamb, all alone in the dark. After an age, we hit a lift and pop out in a din of chattering voices and shuffling feet. The goons cut the cuffs, pull my hood and toss me in a makeshift chain-link pen with a dozen other low-life mooks. Then they split.

We're a slapdash group, my new cellmates and me, sporting as many different styles of cloth as we've got faces. There's one guy in a dirty tux. Another in swim trunks and a tropico. Most of the others are dressed for fun in the sun too. I feel out of place, in my sturdy second-hand coveralls. A sloppy scrawled sign is fastened to the fence behind me. It reads *Fish Markgit*.

A small crowd mills about outside the cage. Hard-faced men in bulky, patched-up EVO suits and bad haircuts. They gab it up in small groups like they're at the pub for a ballgame—until a big Noodle with long, white moustaches puts both hands to his lips and whistles attention into everyone. He approaches the cage and suddenly he isn't so big after all. He's just a tall turnip in a sea of shorties. Maybe reaches my nose on his toes, on a good day. I scan the crowd and count four times as many Oriental faces as anybody else. Curious.

Papa San pries the cage gate, walks in, and orders the fresh fish to line up across the front of the fence, facing the crowd. Each of the small groups outside erupts into debate, with a leader for each one weighing opinions, nodding slowly and staring down the line. They take turns pointing out fish and Papa San tosses us from the tank, one by one. Picking teams. A schoolyard muster if I've ever seen one.

To my surprise, I get taken near the top. But then there must be a first time for everything. I'm selected by an ox-jawed Boogie brute with a scarred, shaved scalp, and half-an-ear missing. He's flanked by three quiet Coolies and a taut, red-nosed Irishman. Looks like I'm the rookie sensation for the International All-Stars.

My big, black boss eyeballs me without blinking as I approach. He's a hard man amongst hard men, and his muscles ripple through his well-worn spacesuit.

"Listen up Gubba, I'm Chief Monti, and we don't tolerate any bluegums 'round here. On my squad, you work, or I put you out." He's got a thick Nozzy drawl and ropes of neck-pump popping out his suit. "You're dressed the part. Do any vacuum welding or zero G bolt-throwing in your day?"

"Fraid not, Cochise," I say. "I was a cop."

"Not anymore," he says.

We file out, while the auction rambles on behind us. I pull up the rear of my new crew, following a steady stream of smileycon neck brands. Some of the burns look fresh, puckered and pink, piled on top of older scar tissue. Second-hand slavery. We duck through a raw corridor, brushing aside careless tangles of cable and conduit. The crew is not too concerned about me 'getting lost' and that's what worries me. I gather that wandering little lambs get the axe mighty quick in a gig like this. The freckle-faced Irishman turns to me as I step around a curious colored stain on the pitted steel floor.

"Bossman's mighty cheesed with you, Chancer," he says. "Figured you handy with a wrench, on account of your knickers." He pinches my jumpsuit.

"That one ain't on me, brother," I say. "These were the only duds I had handy."

The Irishman smiles. "Just be wide. Don't show a hard neck and Ole Monti might give you a nip at the diddies."

"Thanks for the tip, pal. Say, what's your handle? I'm Stockton Ames." I put out my paw for a shake but Freckles laughs at me.

"Lay off, Bowsie!" he says. "No names till we know you'll be around for breakfast. Chief's crew been bucketing boggers of late. You're the third wank in as many shifts, and I don't expect you'll do much better than the rest."

We follow the squad around a tight bend into more of the same unfinished hallway. A bare diode flickers just above the big chief's head.

"I read you, pal. Just one question, though."

He turns an ear.

"What's the story with all the Chinamen?"

He laughs. "A gas, that," he says. "Years back we picked up a whole hull's worth of the hockeyed slints. An orbital FabPlant shut

328

her doors and sent the union doles packing for a Yangtze cruiseliner. Layoff package. 'See the stars' and all that gack. Hoped the plant'd be reopened when they got back. Course, they never did get back. Big Chief Nyxo nicked the lot of them on the cheap, and the brutal buggers refuse to bunk off, on account they're all hardchaw knackers already, see?"

I catch the gist of it, but not much else. Here's a fella what runs his gums stranger than I do.

"That's some severance," I say.

He nods with a blank look on his face and a twitch in his eye.

"How about that Nyxo?" I say. "Decent guy?"

The Irishman just turns back around.

"How 'bout him?" he says quietly.

Our squad rounds into a bright place in the hallway and Chief Monti calls for an all-stop from the front. A dead-eyed, wild-haired holy man squeezes his way down the line. One of my own, a Muni Catholic, by his white collar and red robes, although the long, matted dreadlocks dangling to his waist tell me he hasn't been keeping up with the Papal edicts for some time. This scuzzy priest sprinkles each one of the team with something wet from a carved-up canteen at his hip. When he gets to me, I don't like finding out that it's a lube job; there's motor oil in that tin of his. Always the optimist, I was hoping for plain old Holy water. He mumbles some mostly made up Latin in my ear as he presses past.

"Ain't it a bit early for last rites, Father?"

He says nothing, but dips his fingers once more and draws a slimy cross on my forehead. My new buddy Mick taps me on the shoulder.

"Fair play, Bowsie. Now He *knows* you're touched."

I can't decide if "He" refers to the priest or to God or to someone else entirely, or if it really even matters either way. The Chief moves us out once more, but it's just a short haul to the next stop: a rust-crusted storage locker. Big Monti rummages through a cracked plastic bin, then tosses me a balled-up EVO suit as the others grab helmets from a crooked rack on the wall.

"Put it on," he says.

I wrangle in one leg at a time, over my jumpsuit and boots. Fits like a sack, bunching at the knees and belly—but that's the least of my worries. There's an eight-inch hunk of gray fabric torn from the gut. I poke at it with grease-fingered gloves. A healthy dose of stiff, dried blood is caked around the hole. The bloodstain cracks and flakes to the floor at my touch. The others are too busy ratcheting straps and screwing on their fishbowls to pay me any mind.

"Hey fellas," I say. Five helmeted heads whip in my direction. "Got anything that's actually gonna hold air?"

Mick chuckles at the gaping gap in my survival chances and shakes his head, his eye still twitching. The three Asians go back to checking each other's getups without saying a word. Chief Monti gives me a blank look before bending over the bin once more. For a second I thought he might actually send me out the 'lock in this deadman's hand-me-down. He digs through the pile of discarded pressure-suits and comes up with something small. Tosses it to me.

A roll of tape.

"You serious with this, boss?" I bounce the roll in my glove.

"You're a tall one," Monti says, crackling through his helmet's radio. "This is good as it gets for you. Use what I gave ya' or bail out in the buff for all I care."

"Small wonder the new guys don't get along," I say, "when you feed 'em gear like this."

"Listen bludger, you're new, so I'll cut you a break and tell you twice. Tape up and shut up, else you'll get what's coming to you. I won't say it a third time."

Monti unscrews his fishbowl and sets it on a peg. He turns to me and cracks his knucks, then his neck. The others scurry to put their backs to the wall, clearing some space around us. A ring.

"Hey now, Monti," I say, hands open. "We're playing for the same team. You've got a brand on your neck what says you're somebody's property, just like I have. I'm not looking for a fight. I just want a square deal, okay pal?"

The Chief looks away, smiling and nodding. His gold-capped chompers twinkle in the low light. Situation diffused.

Or maybe not. Monti explodes at the elbow, reaching out at me with all he's got. Really puts his back into it. A full-bodied right hook catches me square on the chin and sends me packing for Blackoutsville. The force of the blow lifts me off my feet and into a row of storage lockers behind me. The cabinets clang hollow, as the back of my head punches into a thin metal door. My bell is officially rung. The Coolies hop on from either side, pinning me at the wrist. There's no fighting their judo grips, not without breaking my arms off at the elbows.

Monti smiles at me and picks up the roll of tape as he approaches. "This is The Heap," he says. "Fraid we're all out of square deals, mate."

He rips a short segment of sticky stuff and sets it squarely over my yap, then turns to fuss with a slidelock panel and walks out of the room. The Chinamen yank me to my feet and drag me out after him.

The big, black chief stops at a second panel just a few yards down a short passage. Another slidelock—with an eighteen-inch circular viewport cut into it—slips open. The chamber on the other side is a bit grisly, to say the least. The sunken cheeks and shriveled remains of three helmetless prunes are pinned to the wall.

Tom, Dick, and Harry look like deflated balloons, although their faces are surprisingly calm. The far door is a clear number, screaming with bright red and yellow warning labels. *Caution! External Airlock. Authorized Personnel Only. Pressure Suits Required Beyond This Point.* I really hope Chief Monti and the boys are reading them too.

On the other side of that hatch, worker bees scurry about in the vacuum, welding floating platforms and riveting trusses from the safety of their fully functioning spacesuits. The shiny steel glimmer of the supermassive twins looms behind them, ready to swallow it all and crush us into dust.

The Asian boys press me low against the wall, next to one of the deflated dummies. Monti pulls a fat, mean-looking rivet-flinger from a holster on his hip, and proceeds to staple my clownsuit to the hull. Each pull of the trigger makes a high-pitched whine, followed by a hollow thud as the bolt punctures the steel behind me. They pin me above and under the armpits, with a couple at the elbows for good measure. I dangle like a puppet, my legs too long to get under me proper.

Monti shakes his head.

"I gave you fair warning, bloke. Here's one last bit of advice. Don't hold your breath when we pop the seal. Explosive decompression of your lungs is not a pretty way to go." He points at the dummy next to me, its face blown out in freeze-dried, bloody chunks. Monti pats my cheek twice and walks out, Coolies in tow.

Mick smiles, reaches through the gaping hole in my EVO suit and frisks me. He raises his eyebrows and pulls out my pack of flavorsticks, taps one free and shoves it in his thin-lipped craw.

"Christ-on-a-bike, you had a short run of it," he says. "If it means anything to you, I'll send the priest in after you're bogged."

I nod once and he shakes the box of picks at me.

You're welcome you twitchy bastard. Mick steps back into the locker room and leaves me to talk it over with the stiffs. The hatch with the viewport shuts behind him and he pokes his pasty, smiling face in the glass. Waves buh-bye, fingertips to palm. The whole chamber shudders as the airlock goes to work, equalizing the pressure. Red beacons strobe a warning. The crimson light bounces off the steel-blue faces of my dead friends. They know the drill. An automated alarm calls out in a coldly pleasant female voicesim, not unlike TimePilot's.

"Full pressure breach in T-minus twenty seconds."

If I'm going to get right with God, I better do it quick. I count confessions from the last day or so.

"Fifteen seconds."

Hidden vents begin sucking the air out. The corpses' matted hair shimmies in the changing pressure like they were in the barber's chair.

"Ten seconds."

The fight in me snaps to life. My feet kick against the floor as I lean forward, using every ounce of juice in my haggard leg muscles to push myself out of this EVO suit death harness.

"9... 8..."

The suit starts to give! This thing was moth-eaten and three sizes too big to begin with. The gimcrack fabric begins to tear from around my elbows with a haughty purr. A glossy, golden emergency cutoff lever twinkles at me from just across the chamber. If I could only pull one arm free, I might have a shot at it.

"7...6..."

Rippppppp. It keeps giving and I keep taking the slack. I stretch out from the wall like the ten-pin that forgot to fall. My breathing gets quick, shallow.

"5...4..."

Remembering Monti's advice, I empty my lungs. Blowing what will probably be my last breath out through my nostrils, I reach for the release handle, an inch short of salvation. I press with all my might. My legs scream out. My fingers graze the handle.

"3...2...1..."

The final message scrolls across a crude dot-matrix display sitting just above the emergency release. The voicesim soundwaves won't carry in a vacuum, and that's what we've got now.

Pressure equalized. External airlock ready for breach.

The door to outside begins to move. My retinas go glossy as a thin layer of ice forms across their surface. The flashing strobes cut off. It's too late for warnings. I can just make out the cylinder-locks spinning on the exterior hatch. Releasing.

THIRTY-FIVE

The emergency lights kick on again.

There's a loud roar as the stale air rushes back in. Tom, Dick, and Harry bob and sway, doing the Dead Guy Mambo as a blast of pressure refills the chamber. I gulp oxygen through my nosehairs and slump back against the wall. The internal viewport and the inside of my eyeballs are foggy with condensation. I'll have to wait to meet my guardian angel but I won't have to wait long.

The interior hatch pops its locks.

I picture the broad brandishing a smoking heater, Monti's crew a bloody heap behind her.

The door slides open.

"Well hello there, friendddddd."

My savior is a fat old man with a dirty beard. That bastard Smitty brushes past the burly chief and grins at me with piano key teeth. He waddles through the open lock. Monti towers behind him like a seven-foot shadow, grabbing at the fat man's flabby arms and growling guttural protests.

"Hold up now, Tubba! This here's my crew!"

Looks like the Nozzy brute isn't too keen to see me survive.

Smitty rolls his eyes and turns with a huff. He draws a speck-sized peashooter from a pocket and plants one right in Monti's big, black forehead. The Chief's eyes flutter just once as he tumbles over backwards.

"Any other pieces of Captain Nyxo's property want to tell me his business?" Smitty says, brandishing the gun with a wild look in his eyes.

The other four flash palms and back away.

"That's what I thought. Now be good little boys and cut him loose."

The Coolies go to work on my suit with pocketplasmas. I breathe a sigh of relief as Smitty peels the tape from my mouth and tosses a pair of cuffs at me.

"Put them on," he says. "You've got a date with the Captain."

"I really appreciate the rescue, Smits," I say, buckling the bracelets around my wrists and snatching the flavorsticks from Twitchy Mick. "But I'm still gonna have to kill you."

Smitty shrugs, then he drops the bag back over my head and marches me out to meet The Man.

"Maybe this woulda been cleaner," Mick whispers as we shuffle by. "Bye then, Bowser. Kisses to Nyxo!"

Smitty leads me to a lift and suddenly we're not alone. I hear breathing. And a faint little humming sound, like a munchkin would make with her head in a sack. It's "No Time for Love," that Dust Bunnies track I taught her back on Titan.

I whistle along quietly, to let her know I'm here.

It's a short ride. Two-verses-and-a-chorus worth: not much in czar-rock bars. I drop the song as we're led out through another winding trail. All of the background sounds and smells are the same. Burning, banging, breaking. Seems this whole ship serves up the same convincing impression of the seventh circle of Hell. It's a tall march through the heart of hooded darkness. The screaming machines and whiffs of brimstone only make my shoes that much heavier. I do my best to shuffle along on gimpy getaway sticks.

Eventually we come to a halt. I hear the distant whiz of a lift falling to meet us, then the quick hiss of a slidelock. Apparently we're going up. They load us in and the door shuts behind me. We shoot skyward. The sudden acceleration rides rough on my bum pins. This is one quick lift. We must have quite the climb to make.

We rise for what seems like an eternity. Finally we slide into a smooth stop, one last door cracks and we're out. Somebody peels my hood. It takes my eyes a moment to adjust to the sudden brightness and my brain another to accept the sudden change in scenery.

Gone are the tangled, boiling bowels of this hellish wreck. We're perched up on a viewing platform high above the side of the ship. Reminds me of the mushroom kingdom back on the resort. A large plexisteel bubble surrounds us. I take a peek down below. We are way up in the clouds—not just above the Tartartus, but towering over the rest of The Heap as well. The slithering station extends out all around us, like the mechanical gizzards of some syntho snake.

Cruisers and dinghies and huge hunks of rock are twisted and tied together in rusty knots, extending out for hours in both directions. Funny thing about outer space, there's no horizon to cut your view short. It's the first time I get a good grasp on the immensity of The Heap. Bright lights burn out in the darkness, as EVO crews assemble who-knows-what with plasma arc vacuum torches. Dilating ports sphincter open and shut, spewing garbage into the hulls of neighboring vessels. Shuttles scurry back and forth, disappearing behind clouds of floating trash and discarded skeletal scraps. The Heap is life and death, all at once. We're insects scurrying over the rotting remains of human civilization. Fleas. Filthy maggots.

I look back up and find us in a hallway of sorts. The lift sits behind us, poking up from the floor where our corridor meets another crossing passage. Ahead of us I find an ornately carved wooden wall with a big brass plaque inlaid in the planks. The plaque sports an image of the ship—long and plump, like a cheap, low-poly cigar—and the text *HTV Tartarus*. Next to the plaque is a matching brass slidelock, polished to a mirror sheen, inscribed with two words: 'Captain's Quarters'.

The door rolls open and we're shoved inside. Self-important orchestra music wafts gently from hidden speakers all around us. This space too is made up of a large glass dome. The floors are a slick glaze of black marble dotted with swanky furniture: a suede sofa, a couple of overstuffed easy chairs, a heavy-looking wooden desk with a high-backed antique leather chair behind it, turned away from us. Rich crimson fabrics are draped from the ceiling in delicate folds, a plush contrast to the sleek, angular architecture everywhere else.

Beyond the desk, the viewport looks out over the great white length of the Tartarus. She's a long lady. A tall drink of hooch. Painted over the hull a half-mile below us are hundred-yard-high block letters. *JANOSCORP*, they read.

"No shit," I say.

The big, leather chair whips around.

"No shit, indeed," says a familiar voice.

∞

My jaw drops hard enough to hurt.

"Proletti!"

I'd recognize that smuggy, snivelling tenor anywhere. But the man before us is more of a memory-leak version of the jerk I remember from Seren Luna.

Stephon Proletti is decked out in full maritime regalia. The peacock peacoat with dangling, braided shoulder tassels. A golden-scrolled, short-brimmed cap. Below that hat, though, his face is nearly unrecognizable. It's mostly metal and plastic now—so many grafts I can't barely tell if he's human under there. Stapled back together from some horrific accident. Come to think of it, last I saw of him, he was wrestling with a pack of SpaceApes. Considering those circumstances, he looks alright.

Slick pops out of his chair like a champagne cork. He stands beside a large anomaly in the window-wall, some kind of orange, staticky portal stuck in the glass, similar to the pot of chips from the grannies' game back at the Zero G Lounge. It flickers and flashes like an angry disco pancake but doesn't make a peep that I can hear.

"Isn't this a tender reunion?" Proletti says with a wicked grin. "Please have a seat. Make yourselves comfortable." He directs his goons to toss me towards the sofa, Bekka and Audrine to the easy chairs. Then he comes to Zee.

It's the first I've taken a good look at our new pal. A middle-aged twist in a tattered rag of a dress. Long, kinky orange hair. Freckled face. And would you look at that front porch! She's got to be eight-and-a-half months pregnant! Ready to pop. Must be why she was down in the dungeon with us and not partaking in 'adult activities' with Slick's goons.

Proletti's plastic face gets cross.

"Who is this!?" he shouts. He grabs Zee by the wrist and drags her over next to him. He's none too gentle about it, bun-in-the-oven besides. Not one of the goons can bear to look him in the eye.

"WHO IS THIS?!" he repeats, angrier this time, cramming a gloved finger in her freckled face.

One of his thugs, the biggest fella, speaks up. "She was down with the other three, sir. We, uhhhhh, we thought you wanted them all, Captain Nyxo, sir."

Proletti shakes his head. He wrenches Zee's wrist tighter. She winces, scared spitless. Eyes wide as walnuts and I don't blame her.

"I requested the man," he gestures to me, "the little girl," Bekka, "and the dark-haired woman that had just arrived." Audrine.

He digs a gloved finger into Zee's cheek. "Who. Is. This?"

"I, uhhh. Well, I dunno, Captain Nyxo, sir," the goon says.

"Well then." Proletti nods. With divebomber speed he flings Zee at the glowing portal in the window-wall. The orange sheen pulsates wildly as she zips through it. A split second later, she floats out in the vacuum, hair wild, arms flailing, eyes frozen with terror. I can see her mouth moving, trying to scream into the airless void.

I shoot off the sofa.

"By all means, go out after her, Mr. Ames," Proletti says. He spreads his arms towards the portal. "You must be well acquainted with the vacuum by now, no?"

But all I can do is stand and stare. A chorus of haunting wood-winds echo my helplessness from the hidden speakers. After about fifteen seconds, Zee no longer moves on her own accord. She spins with the initial force of the toss, but all the life inside her is gone.

I round on Slick.

"No, no, I don't think so, Mr. Ames," he says. He produces one of those remotes for the puppet patch in my neck and I'm a stone statue again. Fists clenched. Teeth gritted. Chafed. He walks over to me, presses another button on the remote and pushes me back into the sofa. The tension leaves my muscles but I'm still not able to move them on my own. He snaps for the goons to remove my cuffs.

"Mr. Ames will no longer be requiring these," Proletti says, tossing the maglocks to the floor. "And I will no longer be requiring you." He motions the goons to the exit. They file out like rats off a sinking ship, and we're left alone with this lunatic.

Proletti turns to face us once more, folding his hands in front of him. The orchestra plays on, drowning every moment in a cinematic, dreamlike quality. "Let's talk business, shall we? Miss DeMarco, always a pleasure." He runs a glove across her cheek. She shudders with disgust. "And I see you still have your young friend with you."

Bekka curls up in the back of her chair, clutching her bear and petting it with reckless abandon. A faint hiss escapes her lungs.

"What do you want from us, Proletti?" Audrine says.

He turns back to her quickly. "Why just to chat with some old friends! Is that so much to ask?" he says, stepping back to address us all. "We have oodles of catching up to do, it seems."

339

He thumbs the remote and I'm free to run my mouth once more.

"Catch a cab to the teeth, buddy. We've got nothing to say to you."

"Oh come now! Is that anyway to speak to your gracious host? After I've gone through all the trouble of finding you? Of rescuing you? Of giving you a home here on my ship? Here in this beautiful future?"

He runs his hands through Audrine's hair. She shuts her eyes and cries out sharply as he gives her locks a tug. "What's the matter, Miss DeMarco? Where's your gratitude?"

"I'm sure I don't know," she spits at him through clenched teeth.

"Cmon Slick," I say. "You can be evil all day long, but there's no reason to be rude to the lady and the kid. Let me up and let's you and I settle this like men."

Proletti laughs.

"Oh we'll get to that part. I assure you, you'll get what's coming to you, Ames." He strokes his plastic chin. "Before it's over, I'll have you begging for death, that's a promise. But there's no need to rush to the end! I'd feel remiss if you didn't understand the full weight of your punishment."

"Punishment?" Audrine says. "You're sick, Stephon. We've never done anything to you! All your misfortune was your own."

Slick clicks his tongue and turns his back to us. His fingers lace together just over the trailing tails of his ridiculous captain's jacket. "Factually incorrect, Miss DeMarco. Patently untrue! Did you not rig the results of the contest at my resort?"

She says nothing, and this excites him.

"Oh that's right," he says. "I was aware of your little tricks. Your feeble attempt to uncover my ambitions? To combat my carefully laid plans? And just how much did you learn? Did you find out what it was I was after? What I've risked so much to find?"

The broad glares at him but still doesn't speak.

"No?" He rests his head on his knuckles and bats his eyes at Audrine. "You employed your womanly wiles best you could, I'm sure. I had half-a-mind to stop you, I really did. That is, until I saw who it was you intended to bring in to assist you. Who it was you intended to bring back into my life." He throws a finger my way and sneers.

"Back into your life? What's the hitch, Slick? I never saw you before I set foot on your crummy, richo rock. You and I were strangers, Proletti, and that's all there is to it."

He sighs and plops beside me on the sofa.

My ragdoll head sways atop a limp lower body as he cozies up next to me. Crossing his legs high, he places his elbow on his knee and his chin on his palm.

"You and Stephon Proletti were strangers, Ames, sure." He slides his metal mug up in front of mine and grins wide. "But I am not Stephon Proletti."

THIRTY-SIX

Proletti's face twists and shimmies, like his skull is reshaping itself under his skin. Audrine gasps, but I'm a little left out of the loop. "What are you loony? Of course you're Proletti. Who the hell else would you be?"

His smirk changes to a frown. His voice deepens, regains the downtown drawl of a voice I haven't heard in years.

"Whatsamatter, pal? Don't you recognize your old partner?"

His face finishes its transformation.

"Mendoza!?" I try to shake my head but can't. "No, you can't be him. Jay Mendoza is dead. He died all those years ago on top of that space elevator."

He shakes a finger in my face. "Until a few minutes ago, you thought Stephon Proletti was equally as dead."

I open my mouth, but I don't have any words.

"And you'd be right of course, on both accounts. Both of the men you've thought me to be are quite deceased. 'Bit the big one', eh Ames?"

Rolling my eyes is about the crudest gesture I can offer him with this chip in my neck, so I make sure to roll 'em extra hard. "Cut to it, bub," I say. "Proletti and Mendoza are dead, and you pretended to be both. A hundred bucks says Nyxo's shoving tulips somewhere, too. And the side bet says you were behind all three bucket-kickings."

"How very astute of you, Detective."

"So who are you?" Audrine asks. "Who are you really?"

The man with Mendoza's face stands. "Names are so fluid, don't you think? Much like faces, voices, personalities? I always found that it was the accomplishments that made the man." He gestures out at The Heap, buzzing with activity. "And I've certainly accomplished much here. But if you must attach a moniker to my being, please feel free to call me Zed. In as much as I've ever had a real name, 'Zed' was how I thought of myself."

His cheekbones begin to crawl around once more in a stomach-churning display. I don't want to watch, but I can't pull my peepers away from the trainwreck of flesh canoodling around his face. His mug meanders a while more, before finally settling on the shape of a man I've never seen before. He's gaunt. Angular and cruel.

"Screw you, Zed," I say. "You haven't accomplished a mound of beans! As far as we know you just knocked off the big kahuna and inherited his craptastic kingdom. For all the airs you put on, you're just the pirate king of a shitheap junkyard. Well guess what, Chief? The top turd is still floating in the bowl, ready to be flush—"

Zed buttons me up with a touch of his remote. He stalks behind the sofa and gives the burnt crust on my neck a good whack, then returns to center stage and takes a seat on the edge of his antique desk, like a professor mid-lecture.

"You're missing the big picture, Detective!" He spreads his arms wide. "A mess this fine doesn't just pop out of the ether. It takes an architect to bring the pieces together. To mold the chaos into such a lovely shape. To meticulously set up the experiment, make the preparations, and push the launch button."

I furrow my brow.

"Let me spell it out for you, then. You never were terribly good at logic puzzles, were you Ames? I became who I needed to be to arrive at where we are today. Impersonating Mendoza gave me access to government networks and investigational tools and—after you left me to die on that space elevator—the keys to an entire organization of criminal activity. Once I controlled the syndicate we had once tried to stop, I was able to establish black market supply caches. We hid weapons, food, vehicles, near TimeResorts all throughout the galaxy, all waiting to be exploited once I arrived here in the future.

"Impersonating Proletti gave me access to Seren Luna and the rich resources afforded by an affluent organization like The Janos Corporation. I very much enjoyed my time there." He smiles wickedly at Audrine. "And most importantly, becoming Stephon Proletti gave me knowledge of the gravity wave phenomenon and the ability to exploit it. In layman's terms, Proletti let me know where to catch a ride to the future."

"Wait, how can that be?" Audrine asks. "Those time frames are overlapping! How could you be both Proletti and Mendoza at the same time? On Earth and on Seren Luna?"

"It took some careful planning—and a lot of very painful facial implants—but if you do the math I'm sure you'll find there was just enough time for Mendoza's career on Earth in the short breaks I took in secret from Seren Luna. Just five minutes away from the resort afforded me more than two days' time on Earth. Relativity is a wonderful ally, don't you think?"

No wonder Mendoza never had a social life. He didn't exist outside of work, at least not by the time I knew him. And no wonder I never trusted Proletti. If I thought he was bad news on Seren Luna, he's become a downright devil by now.

"There were countless other careers mixed in as well. I had to be absolutely certain I'd have everything I needed to seize control once I arrived here, seven billion years in the future. The preparations and sacrifices I've made to achieve all of this..." He lets out a wistful sigh and folds his hands neatly in his lap. "And to think, years of perfect execution nearly tossed aside because of the meddling intrusion of the two of you."

"Perfect execution for what?" Audrine asks. "This was your big scheme? To run to the future and drag a bunch of innocent people along behind you? What's the point, asshole?"

He clucks at us and wags a white-gloved finger.

"You have the right idea but the spirit is all wrong," Proletti says. "I'm looking for something, Miss DeMarco. Something you of all people should know is very, very difficult to find."

"Yeah and what's that, Zed?" Audrine says. "A conscience? If you couldn't find one back home I doubt you'll have much luck here."

"You jest, Miss DeMarco, however I didn't just show up here and pray for the best. I chose to create the world I wanted to rule, the world I was born for. I set the stage to best equip myself to achieve my goals, lofty as they were. To find my prize. This world and the work I want to do in it, the things I need to find here—it all requires inhabitants to help me in my search. So naturally I had to bring along some of my closest friends." He pats Bekka on the head and smiles at her. "And after all, what is an emperor without his subjects? A king without his servants? What's that? You have something to say, Detective?"

He clicks me free.

"Some empire, Napoleon," I say. "You've got a loose grip on a tangled wreck of savages!"

"Au contraire," he counters. "I agree that things may have turned a touch towards the negative, but I'm thoroughly committed to bringing civilization back to the unwashed masses." He produces some plastic confetti chips from a coat pocket and sprinkles them across my lap. Red. Yellow. Blue. Green. White. Just like Smitty gave the goons that nabbed us. Each has a silver transistor stuck on the tail. "Economy, for instance. Trade! Each of these chits represents a different basic human need." He picks up a green one and tosses it at my chest. "Food." A blue one. "Water." He steps over to Audrine and tosses a white one at her. "Shelter. And let's not forget our favorite—" He flings a red one in her eye. "—companionship."

Audrine shakes her head violently.

"Big deal, hotshot," I say. "So you gave your chimps some cabbage to play with. You want an award for coining scratch? Hate to break it to you, Slick, but folks have been slinging cheddar for ages. So save the awardstream speech for an audience that'll hear it."

Zed shrugs.

"Perhaps you're right, Mr. Ames," he says. "Maybe we are just wallowing in the memory of our once great civilization. Maybe we should set the bar higher. Aim for something a bit more… inspired, perhaps? Something better than a mere shadow of humanity's former glory. Is that what you have in mind?"

"Cut the cute stuff, Zeddy Boy. I'm not in the mood to worm it from you. What's the grift?"

His smile widens. Gaps stretch between the plastic plates piecing his mug together. Patches of scar tissue, like flaky, baked whitefish, peek out.

"Patience, Mr. Ames. Patience! We were just getting to that."

The music gets louder. He spins around the desk and keys something on an embedded terminal before gesturing out the window. One by one, a series of lights blink on in a grid over the darkness outside. The lightshow squares up nicely to the shiny spheres behind it, the pair of bad-mother neutron stars. These new lights surround the silver stars, and an orange shimmering sheet grows between them. It looks like the same stuff he pushed Zee through, still glowing in the window-wall, pulsating with wild fury. Soon the orange stuff's spread out between all of the beacons, creating a great big glowing beach ball with both silver stars trapped inside.

"Behold," Zed says, "the inertial containment field."

Cascading timpanis rumble the hidden speakers as the musical accompaniment crescendos.

"Behold my asshole," I spit at him. "You've milled up glorified wrapping paper."

He laughs.

"Oh, but Mr. Ames, it's so much more than that. You simply don't understand. Technology has come quite a long way since your day. And you always were terribly old fashioned, weren't you? A touch... unsophisticated?"

I growl at him.

"But I can help you see the light." He clears his throat. "You see, the containment field is more than just a wrapper for our supermassive friends out there." He picks up a pair of stuffed olives from a bowl on his desk. "It's also the hand that squeezes the wrapper."

He presses the two olives together until the cheese filling spurts out onto the floor.

"So what," I say. "You're going to press a pair of twinklers together? Create one big-boy star? What's the racket? Shake your business up and pour it, Slick. If I wanted a lecture I'd go back to school."

"Perhaps you should improve your education, Mr. Ames," he says. "As Miss DeMarco, or perhaps even your young friend here could tell you, when two massive bodies—neutron stars, for instance—are forcibly combined, they will collapse into a brand new black hole." He smiles. "The resulting flux in magnetic fields will rapidly expel an enormous amount of energy and matter from the newly-formed core. Very hot, very volatile plasma will explode out with tremendous force. *Kaboom. Kablooey.* So long and goodnight."

It's still a shaggy dog story to me.

"So you've built the galaxy's biggest bomb right on your own doorstep? I'll bet your folks would be proud."

Slick's eyes go wide and his mouth curls into a snarl. He's absolutely rabid. Even the music seems to get angry. Trumpets blare and cymbals crash. Apparently his lineage, or lack of it, is a sore subject.

"What's the point, Zed?"

He quickly regains composure and tries to cover by straightening his sleeves. The music calms as well. He must have the tunes linked to his emotional state, the pretentious bastard.

Zed stands silently. Waiting for us to buzz in. Answer our own question, like he's some kind of villainous quizstream host. What would a weasel like this want with that much firepower? It comes to me in a flash.

"Extortion," I say.

Zed smiles at my answer but Audrine frowns.

"Sure, but why would all of these people be willing to work on a weapon that was just going to be used against themselves?" she asks. "That's a big project out there. It doesn't make any sense."

"Unless they didn't know what they were building," I say.

Slick is very interested now.

"Or they aren't planning to use it here at all," Audrine adds.

Zed is pleased. He shuts his eyes. "Well done, well done indeed!"

"But who are you planning to use it against? There aren't any other civilizations out there!" Audrine says.

Zed plays coy. He purses his lips and looks away, pretending to be bashful. "Well now that's not entirely accurate," he says.

"But there weren't any other radio signals!" Audrine says. "Everyone we've met said that the only beacon they found was here at The Heap."

"Is that so?" He raises his eyebrows. "All part of the plan my dear. You see, once I escaped from Seren Luna and commandeered this vessel, I needed a large workforce to help me bring my plan to fruition. The crew was of some help, yes, and we had the raw materials, of course; the Tartarus was a world-building ship in her glory days." He tosses one of those stuffed olives into his metallic mouth. "Incidentally, a *prison* world-building ship. Perfect for the job. Plenty of metal, electronics, high-tech materials. Containing massive cosmic forces and keeping people locked up aren't all that different after all, it would seem."

He ponders this wisdom for a moment.

"But what I needed was labor! A crew to carry out the sweaty, unpleasant parts of my plan. Unfortunately those marvelous little Hags chewed up most of my guests at the resort. And I wish I could take credit for the beasts, I really do. Effective and efficient. But alas, they were someone else's miracle."

He runs his hand along a crimson curtain and stares out into the stars. The orchestra becomes muddled, confused. The instruments play over each other and against the time signature for a moment, before returning to a slow symphonic anthem.

"Now where was I? Ah yes, the worker bees! I placed some jammers around the old home system and some other points of interest along the way and began broadcasting my own message from here. 'We are humanity's last hope! Help us rebuild the world we lost!' Blah, blah, blah. They ate it up like so much caviar." He pops another olive and his face twists into an evil smile. "Voila! The Heap is born and my labor crisis averted!"

"You're a sick chicken, Zed," I say. "These people turned to you for help and you enslaved them!"

"To be fair," he says, "I merely fostered an environment that encouraged the enslavement of others. Grand old human nature took care of the rest. Very few of the guests actually belong to me personally, when you look at the total population—but I do see your point.

"Nonetheless, my needs were met. In the end, that's all that really counts, isn't it? I have my little kingdom and my doomsday device and there are plenty of extrastellar colony worlds out there for me to have my way with. I can destroy all of blessed creation in a great ball of cosmic fire if I so much as get a whim to let it burn."

Audrine shakes her head, disgusted.

"Why?" she asks. "Why bother?"

"Oh, the usual," Zed says. "Money. Power. Respect."

He turns to face her. Stares. "Women," he says. "Also, perhaps most importantly, I have a hankering suspicion that what it is I am seeking is currently in the possession of one of these civilizations. With my weapon at the ready, I have the means to extort my prize from whomever is hiding it from me."

"Did you try asking nicely first?" I ask.

He shrugs. "Frankly, once I set the stone rolling, much of the thrill was the challenge of it all. I wanted to see if it could be done.

If I could succeed in such a monumental endeavor. And it does feel marvelous to see it all coming together so smoothly, I assure you. There's nothing quite so delicious as seeing carefully laid plans bear fruit billions of years down the line. My achievement here represents mankind's single greatest feat of engineering. I've harnessed the raw force of nature's most powerful celestial objects, and bent them to my will. Your arrival here to witness my moment of glory is just the proverbial cherry on top."

He makes a disgusting lip smacking gesture with his broken face. Some sort of white goo oozes out from under the plates of his left cheek.

"And I think those SpaceApes damaged your brain once they got sick of chewing on your chin," I say. "You've got a God complex that the Old Man himself would be jealous of, bud. You sound like a third-rate villain from a bargain bin actionstream to me."

He shrugs it off.

"Well that's your prerogative I suppose. My reasoning is inconsequential once the plan goes into action," Zed says. "I don't need any excuses to hold the universe hostage. Or what's left of it anyway. And on that note..."

He turns to the terminal at his desk.

"Wait!" Audrine shouts. "I still don't understand. The explosion will be right out there and your colony world hostages aren't. How can you threaten them with a weapon that's so far away? How are you going to transport a bomb the size of a black hole?"

"Ahhh," Zed says. "My favorite part, really." He dances to the desk and flicks a few relays. Suddenly a whole new batch of lights are illuminated in the center of the orange field. They form a giant luminous ring. Wide and thin. "The convergence node," he continues. "More affectionately referred to as the Funnel."

The ring of lights begins to spin like a perfectly thrown pass, and the shimmery pulsing intensifies along the orange net around it. The orchestra blares triumphant. A majestic blend of brass and strings and percussion sounds off.

"In a stunning display of genius, we will concentrate the plasma explosion into a wormhole generated by the convergence node here. Squeeze the danger right into the Funnel. Nice and easy. Then we can pass it along in a wormhole relay until we are ready to make a few examples.

"Think of it as a deadly game of hot potato, tossing the plasma back and forth between wormhole gates."

He makes a juggling motion with empty hands.

"From there it's just a matter of deciding what to destroy. I'm leaning towards one of the civilizations in the late sequence Gliese systems. Scorpii G, would be lovely, don't you think? A triple system with plenty of targets. Plenty of witnesses, and they most certainly do *not* possess the trinket I seek. But perhaps some of their friends do.

"Once we've begun, I can unleash a little at a time. Sprinkle a dollop of destruction here. A dash there. Everywhere! After we've vaporized a few of the larger planetary settlements, the others will have no choice but to meet our demands. To hand over the object I so desperately seek."

He gloats in his cleverness and closes his eyes, content. Zed hums along with the music and giggles softly to himself.

"Ughhh. Alright, Zed, I'll bite—if it will shut you up about it already. You're practically begging us to ask, aren't you?" I sigh and shake my head. "What kind of rusty McGuffin have you been chasing halfway through time? What's so important you've gone to all this trouble?"

He opens his mouth but doesn't say a word. His brow furrows and he starts again. "It's— well, it's none of your concern, Mr. Ames."

I blurt a single bleat of laughter. "Ha! You don't even know what it is your looking for, do you? You're as clueless as I am!"

He squinches his face up tight and shakes a finger at me, ready to tell me off right. He's distracted. Angry. Audrine sees her shot and takes it. Bumrushes him. She's out of the chair in an instant, knocking him away from the terminal and tackling him behind the desk. My view is obstructed, but it sure looks like she crawls on top of his chest. The orchestra is angry. Skips in and out. Taut strings squeal and break. I watch her chained hands come up above the desk, then disappear below it. Then again. And again. Driving stakes. Turning his metal face into melted mush. That oozing white goop sprays into the air with each crushing blow, accompanied by a discordant howl from the symphony.

After a handful of pummels, though, Audrine rockets off of him, somersaulting backwards into the far wall. She collapses onto the marble floor with a thud. Zed stands up gracefully and dusts his sleeves off before removing his peacoat. He folds it neatly and lays it across his desk.

Underneath the jacket, his arms are synthetic, and not the kind you mistake for human. These are no LexSynth model prostheses.

He's all steel conduit and chrome pistons.

No wonder she caught so much hangtime. This guy's more jacked than a crankhead blitzbacker, draped over the throttle of a less-than-street-legal hoverchopper. He very calmly, very slowly walks to where Audrine lies crumpled against the wall. His newly pulverized puss gushes waxy goop, leaving a globby trail on his undershirt and the floor behind him.

Audrine struggles to get back on her feet but Zed gets there first, reaches down with one arm, and snags her by the wrist. Without breaking a sweat, he hoists her up into the air. Her legs dangle below, toes barely scraping the marble. Hooking her cuffs around an ornamental brass wall sconce, Zed holds her in place, a fish on the line. They're eye-to-eye now. A half-inch between the tips of their sniffers. He leans in and gives her a sloppy kiss with his dripping metallic lips before letting her go. She spits in disgust as he walks away laughing, leaving her to flap against the wall.

"No more interruptions, please," Zed says.

He stands next to his desk to catch the show. The pulsing of the orange containment field gets faster and faster, until it quivers in one continuous wave. Likewise, the Funnel-ring's rotation gains velocity until it's just a blur of spinning light. The music rises in volume and tempo. A choir of angelic voices joins the orchestra. In a flash, cymbals crash, the containment field convulses, and the silver spheres contract and rebound with a slow jiggle. They melt into each other in rapid spasms, shrinking as they merge. They get smaller and smaller and smaller as they become one, until they disappear from sight altogether and the darkness around them begins to wiggle instead. This must be that baby black hole Zed promised. It doesn't look like much to me. Like somebody dropping the world's biggest cup of black Jiggle-Oh gelatin on the floor. A little bit of a letdown for the end of the universe, if you ask me.

Everything is quiet and still for what feels like an eternity.

∞

Then it begins.

There's a flash of light that burns through my closed eyelids, then a steady stream of blinding hot gas pours out from the darkness. It sputters and spits out from the center, vomiting waves of multi-colored discharge into the spinning ring of light. Like a sailor at an open bar, the Funnel swallows every drop of firewater. For five, ten minutes, the fireworks go on. If you didn't know what Proletti planned to do with the stuff, you might say it was the most beautiful show you ever saw. Waves of brilliant neon fury dance and dash against each other. Eventually the cosmic vomit slows to a dribble. The newly formed black hole burps up the last tramloads of steaming goo and the ring stops spinning. The orange net disappears into the darkness and everything returns to the way it was.

Zed claps slowly as the music fades. He turns to face us once more, wiping white gunk from his chin with the back of his glove.

"Bravo," he says. "Well done. Now on to more… worldly matters."

He licks his lips and steps towards the broad.

THIRTY-SEVEN

Zed stomps back over to where Audrine hangs helpless by her cuffs. Bekka curls up tighter in the easy chair, squeezing the bejeezus out of that stuffed bear and blabbering at a full boil to herself. I pray that she keeps her eyes closed through the worst of it. Audrine kicks fits and spits at the metal monster as he approaches. And here I am, pinned to this damned sofa, with only my smart mouth to save the day.

Zed runs a robotic claw down Audrine's body, ignoring her kicks. He carelessly caresses the curves of her torso with the back of his hand before he reaches up and grasps one of the zippers at her neck. She squirms like crazy, wriggling for freedom, but there's none to find. She's fouled on his hook something fierce. With a quick jerk, he slides the zipper down to her hip.

One down. Two more to go.

"Zed, you bastard," I say. "So help me if you touch her!"

He flips around and stomps towards me.

"So help me you'll what?" he says. "What will the mighty Stockton Ames do?" He grabs me by the neck and lifts me off the couch.

I stare right into him, a fusion furnace burning behind my eyes.

Zed drags me over to the orange portal, holds me next to it like a sack of trash. "Do it, you coward!" I scream in his face. "Just off me now and get it over with!"

He contemplates this for a moment. One free hand scratches his dripping chin. Finally he smiles. "No," he says. "I'd rather make you watch. First Miss DeMarco," he hisses. "Then the girl."

He sets me down next to the portal and grabs a hold of my wrist. "But just for good measure…"

Zed jerks the seam off my sleeve, exposing my bare flesh down to the shoulder. He shoves my arm out the orange portal, into the icy vacuum beyond. It's frigid. Colder than I could ever imagine. I can feel my blood slow, slushify. My skin sizzles as it's exposed to a barrage of freerange cosmic radiation. My arm is simultaneously being deep fried and flash frozen, and there's not a lick I can do about it.

Zed hops back on Audrine in a blink, this time sucking at her neck as he unzips one more of her fasteners. She fights him, but without much luck. White oily muck dribbles down his chin and onto her chest. Deep down, I know none of this is for him. He's not enjoying this act, other than seeing her suffer. Somehow that doesn't make it any better.

"Zed get back here and finish me!" My voice is getting hoarse. My arm is going numb from the inside out. I can see my fingers swell and bulge unnaturally, like sausages left on too long. They turn a horrible shade of blue-gray at the tips.

Zed turns his head around to look at me. Smiles. Then goes back to Audrine. He's got her third and final zipper in his grubby paw.

SmallFry frantically shouts gibberish to herself, eyes squeezed tight. I'm out of options.

"Bekka!" I shout. "Bekka!"

No response.

"Bekka!"

Proletti has got Audrine's last zipper undone. His robotic hands disappear into her jumpsuit as she looks away, sobbing.

"Bekka." I whisper this time. Softly.

Her head whips around to look me square in the eye.

"Bekka, please ask your friends to help us. Tell them we need a hand."

Maybe this'll ignite some defense reflex in her. Some fight or flight response. Maybe she'll book it out of here before that bastard gets his paws on her.

No. She just goes back to babbling, talking to herself, clutching that damned bear. I groan. Decide to call it a life. At least I can close my eyes now. Maybe if I start humming I won't be able to hear any of it either. I shut the world out and prepare to meet my maker.

Suddenly there's a crash above me and I'm knocked flat to the floor, face down. That distinctive depressurization whistle fills my ears as a gale-force gust sucks the air out of the room, out of my lungs. I'm lifted and dropped back to the mat, but I can't move anything below my neck to see why. My view consists of a couple feet of dark marble floor and the legs of Bekka's chair, which start to slide towards me and the busted window behind me. Then, just as suddenly, they stop.

It all stops.

ShortStuff's tiny shoes skitter across the floor before me. She practically steps right on my head. "Where are you going?" I get an answer when my muscles return to life. I pop up to assess the scene, frantically rubbing at the frozen arm hanging lifeless beside me. I'm not so sure it will ever work again.

Bekka stands behind me, smiling at the desk, waving the SI remote in a tiny hand. Audrine is still dangling from the wall sconce, looking more than a little windblown. Zed is gone, emergency recovery foam is spraying all over the broken window glass from hidden emitter nozzles, and there's a five-foot silver sphere where the sofa used to be.

I peer out the viewport and quickly scan the sky. A sparkly, white bubbleship stretches into view above us with a steady stream of chrome marbles pouring out into The Heap.

I turn to Bekka. "Your friends?"

She nods with a big smile.

Rushing over to Audrine, I use my good arm to lift her up off the lamp and gently set her back on the balls of her feet. It's more of a glorified hugging motion than anything heroic. My right arm is still swollen, blue, and limp. Looks like somebody made me into a meat popsicle after all. Or at least one of the better parts of me. "You okay?"

She nods quickly, giving her suit a quick zip.

"What happened to the asshole?" I say.

She points out the viewport.

"He was sucked out when we lost pressure. Spaced."

I run to the glass and scour the field. Lots of silver spheres, plenty of damage. A couple of floating bodies even, but none that fit the bill enough to be our main man Zed.

"Are you sure?" I say. "I don't see him."

"He definitely went out," she says, walking over to help me look.

Bekka nods in agreement.

I place a hand on the window and something cold wraps around my ankle. I back away, or try to anyway. A metal skeleton claw has me vise-gripped, and its frigid twin digs trails into the marble floor. That robo-bastard is crawling up through the orange portal! And if I kick him out, guess who's going with him?

He lets go of me for one single instant... my chance! But the next nanosecond he hurtles up towards me, launching himself back inside with those atomic arms of his. My mistimed roundhouse misses him completely, and he sends me flailing with a kick of his own. I land flat on my back. The wind empties from my already tattered sails.

He's on me in an instant and boy-oh-boy-howdy does he look huffy. Zed lifts me up by my lapel so he can have a better angle to pummel me from. I try to get a few jabs in, but it's tough to tango with one arm frostbitten dead and his metal face doing more damage to my good fist than the other way around.

He screams as he wallops me to little bitty pieces.

After three rounds of verbal and physical abuse, Audrine smashes him with a lamp. It doesn't do much damage to his steel-lined skull, but the move draws his attention away long enough for me to duck out of Dodge. I crawl away, bleeding. Zed's quickly keen to our ruse, gives up on the broad, and goes back to stalking Stockton. I don't have much of a hand to play in here and he quickly herds me up against the mirrored sphere. I can feel the warmth flowing from it, soothing the dustgun damage on my pickle-peppered backside.

My rear is on the mend, but my face feels a hundred times worse as what's left of Zed attempts to dig a fresh hole clean through my skull with rocket-powered punches. My vision goes foggy, dreamlike. I turn my head one last time to spit some teeth and catch Bekka staring at me, a big smile on her face. She's got her hands together in the shape of a circle. "The sphere?" But what does she want me to do with—

Proletti winds up for a howler of a haymaker. A real-deal, career-ending kick-punch, if I've ever seen one coming.

I scrape up just enough time to fall out of the way. His fist flirts with my jaw and goes straight through the surface of the ball behind me. He ends up elbow deep in the silver sphere and spitting mad.

I stumble away like a drunk on payday and try not to throw up anything I may need later. When I get the guts to turn back around, he's still stuck. The Collective sphere won't release him. It glows, warm and red around his wrist. Pulses slowly, like a heartbeat. Zed yanks at his arm feverishly.

Finally he rips his fist free with a splash of black goop from inside the ball. The sphere knits itself together again almost instantly. He shakes off more of the black stuff and comes looking for me, shoving the big ball aside like it's a toy. Zed leaps over the remains of the couch as I scurry away and look for someplace nice to die.

He shakes his fist again, but no more of the goo flies off. I glance around to where the first bit dripped out of the sphere. On the glossy marble floor, a little patch of greenery grows from the spill. Some grass, some flower stalks, a couple tiny trees. It's all sprouting right before my eyes, shooting skyward at an incredibly exaggerated rate. A miracle garden.

I check back to Zed. He flails the once-stuck arm wildly, ripping at it with his other claw. Tearing it apart. The same kind of vegetation pours out of his metallic crevices as he claws away couplings and braided cables. The drippings and shakings sprout on his feet. Finally he rips the robotic arm clean off and tosses it aside. He stomps towards me, shooting sparks across the room.

But more sprouts just erupt out of the new hole in his shoulder. Viny ringlets wrap around his pistons and pull him down towards the deck. He coughs. Fluffy white seed pods escape with each hack.

His coughing turns into a choking laugh.

"You haven't changed anything," he croaks as he's pulled downward. "You might have stopped me for now, but the—" He erupts in a fit of phlegmy coughs. "—the other station chiefs will finish it. My weapon is still out there and The Heap is full of worse men than me. Someone will use it! Someone will find the—"

The vines grow over his face as he is smothered into the plants on the floor. He lies still. Motionless. The little garden of his body blooms. A single white flower blossoms from his chest. An iris. I'll be damned.

"You weren't big," I tell his lifeless corpse. "Just loud."

Audrine spits on the sprouts Zed's become.

I walk to the viewport, careful to avoid any of the plant patches—just in case they're still biting—and stare out at the ominous ring. Something catches my eye on the desk and I snatch it up and tuck it under an armpit.

He's right. Even though it's not my fight, the threat is still out there. Waiting to destroy entire worlds. Entire civilizations. Entire peoples.

And maybe the victims won't look like me. Maybe they won't speak English or like to eat greasy McBeefers while they watch the ballgame. Maybe I wouldn't care for them at all. But right now, none of that matters. For the first time in a long time, I've got a chance to give a good goddamn about something other than my own hide and someone other than myself.

Audrine stands at my side. Bekka too. Together we silently stare out into the darkness, trying to take in all the hate behind Zed's black hole bomb and all the suffering ahead of it.

ShortStuff reaches up and places her BuddyBear in my hands. Damn! This thing is a sack of rocks! I must have tripped the on-switch, because the damned thing starts to come to life in my arms. It stretches and yawns like it's been asleep and starts to make a robotic mewling sound from its fuzz-stuffed bear-mouth. Bekka ignores the robo-beast's tiny cries, takes her little mitts and works at a seam on his woolly neck. Eventually she rips the squawking head clean off, tosses it aside, and grins big. I glance at Audrine.

Maybe the pipsqueak has finally lost her last marble.

But hold on now. A dull, metallic sheen pokes up through the stuffing. I turn the bear over and wouldn't you know that old tallboy BabyNuke falls right out of the shredded neck-hole and into her tiny outstretched palms. "I'll be damned."

Bekka looks up at me and smiles. Makes a throwing motion, then hands the can to me. I look over to Audrine. She nods. We step over to the portal. It's a long shot. That collector ring is a good ways off and not very wide. It's a throw a pro would be pressed to make. Like throwing out a runner on second from the parking lot. Like tossing a touchdown to a tight end in triple-coverage, in the next town over. Lucky for me, I'm tossing a ten gigaton warhead and not a ball. Close only counts in horseshoes and hand grenades, right? I kiss the can for good luck. Audrine and Bekka smooch it too. Then I flip the arming mechanism with my thumb, give it a twist, wind up, and hurl it out the orange portal.

"Bombs away!"

She's a real beaut of a toss, too. We follow the pulsing strobe as it spins out into the darkness. Big Chief Wallace would be proud; I'm right on the money. Or close enough anyways.

It detonates in a glorious bloom of brightness. A double mush-room of screaming daylight vaporizes a six-mile swath of space. The convergence node is bopped. The black hole bomb is utterly out of commission. Zed's plan is all washed up.

I look down at the garden blooming from his body on the floor. Zed's dead too. So are Proletti, and Mendoza, and whoever else he wants to pretend to be. I bask in the blinding brilliance of the warhead, as the last of this goat's great accomplishments fizzles and pops.

There's no room to gloat, however. Bekka tugs at my sleeve. I turn around in time to frown at the window.

With the ring gone, the wormhole tears open again and all the hot guts come pouring back out. "Whoops." I hadn't quite considered the consequences when I made the toss, and now I sorta wish I had mulled it over.

A river of fiery plasma and deadly radiation jets out from the vaporized funnel, just like it went in. Except now the containment field is down. There's nothing to keep the burning goop from destroying the entire Heap, and us with it.

I grab the girls and brace for impact.

The plasma burp rips into the junkyard station like a fat guy at a buffet. Entire clusters of ships melt to matchsticks, engulfed in waves of steaming cosmic gravy. A smattering of slaggy, smelted shells lie left in its wake. Vessels are cut free from their moorings. They drip down into the deep darkness of the black hole's gravity well. No man's land. The point of no return. Our view is riddled with debris, and rapid-fire explosions pop off all around us. It's pure, unadulterated chaos, and it's heading right this way.

Even high up in our perch, we're rocked by a ship-shaking tremor. I look down to the hull, seemingly so far below us. We've taken a healthy shot of firewater midship. A large hunk of Heap presses into our bow, pries us free from our mooring, and pushes the stern—and us with it—up into the danger zone. In other words, the Tartarus is flipping screwed.

Some of the vessels caught in the black hole's pull—those with functioning engines—try to burn their way out, but it's no use. They crash into each other, or into clumps of floating wreckage, creating brand-new hazards for other ships to pinball into. Three separate bar-rages of escape pods eject from a nearby pleasure liner. Most of the life rafts bang into each other like billiards on a bad break. A few others fall into the big, black, corner pocket. More ships and sailors follow suit, vomiting pods into the maelstrom. It's a symphony of destruction and the maestro's gone missing.

Our little perch on the bridge of the Tartarus begins to boogie, tilts up towards all that chaos out there. It's unnerving. Partially because the artificial gravity tells us that 'down' is still below our feet, and it's the entire world outside that's flying up to greet us, all at once. It's enough to make a guy seasick. I lean over the desk and shut my eyes for a moment, sparring with the vertigo, until we're whacked by something big enough to shake me to my knees.

I decide it's better to see it coming.

Large hunks of hulls and girders, and the occasional escape pod careen around the viewport. I grimace as a titanic red frigate breaks free to our left, and begins to spin towards us up in the crow's nest. The crimson ship gets larger and larger, filling up our little window to the outside world, until a chunk of derelict cabin swings in and knocks the boat off our course.

I swallow hard as what's left of the kamikaze vessel disappears into the stalk of the bridge platform below us, cutting us free from the rest of the Tartarus. We're suddenly set adrift and the inertial dampeners go haywire. All three of us are beat down to the floor by a wave of artificial gravity. My cheeks press into the dark marble.

Looking out the window is like watching a magtram crash in slow motion. I don't want to see it go down but I can't take my eyes away. The Heap is a broken beehive, knocked from a falling tree. Smashed. Angry. Swarming with life and violence. Somehow Audrine breaks the spell. She grips my shoulder and shakes me like a savage.

"I think we should get the hell out of here," she says.

I nod furiously.

"Couldn't agree more, doll."

THIRTY-EIGHT

The lights flicker on and off as the power surges. That sconce the broad was pinned to pops with a shower of sparks and expensive crystal. Lucky for us, the emergency evacuation routine still works. A trail of runway lights wink on, leading us out towards the life rafts, or so I hope.

We pop to our feet and sprint towards the door, but Audrine stops short. She runs back to the desk, frantically throwing open drawers as sparks shower around her.

"Looking for this?" I wave Proletti's precious notebook at her and point to the exit.

"Stockton, I ne—"

"Later," I say, and lead the way out of the captain's quarters.

We stumble out, right into a warzone. Thugs fight with goons over armfuls of loot and supplies and loose women. A pack of SnotBabies gives chase to some of Slick's slower cronies in the distance.

There's gunfire. Shouts. Screams. We rush into the fray, heads down but eyes up. Careful to keep our distance from anything dangerous, but also hot-footing at full tilt. It's a tough act to balance in such a narrow, crowded passage.

After a minute or two, a lanky, mustachioed goon drops a crate of canned potatoes and hooks Bekka's neck as we race by.

"Mister Stockton!" she cries as he throws his dirty paws over her yap.

I skid to a stop and lay out the kidnapper with a single leaping left to his temple. I decide it's much easier to clean clocks without metal faces. Bekka hops up into my arms and I catch her with the one that still works. Looks like I'm towing her the rest of the way.

Audrine takes the reins now, trying her damnedest to navigate us down a corridor that's strewn with debris and lousy with goons, SpaceApes, and God knows what else that wants to kill us. Dark smoke billows out from the floor vents in thick, choking plumes. Emergency strobes beam through the fog in blinding flashes. It's hard to make out my own feet below me, let alone the broad dipping and ducking through dangerous traffic up ahead.

I pray that our passage stays pressurized.

Audrine darts into a crossing corridor, although the lights blink onward. There's no time to second guess her now. I follow behind her, swift and silent, hugging ShortStack tight. We press up flat against the wall next to her, panting for breath with smoke-singed lungs.

A troop of goons sprint past our hidey-hole, with a SnotBaby complement in close pursuit. The monsters dive into the goons as they dash by, bringing them down with brutal efficiency. For an instant, the chaotic din of breaking glass, gunfire, and groaning girders is pierced by screams and sloppy slurps. We shimmy out slowly, trying not to attract attention, but we don't try hard enough.

A pair of SpaceApes has us made. I watch their crusty, eyeless faces turn towards us from over a pile of half-chewed pirate-bodies. We hightail it down the hallway and don't look back. The machine gun staccato of our footfalls fills my head.

I make like a rabbit, until I get a foot-full of something squishy and soft under my sole—something better left unidentified. My grip on the floor gets tenuous. I begin to skate on one wobbly clog, ready to crash and burn. Bekka dons a deathgrip around my neck as we capsize.

Not on Audrine's watch though.

The broad catches our distress signals, grabs me by the shoulder and back of my lap and straightens us out. She topples a few crates behind us before sprinting out ahead of me again.

This twist has some serious tread on those gazelle gams of hers. I'd eat her dust with a knife, a fork, and a ten second head start. I can just begin to see the cluster of escape pods through the smoky haze ahead of us. We're in the home stretch! Unfortunately, the SnotBabies are right there with us. It'll be a photo finish, if we even make it that far.

My ears ring with the *pitter-patter, skitter-skatter* of their poisonous little claws. Audrine ducks some dangling duct and dives headfirst into an empty pod like she's stealing third. I follow suit, toss the kid after her and turn for a fight. The lead beast leaps feet first, right for my jugular. I lean back and feed him a boot sandwich before slamming my fist down onto a big red button beside me. The hatch slams shut, cutting the first SnotBaby off at the neck and blocking the path of his buddy, who barrels into the now closed door with a headful of thump. I sweep Numero Uno's still twitching torso into the corner and bash at him with the fire extinguisher until he doesn't twitch any longer. A battery of release charges fire around the outside of the hatch, severing our link to the ship and shoving us off.

"Adios," I say, wiping SnotBaby gunk from my forehead.

We rocket from the onboard carnage, floating in a tiny tin can of a vessel. It's one step up from the model that comes free in a box of McTasty Flakes. Brand new and cheap as hell. Single-ply, all the way around. A handful of rivets pop loose when I take a seat. I grab for the 'oh-shit' bar, pray it doesn't come off in my hand, and take a peek out the bubble in front.

The bridge of the Tartarus sinks away below us, erupting short bursts of flame that fizzle quickly when they reach the vacuum. A handful of escape pods pop off just behind us. Others aren't so lucky. Unfortunately, we haven't quite reached the clear just yet ourselves. A maelstrom of metal and fire swirls all around us. The castoff debris from the corpse of The Heap threatens to swallow us whole and tear our rickety little boat to pieces.

Audrine hops onto the life raft's control sticks lickety-split and maneuvers us between spinning junk and belching fireballs. We watch out the window as a couple of goons float by in a sealed somnopod. I think I can just make out Smitty's crusty beard and considerable paunch from under the bubble. Bekka waves to them. Hello and goodbye.

A spacewalking pedestrian in street clothes bounces off the windshield, leaving a bloody smear across our view. And here we are without any wipers. Makes me glad I never drove a cab.

"This thing flies like a brick!" Audrine says, steering us around a house-sized hunk of rusty hull. A single bead of sweat hugs her brow, threatening to take the plunge.

"You're doing fine, doll," I say. "Just keep us out of the drink."

As if summoned by my words of encouragement, a massive truss nudges into us from above. Luckily, it's short on force and forgets to pierce our hull. Showers of sparks rain down on our heads and the lights flicker a few times, but we pull out from under it in one piece.

The truss bullies us out of the worst of it and into a little clearing of sorts. A safe zone. For the next quarter mile or so ahead, we've got nothing bigger than a few stray armchairs to worry about. Beyond that though, we're looking into a hornets' nest. A real no-fly zone. A swarm of fusion-core fuel cells pour out of a limping freighter up there. They ignite like popcorn in the near distance, a daisy-chain of bang-bangs that manage to catch every last bit of debris floating their way in a ball of lightning-fire. It's a minefield, and it's our only way out. I trace the path of another escape pod as it attempts to navigate the fruckus ahead of us, hoping we can follow her path to safety. I wince when it goes boom too. A human arm, cut off at the elbow, ejects from this fresh mess and bounces off our bubble windshield.

"Well, it was nice knowing you two," I say, giving each of the ladies a gentle pat on the back.

Audrine takes a deep breath, grits her teeth and guns us into the swarm. She does her best to avoid the exploding fuel cells better than the fellas ahead of us, but it's a losing fight. The little canisters explode all around us. Each near-miss rattles our can, shaking loose ceiling-screws into my lap. As we get closer to the freighter spilling the popping porridge, the blasts get closer to us. There's too many to avoid. We'll never shake them all. Two cells pop directly below us and we're all three lifted from our seats by the shockwave. Clusters of hydraulic pump-housings come unseated above me and hiss furiously. Each one is a little hydra head, its neck flapping wildly with the escaping pressure. I reach up and wrangle them one at a time, tying off the hoses in hasty half-shanks. We're falling to pieces faster than I can patch us up.

"We can't keep at it, doll," I say. "Somethings going to give and I've got a hunch that it's going to be us and this raggedy-ass life raft."

Audrine ignores me, keeping her peepers glued to the bubble, scanning back and forth for any way out of this exploding nightmare.

"There!"

She points to the lifeless husk of a massive, cocoa-colored mining barge. It's marked X-467 in bright yellow paint. One of the exploding fuel cells has cracked a tiny pothole in the enormous storage-pod assembly train, just maybe big enough for us to squeeze through. Not exactly what I'd call a sure thing, but it just might be the *only* thing.

Audrine rips the sticks and we begin to bank for the barge. I've got faith in the broad's driving record—she's kept us alive this long after all—but this plan is for the birds. It's like threading a speeding needle with a spaghetti noodle and a bad case of the shakes. But telling her what she already knows won't help our sitch any, so I keep my mouth shut and silently make my peace.

She sweeps us wide-right to come at the cavern head on, side-stepping fuel cells and other fresh flotsam along the way. If just one of these bad boys pops, we're getting a faceful of brown barge for a last meal.

Lucky for us, the bang-bangs keep their lids on.

Audrine holds it steady and we creep up to the barge-hole slow-like, ready for the break-in. I hold my breath and duck low in my seat, hands on my head, as she steers us into the narrow gap. There's a horrible metallic screech as our hull bumps uglies with the barge. Something snaps off above us. Fissures sprout along the edges of the windshield. A sequence of warning lamps and angry alarms whine to life, shouting their protests across the dash. I slide my hands down over my eyes. I can't watch. If only I had an extra pair of hands to plug my ears. This concerto of shrill squeals and threatening emergency chimes is about all I can take.

And then it stops.

We've squeezed through.

I exhale. Remove my blindfold. We're alive! Unpunctured! Audrine eases us into the long, empty storage hold. After the chaos outside, the confines of the barge are cozy, nice even. We're down to one headlight but it's enough to get by. Our lovely pilot skirts us around a random stack of round, quarried asteroid ore and we've got a straight shot down the length of the cylindrical pod. Starlight pours in from the open bay doors at the far end. Starlight! Sweet, beautiful, precious starlight. Not explosions or debris or other rotten stuff that wants to end our existence. Just the sweet twinkle of near-forgotten freedom.

Audrine glides us out into that open range. The clutter and madness fall away behind us like a bad dream.

"Now what?" I say.

"Now we cut on the built-in wormhole generator and get the hell out of here," Audrine says, pointing to a gleaming green lever. "Escape pod technology has come a long way since our day!"

"Cut away, lady."

She gives me a wink. "You got it! I'm picking up at least six different hailing frequency transmissions from across the galaxy. Seven! Eight! Nine! They're lighting up our switchboard left and right! Looks like those colony worlds are getting their message through now that Zed's jammers are down." She points at a series of tiny blinking blips on the screen. "Which one should we shoot for, Stockton?"

"Pick one," I say, patting around for my box of chewsticks. I find it and pour myself a good one. Sweet green apple. Smiling, I lean back in my chair, arms behind my neck.

She nods, flips some switches and racks a large lever down into the dash. A swirling array of nebulous light opens up in front of us. It quickly spins itself into an irregular tunnel with shimmering spiderweb walls and plenty of room for us to twirl right in. A beautiful blue planet coated in turquoise seas and dotted with lush-looking islands awaits us on the other side. It's a paradise. Jungley and perfect.

Audrine puts both hands around my neck, kisses me on the lips, then turns to take in our new home. She begins to sing. Her singing voice is far lovelier than I would have thought from the gruff, toad-in-her-throat way she speaks.

Little Bekka giggles and splashes in the water. A gentle, sapphire wave chases her up the shore. She collapses into the snow white sand before us, her tiny glasses gone crooked once more. Audrine laughs and wipes a smudge of sand away from the girl's cheeks, then sends her off to make castles in the surf. I wave to the munchkin with a coconut-cup cocktail in my surgically repaired right hand.

"Wasn't it all worth it?" Audrine says. Gleaming glass towers rise above the swooping palms, into the deep blue sky behind her. A bright yellow sun smiles down on us through a break of big, friendly-looking clouds. "Would we appreciate this half as much if we hadn't been dragged halfway through hell to get here?"

I pull her close to me and press her lips to mine. She tastes like pineapple and homemade rum. Her oiled skin slips and slides over mine as she nestles against me on the blanket.

"I'd appreciate you anywhere, doll," I say.

She stares into my eyes, then throws the thrusters forward.

Nothing happens. The wormhole is still floating in front of us, the ocean-world urging us on, waving like a sultry dish. But we're not getting any closer to her sweet embrace.

Audrine's song dries up in her throat.

"What gives?" I ask.

She fusses with the controls. Hits the gas again. We go nowhere.

"I... I don't know," she says.

Then she looks into the rearview monitor. Beyond the debris field, past the popping-fresh fireballs and slamdancing shipwrecks, the brand new, ultramassive black hole still looms behind us. That bitch. The Heap and all of its rubble swirl slowly, sinking into her massive maw like a truckful of garbage flushed down the galactic john. Audrine sees it too. All the hope flees from her face, all at once.

"We're too close," she says. "We're caught in the gravity well. The black hole is pulling us in!"

"Well motor us on out a ways and crank it up again," I say with a shrug.

"It doesn't work like that, Stockton," she says. "Our engines aren't strong enough to pull out!" She points to a display readout with a gigantic, gridded funnel: the black hole. And inside the funnel there's a flashing red dot, blinking its way slowly down the drain: us. Along with everything else in the neighborhood.

"We crossed over," she says. "We crossed over and we didn't even know it."

"Now what?" I ask. "Just sit here quietly and wait to be sucked in and crushed to death?"

She covers Bekka's ears.

"Stockton, we were goners the moment we slipped inside the gravity well. But we won't be crushed. At least, I don't think so. It's far more likely we'll be pulled into pieces by extreme tidal forces."

"Tidal forces? Like in the ocean?"

"Almost," she says. "The pull is so strong that the parts of our bodies closest to the black hole will get tugged on harder than those farther away. When we get close enough, it'll stretch us into taffy ten miles long before the gravity rips us to shreds at a molecular level. Or at least theoretically that's how it should happen."

"What, you don't know for sure?"

"Like I told you before," she reminds me, "no one's ever come out the other side to tell us about it."

"Well thanks for the science lesson anyway," I say. "Your version of our looming destruction sounds much better than my own."

We sit in silence for a moment, contemplating our fleeting mortality. After a solid thirty seconds of soul searching, Audrine's eyes light up. "I've got it!" she says. "Bekka, can you ask your friends if they will come and get us? Their ship must be more powerful than this piece of crap escape pod."

"Thattagirl! They bailed us out before and by my book they still owe us a solid or two." Bekka nods her head with a smile. She closes her eyes tight and squinches her little face, deep in concentration. After a few seconds, she straightens her glasses and nods once. Shakes her head. Then nods again. Her eyes pop open.

"They say that we are in the—ummm—in Schwart's child's radius. They say they can't get to us without them getting sucked in too."

"Damn!" I say.

But Bekka's not done.

"They do have a way we can get out. But they say you won't like it." She frowns.

"Well what is it, sweetie?" Audrine asks.

Bekka's eyes are closed again. She's talking with them inside her mind. Nodding. No head shakes this time, that's promising.

"They say you need to aim the worm's hole right at the—umm—right at the single lady." She closes her eyes once more. "Right at the singularity," she corrects herself.

I look at Audrine for an explanation.

"They want us to pass right through the center of the black hole."

My head starts to shake.

"Whoa, whoa, whoa," I say. "Hold your horses there beautiful! I thought playing with wormholes near the black hole was a bad idea! I thought nobody ever made it out the other side!"

Audrine sighs, a concerned look on her face. Bekka closes her eyes again. Nods one more time. "They say it's our only hope," she says. "What does that mean, Miss Audrine?"

Audrine pats her on the head and smiles.

"It means we're going to get out of here, sweetie."

She cranks the lifeboat around the other way and begins fidgeting with some tiny control knobs. Our orientation flickers up on the cockpit holodisplay. Audrine gets us lined up at an angle right through the heart of the maelstrom and the big black nothing behind it.

A thousand and one warning lights pop to life on the windshield. "This is a very bad idea," the lights say, but this broad actually intends to go through with it.

"You can't be serious about this!" I say. "The last time these guys took us anywhere we ended up getting sold into slavery!"

Audrine stops with the controls for a moment. Stares me down.

"Do you have any better ideas?"

"Well, no but—"

"Would you like to get out and wait for another ride?"

"No, I wou—"

"Then shut up and hold onto your ass," she says. And with that she throws the generator back on.

The wormhole opens up before us. But there's no blue paradise on the other side this time. Just a long, twisting tunnel of stammering, silky ether. It bubbles and spins around itself angrily. Even the opening fizzles and spits out tiny, shining tendrils that quickly dissolve back into the sputtering mess. Not the most inviting rabbit hole I've ever intended to dive down.

I pull her hand away from the controls.

"Not so fast, *sweetie*," I say. She's not happy but she hears me out. "If we're gonna die today—and it sure looks like that may be the case— I'd like a couple of answers out of you before we go through with it."

She stares into the wormhole, sighs, then throws a switch to cut the thrusters. She spins her chair to face me. The angry tunnel crackles behind her. "What do you want to know, Stockton?"

"For starters, what about the girl?"

I throw a thumb towards ShortStack.

"What about her?" Audrine says.

"Who does she belong to? How come she can talk to those freak-shows in her head?"

Audrine crosses her arms. "Ask her yourself."

I turn towards LittleBritches.

"Hey kiddo," I say. "What's your name? Your *full* name."

She looks at me, puzzled, then blinks twice.

"Rebekka-Ann Iris DeMarco," she says.

I slap at my forehead.

"Well I'll be damned. Why didn't you tell me that before?"

"If I remember it correctly, Stockton," Audrine says, "you interrupted her when she tried to tell you the first time."

I look at the broad and scowl, then back to the girl.

"This your ma?"

"No," Bekka says. Audrine puts an arm around her. "But she looks like mommy. Sounds like her too. Mommy told me she would. She said I could trust Miss Audrine and her grumpy friend."

I squint at the two of them, then turn to Audrine. "And you didn't find any of this the least bit curious?"

"We live in a curious world, Stockton."

"I'll say. Curious, my foot. How about your friends, ShortStuff? How come you can hear them inside your head? How come you can talk to them when they're not even around?"

Bekka shrugs.

"They say it's because I know how to listen. They say you and Miss Audrine can do it, too. If you listen close enough."

Audrine shakes her head. Her hands go back to the flight controls. "Alright Stockton, if you're done interrogating the little girl I—"

"Sure," I say. "Her I'm done with. But you've still got some talking to do. Some answers you still owe me."

She shuts her eyes and nods.

I pull out Zed's little green notebook.

"What's so important about this? What did Slick put in here that's worth dying for?" I flip open to a random page. Inside is a neat listing of my first few days at the resort. An almost hourly itinerary of my activities. A play-by-play script of every conversation I had at Seren Luna. With Slick, the broad, the help. After Audrine gives me the bottle of hooch though, the pages go blank. I turn towards the end.

The words stare out at me, a slap in the face of everything I've ever known possible.

0900 hours they say. *Turn escape pod around. Fly ship into wormhole, directly through center of black hole.*

"Stockton," Audrine says. "Stockton you wouldn't have believed me if I'd told you."

"This isn't a journal," I say, shaking my head. "It's a set of instructions." My fingers absently trace the neat, looping script plastered across the pages. "And it wasn't Slick's either."

"Stockton, I—"

"Did you think I wouldn't recognize your handwriting, doll? Did you think I wouldn't recognize this for exactly what it was the moment I laid my eyes on it?"

She looks up at me, defiance in her eyes. Even caught red-handed, she won't say 'sorry'.

"And just what do you think it is?" she asks.

"It's a set-up," I say. "You were pulling Slick's strings all along, just like you were pulling mine. You set this whole house of cards up, like some kind of sick, twisted game. Used both of us as pawns, even though you knew the whole thing would come crashing down on our heads. But at least Zed or Proletti or whoever the hell he was, at least he knew it."

She grasps my hands, pleading. The distorted tunnel of the worm-hole twists and shakes at the edge of my vision.

"Stockton, you're right. We *are* pawns. But what you can't see written in those pages is that I'm a puppet too. We all are. Every last one of us. You and me, Bekka and Zed, and everybody else you've ever met, too. We all have a role to play. Turn back a few pages. You'll see that not everything went the way I thought it would."

I do like she says. Scan through a dozen sheets filled with names and places I don't recognize. Things that never happened, at least not to me.

"Zed wasn't following my orders," she says, gently trying to close the cover of the book. "He was trying to stop them. He stole this book from me. He wanted to make sure I didn't get what I wanted, and he had a play-by-play gameplan of everything I needed to do, and everywhere I needed to be. We had to jump off-script, just to survive."

"And yet here we are, right where you planned."

She smiles meekly. "I'm just as surprised as you are, Stockton. Zed was thrown off by the appearance of the SnotBabies, just like I was. They weren't part of the plan: his, mine, or anybody else's. They changed everything. Everything that came after them was a surprise to me, too. But maybe there is a divine plan for the universe after all. Because somehow, we made it here, right back where we needed to be. Staring down the barrel of this big, black mystery before us."

I pull my paws from her and rub them over my temples.

"Let's say I believe you," I say. "What in the world would possess you to carry out a plan like this? Why would you throw yourself—and the kid too, don't forget about her—why would you drag yourself into such a hot mess?"

"Because I had to," she says, ruffling ShortStuff's mop. "I had to stick to the script. To make sure that the three of us fulfilled a destiny that absolutely has to happen. I knew I had to get you here and I had to let you think it was your idea."

"And how could you possibly ever know a thing like that?" I say.

"I remembered it," she said. "I remembered it for you because you aren't able to. Not yet. It's my job to get you where you need to be, until you can remember for yourself what it is you are supposed to do. Who it is you're supposed to be."

"Your job, huh? And just who hired you to do this job of yours? Who is pulling *your* strings, princess? Who decided you needed to drag me into all your fun and games?"

She shakes her head.

"That fella at your table? The first night I met you for dinner? Your rude friend?"

She winces.

"Who was he? What does he have to do with any of this?" I grab her by the arms.

She opens her eyes and speaks softly.

"You wouldn't believe that either," she says.

"There's not a lot you could tell me that I'd be inclined to take at face value at this point, honey. So far, I've heard a lot of improbable excuses and not much in the way of apologies, or rational explanations for all the impossible lines you're feeding me. You haven't given me much reason to trust you."

"Stockton, I wish that it could be any other way."

She tugs on the notebook, but I yank it away from her grasp, and stare blankly into the cover of the damned thing. It's worn and faded. Old.

"Just what was Zed after?" I ask her. "He didn't know what it was he was looking for, I know that much. He would have killed us outright if he did. But I've got a feeling that you do. My gut tells me you know because the two of you were after the same prize."

She smiles and sits up straight. "The funny thing is, he had it all along. He had it right under his nose the whole time, and he was just too proud to realize it."

I motion for her to continue as I thumb through the pages.

"It was you, Stockton. If I had any doubts before, I know it's true now. *You* are what we've both been looking for. You are the only thing that can help us uncover the answer to the ultimate question. You are the only one that can find it, shoddy detective work aside."

I look up and shake my skull at her.

"Listen lady, I was just trying to keep us both alive back there. Sorry there wasn't much time for a crackerjack investigation. But I think you've got me confused for some other guy. I can't help you find any answers. Hell, I don't even know the damned question."

She kisses me on the cheek.

"Someday you will," she says. "Someday soon you'll—"

My fingers catch on a dog-eared corner of her journal, and the look that jumps across her face tells me that I've stumbled across something she hoped I would never find.

She tries to stop me, to take the book away before I can look, but I spin in my seat and glance over just what she doesn't want me to see.

It's a list. A list of names, with her's printed neatly at the top.

Below that, some of them are familiar and many of these are already crossed out: *Doctor Stephon Proletti. Detective Second Class Jaxon Mendoza.* A few others before these I don't recognize, some I can hardly even pronounce: *Major General Francois Hebert. Davison LaFayette IV.* Someone or something called *AJAX.* Most of these aren't crossed through, not yet.

There's one name though, tucked away at the top, just below Audrine's, that eats at me worse than any of the others. A name that has no business being in a list like this at all.

Irene Ames. Struck through, just like all the others on this list that I've known Zed to be in the past. All the other poor souls he knocked off and impersonated over the years.

I stab my finger at the list like a knife.

"Why is my mother's name on this list?" I scan it some more. This is not Audrine's handwriting. Could belong to Zed, or anyone else in the whole goddamned lonely universe for that matter. "Why is yours? Who wrote this?"

The look on her face is pure panic.

"Stockton, I didn't want you to see that. It's not what you think..."

"Yeah then what the hell is it? Because to tell the truth, doll, I don't know what to make of it. I don't know what to make of any of it. I'm half-ready to hurl this book out the window and you along with it."

She closes the cover and when she moves to take the book back from me, I don't try to stop her. With her other hand, she throws the thruster switch forward, and we begin to slip in towards the angry, distended wormhole, and the heart of the black beast on the other side.

"Some things are best left for another day," she says. "You'll get the answers you want, but only when you're ready to hear them."

I glare at her for a moment, then let it go. I kick my feet up on the dash and stretch my arms back behind my head again. Lace my fingers loose under my neck.

"Whatever you say, lady. I'm all done playing detective with you. We'll only have a few more minutes to worry about it anyway." I stare out into the twisting madness as the wormhole begins to swallow us. The distorted shapes of broken ships and stars, fire and light, shine across the wet lips of the swirling vortex.

I turn to Bekka and pat her on the head.

"Nice knowing ya', ShortStuff."

She just smiles wide, until her eyes are nearly closed, and grasps my hand in hers. "Don't worry, Mister Stockton," she says. "Everything will be just fine."

I raise a single eyebrow. "Yeah?" I say. "What makes you sure?"

She squeezes my hand tight.

"It's not my first rodeo," she says.

We fall in.

The ride gets bumpy.

Bekka drops my hand as our little tin can starts to rattle and shake. The distorted hunks of the heap outside stretch towards infinity. They disappear into a single point of absolute darkness at the end of the tunnel.

We start to spin.

The black blob before us gets bigger. Streaks of brilliance blaze by us, on their way down the tube. Faster we twist, turning kamikaze curlicues that get tighter and tighter until I'm not so sure we're even spinning at all anymore. If I'd had any lunch, I'd be losing it.

The blackness swallows everything outside.

Things inside the raft start to look strange too. Like we're a wet painting, being smeared across the canvas. Audrine's emerald eyes stay burned into my retinas, until they too get loopy and loose. I reach out for her, but all I see is a hundred hands extending out from my elbow into the black. I grab a hold for something, anything, before I realize I have a hold on the back of my own neck.

The air gets heavy. My arms get heavy. Existence gets heavy. Unbearable. I let go. Just when I feel like I'm going to be crushed into a single grain of dust, there's a blinding flash of light and a boom that shakes me apart.

Then darkness.

THIRTY-NINE

There's nothing.

Only darkness. Only emptiness.

Until Skip McKendrick appears before me in a poof of smoke, just like we're in the 'streams. He wears the full StarCaptain getup. From the bubble helmet, propped-open, to his trademark steel blue eyes, right down to the fat straps on his shiny black boots. He lights up a Benton Blue, full-flavor, and offers one to me.

I reach out to grab it, but I don't have any hands. I glance around. I don't have any arms or legs either. I'm nothing. A floating pair of peepers, if that.

He chuckles.

"Sorry about that," he says. "Old habit."

He climbs into a folding chair with his name printed on the back, like the kind they keep on set. Are we between takes here or what? As far as I can see, there is no set. It's just him and the chair and the darkness.

Slowly though, the scenery materializes around him.

Like someone just got around to flipping on the stage lights. He sits in front of a great big window. So big in fact, that I can't see the edges. And behind that window, the burnt-out husk of my home planet floats before a dying sun. A swollen red ball of fire. Angry. Distended. Earth as I last saw her.

No body appears for me though. I'm still a ghost. A spirit.

Skip takes a long pull on his smoke. Here's a man that knows what pleasure is. His eyes shut, he exhales slowly. "You can talk, Stockton," he says. "I know that don't make much sense, as it were, but I can hear you just the same."

I give it a test. "He-hello?" I say.

It's really more like thinking out loud, seeing as I got no lips to move and no ears to hear. But I make out the sound of my thoughts alright, and apparently he does too.

He nods, and continues smoking.

"Goddamn!" I say. "Are you—ummm, well—you aren't *Him* are you?"

He laughs and glances at the scene behind him. Ever so slowly, the angry red sun begins to fade and shrink. It goes fuzzy, gets lighter.

"If I were," he says, "would you want to be talking to me that way?"

He's got a point there.

"No, I guess not."

He nods.

"No I ain't God, Stockton," he says. "Least not in that Old Testament, benevolent creator way you think of Him."

The view through the window continues to change. The sun is returning to a normal size and color, the sun I remember. The red cracks on the rocky surface of the planet start to dry up.

"Well then who the hell are you?"

He stares at me, at least where I should be.

My mind becomes so filled with sensation and knowledge and emotion that I start to black out. Everything goes white. My brain is bursting. Breaking. A deluge of information overwhelms my consciousness, to the point where I no longer exist. Even in my current invisible state, I'm disappearing under a sea of synapses, not that I can make any sense of it. The very idea of 'me' starts to fade. It's almost pleasant. Almost.

He snaps his fingers and suddenly it's all gone. My own thoughts return and none too soon.

"I ain't Skip McKendrick, that's for damned sure, Stockton. Let's just say that's a tough one to answer and leave it at that for now."

"Well if you're not Skip, why do you look like him?"

He laughs again, and stares into his smoke.

"As clichéd as it sounds, I didn't choose this form. I look and sound like Skip McKendrick because that's how you choose to experience me. As for why I'm StarCaptain Skip and not Sheriff Skip, that's a question you'll have to answer yourself, partner."

I nod internally.

The Earth is slowly but surely returning to normal behind him. The whole globe spins around in a blur, but not so fast I can't make out the familiar details. The oceans reform from tiny puddles. The continents bounce around each other like bumper cars. They get green again. Mountains poke up from the collisions.

"It's going backwards, isn't it?" I say. "Time, I mean."

He nods and stamps out his smoke. Flicks another out of the cylindrical pack but doesn't pull it just yet. "I suppose you'd see it that way, yes," he says. "I'd be lying if I said that's how it really works. But it won't make much difference to *you* now, will it?"

I shake my head no. I suddenly get the feeling that this whole conversation is only for my sake. Like he knows everything I'm going to say a lifetime before I even begin to think it.

"Wow," I say. "It sure is beautiful."

He smiles.

"Thanks," he says.

The Earth is nearly back the way I knew it. Cities and roads crawl across the continents. Space elevators stretch up into the atmosphere and beyond. Ships and satellites buzz around like bees, pollinating the planet with civilization once again.

Skip lets the second cigarette fall back into the pack, but doesn't take his eyes off it. He wants another, but won't have it. Not yet he won't.

"Well go on then," he says, still staring into his lap. "Ask it."

He's in my head alright. I spit out the query that's been eating at me for this whole damned conversation. "No offense here, fella," I say. "But what the hell do you want from me?"

He smiles wide and looks up at me. It's a billion-dollar smile. A Hollywood landmark in its own right.

The Earth's rotation slows to a stop.

"Did you find it, Stockton?"

I shake an invisible head and shrug invisible shoulders.

"Everybody's looking for something, aren't they Skip?"

He nods.

"Sorry, bub," I say. "I have no idea what anybody's looking for, and I don't know why anybody thinks I can help them find it."

He pulls that smoke after all.

"You're a pretty resourceful guy, Ames. That stunt with the nuke? I didn't think you had it in you. That move surprised even me. Maybe that's why everybody believes in you. You've got gusto."

I shrug.

"Aww shucks," I say.

He points at me and winks.

"So what is it then? And please don't make me ask again. What do you and the girl and that face-changing asshole all need me to find?"

He lights the cigarette and smiles.

"Oh nothing much," he says. "Just the most important thing in all of existence."

"Yeah, and what's that?" I sigh.

"The beginning," he says.

"The beginning of what? For crying out loud won't someone just come out and say it? Why do I have to dig this out of everyone I meet?"

He takes his gaze from the smoke and stares right into me.

"The beginning of everything," Skip McKendrick says.

I shake my head and laugh.

"Now how did you all go and lose something like that?" I ask.

He shrugs and blows a cloud.

"Never had it to begin with," he says. "That's what we need you for."

"Well I appreciate the offer and all," I say. "But I haven't seen anything like that lying around."

"That's alright partner." He stands out of the chair and turns to look out on the Earth below. "It's out there somewhere." He smiles one last time, and reflected in his teeth I find the answer to everything anyone could ever ask, in the last place I'd ever think to look for it. "You'll know it when you see it."

Everything fades into nothing once more.

FORTY

Rain. It's raining outside.

"It never rains in space."

My eyes open slowly. It's dark. Fat drops streak down a window beside my somnopod. Outside the sky is gray. Gloomy. There are buildings out there. Honking magcabs. Traffic. I'm in the city.

Space? Why would I think I should wake up in space?

I flip the release on my somnopod and sit up with a yawn. Big Chief Wallace stares at me from across the room with a cigar in his teeth. Gives me a thumbs up. A Knights poster. *My* Knights poster.

"Stockton, honey, get up! You'll be late for class!"

Mom? I smell pancakes. Bacostrips. Home. I stand up and stretch. The alarm is chirping on my MPD. Vibrating my whole arm. I roll up the sleeve of my PJs and swipe the buzz away, but my right hand is cold and tingly, like it's still asleep. I must have been sleeping hard. What a weird dream I was having. Something about flashing lights. A tunnel. StarCaptain Skip and—

A buzz at the front door interrupts my thought.

That's strange. Who would come calling this early? I hear mom set down her cooking to answer it. Muffled voices from the living room. I can't quite make out the words.

It's quiet for a bit, then mom is at my door.

"Stockton, there's someone here that wants to talk to you," she says with a smile. "You be friendly to the nice lady, then we'll get you some breakfast. Okay, honey?"

I nod and wipe the sleep from my eyes. Mom steps away and a lady walks in. Younger than Mom, but not by much. She's got a green dress-suit on. Lots of ribbons and shiny brass buttons.

She's dressed like the soldiers down at the station. Like the ones on the mediastreams. Right down to the little hat. It sits above her dark hair, her sparkly green eyes. She's very pretty. Very nice looking.

I decide all at once that I like this lady very much.

"Hello, Stockton," she says. She extends a hand to shake. I give her a good one. Mom always says you can tell a lot about a man by his handshake.

"Hi," I say.

"Stockton, I'm here to ask you a question," she says.

She bends low to look me in the eyes.

"Okay," I say.

"Stockton, what do you want to be when you grow up?"

"Gee, I don't know," I say. I look over at the Knights poster. "A ballplayer maybe? Or a detective. Yeah, definitely a detective!"

"A detective, huh?" She puts a finger to her ruby red lips, contemplates my answer for a moment.

"How about a soldier, Stockton? Would you ever want to be a Marine? In the Orbital Defense Corps? Fly around in spaceships? See the galaxy? Save the world? That kind of thing?"

I think about it.

"Yeah, that seems pretty good too," I say. "I think maybe I'd like to be a Marine someday."

She smiles and gives me a pat on the head.

"I thought so," she says, standing up straight once more. "Stockton, I want you to remember this conversation." She reaches into her hip pocket. "And to make sure you do, I brought you a gift."

She pulls out a little metal token and presses it into my palm.

"What's this?" I say, flipping it over.

She winks at me.

"It's a homing chit. For your new friend."

A brand new PackBot® P280 comes floating through my door. There's a little red ribbon tied around him, with a big, floppy bow. He comes to a stop right at my feet.

"Wow, thanks!" I say. "This is a nice one! The latest model, with the maglevs and everything! No wheels for me! The other guys will be so jealous!"

She smiles.

"He'll come in handy," she says, turning to go, "when you're ready to find me. When you're ready to save the world."

She steps out into the hallway and out of my life.

ABOUT THE AUTHOR

Henry Abner is the pen name of hard-boiled fiction author Henry Abner Sturdivant. Henry Abner the author was a staple of the early era of pulp fiction crime stories, writing many tales of action and intrigue that take place in his native Georgia and other areas of the rural south.

Henry Abner Sturdivant the man was more than a crime writer, however. He had a long career in law enforcement, and served as the chief of police of tiny Washington, Georgia from 1921 until his death in July of 1935, when he was killed in the line of duty while apprehending a suspect. He was survived by his only daughter Sara and wife Lora, and is laid to rest at Sharon Methodist Church, in Taliaferro County, Georgia.

The text you have just read was compiled from previously unpublished notes and manuscripts found in sealed evidence files from the Washington Police headquarters. These materials were discovered by accident when the municipal police department was being closed and merged with county law enforcement, some eighty years after they were written. The text was edited by members of the Janos Corporation publications team, under the approval and guidance of the Henry Abner estate.

Relativity and the rest of the *Goddamned Lonely Universe* stories represent his only known works of science fiction.

MORE FROM HENRY ABNER & JANOSCORP

Stay up to date with the latest news and future releases by signing up for the JanosCorp Publications Mailing List at:

www.janoscorp.com/signup

Get a FREE EBOOK just for joing the mailing list!

Follow Henry Abner on Facebook at:

www.facebook.com/henryabnerauthor

Find more work by Henry Abner, including the standalone short fiction series: *Tales from the Goddamned Lonely Universe* on Amazon at:

http://www.amazon.com/Henry-Abner/e/B018W4VBA8

THE JANOS CORPORATION
FROM THE PAST & TO THE FUTURE